# ROBE[RT]

# RE[LICS]

*The Chro[nicles]*

**Book 1**

BARRINGTON AREA LIBRARY
505 N. NORTHWEST HWY.
BARRINGTON, ILLINOIS 60010

*lomon Drake* is a work
ces and incidents either
imagination or are used
n actual person living or
, events or locales are

'k

.....s Reserved

Published by Robert York
www.robert-york.com

**ISBN: 9781983358029**
Fiction-Urban Fantasy/Adventure

Cover Design: Robert York

Except under the U.S. Copyright Act of 1976, no part of this publication may be reproduced, copied, scanned, recorded, distributed or transmitted in any form by any means, or stored in a database or retrieval system without the prior written permission by the author.

Sale of this book without a front cover may be unauthorized. If this book is coverless, it may have been reported to the publisher as "unsold or destroyed" and neither the author nor the publisher may have received payment for it.

Dedication:

This is to my dearest love Kelly.
You found me in the dark and brought me into the light.
Without you life would hold no meaning.

I Love You

To You Intrepid Reader,

I would like to **Thank You** for reading this, my first book, which I hope flourishes into a series of books. I discovered that I enjoyed reading at an early age thanks to the encouragement of my mother. She was instrumental in helping me discover and nurture my creative side. Reading became an escape and a way to fuel my imagination through frightening tales of horror, swashbuckling adventures, which included cutthroat pirates or heroes on other worlds battling evil in all of their guises. I hope you enjoy **Relics: The Chronicles of Solomon Drake** as much as I enjoyed writing it.

Robert York

*"What the eyes see and the ears hear, the mind believes."*

**Harry Houdini**

# Chapter 1

I don't know why I'm writing this. I keep asking myself that question over and over again. Articulating my thoughts and emotions through written word has never appealed to me in anyway. It's ironic because I absolutely love to read and there's the duality of it all. I've never been much of a writer to begin with, punctuation being a major area of weakness for me. OK, to be honest I'm horrible at it. I sort of know where periods are supposed to go and I use apostrophes infrequently. As for commas well, they look nice here and there, yet I have no clue what they're for. I think my high school *English* teacher may have retired early from the stress of having to grade my composition papers. So for those of you still brave enough to read this after expressing my opinions on my writing abilities, I'd like to apologize in advance for all the bad grammar and punctuation errors.

I'm not a professional writer by any stretch of the imagination and this manuscript is being written in secret. There are some people, powerful people that wouldn't be too happy with me if they knew I were writing a book about the goings-on in our world. In point of fact they'd probably kill me and I don't mean that figuratively. Anyway, perhaps the real reason I'm writing this record is so that I can better understand things that have happened or things that have yet to happen. To be honest, maybe it's because I'm trying to prove to myself that there's a part of me that's still sane. It's not that I'm insane, but from what I've been through so far, I should be.

My name for those of you who are interested is Solomon Alexander Drake and I'm a Wizard, a real one in fact. I was named after two kings. One of which was known for great wisdom and strength, the other known for cunning and a fearless nature in battle. I've sometimes thought that someone, be it my mother or my father had high hopes for me and of what kind of a man I'd become when they decided to give me those names. I only hope that I haven't yet let them down. Now for all you observant readers, I do realize that my initials spell S.A.D. Something that's never been lost on me from the very moment I could read. So before you decide to come up with clever sayings or jokes at my expense please save your time, because I've heard them all before.

The world that I am referring to isn't the normal world you're familiar with. There's another world that people don't see or more accurately don't care to see. A strange world in which the "normal" rules that govern our perceptions cannot be adequately explained through science or the rational mind.

Have you ever been walking down a street, whether it is during the day or the night when you could've sworn something darted out in front of you only to dismiss it as a trick of the light or your tired eyes?

Have you ever been home alone and experienced strange sounds which at first you can't explain only to decide that it was nothing more than the house settling or the furnace resetting?

Have you ever felt as though you were being watched when no one else was supposed to be around?

Have you ever walked through a cold spot in an empty room that sent goose flesh all over your skin?

If you've answered yes to any of these questions I wouldn't panic just yet. It may shock you to learn that there's a supernatural or magical world, which exists and is real. It isn't hidden by magical spells or managed by departments of magic. There are creatures and beings that mankind comes in contact with everyday which most people don't even notice. There are also those other beings that live in the dark places of the world. They hide in plain sight, watching and in some cases waiting. You can blame a high percentage of unexplained disappearances on some of the nastier creatures, like Ghouls, Vampires and Wraiths. Hell, I wouldn't be surprised if there were a Dark Fairy or Snotling watching you from the shadows as you read this.

I'm twenty-seven years of age and like many people my age I find myself adrift between the mental state of high school and adulthood. Knowing that I should be more responsible while at the same time not wanting to let go of those carefree days of uninterrupted sleep and long hours of playing video games. I never went to college, which some would argue is a detriment to my upward financial mobility when it comes to advancing my career or making money. I however don't agree. I have yet to find a college that offers degrees in potion making or spell casting. At least I don't have thousands of dollars in student loans crushing me financially, a crime in my opinion. Knowledge shouldn't cost exorbitant amounts of money. I've been able to further my own education through PBS, experience and the public library; not to mention I've been able to do it without the influence of jaded professors. Besides, I've already served my time in lock up. I mean school. Thirteen years to be exact, kindergarten all the way up to my senior year in high school. Why would I tack on another four when I loathed every minute of the previous thirteen?

I work in a magic store. I know what you might be thinking.

"How smart can this guy be if he's working in retail,"

The only thing I have to say to that is read on and find out. *Blackmane's Magic and Potion Shop*, the place where I work is located on *Michigan Ave.* in the greatest city in the world, *Detroit, Michigan*; my hometown. If you'll allow me to indulge in a little shameless advertising I'll tell you a bit about my job. *Blackmane's* isn't your ordinary run of the mill magic shop. There are no card tricks, no magic rings and no top hats with rabbits hidden inside or cabinets to saw the unsuspecting lady assistant named Trixie in half. We do however sell trick handcuffs. I never figured out why we carry them, but you'd be surprised at how many "normals" with *BDSM* fetishes come in and clean us out of our whole inventory. Takes all kinds of people I guess.

*Blackmane's* is a real honest to God magic store. We carry wands, we carry staves, we make potions on demand; a very lucrative business, especially around *Valentine's Day* or when the occasional middle-aged balding man decides to come in looking for something to restore hair to his barren head or as it turns out more often than not, his virility. We stock exotic, yet sometimes illegal ingredients. *Blackmane's* also carries a large selection of spell books, potion books, reference books, books on charms or just about anything connected with the world of magic, we stock it and sell it all for a reasonable price. It's not exactly the work environment of Walmart or Starbucks, however my job has a coolness and wow factor the others don't have.

Anyway, the story I'm about to relate to you is an unusual one. One in which many reading this have never experienced and I hope you know how lucky you are to have never fallen down a rabbit hole even *Lewis Carroll* would be too frightened to write about. My story for you begins on a Monday and we all know how much of a maligned day Mondays are because it heralds the end of our weekend and the beginning of a potential five-day hell. I've often thought there should be an eighth day to the week. A day between Sunday and Monday, because let's face it, we all need a few extra hours to prepare us for dealing with the people that try our patience in the upcoming days. One other thing I forgot to mention, I tend to ramble on occasion. I don't mean too, it's just that I like to tell stories and don't get the opportunity as often as you might think. I promise that I'll keep my ramblings brief and to the point because the information I have for you is important and might just save your life one day. But I digress, like any good story; mine has a beginning, a middle and end, however my end has yet to be written. I've been through so much already; sadly I don't think I'll be fortunate enough to see how my story ends given the dangers I must face. As you read this you will come to understand why that might be the case. On this particular Monday my journey begins simply with a dream. Not a dream of hope or a dream of inspiration, but a dream of survival.

# Chapter 2

I enjoy exercising about as much as I like to do chores around the house. It's not that I don't exercise, because I do. I ride my mountain bike nearly everyday, weather permitting of course. I'll do a little *Tai Chi* to keep myself limber. Maybe I'll do a few reps here and there with some free weights, but what I absolutely dislike is running. Some out there reading this are probably asking,

"Well, what's wrong with running?"

I'm well aware that it gets you up and out of the house and it's good for your heart. Frankly if I'm going to travel three to five miles distance from my home and sweat in the process, I'd rather sit and pedal my ass there. Then again, on further reflection, running does come in handy if you're running for a train, have to run out and grab a bite to eat, if you're being chased either by the authorities or by someone or something that wants to do you harm. That last one I can really relate to and take to heart. To know what I'm referring to, I'd have to tell you what happened; so let me set the scene for you.

It was winter at the time and abnormally cold. It was getting dark. I looked to the horizon to see the last fleeting rays of the sun disappear behind distant tree lined hills, silhouetting the mountainside in darkness. A feeling of fear and isolation fell over me at the sight. Anyone that's ever been in a forest alone at night knows what I'm talking about. A feeling of primal terror and dread of what lurks in the shadows by day, but prowls in the open when the blanket of night descends over the land.

*Detroit*, over the years has been known for it's harsh, unpredictable weather. Sadly, everything that I've ever experienced about winter's fury in my hometown pales in comparison to the monster of a storm *Mother Nature* cooked up this night. Snow carried by high frigid winds swirled about me; biting through the winter gear right through to my skin. Snowflakes the size of popped popcorn fell from the sky, pelting my exposed face. Ice formed on my eyebrows and four days worth of stubble. The temperature felt like it must've been more than ten degrees below freezing. My face had gone cold hours ago; I could no longer feel any sort of sensation on my skin and I was struggling to breathe. The snow, knee deep in most places meant moving through it was difficult at best. If being tired, hungry and trying to survive the stinging cold of this storm wasn't bad enough, I was running for my life.

Three huge shaggy white creatures plowed their way through the snow behind me, like it was nothing more than piles of freshly raked autumn leaves. I heard their ground shaking bellows of angry challenge over the howling winter winds, which frightened the crap out of me. I turned this way, then that, frantically stealing glances behind me.

Each time I spied them my heart pumped faster. They were closing the distance rapidly. Their nostrils flared with each deep breath, large canine fangs bared in what I assumed was the anticipation of sinking them into my flesh, a chilling yet motivating thought to help move my legs faster. Frozen breath huffed out of their mouths like smoke from a chugging steam locomotive running at full speed. There wasn't time to get a good look at them, but they appeared to be apelike in appearance only with longer hair.

Distance.

I needed to put as much distance as I could between my attackers and me quickly. It was difficult to do in this snow to say the least, it didn't help that I was close to exhaustion either. I managed to put fifty or so yards between the creatures and myself. I huffed like an out of shape cop chasing down a purse-snatcher. My chest ached; shooting pain went through my burning lungs with every labored breath.

These things moved fast, faster than I would've believed possible had I not witnessed it with my own eyes. If something wasn't done to get their interest off me, they were going to overtake and kill me. Dying wasn't something I really wanted to do at that moment. I turned, glancing hurriedly behind me, out of fear more than anything else. They were about twenty-five yards away now. My heart pumped faster at the sight, almost like I had been injected with a syringe of adrenaline. I could feel the fright filled beats pounding against my sternum. Fueled by fear and a sense of self-preservation, I turned again in mid-stride, leveling the head of my battle staff at the ground ten yards in front of the closest of the charging ape creatures. With an unspoken Latin phrase.

"*Puter Navitas Telum,*"

A ball of blue energy erupted from the end of the staff. It rocketed toward the ground at the oncoming ape creatures, exploding on impact, hurling them away from me in a tangled heap of snow mingled with chunks of frozen dirt.

It worked!

I thought somewhat amazed. I put a bit more power than I'd intended into the spell, but I was satisfied with the result nevertheless. The powerful blast of blue energy wasn't meant to harm the creatures only to give me a little breathing space.

Stopping in my tracks, I turned to face them, thrusting off my coat hood in one fluid motion. Taking a firm grip on the head of the battle staff with my right hand, I gave the shaft a twist unsheathing a concealed thirty-two inch blade. The straight blade, about an inch thick, was similar to a *Japanese* Katana, but devoid of the characteristic curved shape. This elegant weapon of war was made from an extremely rare black metal called *Damasca*, forged in the foundries of the Mountain Dwarves that resided in the Alps of *Switzerland*. Magic runes etched into its length ran down the blade edge on both sides. I held the sword brandishing it in a loose *En Garde* posture uttering the Latin phrase *"Mucro Suscitatio"* as I did. The runes erupted into a white-hot fire, which glowed with a spectral incandescence.

    I didn't have long to wait for them to come at me again. The larger of the three ape creatures bounded over the crater made by the energy blast, another ran around it coming at me from the left. I didn't see the third ape creature. I speculated that it may have been killed by the blast or just rendered unconscious. A thought that made its way into my brain which made me uneasy, was that the creature at this very moment was circling its way around the action to get the drop on me. I doubted whether it would run away. These creatures didn't seem to know the meaning of the word retreat.

    I had to concentrate on the two immediate threats before me; I didn't have time to think about the third ape right now. Moving to the right as well as I could in the drift of snow, I leveled my battle staff at the creature coming straight for me. I thought the Latin phrase "Nisi

Incendia" A lance of white-hot fire, thicker than my forearm erupted from the end of the staff, sending it hurdling at the ape creature closest to me. The intense heat caused the air around the lance of fire to vaporize turning to steam. The fiery blast hit the ape square in the chest lighting it up like a high school pep rally bonfire. The beast let out a pained agonizing roar, grunting and writhing in horrified pain as the blast knocked it off it's feet, sending it hurdling backwards about forty-five feet into a stand of nearby trees. I heard a loud crunching sound, figuring it was probably bone breaking against the frozen trunk of a tree.

Silhouetted by the light from the fire I could just make out a tall tree mantled with snow falling to the forest floor with an echoing crash. The force of the fire blast and the mass of the ape creature's body striking the tree must've brought it down. I let out a sigh of relief, one of my attackers out of action; that left only the immediate threat and a possible third.

The second ape creature raced furiously around to the left, out of my peripheral vision. I made a clumsy step in that direction nearly losing my footing. Hindsight being twenty-twenty, it was a lucky thing that I stumbled. Had my head remained in the place it was a millisecond before, the ape creature's fist would've knocked it off my shoulders. Fortunately, his massive fist only grazed the left side of my face, but it still hurt like hell. Stars danced around in my vision mockingly. My body went limp; I slumped forward, succumbing to the blow, my balance wavering, however I held on to the sword and lower part of my staff.

"Stupid!" I snarled.

I allowed myself to become distracted, letting him get to close. The creature's momentum sent it barreling past me. I went down on one knee gasping in pain. Droplets of blood dripped onto the snow freezing on contact. I must've gotten popped harder than I thought. Through a dizzy haze, I watched the creature turn in the snow, kicking up a wall of drift twenty-feet high. It skidded for fifteen yards before it's hands and feet gained purchase on the frozen ground. It raised up on it's hind legs beating its chest with huge balled fists letting out an ear splitting roar as it leapt forward charging. I shook my head trying desperately to clear it.

Everything around me was out of focus and seemed to be moving in slow motion. I didn't have the time or the focus to let loose with another magical strike, the creature moved too fast and would be upon me in moments. I didn't think I could clear my head in time to gather the magic I'd need. Struggling to get on my feet, I realized that I'd inadvertently moved into a deeper drift. My attempts at regaining my balance only managed to cause me to sink deeper into the snow. There wasn't much I could do except die. I know that's an overly dramatic statement, but when you're in a situation like this you have few options.

Wait.

There's one thing I could do that might keep me alive. I needed to work fast though. The creature closed the distance quickly. When it was about five yards away it leapt into the air, it's tightly clenched fists raised over its head in a (I'm going to pile drive your ass into the ground) sort of posture. Taking the end of the battle staff, I drew a rough circle in the snow around me, about thirty-six inches in diameter. I planted the shaft of wood into the snow next to me being careful not to mar the ring I'd made. I hurriedly pulled the glove off my right hand, held it over the circle with out stretched fingers uttering the Latin phrase *"Propinquus Orbis"* closing it. A distant snapping hum, audible enough to hear over the storm told me the shield went up. The sound and fury of the storm immediately died away. I'd gotten the shield up in time.

Barely.

The creature hit the shield hard like a pigeon smacking against a newly washed plate glass window. I could feel the impact inside the circle, however it was greatly diminished in strength given that the invisible barrier of magic protected me. The creature slid down the curved invisible wall of energy into an unconscious heap not more than a foot in front of me. A trail of drool streaked down the outside of the barrier ending at the creatures open lip where its head lay against the circle. Shallow puffs of breath escaped its nostrils, it wasn't dead, but I knew it was going to be hurting with a hell of a headache when it finally came to. The great beast lay motionless, sinking into the soft drift of snow.

I gasped in pain and frustration, taking stock of my injuries. The creature's fist had scraped the entire left side of my face, from ear to lips. Part of the skin over my eyebrow was torn and bleeding liberally. Not too bad I thought. The sword was still a light casting a welcome, warming glow in the dank forest. I scanned the area around me as far as my eyes could peer through the raging storm. There was the faint diminishing glow of the other creature's body being reduced to ashes off to my left. Then something caught my eye over to my right. I thought I saw something, movement of some sort. I jerked my head in that direction. Shadows, three distinct shadows moving among the trees. I was certain of it. One of the forms appeared to be carrying a Wizard's staff. Was someone else here watching the scene or were they possibly responsible for these creatures being here. I inched forward squinting my eyes trying my best to discern more detail. The shadow with the staff halted. It appeared as though whatever it was had locked eyes on mine and was staring back at me. I strained to look closer; my eyesight however went out of focus. Fatigue was setting in, my balance wavering. I shook my head to clear my vision. When I looked back where I thought I saw the shadows, they were gone. Maybe my mind was playing tricks on me. I did after all sustain a staggering blow from the beast. The pain of my injuries started to trickle into my awareness, making certain I was acquainted with its presence. My first thought was to find my pack and take a few aspirin. I think I discarded it a ways back in the haste of escaping my attackers. After that, I'd find a place to wait out the storm so I wouldn't freeze to death.

I took another long look at my surroundings, satisfied that there'd be no threat from the third creature or the shadows, I ran the handle of my sword across the line of the circle, breaking the spell. The magic melted away and the stinging bite of the storm came rushing back against the exposed skin on my face. I pulled the other end of the staff out of the snow. Using that and the unmoving body of the ape creature I managed to free myself from the snowdrift. Sitting a few feet away from the creature, exhausted and gasping for air, I took a good look at my attacker. Its face was turned toward me. My eyes stared unblinking at it for a few moments. I was right in my initial assumption, the creature was ape-like in appearance.

In some weird fashion I'd hoped that these things would turn out to be people in elaborate costumes, like the villains in *Scooby-Doo* cartoons. Sadly however this was real life and not Saturday morning when I was a kid. My eyes continued to rove over the body. If I didn't know any better I'd say the creature was Bigfoot's cousin, the Yeti. While distracted in the midst of my zoological pondering, a great hand closed over my head squeezing it, a large finger covering my left eye. I went rigid; the hand lifted me off the ground turning me in mid air. It was the third ape I'd overlooked; it held me in its right hand. You'd think something this large would make some sort of sound creeping up on a person, but it didn't.

The creature eyed me. The way a cat corners a mouse right before it eviscerates it. Breath billowed out of its nostrils in quick angry huffs. This smart bastard stayed away from the scene of the action waiting for me to make a mistake, which I ultimately did. Obviously, this beast was the brains of these creatures. The creature simply glared at me, I think daring me to do something, anything that would be provocative. It finally opened its mouth letting out a roar of anger that almost made me lose all my bodily control. The breath of this creature was foul. It smelled bad, like rotten meat mixed with the pungent aroma of *Limburger* cheese and a hint of high school locker room after a football game. This thing needed a breath mint in the worst way; correction breath mints - *plural* - one wouldn't do the job. It was at this moment that I remembered that I held a magic sword. Lifting it, I drove the point deep into the creature's left shoulder. It growled in agonizing pain. The hair and flesh around the wound burned and blistered.

Only beings from Mid-Realm reacted in such a way to magical blades. It was one of their few weaknesses in the mortal realm. Ten millennia ago the temporal barrier between the mortal world and Mid-Realm was fluid, meaning that beings from either reality could pass between worlds without any trouble. Which is where many of humanity's myths, legends and folklore originated. As time passed, the borders between our worlds solidified preventing easy access from one to the other. There are a handful of doorways around the world remaining to this day, which allow passage between realms. We hear about these doorways occasionally through stories or eyewitness accounts such as weird goings on in the *Bermuda Triangle*, strange colored lights in the sky or tall mysterious beings lurking in wooded areas.

Great... I thought, what the hell were Mid-Realm creatures doing here?

The creature moved in a blur of motion, grabbing the blade of the sword with its freehand, hurling me away from itself with the other. I flew through the air like a limp rag doll landing in the snow cutting a long path through the drifts not unlike a path a plane might make crash landing back to earth. Luckily I missed hitting the trunks of two rather large trees, coming to rest on my back between them. Snow packed into the neck of my coat, covering my shoulders and part of my head.

The pain was excruciating. Everything hurt, but I managed to raise my head just enough to watch the creature pull the dimming sword from its shoulder, discarding it petulantly into a nearby snowdrift. The creature turned in my direction. Our eyes met. His were filled with unbridled rage. He crouched into a tight ball, launching himself at me. In two mighty bounds he was on top of me. His ponderous weight pressing down on my chest.

Damn. This thing weighed a lot.

The creature glared hatefully into my eyes. Blood from its wound dripped into a pool beside me. The drip... drip... drip... pattering sound was maddening.

"Hey there buddy." I said in an absolutely terrified tone. "Nice day huh?"

O.K. you try saying something witty with a thousand pound Mid-Realm gorilla beast sitting on your chest bent on killing you. I bet you would've failed as spectacularly as I did just then. My heart thumped furiously against my sternum as I watched in helpless horror. The creature growled, opening its mouth wide, with a quick movement of its head and upper body, it leaned its cavernous mouth down over my face. I felt its large canine teeth sink into the soft flesh of my scalp, its jaws closed around my face and head. The beast gave his head a savage jerk. I felt and heard the bones in my neck shatter, splintering into tiny fragments.

My throat began to close up. I choked gasping for air; I wasn't able to take another breath. I've never felt pain like this before. I started to panic, but all I could do is watch and listen. My vision began to lose focus then, slowly faded to black, I fought uselessly against the encroaching darkness. My hearing failed me. I could hear everything clearly then, poof. Nothing. It was almost like someone slowly closing a sliding glass door to drown out unwanted noise. Then the moment I was dreading happened, I could literally feel the life draining out of me. Escaping. There was no light to guide me to the next life. There was no out of body experience. There was only the feeling of complete and total nothingness. I was dead and that's all there was to it. Eternal sleep fell about me like a warm blanket and I knew no more of the world of the living.

# Chapter 3

"Solomon..."

I heard my name. It was a faint, but tangible echo in the deep recesses of my mind. Almost like hearing your name in a hazy dream, far off yet drifting on a wisp of wind. That was impossible. Wasn't it? How could someone be calling my name? I died. I know I did. My lifeless body lay in the middle of that forest. The snow has probably covered my body and it wouldn't be found until the spring thaw if at all. That is unless the snow creatures - the remaining ones that is - devoured me as one final indignity. As far as I knew, there's no possible way to converse with the dead. Right? So how could I be hearing my name?

"Solomon..."

There it was again.

My name, I heard it. I was sure of it this time, louder, more clearly. Yet, somehow the voice was familiar, heard through the lifting haze in my mind. Maybe my neck wasn't the only thing to be savagely mangled. What if for good measure, the ape creature decided to eat my face off? Leaving me not only broken in the snow with shattered bones in my neck, but with an exposed skull to look at for the rest of my life. That definitely would be the cruelest joke fate has ever played on me and let's face it, fate has played some real doozy's over the years.

"Solomon, my boy... Wake up."

My eyes snapped open, adjusting to being abruptly brought back from sleep. I inhaled deeply looking around me. I didn't die. I was alive. I lifted my hands touching my chest and face making sure there were no injuries. I was alive God dammit! Alive and intact.

I stood behind the front counter of Blackmane's Magic and Potion Shop. It was *December* fifth according to the calendar on the wall and I was alive. Familiar aromas came flooding into my nostrils. Such as the sweet and metallic smelling potions brewing carried up from the basement through the heating vents. The aroma of well aged oak wood, a smell that permeated the entire shop because every cabinet and shelf was made from that very material. The odor of all the different ingredients wafted about me overwhelming my sense of smell. Ingredients like stagnant cypress stump water, shavings of rainbow bark or the briny tang of *Dead Sea* water along with the smells of various roots and plant clippings, some smelling pleasant like newly mowed grass or lilac. While others tended to be more foul smelling like the scent of unwashed armpits or beer-soaked ashtrays.

    I looked to my left. On the wall hung the same old woodcarving I'd seen many times over the years depicting *King Arthur* pulling *Excalibur* from a squat stone while the Wizard *Merlin* looked on. Within the tarnished etched silver frame arranged over the scene in an arch were eight emerald green stones roughly the size of *U.S. Quarters*. Above the framed woodcarving hung an extremely old yet somewhat creepy wooden gothic style *German* cuckoo clock. Instead of the traditional cuckoo that popped out marking the top of the hour this particular clock had a dragon's head which burst angrily from it's lair bellowing a deep threatening roar, spitting plumes of fire. The clock chimed a sullen tone to all who were within earshot that the time was now twelve-thirty in the afternoon. A dawning realization came to me. Slowly, but it came nevertheless.

    Damn it! I thought.

    I fell asleep again. It was all just a dream. A freaky real feeling messed up one at that. Thank God! A relieved smile crept onto my face as I turned back to the counter. Standing on the other side were three people. Well, two people and a Troll. The first person was a short stout man, Oswald Gleason. He had a concerned look on his face. Standing directly behind Oswald to his right

23

was Glum, Oswald's Troll. The second person I mentioned was Orm, a good friend of Barnabas Blackmane, the owner of the magic shop and a friend to Oswald Gleason as well.

    The first two were an odd contrast to say the least. Oswald was short as I've said, around five feet tall and plump. He once remarked to me *"That he never met a meal he didn't like."* Judging by the size of his midsection I didn't have any doubts about the truth of his statement. He had a broad face, wide set eyes and a thin pair of lips, which stretched nearly to both of his ears when he smiled. He looked an awful lot like a frog that had just caught and eaten a nice juicy insect of some sort. His skin was pale in color, not a sickly pallor just that of someone who tended to shun sunlight and Wizards quite often did just that. His white hair, which was thick for man his age - five hundred and thirty two his last birthday - was combed back into a neatly kept ponytail. His style of dress never varied much in any noticeable way reminding me of an eccentric late eighteenth century villain dressed all in crushed black velvet. The only splash of color he accented his outfit with was a red and gold vest he wore under his long coat.

    Glum on the other hand was nearly eight feet tall. He was usually dressed in loose fitting sweatpants and hoodies. Today however he wore a *Detroit Lions* jersey that was almost too small for his ample frame. On his feet was a pair of shoes sized thirty-eight specially made by an Elf family. I haven't any idea how much they cost to make, but I know they weren't cheap. His skin was ashen gray in color. He looked like a typical run of the mill Troll, large hairless head, protruding brow ridge and a pair of deep-set black eyes, which seemed tiny when you looked into them. His shoulders were broad, which made him appear even larger than he actually was. If you were to lay eyes on Glum you'd swear he was dangerous with his huge powerful arms and legs. However in reality Glum was quite gentle. Unless of course you decided to make trouble for Oswald, then he would tear you apart.

No questions asked.

You'd have to meet Glum to understand him; he has the mental maturity of a ten year old. He loves and worships Oswald, the way a son loves and worships his father at a very young age, when the veil of innocence is still intact. It's an unusual sort of relationship, but it works and they're both happy.

Orm, the third person I mentioned was as different in appearance as a watermelon is to a banana. He's tall. Not as tall as Glum, closer to average *NBA* tall as well as being rail thin. If he ate a grain of rice right now I guarantee there'd be a noticeable bulge under his tight fitting shirt. He's one of those people that could eat copious amounts of food, yet never gain an ounce. His long face was framed by thick jet-black hair that fell just below his jaw line. His hawkish nose perched atop his thick brush like mustache. He paid me little attention as he checked his list to the ingredients Barnabas collected out of the magic shop's inventory.

"Are you alright?" Oswald asked concerned.

"Yeah," I replied through a stifled yawn. "Sorry, Barnabas kept us out late again last night. A character building exercise he called it."

A knowing smile played in Oswald's features.

"Ah... Looking after the needs of Abner Dempke and his followers again... Barnabas pushes himself far too much, I fear he's spreading himself thin."

"You could say that, but as you know it's his way. We didn't get back until nearly three a.m." I said in a complaining tone. "You'd think Abner's people would learn by now to lay off that stuff."

"Werewolves are creatures of excess, you know that as well as I do. Asking them or trying to make them give up addictions is like asking a fish not to swim... It's in their blood." Oswald said philosophically.

Abner Dempke - in case you were wondering - is the alpha male or leader of a small pack of Werewolves that reside here in *Detroit*. There are fifteen in his pack all together. They're nice enough folks, hard working and full of the joy of living each day like there's no tomorrow.

About two years ago half of Abner's pack was infected with a disease called the Bane. Being a Werewolf and long lived with a very high metabolism they can't get drunk or high on all the normal drugs that humans take for granted. That makes them essentially immune to most if not all diseases known to man. Hell, even tranquilizers formulated for big game like rhinos and elephants can't easily put them down. So, for recreational enjoyment Werewolves have turned to ingesting *Wolfsbane* to get a buzz.

*Wolfsbane* to humans and other animals is poisonous, but to a Werewolf its like taking heroin or crack with similar effects. The Bane is a disease that only affects Werewolves. The disease exists within the cellular walls of the *Wolfsbane* plant. When the plant is ingested the disease goes to work destroying the digestive system causing the one infected to essentially starve to death no matter how much food is eaten. It's an exceedingly nasty disease. About forty percent of the world's Werewolf population died off because of the Bane disease. There's a lot of speculation of its origin and many in the magical community believe that it was developed specifically to target Werewolves.

The origin of the Bane is still unknown, but many point the finger at the world of Normal's and their "so-called" scientists. I on the other hand don't agree with that line of thinking. Most of the world's population doesn't know of the existence of the magical community or the creatures that are part of it and those Normal's that do, choose to ignore us all together. For some reason people in general will choose denial over facing the truth. I can't say I blame them. If humanity knew what sorts of weirdness and danger existed so close to them, they'd freak out on a scale that hasn't been seen since the witch hunts in Europe centuries ago. For what it's worth, my money was on the Vampires. Those two races have never

27

gotten along and I know the Vampire's would love to see all Werewolves' dead. If it weren't for the efforts of Barnabas and a few other Wizards' like him Werewolves would've died out altogether. Sadly, many Werewolves are so addicted to *Wolfsbane* that many continue to get sick from eating the plant. Which is the main reason that Barnabas and I were out until all most three this morning.

"Is this all the Goblin hair you have," Orm asked in his thick *French* accent thrusting a small glass bottle under my nose.

I recoiled away from the bottle when I got a whiff of what was inside. Goblin hair smells like ammonia with a hint of almond, a fragrance *Glade* won't be offering as an air freshener anytime soon. I was glad my stomach was empty at the moment.

"Yes," I said. "Barnabas gave you all we had,"

Orm shook his head disappointedly corking the bottle.

"This won't nearly be enough," he complained.

"You can get more at Nabi's in Stumpwater's," I suggested.

He made a disgusted sound.

"Nabi's," he said offended. "They are far too expensive and the quality is not as good,"

I nodded sympathetically even though I really didn't care where he got his ingredients. He wasn't exactly the best customer and let's face it the man was cheap.

"Where is James today," Oswald asked curiously. "Doesn't he usually fetch your potion ingredients for you,"

"Humph, that no good clumsy oaf," Orm scoffed contemptuously. "I would not trust him to fetch water,"

He placed a small wooden box filled with dragon fire ash down a little to forcefully onto the glass case startling Glum from his examination of a scuff on the hardwood floor.

"I have him perched upon a fifteen foot high stone pillar practicing his wand balancing technique over a pit filled with shards of broken glass and rusty rug tacks, that should keep him busy until I return," Orm said amused.

Oswald and I exchanged perplexed looks of incredulity.

He went back to checking off the items on his list.

God I was tired. Judging by the look on Oswald's face I could drop to the floor at any moment.

"Why don't you just make an executive decision and put the "Out to Lunch" sign in the window, lock the door and take a short nap?" Oswald said with a noticeable - I won't tell inflection in his fatherly tone.

I chuckled halfheartedly. It was tempting. Very tempting. Hell, why not? Business had been slow all day, but then again if I did close the shop, Barnabas would have me do some unpleasant chores for the next two months. Such as, cleaning out the brood worm tank, God how I dislike even looking at those nasty things. Brood worms are black in color, but turn bright red when they've fed. They're seven inches long before they feed, expanding to over thirteen inches when full. They can ingest a pint of blood at a feeding. Brood worms are roughly an inch in diameter, eyeless, but equipped with three circular rows of jagged teeth in their mouths. Makes my skin crawl just thinking about them. The only reason we keep them in the shop is because their blood contains high levels of sulfur, which is used in potion making.

"No. I'll tough it out. Barnabas wouldn't appreciate it if I did that. Besides he should be back at any moment with lunch and my hunger outweighs being tired."

"Food?" Glum smiled, his ears perked up at the mention of his favorite subject, food.

"Glum hungry."

Oswald and I exchanged a grin. Then Oswald turned patting the big guy on the forearm.

"Soon Glum... Soon." He said to him reassuringly.

"Food..." Glum said once again only softer this time. I think he meant the word only for himself.

I was waiting patiently for Barnabas to get back with our greasy and extremely unhealthy fast food lunch, when Oswald walked into the store with Glum followed by Orm a short time later. Being up since five thirty that morning I never really got to bed after a long night. Skipping breakfast was something I did on a far too regular basis. Working on only a few hours sleep made my mind wander again. I could hear the echoes of an old public service announcement playing around in my head with a slight mocking undertone.

"Breakfast is the most important meal of the day,"

"Bite me," I thought in a not so humorous mood.

Orm packed the last of his ingredients back into a cardboard box after painstakingly checking the items three times. Sometimes I wonder if he suffers from OCD or he's just a jerk. He picked the box up off the counter tucking it under his left arm.

"Put this on my bill," he said. "I will settle my account with Barnabas at the end of the month,"

I opened my mouth to reply, but he made a gesture with is free hand abruptly vanishing before our eyes.

"Someone should teach him some manners," Oswald said disappointed.

I shrugged sighing. Orm always did things like that. He treated everyone like they were beneath him, well not everyone. He'd never treat Barnabas like a peon. I really didn't need this crap at the moment. There were a thousand different things I could've been doing right at that moment. Well, maybe not a thousand, but a few to be sure came to mind; catching up on my movies and book lists, riding my mountain bike or rebuilding my *1969 Buick Skylark Custom Convertible* that sat in Barnabas's garage. The car was in bad shape. Bad might be too generous a word for the condition it was in, but all the parts were there. Sadly I knew next to nothing about cars or how to rebuild them, but it was free. I mean how could I pass it up? I really enjoyed working on it and so what if it took me years to make it cherry again, it was mine. When it was finished it would be a head turner. I won it playing poker a few months ago at the Laughing Goblin Tavern. One of the few times I actually won at the damn game. I'm well known in gambling circles for my long losing streaks and my money is highly sought and welcomed at any poker table.

Barnabas thought I was insane for bringing it home, he'd have rather seen it taken to a junkyard. The man has absolutely no imagination. However sleep, glorious sleep was at the top of my list of things to do. Followed closely behind was devouring two hot dogs just the way I liked them with mustard, relish and extra onions. The fries are wrapped inside with the hot dogs combining for a perfect storm of greasy delight. Washed down with a medium *Dr. Pepper* from Deli Dogs, one of the best hot dog places here in *Detroit*. The antique clock on the wall ticked by painfully slowly. The hunger pains, though unpleasant wouldn't have been so bad had it not been Monday, twelve thirty in the afternoon and I was engaged in a lengthy, yet somewhat boring conversation with Oswald Gleason; our most regular and devoted customer. He never missed a Monday.

Ever.

Now, let me start off by saying, Oswald wasn't a bad guy. He was just very old, very dull and a tad on the peculiar side. Then again, who isn't. Oswald was always kind and generous toward me however. He's sort of like an uncle to me. I've known him since the age of fourteen when I came to live with Barnabas. The more time I spent around Oswald a soft spot developed in my heart for him, so I'd listen to him prattle on about any subject, until he was ready to go on his way.

On this particular Monday he was talking about how difficult it was to find good apprentices these days. The only thing that kept my mind in the conversation was the painful gurgling sounds emanating from my stomach, almost like the noise two dogs make fighting over a piece of bacon.

"Well," he said interrupting my musings. "I'm sure that Abner and his followers appreciated the time and effort you and Barnabas made on their behalf."

"I know," I said. "But..."

"But nothing," he said briskly cutting off my complaint. "Don't ever take lightly what you do to help others... Abner and his followers will never forget your kindness and that is something you should never discount, because,"

Something caught Oswald's attention and he abruptly broke off the conversation. Whatever it was, his attention was concentrated on the woodcarving to his right. It made him an even paler shade of white than I was use to seeing. My brow furrowed in contemplation. Oswald raised his hands, glancing at his rings. Eight gold rings with green colored stones set in each rode on the four fingers of each of his hands. I noticed one of them had changed color, from green to red, very peculiar. As long as I've known Oswald the stones in his rings have always been green. His eyes returned to the woodcarving, his lips parting in apparent dawning realization. Then again I was tired and could've been misreading his expression. I turned looking to where Oswald's attention was concentrated. The wood carving depicting *King Arthur* removing *Excalibur* from a stone appeared to be exactly the same, except one of the eight emerald stones arranged in an arc had turned from green to red. That was odd as well. I never knew that the mural was enchanted, but living and working in the world of Wizards I wasn't really surprised.

    I turned back to ask Oswald if he knew about the woodcarving, however to my surprise he and Glum were gone. They'd just vanished, not even making a sound. I wasn't startled at Oswald and Glum's abrupt exit. They'd often do things like this, popping in and popping out of the store all the time. His rings though, that was odd. Along with what happened with the woodcarving, that stone had changed color as well. I turned back to the woodcarving to find another of the green stones blinking to red. I still didn't have a clue as to what any of this meant, but like the check engine light on a car, this couldn't be good. At that precise moment the mailbox bell rang. I heard a metallic tang of a letter dropping into the bottom of the empty metal box. The mailman wasn't normally due till three o'clock so it had to be some sort of magical correspondence. I paid the letter no mind. Barnabas could get it when he got back with lunch.

I blearily blinked my eyes, sleep driving the thought of the changing stones from my mind. I'd ask Barnabas or Oswald about them later. I sighed in relief that I was finally alone, that I didn't have to listen to Oswald any longer. I pulled up a nearby stool sitting down on it. I leaned forward on the counter, folded my arms and laid my head down on them closing my sleep-deprived eyes for a few minutes of peace.

I started to drift away into the river of sleep; sadly a loud crash of glass shattering in back of me startled me out of my doze. So much for my few moments of peace, I groaned thumping my forehead frustrated on the counter before lifting my tired head. I had to investigate what happened and clean up whatever it was before Barnabas returned. I got off the stool walking down the dried ingredient aisle to my left. There I found a glass jar containing dried toadstools had fallen off the shelf and shattered, scattering its contents everywhere. Right beside the broken glass and toadstools was the unconscious form of a Cob Elf sprawled on his back with a nasty bump forming on his forehead just above his left eye. The Elf possibly snuck in and somehow was able to get through the shops defensive wards.

Great, another shoplifting ingredient thief.

It happened from time to time. Ingredients for magical potions tended to be rare, well some of them anyway and very expensive. Sadly if you couldn't afford the prices for them, a person either looked for the ingredients on their own, which was a dangerous endeavor or they would try to steal them. However, no one had gotten so far into the store like this before. Ordinarily the store's wards would immobilize any would be thief, setting off alarms notifying us that an intruder had been caught. Fortunately, he had some trouble opening the jar. Which resulted in him knocking himself out cold.

The Elf was about twenty-four inches in height, on the short side for a Cob Elf. Dressed in a deep red suit, reminiscent of the fashion a man might have worn during the late eighteen hundreds. The condition of his clothes and the Elf himself appeared to have been through a hard scuffle. The fabric of his red coat was torn in places; there were black scorch marks around his head and shoulders. As he lay there I took in his facial features. He had the face of a kindly old uncle, full of life with a hint of good-natured mischievousness despite his haggard appearance. Surely he wasn't a threat to anyone. What was he doing here? How did he find himself in this state, more importantly who did this to him? I knelt down beside him taking hold of his left wrist checking for a pulse. He was still alive. His pulse was slow and steady.

I lowered his hand gently; the back of it touched the floor causing the fingers to open. A small yellow crystal rolled out onto the floor making a faint tinkling sound like ice being dropped into a glass tumbler. My attention was fixed on the crystal. It wasn't very large, maybe a few inches in length, no more than a half inch in diameter. I could feel power pulsing inside it. I hesitated, not wanting to pick it up. All the warning bells inside my head went off at once, warning me that it wouldn't be a good idea to pick it up. Before I realized what I was doing I watched my hand reaching for it. A compulsion I couldn't resist pushing me not to listen to the warnings sounding inside my brain. I couldn't stop myself or stay the motion of my hand. It acted separately of my consciousness, the thing mesmerized me and I wanted to pick it up.

No, check that… I needed to pick it up.

My fingers wrapped around the crystal. A brilliant warm light blazed from it. I averted my eyes. I felt dizzy, like the feeling you sometimes got when you were a child, spinning around in an office chair too long. My body tingled with an overload of sensation. Though uncomfortable the feeling wasn't painful. My stomach churned. I could feel bile rising in my throat. My skin felt like there was a river of hot wellspring water flowing beneath it. My vision blackened around the edges, dimming. At one point the sensation of fire was so intense, I thought my skin was going to melt. Then as suddenly as it began the sensations I was experiencing simply vanished.

The crystal's yellow color dimmed giving way to a clear color. I shook the cobwebs out of my head. I placed the crystal inside the Cob Elf's coat pocket with shaking hands. I picked him up moving him away from the mess of toadstools and broken glass. I placed him gently on a stack of neatly folded packing pads, which we kept in the back. He was still out cold. I turned to clean up the mess, but something caught my eye. Turning back, I noticed a thick braid of metal around the Elf's neck. A medallion was attached to the end of the metal braid. I reached down to see if there was an inscription upon the medallion. Grasping it with my thumb and forefinger I turned it over. An intense bolt of electricity shot up my arm right through my body down to my toes. You'd have thought that I'd learned my lesson about touching strange objects after the crystal incident. No... not me. Not Mr. Thickhead. I blame the lack of sleep. This just wasn't my day.

  The front door opened, chiming the strand of tarnished brass bells. Sweet! Barnabas had returned with lunch. Cleaning up the mess would have to wait. I was hungry. Walking to the front of the store something didn't feel right. There was a cold energy flowing around me. A dark energy. Goose flesh rose on my skin causing me to shiver. I stopped a few feet away from the counter realizing where the feeling I'd been experiencing probably originated from. It wasn't Barnabas that came in, but a tall albino man flanked by rather attractive identical twins of the female variety. He smiled when he saw me. His teeth however were not something he should've been proud of. They were yellowish brown almost the color of *Dusseldorf Mustard* along with having large gaps in between each tooth. Obviously he hadn't heard about the advances in modern dentistry or simple teeth whitening products. I couldn't see his eyes;

he was wearing a dark pair of round-rimmed glasses, which wrapped around his eyes like fancy ski goggles, concealing them.

"Good afternoon'" he said in a gruff high-pitched tone. "I was wondering if you had seen a Cob Elf anywhere about? He took something that doesn't belong to him and I'm here to collect it.

# Chapter 4

Cob Elf?

How did this guy know there was a Cob Elf here? I thought. Rather puzzled by his question, trying my best not to show it. The Elf took something. That crystal. Maybe that's what he was after. This guy, whoever he was had the look of someone that didn't like to play games. So it might be a good idea for me to just bite my tongue and be a good magic shop employee.

"Pardon me, I don't recall you or your friends…" gesturing to the twins. "…Ever being in the store before, who are you again?" I said moving to the counter, placing both hands palms down on its surface.

The albino took a step forward. He tapped the end of his cane once upon the floor before lifting it to a horizontal position at his side. The man's skin and hair were the color of new fallen snow. I can honestly say that I've never seen lustrous chin length hair quite like his. He must've used some sort of professional hair care product and spent a lot of time in front of a mirror to get it that symmetrical. He was dressed in an unremarkable black business suit, a gray over coat draped over his left forearm. The cane he held looked to be an antique, ornately carved wood with a gold handle in the shape of *Medusa's* head. The snakes in her hair coiled down wrapping around the shaft about three to four inches where the metal joined the wood.

The twins mirrored the albino's movements, however they moved more gracefully and more fluid like smoke moving on a light breeze. Both were about five seven in height, dressed exactly the same in red and black leather jumpsuits covering their bodies from their necks all the way down to their feet. The suits made a distinctive sultry creaking noise leather makes when a person moves in it, a very distracting sound.

To be perfectly honest they filled out those jumpsuits nicely. I had a heck of a time keeping my eyes off their more interesting features. Each had long blonde hair, braided into high tight topknot ponytails. They possessed the kind of faces and bodies you might see gracing the pages of popular fashion magazines. Their skin, also pale, but not as pale as the albino's was very attractive. I couldn't see their eyes because they were wearing dark wraparound sunglasses as well; theirs however looked more stylish and far more expensive.

"Who I am is inconsequential... The question I asked was have you seen a Cob Elf?" The albino spoke slowly and precisely talking to me as though I were a child of five.

"No I haven't," I answered mimicking his tone and inflection.

Of course I saw the Cob Elf, he was lying unconscious in the back room, but he didn't need to know that. Besides I didn't know who the hell this joker or these women were.

"That's strange," the albino said mockingly. "We tracked him to this location,"

"He's lying to you my Lord... Yes, lying through his mortal teeth." The twins said in unison, like they were sharing the same brain and mouth.

That wasn't creepy or anything.

They said mortal teeth. Which meant that they probably weren't mortal themselves and if a fight broke out I'd be at a disadvantage. The twins took a few steps forward fanning out away from the albino, attempting I supposed to position themselves in such a way as to prevent me from escaping should I try to beat a hasty retreat. The way my heart was pounding in my chest the thought was tempting. The albino's lips tightened turning a dark pink color then he said.

"Are you lying to me young man? If there is one thing I cannot stand is to be lied to," his eyes fixed on me. "My companions are very good at knowing when someone is lying to me... I hope for your sake this is the first time they're wrong,"

His fingers squeezed tighter around the shaft of the cane.

"However, if my associates are correct and you are lying to me, I would have no other choice but to let these lovely ladies have a private talk with you. Wringing the truth from difficult people is something they enjoy immensely. We can be reasonable here however," he paused brushing a bit of lint from his jacket lapel.

"All I want is the Elf nothing more... Now be a good young man and tell me where he is."

The twins grinned, each mirroring the others movements, showing their perfectly white teeth. Whitey should ask them where they get their teeth cleaned and polished. I also noticed one other thing about the twin's smiles; their long pointed canine teeth.

Vampires.

Great... As long as they didn't try to use their glamour on me I should be fine. Whitey however, was far more dangerous of the three. I could feel dark oily energy swirling around him the longer he stood in front of me. He was gathering magic, which was bad. It meant he was anticipating a fight or more accurately wanting to start one. I really didn't want to have to get into a fight here in the store, but there was no way in hell I was giving the little guy up to these three. Sigh. Having a conscious can really suck at times.

"Look, I don't want any trouble."

"Then give me the Elf!" Whitey barked cutting me off, an icy threat contained in his words.

"Can we have him now? Yes, can we? We think he would be so much fun and very tasty." The Vampire twins said in uncontrolled anticipation.

They were looking at me like a pair of hyenas waiting for a lion to get finished with its kill so they could swoop in to finish up the remains. They wanted me and not in a good way. I didn't want to think what would happen if they got their icy hands on me.

"Patience ladies... Patience... I'm sure this young man will do the right thing and if he doesn't then you will have an opportunity to persuade him,"

The albino raised his left wrist glancing at his watch.

"I'll give him approximately nine seconds to produce the Elf," he said.

The twins shifted their weight anxiously waiting for Whitey to give the word. I really didn't have time for this.

"Look Whitey..."

Oops.

Did I just call him Whitey? Yeah... By the angry expression on his face I'm afraid I did. For some reason the editing feature that controlled what I was thinking and what I should be saying wasn't working today. OK, it rarely ever worked. Maybe it's because I was hungry and in turn made me a tad grumpy. That wasn't true either; I speak my mind and have absolutely no tact, besides he's trying to intimidate me. I don't like being intimidated.

"I haven't seen any Elf." I continued. "If I do I'll be sure to let you know. In the meantime this is a store, either buy something or get the hell out and take the young ladies with you."

Whitey's face clouded over in anger. As I have said, I couldn't see his eyes, but I knew he was pissed. I made sure my left hand rested on a round magic symbol carved into the wood of the counter. It was a defensive spell I came up with a while back in lieu of keeping a gun under the counter. Barnabas disliked guns and wouldn't let me keep one at hand. He always said,

"We're Wizards, guns are beneath us,"

Sometimes a gun would come in handy, I don't care how powerful a Wizard he or she thinks they are, a jacketed round to the head will kill your enemy just as quickly as a spell. Anyway, this particular spell was designed to immobilize an attacker with fine spider web like strands. The more you struggled the more entangled you'd become. Most spells, however require you to put energy into them to work, which sort of tips your hand to the Wizard you're facing off against. Any Wizard worth their salt can feel an opponent gathering magic for an attack. This one didn't need any energy channeled through it to work. I made it sort of like a mousetrap. All I had to do was take my hand off the magical symbol and the trap would activate.

Pretty cool huh?

The way this conversation was heading I'd need to activate it soon. The Vampire twins looked like they were going to lunge at me at any moment.

"You killed my Master!" Came a furious high pitch voice to my right.

I paused blinking, stunned by this new voice. I think we all looked to the spot where the voice originated, however I wasn't sure. I didn't see anyone, so I lowered my gaze. There stood the Cob Elf. He was awake though he appeared to be in pain, a visible knot on his head. He stood next to the counter, his feet firmly planted, right arm raised. I could see magical energy swirling around his out stretched hand. It was like looking through heat rising off an asphalt road on a scorching hot day. A hate filled expression on his face. Whitey tensed.

"Well... well... well... There you are you troublesome little creature,"

Whitey turned fixing his eyes on me.

"I'll deal with you in a moment,"

He turned his attention back to the Cob Elf. Gripping his cane harder, he leveled it at his diminutive foe. The Elf raised his left arm. A faint shimmering blue shield emanated from the palm of his outstretched hand. A half dome of pure defensive energy sprang to life. I can create shields and barriers with various forms of energy to protect myself as well. However my abilities were not in the same class as this Cob Elf's. Elves are magical creatures, meaning they're born with the ability to wield magic. High and Dark Elves are the most powerful respectively, followed by Forest Elves, then the Cob Elves. They're sort of the blue-collar members of the Elf family. Basic magic spells, disappearing, fixing things, healing, cooking, making toys, pretty much everything you've read or seen about them in movies and books.

"Let's all just take it easy now," I said with absolutely no confidence that any of us were going to be taking it easy.

The tension in the store was so thick you could cut it with a knife. Whitey and the twins were poised, ready to pounce. The Elf was as unmovable as a granite mountain and my palms were sweating profusely. I was scared to death trying my best not to show it. My weapons and focus items were nowhere near me, however there were a couple of *Louisville Slugger* baseball bats under the counter to my right. If I could only get to one, I'd feel more at ease. I concentrated intensely on a bat; I could feel a nervous smile appearing on my face. In retrospect I could see how that smile could've been misinterpreted in this delicate situation, because Whitey and the twins were not amused at all.

"Kill them!" Whitey hissed through clinched teeth.

"Crap!" I exclaimed.

Actually I think I used a word that sounded a lot like "Spit"

The twins lunged straight for me; their motions were lightening fast, like the strike of a coiled rattler.

Two pairs of five-inch straight double-edged daggers blurred into view from sheaths I assumed were worn behind their backs. The twins spun the blades weaving them through their fingers with practiced skill. I had only a split second to act. I took my hand off the magic symbol, ducking down to the right, reaching for one of the baseball bats. This was an excellent opportunity for me to see if all those hours I spent at *Macomb's Batting Cages* paid off.

Thousands upon thousands of delicate clear strands of spider web like material exploded from the walls, the ceiling and the floor. The sunlight shone through the front windows hitting the strands in such a way creating a prismatic effect that bathed the inside of the store with a rainbow of color. The strands looked like spun glass seeking out any movement on the other side of the counter. The twin closest to me on the left became entangled in a mass of strands. She was pulled to the floor screaming and thrashing. The other twin dodged the strands ending up near the store's front door with such a graceful display of tumbling and acrobatics that would make the entire US gymnastics team envious.

Whitey on the other hand took a different approach in dealing with my trap. He unleashed a strike of dark tendril magic from the end of his cane at the Elf. No sooner had the strike been released, his overcoat was in his left hand using it like a matador's cape tempting a bull. He swept it in a circle around him, gathering the strands like they were spun cotton candy. He made one

49

complete circle then discarded the smoking coat to the floor. Facing the Elf once more. The coat bubbled and melted before my eyes. Dark magic struck the Elf's shield, exploding into a white light forcing the little guy back two or three feet before it dissipated. The Elf let loose a magical strike of his own. Hundreds of ice shards the size of golf tees shot from his fingers hurdling at Whitey.

Whitey lifted his left hand palm out moving it in a counterclockwise circle in front of him. A wall of green fire appeared. The ice shards turned to steam on contact. I caught a blur of motion to my left. I turned just in time to see the Vampire twin that avoided my defensive spell running along the wall as if it were a stadium track. I raised my left hand and thought the Latin words,

"Erigo Contego,"

A translucent blue shield roughly forty inches in diameter appeared in front of my out stretched hand. The Vampire twin launched herself off the mural of *King Arthur*, throwing both arms above her head aiming her daggers straight at me. Her body was straight and rigid; she had the look of a missile zeroing in on me. I leaned into the shield bracing myself for the impact. The baseball bat I held was back and ready to be employed in an old fashioned yet still useful clubbing motion. However as what usually happens nothing really goes to plan.

The Vampire used the counter as a springboard. Her hands made contact with the heavy flat surface allowing her to flip over my shield landing behind me. I dropped the bat and defensive shield moving into a crouch scything her legs out from under her with a low sweep kick. I'd say watching all those *Kung Fu* movies on television when I was an impressionable little boy finally paid off. The Vamp was fast, too fast actually for my mortal reflexes. She was up and coming at me once again. I raised my hand palm out facing her thinking the Latin phrase,

"Conicio Incednia"

I pushed my hand toward her. A ball of yellow fire the size of a basketball hurdled toward her head. The fireball hit its mark, impacting square in the middle of her face. Her painful screams were almost too much for my ears to handle. She dropped the daggers bringing her hands to her face. I could see the remains of her melted sunglasses dripping from between her clenched fingers. I knew I only had moments before her face began healing and she'd be at my throat wanting to tear it out. So I picked up the baseball bat swinging hard, cracking it right across the right side of her face. The bat broke off at the handle right above where I gripped it sending the head of the bat sailing into a shelf of magical reference books. She went down in an unconscious heap. I turned to see the other Vampire twin almost free of her bonds. *

I blinked taking my eyes off the scene around me. The whole situation gave me pause. I'd dodged death's icy hand by the barest of margins. I turned my attention to the front of the store. There I saw Barnabas wearing his well-worn brown winter jacket and a look of concern planted on his face. His thick brown hair peppered with streaks of gray was tousled by the mild *December* wind. He and Oswald stood just inside the door of the magic shop. Their right arms out stretched; motes of white wisps of subtle power swirling around their fingertips and hands were evident. They'd used an immobilizing spell on everyone in the store but me. Behind them towering over my two rescuers stood Glum, itching to get in on the fighting.

He loved a good brawl every now and then. In matter of fact all Trolls enjoyed brawling. They lived for it. To Glum's left was Sister Marianna. She was head of the *Catholic* orphanage where I lived until the age of fourteen. She'd left the Order many years ago because she was smitten with one Barnabas Blackmane. Her religious beliefs and personal desires just didn't mesh, so she had to give something up. The church lost a good nun, however I gained a mother figure. Though I still can't seem to break the habit - see what I did there - of calling her Sister Marianna. She stood a little over five and a half feet tall, however her outspoken nature made you think she was a lot taller. In spite of the tableau she was now witness to, her face bore her signature heartwarming smile. At times like these her demeanor reminded me of a kindly old aunt instead of the battle-hardened nun that now stood in the doorway. I noticed in one of her hands she carried two huge grease stained brown paper bags. In the other a beverage caddie with four large soft drinks seated inside. The cavalry had arrived in the nick of time and they brought lunch. There is a God.

"Solomon?" Barnabas began, concern laced in his thick English accent. "Can you hear me?"

"Yeah... I'm fine." I said. "When did you all get here?"

"Right when the young lady over there intended to give you a close shave." Barnabas said, a reproving tone in his voice.

"Haven't I taught you to immobilize your opponent with a spell to prevent them from attacking you when your attention is elsewhere?"

"Yes... I just didn't think..."

"Didn't think?" He said abruptly cutting me off. "Your careless disregard for the basics of magical defense will get you killed one day..."

"Barnabas." Oswald said in a calming voice. "Perhaps it would be best if we left Solomon's performance evaluation for another more appropriate time."

Barnabas turned scowling at him. Oswald met his eyes indicating the scene in front of us with a subtle gesture of his head. Barnabas looked at the state of his shop and the combatants. He cleared his throat puffing out a quick burst of air sounding like a frustrated horse being denied a cube of sugar.

"Yes... Quite right my old friend. Best to take care of this problem first."

Barnabas leveled his outstretched hand at the albino facing away from him.

"Let's get a look at everyone shall we."

He made a gesture toward the ceiling extending his index and middle fingers, turning his hand in a half circle. The albino's frozen form turned around facing Barnabas. Recognition filled Barnabas's expression; his eyes grew wide in shock. He'd seen this man before.

"Rahm..." He gasped.

Even though he was immobilized, you could sense the sadistic satisfaction at Barnabas's recognition.

"But you're dead... You shouldn't be here... I watched you die." Barnabas said, recovering from the shock of seeing this man again.

Barnabas made a slight gesture with an index finger. The albino's head moved with a subtle shudder then he smiled at Barnabas.

"Hello Barnabas... Yes, I remember that day very well. I almost died. You, Bialek and that fat body standing beside you just stood there watching as I was pulled into that magical rift..."

"Which you conjured using black magic!" Oswald spat interrupting. In all the years I've known him, I've never heard him speak to anyone like that.

"Yes, I did and it would've worked if it hadn't been for you two, Hans Bialek and that Troll meddling in my business,"

Rahm chuckled maniacally then spoke again.

"All I wanted to do was learn all that there was to learn about magic, but you Oswald and this self-righteous hypocrite beside you denied me at every turn. How was I Barnabas, your apprentice to learn when you decided that certain arts were too dangerous,"

He looked to Barnabas meeting his eyes. Absolute hatred burned within them. He wanted Barnabas, Oswald and Glum dead, just like Bialek. Rahm then looked to me.

"My old Master is just as pathetic now as when I was his pupil,"

Rahm turned back to Barnabas.

"Where did you get this one? Off the street like you found me? Trying to rehabilitate him as well? Showing him the ways of magic and all that other tripe you tried to make me believe?"

He laughed again. No humor contained in the act, only contempt.

"If I were you I'd get as far away from these two as I could. They'll only hold you back, then when you least expect it... They'll betray you."

Rahm looked at each of us in turn. A smile reserved only for a condemned man heading to the electric chair plastered on his face.

"I'm enjoying the looks of surprise on your moronic faces... They remind me so much of the look Bialek gave me right before I killed him... I'd imagine that there's a dull witted look still etched on his dead face." Rahm said thoughtfully.

Barnabas shook his head regretfully.

"I should've turned you over to the Black Guard when I discovered what you were up too,"

Rahm chuckled again.

"You'd never have done that Barnabas… We both know you're far too sentimental to turn me over to the council's war dogs. You were more worried about what other Wizards would say if they found out that one of Barnabas Blackmane's apprentices went bad… The scandal and all that whispering behind your back would've been too much for you to handle," Rahm said mockingly.

Barnabas's expression hardened though one could see pain in his eyes.

"I won't be making the same mistake twice Rahm,"

Rahm laughed derisively.

"That won't happen today old fool…"

Black flames rose up from the floor engulfing the albino. Deep hues of bright yellows and oranges lapped chaotically at the air from the outermost edges of the flames. There was no light to speak of, however the heat was so intense that it scorched the hardwood floor underneath where the albino was immobilized. The flames undulated roiling inward. A loud cackling laugh strong and harsh could be heard coming from within the flames.

Then… Poof.

The flames along with the albino were gone. Leaving scorch marks on the floor along with an intense smell of sulfur. I looked about the shop spying my twin attackers right where I'd seen them before. Immobilized by Barnabas and Oswald. Rahm escaped leaving his Vampire backup. Why would he do that? Were they an expendable part of his plan? I didn't have the answers to those questions, but perhaps the twins did. The Cob Elf was still here as well. What in Gods name was going on?

All I knew for certain was that the albino wanted something from the Elf and was willing to kill him or whoever stood in his way to get it. The albino, according to Barnabas and Oswald should've died a long time ago by his own blind thirst for power. Then he shows up here startling the hell out of Barnabas and Oswald. The bigger mystery for me was Rahm was once Barnabas's apprentice. Barnabas has never said anything about having an apprentice before me. I knew Barnabas was old, so it was conceivable that he had another pupil during his lifetime only this one wanted revenge.

I sighed.

This was way too much for me to be thinking about on only a few hours sleep and an empty stomach. I hadn't noticed while I was musing about the happenings of a few moments ago that Glum had disarmed the twins, binding them securely using steel shackles made by the Dwarf Lords. I watched numbly as he hung them side-by-side on hooks behind the counter. They protested in language that would've made a retired truck driving sailor blush. Glum being the polite troll that he is and being a fan of silence produced a table size cloth handkerchief from his back pocket. Which he preceded to tear into mouth sized pieces stuffing them in the twin's mouths, all the while being mindful of their sharp Vampire teeth. I hoped the handkerchief he was using was a clean one, but then again... I really didn't care.

Sister Marianna... I mean Mari, took the bags of food and soft drinks placing them down on the counter. She proceeded to open the grease stained bags removing neatly wrapped hot dogs. My mouth watered. I lurched mindlessly forward like a Zombie craving brains, however a noise to my left caught my attention.

I turned to see Barnabas and Oswald helping the Elf to the floor. They laid him down gently on his back. Oswald removed his black velvet coat, folding it and placing it under the Elf's head. Barnabas spoke in hushed tones. I moved closer to hear better.

"Where's your Master Tilly? Where's Hans?"

"Dead..." Tilly said with difficulty. "That white man killed him. He somehow got through the Master's defensive spells undetected. He fought bravely, then one of those Vampires distracted my Master and the white man stabbed him through the heart."

"Do you know how they got into the fortress Tilly?" Oswald asked urgently.

"No sir, one moment I was serving the Master his tea and the next moment the white man and the Vampires were rushing through the doorway of the Master's study..." He trailed off, emotion choking off his words.

"Tilly, Did Bialek give you something? Something you were supposed to give to me?"

"Yes." Tilly groaned touching his head. "A crystal, during the fighting my Master opened a portal and pushed me through... I watched them kill him as the portal closed."

He patted searchingly over his coat pockets, tears in his eyes. He produced the crystal I'd originally seen when Tilly was laid out in the back of the store. Barnabas took the crystal from the Elf holding it in his right hand. It appeared as though he was waiting for something to happen. But it didn't. He opened his hand looking curiously at the crystal.

"Tilly." Barnabas began. "Did anyone else besides you handle this crystal? I know the albino wouldn't have waited around had he gotten it,"

Tilly thought for a moment his brows knitting together.

"No sir, I'm positive. I came through the portal my Master created... When I arrived here, I found myself in one of the isles looking at him napping with his head down."

Tilly pointed a shaky finger in my direction.

"When the portal closed. I bumped into a shelf knocking a jar down on top of my head. That was the last thing I remembered before I heard the white man threatening your apprentice."

Barnabas and Oswald turned their questioning glances in my direction. Barnabas stood moving over to me holding the crystal in plain sight. I started to say something, but Barnabas raised a silencing finger. He lifted his free hand, palm out and open, slowly moving it over my head and chest. The corners of his mouth quirked up into a relieved grin, he exhaled closing his eyes.

"It's OK, It's safe for now."

Barnabas turned away moving back over to Oswald and Tilly. Oswald moved in close to Barnabas speaking in a hushed whisper.

"Who do you think is behind this Barney?" Oswald asked concern in his voice.

"I haven't a clue..." He broke off pausing in thought. "But we need to move quickly."

"Excuse me?" I said interrupting. "What are you talking about? What is "it" and who is this little guy?" I pointed to Tilly. "Don't hold back on me Barnabas. Tell me what's going on?"

"In due time. There are things that must be done quickly as well as questions that must be answered for us to understand what is happening. You must trust me Solomon and do as I ask."

"Yes there are things that must be done. But first you are going to eat before all this food gets cold."

I turned to see Mari standing at the front counter smiling her reproving nun smile with two wrapped hot dogs held out for each of us. I noticed the grease from the fries blotting through the paper wrapping, a sign of a good hot dog. My mouth watered at the sight. If you've never had a hot dog from Deli Dogs, I definitely recommend that you do if you have the chance the next time you find yourself in the *Motor City*. Our question and answer session could wait until we all had something in our stomachs. Barnabas smiled a smile of surrender. Mari had a way with him. She could get Barnabas to stop and listen to reason like no other person could.

# Chapter 5

We finished our lunch in silence, which was never the norm. There was always something to discuss or mindless banter to be heard over any meal, however this particular one was decidedly different. I felt better nevertheless even though I was still exhausted. The grumbling in my gut retreated for the moment but would be back. Wizards in general eat a lot. We have the forces of the universe at our command that takes quite a bit of exertion both mentally and physically. Which is why I think you rarely see an overweight Wizard, we just burn through calories too quickly. Glum sat on the floor leaning up against the front door finishing off the last of eight hot dogs he was given to eat. He even unwrapped them first, a surprise even to me. Mari sat next to him talking all the while affectionately patting his large baldhead. I think Mari genuinely liked Glum. Trolls aren't known for being cuddly or for having a soft side. They're not unlike bulldozers that can think. It takes a special kind of person to look past their nature to see what lies beneath. Mari is just that sort of person. She'd often bake huge chocolate chip cookies to give to Glum as treats. Seriously, these cookies were enormous. They were the size of old twelve inch LP music records, It was a good thing her oven was on the small side or she'd probably try baking manhole cover sized cookies. Oswald however strongly disapproved of Mari and her treats. His main reason always being that he didn't want Glum to get fat. Funny thing is I've yet to see an overweight Troll and I've dealt with a few off and on over the years. They're like garbage disposals and can eat their weight in food each day. Truth be told I think the real reason Oswald frowned upon Mari's cookies was that Glum would never share them with him.

  The two Vampire twins hung on the wall where Glum placed them for safekeeping. They glared down at us, eyes unblinking while we ate. If looks could kill, I do believe we'd have all been burned to ash right where we sat. It's entirely possible they were in need of an intensive round of anger management therapy. But who am I to judge, I have anger issues of my own dealing with all the stupid people in this city. Tilly sat leaning against the counter next to my legs, finishing the rest of his meal. He wasn't eating much, which was understandable after what he'd been through. The curious thing though was that he'd become rather attached to me over the last half hour, never leaving my side. He'd jump to his feet every time I moved, almost as though he were waiting for me to give him an order or something.

Weird.

Barnabas and Oswald sat as far away from me as possible. Sort of made me wonder what the hell was going on and why they were giving me the silent treatment. They'd never kept me in the dark like this before. I took note however that they found Tilly's newfound attachment to me amusing. Mari got off her stool next to Glum and began clearing the front counter of the remains of our fast food repast. I finished the last of my soda as I looked on. It was then that something caught my eye. I turned back to Glum; my eyes were drawn to the top of the door. I watched curiously as the transom above the door opened completely on its own. Three larger than average crows flew into the store through the open transom landing on the counter a foot or so away from Barnabas and Oswald. On the backs of the crows rode three tiny human like figures.

The first little person was about six inches in height and male. Blessed with a strong stocky frame he exuded leadership. He was dressed in a full-length chain mail shirt, worn under a black front and back metal chest plate. Thick leather gauntlets and boots made of the same sturdy material adorned his hands and feet. A wide black leather belt studded with tarnished metal studs encircled his middle. Tucked into that belt was his long graying brown beard. On his left, hanging from the belt was a well-used scabbard that contained a crusader style sword. On his head rode a metal Viking style bowl helmet minus the horns.

The second person was a woman. She possessed a warrior's build, however it was softened by well-defined feminine curves. She may have been a half-inch shorter than her counterpart, but she was in every way his equal. Her long brown hair braided into a tail fell to the middle of her back. Her features were very lovely and striking. She could both captivate and decapitate and neither would seem out of place. She was similarly armored as the first person I described except in lieu of a helmet adorning her head she instead wore a thick band of silver about her forehead. She also opted for a pair of metal shoulder pads, which matched her breastplate in style and color.

The third person towered over the other two by a full two inches. His frame was ample to the point of being fat, though I suspected a strong, formidable warrior lurked beneath that double chin and gelatinous belly. The crow, which he rode upon, looked a bit shaky and winded, I'm guessing from the weight of its passenger. This person was dressed similarly as the other two though his weapons of choice were markedly different. He carried a heavy looking spiked mace strapped to his back along with two tiny daggers shoved into his belt with nothing adorning his head. He lacked the long beard as the first person I described, but his thick walrus mustache and matching eyebrows complimented his chubby cheeks. Held in his hands like an ear of corn was what looked like a hot wing, which he savored with every mouthful as if it were ambrosia prepared by the Gods.

    It was Bobum, Tish and Earl our Guarding Gnomes. Yes, that's right. I said Guarding Gnomes, not Garden Gnomes. Gnomes contrary to popular belief are fierce warriors that up until recently lived mainly in forests. However today - due to deforestation and urban crawl - they can be more commonly found in neighborhood flowerbeds or gardens, if you know where to look. When a group of Gnomes takes up residence in someone's garden it is in their nature to protect not only the garden, but the home as well. Over the years mainly through miscommunication, cartoonish lawn statues and badly written folk tales has the true name for Gnomes - *"Guarding Gnomes"* - been lost.

    A few years ago Bobum and his people were displaced from their home here in *Detroit.* The reason was due to the financial pressures placed upon the city through bad fiscal policies as well as residents leaving in droves for better places to live. The yard in which they made their home was eventually bulldozed over as part of a plan to make the actual footprint of the outlying city much smaller. So Barnabas invited the Gnomes to come live in his garden that he built on the roof of the thirty five hundred square foot garage, which is literally right next to the magic shop. It's actually a very good arrangement. The Gnomes tend to the garden and keep out any unwanted creatures like brood worms or Fairies. Did I mention that Gnomes hate Fairies?

They're mortal enemies.

I found that out purely by accident one night while watching a movie with them. Never, ever watch *Peter Pan* with a room full of armed Gnomes. They nearly destroyed my television that night.

Bobum dismounted his crow with the expert skill of a man being as comfortable in the saddle as he was with breathing. He removed his helmet as he approached Barnabas bowing respectfully. Then he spoke.

"My Lord," he said in a tiny gruff voice, sounding an awful lot like the *Mayor of Munchkin Land* from the movie *The Wizard of Oz*. "We have scoured the area as you ordered us to do and have chased away three Vampire retainers observing your store."

Retainers.

He was talking about Familiars. Familiars are essentially walking blood banks for Vampires. Many Vampires - especially the older ones - don't want to drink cold-bagged blood supplied by the huge network of blood farms run by the various Vampire houses. They would instead seek out humans willing to enter into a servile relationship with the hopes of one day becoming Vampires themselves. Familiars in many ways are sort of like walking wine cellars. All Familiars have marks -

usually in the form of a tattoo - indicating which individual Vampire or Vampire family they belonged to.

"How do you know they were Vampire retainers, Master Bobum?" Barnabas asked.

Bobum walked over to a discarded hot dog wrapper lying close to him. The wrapper still had a few fries left on it along with a smear of ketchup.

"One of them had this mark on the back of their neck behind the right ear my Lord," Bobum said picking up a *French* fry.

He drew a symbol in the ketchup, at my vantage point I couldn't make it out. He then picked up the wrapper showing it to Barnabas and the rest of us. The symbol that Bobum had drawn I wasn't familiar with. Over the years Barnabas has taken the time to instruct me about the Vampire houses, their leadership and of course their family marks. This one didn't resemble anything I'd seen before. The mark consisted of three capital "X's" in a line, the middle "X" being slightly larger than the two on either side. Barnabas glanced over to the Vampire twins hanging on the wall. His look was unreadable, however I knew his mental gears were working. After a moment's consideration he turned his attention back to Bobum.

"How were you able to see this on one of their necks if they were running away?" Oswald asked.

Bobum dropped the fry and the wrapper turning to address Oswald.

69

"It was Earl who found the mark," Bobum hooked a thumb at his companion.

"He leapt from his mount giving our quarry a massive blow to the head, knocking him to the ground. Tish and I flew in to assist. Unfortunately our quarry escaped, but not before we gained the information."

"You tackled him Earl?" I asked impressed.

The size ratio between him and the Familiar was astounding. Talk about *David and Goliath*.

"Way to go buddy!"

Earl paused in mid nibble turning his head toward me. He inclined it regally, acknowledging my compliment then returned to eating the chicken wing.

"Yes we would have returned sooner had Earl not decided to enter a fast food establishment and abscond with some of their fare," Tish said disapprovingly.

"Honestly Earl can you not think of anything else but filling your belly?"

In reply Earl let out a loud throaty belch.

"Swine," Tish muttered under her breath.

Bobum turned to the Vampire twins hanging on the wall. He placed the helmet back on his head, contempt in his manner and expression.

"I see you have captured two of the Vampire fiends my Lord, shall I send them to the dark abyss that awaits them and all their kind?" Bobum said truculently, placing his hand on the hilt of his sword.

"Not just yet Master Bobum, we still must question them." Barnabas replied.

"As you wish my Lord… Later perhaps,"

Barnabas gave thought to the question then answered.

"Perhaps,"

Bobum inclined his head in understanding.

Earl finished the chicken wing, licking the sauce from his pudgy fingers. In mid-lick, Earl turned his attention to the Vampire twins, regarding them. After a moment he shrugged turning away, tossing the chicken wing bone carelessly in the direction of one of the twins. The bone sailed across the space between Earl and the Vampire, bonking the twin hanging on the left between the eyes leaving a greasy stain of sauce before falling to the floor. The Vampire glared murderously at Earl. After a few short moments he turned his attention to a half eaten hot dog lying on a wrapper near him. He hopped down off his mount - the crow looking more than a little relieved that the weight was off his back - Earl rushed eagerly over to the half eaten hot dog. He gazed at it with a gluttonous gleam in his eyes. I watched him with an amused curiosity as Earl picked up a white paper napkin, tucking it under his chin into his breastplate. He seized the hot dog in both hands raising it to his wide-open mouth.

"Earl!" Bobum and Tish said in loud reproving tones.

The sudden outburst startled Earl causing him to drop the hot dog. He wiped his hands absently on the napkin covering his breastplate; he cast his eyes in Bobum's direction.

"Mind your manners. We haven't been asked to eat at Lord Barnabas's table. We have much work ahead of us and cannot lose sight of our duties," Bobum said.

Earl's eyes returned to the hot dog. He gazed at it longingly like a forlorn lover standing on the opposite side of an uncrossable river. He let out a defeated sigh turning away from the hot dog sulking back to his crow. Out of the corner of his eye he watched Bobum. When his leader looked away Earl scurried back to the rapper scooping up two *French* fries, cramming them into his chipmunk like cheeks. He then discarded the napkin as he scurried back climbing up onto the back of his mount.

"Have you heard any word from Zeg?" Barnabas asked Bobum.

Before Bobum could answer, another black crow flew in through the transom. It circled above the counter once landing next to Bobum. A small Gnome about four inches tall jumped down from his mount approaching Barnabas then knelt. The Gnome was younger than the other three. He had no facial hair. He was dressed in a long vest coat green in color, a sash of mustard yellow wrapped around his middle, a white loose fitting shirt, white pants and black leather boots. It was Zeg, Bobum's oldest son.

"My Lord I have news," Zeg addressed Barnabas.

Barnabas cast a brief look in my direction before he spoke to Zeg.

"What was his answer Master Zeg?"

Zeg stood continuing.

"My Lord, he said he will help you no matter what needs to be done."

Barnabas was silent for a few seconds, though they felt like they ticked by like minutes. He turned to Oswald. Oswald gave him a slight nod then they both glanced at me. Barnabas turned back to Zeg.

"Did you give him my instructions?" Asked Barnabas.

"Yes my Lord," Zeg responded, bowing.

"He said they would be there."

"Excellent... You and your people have done well Bobum."

All the Gnomes present bowed respectfully at Barnabas's kind words

"Thank you my Lord. What are your orders?" Bobum asked with a proud inflated chest.

"I want you and your people to stay on alert and continue to be on the lookout for anyone or anything that does not belong around here. I am counting on you to be my eyes and ears, do you understand?"

"Yes my Lord!" Bobum said with renewed excitement. Bobum, Tish and his son Zeg hopped back onto their crows. All four crows took wing. OK, to be honest it took Earl's crow a bit longer to take wing. I think we need to look into getting him a bigger bird to travel around on. A great horned owl or maybe even a *California* condor, you know something big like that.

The birds and their diminutive riders circled the front of the shop disappearing through the open transom. Earl's crow was the last to make it through the opening. When the crow's tail feathers cleared the frame, the transom closed shut with an audible wooden click.

Mari went back to cleaning up the rest of the wrappers and cups from off the counter when she let out a disgusted sound.

"Yuck. Why do you let those nasty birds in here? All the do is poop and leave their dirty feathers all over the place." She said annoyed.

Mari reached under the counter producing a roll of paper towels and a half filled squirt bottle of all-purpose cleaner. She sprayed the cleaner on a whitish green pile of what I could only assume were bird leavings. Mari scrunched up her nose cleaning the pile of crow poop off the counter.

"What would you have him do Mari, cast a constipation spell on the birds every time they fly into the store?" Oswald asked humorously.

Mari glared at Oswald.

"You won't think this is funny if I make you come over here and clean this mess up," Mari said in reply.

Oswald raised his hands in supplication attempting to diffuse her quick temper.

Mari wasn't much of an animal person. "Animals were not meant to be in doors, they belonged outside." I've heard her say more times than I can remember.

Glum stood letting out a low deep-throated chuckle getting to his feet. His chuckle was reminiscent of the sound a car tire makes rolling over the grooves of a warning median pulling into a tollbooth on the highway.

"Poop," said Glum between chuckles.

What can I say, he amuses easily.

He walked over to Mari behind the counter handing her all his wrappers. She smiled rising up on her tiptoes giving him a pat and kiss on the cheek. She took the wrappers promptly stuffing them into a garbage can that stood next to the register. Glum walked over to stand in front of the Vampire twins. He cocked his head staring at them blankly with a slack jawed expression. He got bored with that activity then made his way over to Oswald. Glum got a hug from his adoptive father before he found something on the floor that garnered a lion's share of his attention.

Barnabas got up from his stool turning to face the Vampire twins. He attracted their attention almost immediately. Barnabas fixed his eyes on the first twin making a subtle gesture with his right hand. He did the same with the second. Their heads drooped, chins resting on their chests. Barnabas had put them to sleep. He turned toward the front door of the shop extending his right hand. He uttered an incantation in Latin.

"Signum Cella."

I felt a blanket of subtle energy descend around me, closing us in and off from the outside world. Barnabas had cast a privacy spell. The spell would prevent anyone from overhearing what was said either through magical or technological means.

Satisfied with his precautions, he faced me. It looked as though he was wrestling with something unpleasant. Either it was something he didn't want to tell me or something he wanted me to do. I was fairly sure whatever it was I wasn't going to like it.

"Solomon," he began gravely. "Oswald and I are not exactly sure what's happening at the moment. All we do know for certain is that our security has been compromised and two members of our organization have been killed,"

He hesitated before continuing to let that fact sink into the minds of everyone present.

"The remaining six of us appears to be safe for the moment,"

He took a reassuring glance over to the woodcarving. My assumption was for him to make certain that none of the other stones winked from green to red during the time he was speaking. Oswald did the same with his rings.

"Is the magic shop any safer than the Wizard's place that was hit earlier," I asked unease in my tone.

"Whitey and the twins over there..." I said gesturing to our prisoners. "Didn't have any trouble throwing down in here,"

Barnabas bristled at my observation. He didn't like that fact any more than me. I knew Barnabas and Oswald spent a lot of time fortifying both of their places. So the shops defenses should've stopped them as soon as Whitey cast a magical spell or when the twins used their weapons.

"Yes, I'm puzzled by that as well." Barnabas said drifting away in thought.

"Well the defenses are up now and hopefully the others have followed the contingency plans that were developed for just such an occurrence," Oswald said interrupting in a tired voice.

"Yes," Barnabas said. "The other four should've gone to the safe houses by now,"

"Have you heard from any of the other members of your organization," I asked. Then added. "Besides Oswald that is,"

Barnabas picked up an envelope that sat next to him on the counter. He held it as he spoke.

"Yes," he said. "This letter is from another of our order, Orm,"

That was a surprise; Orm was part of this secret organization. Maybe that's why he was here so often. Perhaps visiting the magic shop on occasion was an inconspicuous way for Barnabas and Orm to get together and talk about their little Wizard club. In fact, Orm was here in the magic shop just this morning right before all hell broke loose. Barnabas paused organizing his thoughts before continuing. Whatever was on his mind was difficult for him to put into words.

"He was paired with another of our order… Hans Bialek, Tilly's former Master. Orm sent this letter to the magic shop right before he died,"

Barnabas went silent for a long moment.

"Well, what does it say," I asked curiously.

"It's an ingredient order Orm wanted me to fill for next week's pick up,"

I nodded. The letter that arrived shortly before Tilly was nothing more than a shopping list. Which possibly meant Orm was hit with a surprise attack as well. Whoever was responsible for these attacks wasn't taking any chances.

Oswald smiled compassionately at his old friend then said.

"Perhaps it would be better if Barnabas and I explained what we can about our organization and how it was structured, since the death of two of our members the spells that kept us from speaking about the Octagon are no longer a danger for us,"

Barnabas nodded thankfully clearing his throat. He turned waving a hand in the direction of the mural.

"See those stones over the scene depicted?" Barnabas asked.

I nodded.

"Each stone…" he continued. "Is enchanted and linked to one of the members of our order. The stones will only change color if one of our numbers has died. Black for death by natural causes and red by violent means."

So that meant two Wizards, according to Oswald's rings and the woodcarving died by violent means. How violent was anybody's guess, but I was leaning toward gruesome.

# Chapter 6

Barnabas rolled up his left shirtsleeve to his bicep. He ran an index finger over the skin of his forearm an inch or two below the crook of the elbow. There a thick black lined circle tattoo about the size of a *U.S. Half Dollar* began to appear. Magical symbols and runes have never been the strongest subject in my studies - mainly because they're boring as hell to learn - but I knew enough about them to know that the symbol was an ancient *Heka* linking charm. How the charms worked were fairly simple. You needed three things; blood from the person you wish to link to an object, the object in this case clear stones and the charm to link the two together, the tattoo. The design on the charm was specific as well. It must contain elements that reflect the sort of charm you wish to make.

"Just like Oswald's rings," I interjected.

"Precisely my boy, precisely," Oswald said beaming. "You noticed my rings earlier when one of them changed color."

I returned his smile, a feeling of gratitude making my cheeks color a bit for the pride he had shown in me.

"Rahm and the Vampires showing up here wasn't a coincidence. His being alive is most troubling as is the question of how he was able to return to this plain of existence," said Barnabas.

I saw this as my opportunity to ask the question that had been on my mind ever since I found out that Barnabas had an apprentice before me. Granted it'd only been an hour since I found out the information. But hey, enquiring minds want to know.

"Who is Rahm," I asked.

"And why does he hate you three so much," I gestured to Barnabas, Oswald and Glum in turn.

"I know that he was your apprentice Barnabas and I also know that you thought he was dead, judging by yours and Oswald's expressions, Rahm appearing here today was a big surprise,"

Barnabas grew silent looking at me then turned pacing around the front of the shop. He'd look in my direction every so often attempting to answer my questions. Then he'd shake his head indecisively and continue pacing. He finally let out a defeated sigh turning to face me.

"It is obvious to me that if I try and evade these questions you will continue to hound me over them, that point not withstanding I feel that you should know about Rahm and as you put it why he hates us so much." Barnabas began slowly.

"Rahm Murlocke was one of many children orphaned during the War Witches uprising," he said continuing. "As was Glum,"

Barnabas gestured to Glum who found mining for nose gold more rewarding than listening to this story. Judging by Glum's progress I'd say that he was close to hitting brain.

"Are you familiar with this dark part of our history," He asked.

I nodded. I knew all about this violent past of Wizard history, but I wish I didn't. Those were dark days for the World of Wizards.

"What is not written in the books of our history is that Rahm Murlocke was the son of Rebecca Redd or who is more commonly know as the "Death Raven". She and Rahm's father, Moran Murlocke were thought to have been killed by Kirk McGregor of the Black Guard, though their bodies were never found,"

Barnabas moved about the front of the store as his story spilled forth.

"Because Rahm was so young the Elder Council decided that he wouldn't suffer the same fate as his parents, so his past along with any record of his lineage was expunged from existence."

Barnabas paused gazing at Mari she offered him a sympathetic smile. I wondered if she knew any of this.

"It was the policy of the Elder Council that the children be placed with Masters that did not currently have apprentices,"

Barnabas turned moving to the front window of the store peering out as he continued to tell his tale.

"As you may or may not have guessed I was picked to be Rahm's Master. From the beginning I noticed something wasn't right about that boy. He was mean and vicious. He enjoyed causing pain to anyone or anything,"

He turned back to me.

"I thought it best to enlist others to help teach him the ways of magic, so I contacted Oswald as well as Hans Bialek and they readily agreed to help. After a few months they came to the same conclusion I did and it was decided that we limit his exposure to various aspects of the arts. Rahm didn't take the news of our decision very well and he began secretly learning the Darker Arts on his own by stealing everything he required. As he grew older we realized that his power was growing far faster than any of us had dared realize, it wasn't until it was almost too late that we discovered where his increased power originated,"

Barnabas bowed his head hesitating before continuing.

"Rahm was using ritual magic in order to summon Hellions from the Dark Realm. The bargain he'd struck with them was simple, power for himself in exchange for the Hellions freedom. The night we four, Oswald, Glum Hans and myself confronted him was the night he had begun a spell to open a way into our world that the Hellions could use. When we found him, at the place his parents were purportedly killed the door leading to the Dark Realm was nearly completely open. The spell he was using was extremely complex and it didn't take much interference for us to disrupt it. Rahm was caught in a magical backwash of the doorways collapse sucking him into the space between our reality and the reality of the Dark Realm, a place where none have returned,"

"Or so we thought," Oswald offered gravely.

Barnabas nodded.

"That's why his being here now was such a surprise, as far as anyone knows it is impossible to return from the Dark Realm," Barnabas said.

"His returning first to Hans would've been a surprise to him as well. I believe Rahm knew enough about the Order to pose a dangerous threat. That's why I believe he picked Hans to attack first, Rahm wanted the power contained in the crystal in order to gain the other three relics for himself or possibly for a third party,"

"All that might be true yes," Oswald broke in.

"But it's my firm opinion that Rahm chose Bialek first because he is deathly afraid of your teacher," Oswald indicated Barnabas with a chubby finger.

Barnabas waved off Oswald's unwanted admiration. Though I detected a remorseful tone in his voice as he continued.

"Hans Carval Bialek was one of the oldest and more powerful members of our order, he was also a good friend. As I have already stated and as you know he and Orm were charged with protecting one of the relics, the crystal Tilly brought to us."

Barnabas held up the crystal for all to see then he placed it on the counter next to him. He rolled down his sleeve buttoning it. Barnabas hesitated for another long moment before speaking.

"What Oswald and I are about to tell all of you are secrets that we and the six others have kept for nearly three hundred years."

He paused to see what sort of effect his words had on me. I will say that I was surprised, but not shocked that there were a few secrets he kept from me. The man was after all over seven hundred years old. He'd have to have a few skeletons in his closet, if not an entire cemetery. My world had already been turned upside down over the last few hours, what were a few more revelations going to amount to. I trusted Barnabas. He's never lied to me or led me down a path that would've ever put me in danger.

My life didn't start out well as many of you may have guessed. I never knew my mother or my father. My mother sadly died in childbirth due to complications or so I'm told. My father disappeared a few months before I was born. I guess he wasn't ready to be a father. To this day no one knows or won't tell me exactly what happened to him. Sometimes I feel that's a good thing. Why have anger issues about events that you have absolutely no control over. I lived at Sister Marianna's orphanage from almost the day that I was born till around the age of fourteen when my magic started to manifest. Barnabas seemed to always be at the orphanage keeping time as they say with Sister Marianna. When he discovered that I possessed abilities like him, he took an interest in me, eventually adopting me as his son. He made me feel normal - despite my powers - and welcome in his home. I always thought of myself as a freak until he showed me the other world that existed alongside the world of Normals. I smiled a trusting smile leveling my eyes meeting his without fear or trepidation.

"OK," I said relaxing on my stool.

Placing the empty soft drink cup next to me on the counter.

"Tell me only what you feel is necessary for me to know."

He returned the smile inclining his head once.

"You were always a smart young man. Today's events notwithstanding."

"Ha. Ha. I had them on the ropes till you walked in and took all the credit."

"Indeed," His smile wavered.

He paced the shop pensively, facing me after ordering his thoughts.

"Are you familiar with the history of *King Arthur*," He continued turning back to face me, waving his hand toward the mural once again.

"Yes," I said. "I think I know the basics of the legend."

"Legend," Barnabas scoffed incredulously. "Far from it, the history of *King Arthur* is very real my boy," he said emphasizing the word "history".

Barnabas turned walking over to Oswald, who sat on a high stool at the other end of the counter. Barnabas settled next to him, leaning on the counter nodding to him encouragingly. Oswald glanced reluctantly from side to side before placing his right hand palm down on the counter. As I watched, a dim orange light appeared under his hand, growing incrementally in intensity. I heard the sounds of wood rubbing against wood creaking, popping and snapping. I watched the wood that formed the top of the counter bend and fold itself into the shape of a mahogany box six inches high and twelve inches square. Oswald removed his hand from the box.

The box itself was unremarkable, just an ordinary wooden box. The decorations that adorned it however were far from ordinary. On top of the lid, a coat of arms roughly six inches by three inches was emblazoned in the center. The "heater" shaped shield was a deep metallic blue in color. On it were three ornate crowns stacked vertically inlaid with metal that I presumed to be gold. Directly behind the coat of arms positioned vertically rested an accurate reproduction of a magnificent *Celtic* style sword with a crusader handle. Barnabas placed a hand on the box fixing his eyes on me. I moved closer to get a better look, as an afterthought I lifted Tilly placing him on a stool because of his height disadvantage. He had every right to check out whatever was in that box just like the rest if us.

"Within this box rests a relic of *King Arthur* that Oswald and I were charged with protecting." He paused.

Turning his gaze to the box, giving just the slightest of smiles. A smile a little boy might flash gazing at a prized possession his beloved sports hero may have owned.

"The Order of the Octagon watched over four such relics from Arthur's kingdom which encompassed thirteen realms." he said turning back to me.

"Merlin, the first of our order enchanted all the objects to aid the King in his rule, for Arthur was no ordinary king."

Barnabas turned the box so that the lock faced him. He placed an index finger over the keyhole. A flash of light appeared for an instant. I heard the distinct sounds of metal tumblers turning and clicking together, then the lid began lifting, opening by itself.

"The Order of the Octagon?" "What's that?" I asked curiously.

"The Order is a group of eight Wizards, charged with keeping the secrets and protecting the relics of Arthur's reign," Barnabas said.

"Merlin originally started the group. Before Arthur's death, Merlin left instructions for the group to have the relics scattered and hidden keeping them safe from the ambitions of men. The responsibility has been passed down from one group of Wizards to the next. Our group of eight has watched over the relics, keeping their secrets the longest, Even the Elder Council is mostly unaware of our groups activities,"

Barnabas reached into the red silk lined box carefully removing a crown holding it gently in his hands. I felt the power contained within it as he drew it closer to us. The crown was beyond description. There were many words I could've used such as beautiful, elegant or even exquisite. None of those words however came close to describing the majesty of this crown. The crown was made of gold and a silver colored metal, perhaps platinum or white gold. It had thirteen points in the shape of crosses. The entire crown was etched with intricate *Celtic* designs and symbols. On the headband set into the gold underneath each point was a brilliant oval shaped blood red ruby about the size of a *U.S. Dime*.

"This..." Barnabas said in a hushed reverent tone.

"...Is the crown of King Arthur. It was made by the Dwarf Lord Burbine Greybeard and enchanted by Merlin to bestow upon the wearer great knowledge and protection. It along with the other relics we hold in our care are as powerful as the next, should they fall into the wrong hands a man might be able to enslave the world."

"Which is why what happened to Bialek and Orm is most troubling," Oswald interrupted.

Barnabas nodded.

"Someone learned of the relics along with those that might know of their whereabouts, they attacked in a coordinated fashion killing both Bialek and Orm, Tilly however escaped with the crystal only by Bialek's quick thinking." Oswald finished.

Both he and Barnabas glanced over to the little Cob Elf. Tilly stood next to me standing on a stool in obvious grief, ringing a handkerchief is his hands muttering "My poor master" to himself.

"At this time however all of this is nothing more than speculation of course," Said Barnabas.

I glanced to Tilly, then to Barnabas and finally to Oswald, a few thoughts had just occurred to me, disturbing and upsetting with unpleasant possibilities.

"Um. I hate to interrupt, but what are the other two relics? I assume Excalibur is one of them. What exactly was contained in that crystal, more importantly how was someone able to foil the privacy spells you put in place and how was he…"

I hooked a thumb at Tilly

"…Able to get past the shops defenses?"

"Well." Barnabas paused in thought placing the crown back inside the box. Glum tried poking a big finger at the crown before it disappeared. Barnabas absently swatted his hand away without looking, as though this were something he'd done on far too many occasions. Glum withdrew his hand looking crestfallen. Mari moved over to the big guy smiling, patting his hand where Barnabas had smacked it.

"The four relics represent the four qualities a king must have if he is to rule over his kingdom and subjects."

"First, is the crown which represents wisdom," Oswald said derailing Barnabas in mid explanation. I swear sometimes they act like two old ladies trying to out gossip the other.

"Yes." Barnabas said eyeing his longtime friend before continuing. Oswald smiled serenely back at him.

"Second, is the sword which represents strength."

"Excalibur you mean," I offered interrupting. Why should Oswald have all the fun?

Barnabas glared as a teacher would at an impudent student. He cocked his eyebrow in a way that always meant be quiet or else. Let's just say I decided to take the high road remaining silent,

"Third," He continued. "Is the crest ring which represents courage,"

Barnabas turned surveying me. I felt uncomfortable believing he was unhappy with me, but as I stared back I thought I saw multiple expressions there. Part regret, part admiration, part envy and part relief. His lips revealed a weary smile. In all the years I'd known him this was the first time he looked old to me, worn out. I noticed lines forming around his eyes and around his mouth as he smiled. He looked every bit his age of seven hundred years and then some. The dark patches under his eyes made his face appear shallow and drawn. My heart sort of sank a bit. It was like seeing your father for the first time after being away for a decade. His smile faded and he spoke again.

"Forth, is the crystal which represents hope,"

"What was the crystal," I asked with an uneasy feeling tingling up my spine.

"The crystal contained the power of Merlin," Oswald offered.

"Before he was imprisoned in stone by the Sorceress Morgana," he continued. "Merlin placed most of his magic and wisdom within the crystal to aid a worthy king should the other three relics fail him during his reign, as they failed Arthur."

I rubbed my tired eyes.

"As I have said there were eight of us in the Order of the Octagon," Barnabas said.

"We structured our organization to have four paired sets of Wizard's living in close proximity to one another watching over and taking care of one of the four items assigned to each pair, Oswald and I are paired as was Bialek and Orm, The tattoo's not only act as a monitor for each of us but prevent any member of the Order from discussing the Order's business with outsiders,"

He placed a hand on the arm that sported the tattoo settling his eyes on mine for effect. Silence fell over the shop. My mind tried wrapping itself around this unsettling news. I'd become the vessel for the wisdom of Merlin and his magical power. That was a level of cool I could hardly fathom and it was also terrifying. I've heard stories about Merlin. He was like a superhero with all the things he could purportedly do. Most of which I will concede was grounded in legend, but as we all know legends usually start out as fact in the beginning. The deed or deeds are told and retold so many times people add details along with embellishments to make the story new and more exciting. There was another thought gnawing at me. One deeper and a hell of a lot more terrifying, if Whitey and the Vampire twins killed two very powerful Wizards over that crystal, what would they do to me, an upstart Wizard, when they found out that I absorbed the power from that crystal? That train of thought led me to another train of thought and even more questions.

How many others are out there right now searching for the crystal and the remaining relics? My mind was advising me strenuously to find a nice, quiet place to hide. Was there a place on Earth or in Mid-Realm I could hide away from these dangers? Probably not, I sighed in pure frustration. It's never been in my nature to run from danger. I'm not a brave man by any means. I don't seek out trouble, but when it finds me I face it. I might be terrified as all hell, but I won't run. I think the reason for that stems from my school days. I was a tall skinny pasty white kid that couldn't run very fast. So when the bullies came for me to make my life a living hell. I had a choice to make. Give them what they wanted, my fear, which they craved like a drug or to take their beatings without making a sound. As with everything in my life I chose the hard road learning to take a beating. While I pondered all this I became acutely aware that there were various pairs of eyes staring at me. Well, everyone but Glum. He was looking up counting the tarnished etched copper tiles attached to the ceiling. He must've found all the talking very boring.

"Are you alright son," Asked Barnabas.

"Yes," I replied. "Just a bit freaked out. It's a lot to take in. How do we get Merlin's power out of me," I asked afraid of the answer.

Nothing seems to ever be easy for me. My question hung thickly in the air and was met by silence. A long silence. Then Barnabas spoke.

"The crystal is the vessel for the power of Merlin to be kept safe for a day of great need. Once the power of Merlin is transferred to a host there is but one way for the power to return to the crystal."

"And that is?"

"The death of the host," Oswald supplied.

See.

What'd I tell you? Nothing is ever easy for me. Do you think that just once, something, anything could go my way? Am I asking too flipping much here? How difficult would it have been for me to drink a potion, or wear a hat made into the shape of a pyramid or kiss a pig? Well, maybe I wouldn't do that last one. I let out a defeated sigh, slumping on my stool then asked.

"OK… Is this power dangerous?"

"No," said Oswald. "From all available information on the crystal, no. As the power settles into you, it will do many things, but it is not dangerous."

"What will it do? Will it change who I am," I asked.

"Over time the power will augment your magic considerably," Oswald continued. "To a degree it will help clear your mind when your thoughts are cloudy, make your reflexes faster. It will also protect you from many dangers and keep you healthy from disease and injury. The power will even extend your life, but in the beginning the power will remain dormant, waiting."

"Waiting? Waiting for what?" I asked.

"For the time when you need it most," Barnabas answered in a detached tone.

"The power, is neither good nor evil," Barnabas continued. "It adapts itself to the personality of the host. If a person is inherently good then the power reflects that. If a person is inherently evil... Well, let's say it wouldn't be good."

I was dog-tired, but there was no way I could go to sleep after all this. I looked to the floor unblinking for a moment then spoke.

"Alright, let me see if I have all this straight. There is a group of egomaniacs running around looking for the four relics that use to belong to King Arthur. These relics were all enchanted by the most powerful Wizard of all time, Merlin. One of the relics has transferred from one vessel to myself and another is in a box sitting on top of the counter over there."

I gestured a hand in the direction of the crown.

"That leaves two relics unaccounted for, am I right about the facts so far?" I said finishing.

"More or less," said Barnabas.

"Good. At least my brain is still functioning."

I rubbed a hand roughly over my face.

"As for Tilly being able to come and go in the magic shop without any hindrances I think the answer is fairly simple," said Barnabas. "Tilly was until recently in the service of Hans Bialek, a member of the Order of the Octagon…"

"And had some sort of charm or talisman to use as a key whenever he needed to come here," I said completing his sentence.

Barnabas and Oswald grinned, pleased with my answers.

"And you're sure about everything you're saying about the power of Merlin," I asked.

Both Oswald and Barnabas stared at me blankly then glanced at each other, unable or unwilling to answer my question. Then Oswald said.

"No we're not. It's been quite a long time since the power contained in that crystal was employed,"

I nodded. At least they were being honest by saying they don't know. It didn't make me feel any better though.

"What happens now," I asked.

"We have many things to do in a very short time," said Barnabas.

"Oswald and I will remain here to question our guests as to whom they might be working for. We also need to get things packed and ready because there are places we must go. Such as ascertaining the whereabouts of the other members of the Octagon as well as making sure the remaining relics are still safely hidden and to search Orm's home for information,"

Barnabas turned to Mari.

"Mari, would you and Tilly take care of gathering our gear together," Barnabas asked.

"Of course Barney, whatever you need," replied Mari.

Tilly's demeanor immediately changed to one of excitement at being able to help.

"I think it would also benefit us to investigate Bialek's compound for any possible answers which might indicate who was able to get to Bialek and kill him so easily,"

Barnabas turned to me.

"The crown must be taken to a safe place and kept out of the reach of our enemies," Barnabas continued looking squarely in my direction. "And you will be the one charged with that task,"

"Whoa. Wait. Why me," I asked.

"Because I said so." Barnabas replied with a wry smile.

I honestly think he loves to bait me so he can force me into an argument. He knows full well that I have difficulty keeping my mouth shut.

"Because you said so," I shot back my anger rising. "You want me to take that crown somewhere safe all by myself," I asked incredulously.

"Why can't either of you do it?" I said gesturing between Oswald and Barnabas.

"Yes Solomon I do, I wouldn't give this task to just anyone. I know you're more than up to the challenge of taking the crown somewhere safe. Oswald and I cannot go because we have to prepare things here. Besides, Bobum and his people are keeping an eye on the shop outside. They'll let us know if anyone is watching."

"Fine," I groaned sagging on my stool.

"Now go get the items you may need for the drop off and meet me back down here."

I reluctantly slid off my stool trudging over to the door leading up to the apartment above the shop.

# Chapter 7

I opened the door to the apartment that I shared with Barnabas and Mari with a little more force than was necessary, causing the door to swing wide striking the metal spring door stop with an audible "Boing!" followed by the unmistakable dry sound of metal hitting drywall.

"Shit," I said through clinched teeth.

I examined the wall behind the door; sure enough a doorknob-sized impression was in the drywall about an eighth of an inch deep. My temper got the best of me and I let out a word in a loud growl that sounded a lot like the word "luck". I breathed in a few short deep breaths exhaling them rhythmically attempting to calm myself down as I slowly closed the door. I would fix the damage later. Here I am a grown man and I'm being treated like a *goddamned* child. I end up having to do all the disgusting backbreaking grunt work. Whether it's cleaning up failed experiments, potions that have gone bad - those are the worst - taking things from one place to another or tending to dangerous foul smelling creatures, which if they had half a chance would devour me in a heartbeat. Coughing up your bones in a globulous hair ball a day or two later. Come walk around in the basement under the magic shop if you don't believe me. Don't get me wrong I'm not afraid of hard work or getting my hands dirty. I know I'm learning a lot from Barnabas and paying my dues and building character along the way. I get that, but come on; I'm in my mid-twenties for crying out loud.

Seeded into all the other reasons I was angry at the moment was the fact that I still lived with Barnabas and Mari. Don't misunderstand me the apartment above the magic shop is extremely nice. Originally this apartment building had four apartments. Barnabas being Barnabas had the whole place remodeled combining all of them into one huge two-story living space. So there was a lot of room for everyone to have their own space including separate bathrooms for each of the six bedrooms and huge walk-in closets. Because I am still an apprentice being taught under Barnabas Blackmane I'm not allowed to live away from my Master.

I'm sure his reasoning can be attributed to his adherence to an out of date code relating to an apprentice and his or her Master. The Elder Council holds a Master accountable if their apprentice messes up. So the closer I am to him the closer he can watch me. Which probably explains Barnabas's actions toward me given his previous apprentice's trip to the dark side. Anyway, I understand all that, however it's still awfully hard to bring a woman home. Especially, when a seven hundred year old man enjoys walking around the apartment in a red smoking jacket with matching fez, puffing on a pipe filled with cherry flavored tobacco. You laugh; I have to watch him walk around in that get up. I have to count my blessings however; at least he doesn't fry bacon without a shirt on. You can sort of see why my love life is non-existent.

    I sulked down the hallway of the apartment, past an original portrait of Barnabas painted by *Rembrandt* on my right - which was personalized by the artist himself – to the left hung an original *Salvador Dali* painting depicting something that only *LSD* could've helped the artist create. The apartment was spacious, as I have already alluded too. Roughly six thousand square feet with six good sized bedrooms, a dining room, living room and a kitchen that would make a TV chef envious. The only one who really made use of it was Mari. She was a master at cooking and hated for anyone to use her cooking utensils. As an *April Fools* joke one year I hid all of her copper pots. OK, I didn't exactly hide them. I used a magical spell to make them disappear. The spell worked flawlessly, Mari however had a conniption fit when she discovered they were missing. She scared the absolute crap out of me, I confessed right on the spot. A vein popped out on her forehead threatening to burst while she yelled a torrent of insane nun threats at me. She rattled me so badly it took me nearly three days to remember the exact spell I used. Needless to say I try not to touch anything in her kitchen that is even remotely related to cooking.

I opened the door to my room and entered. Deciding to make a little detour I headed into the bathroom flicking on the light. I took a good look at myself in the mirror. I looked like hammered shit. I ran some cold water into the sink basin not bothering to flip the stopper down. I held my fingers under the flowing water as I took stock of my appearance. My skin looked pale and unhealthy. I hate winter. You never get any good sun around this time of year in *Detroit* and I refuse to get a tan with a bulb. My eyes are normally the color of a clear summer sky at noon, right now however they looked dull and gray. The dark bags under my eyes weren't helping my appearance either. My brown hair was longer than I liked and I was in desperate need of a hair cut. My five o'clock shadow was quickly moving into the twelve o'clock hour. I really should shave, but I just didn't have the time. I cupped my hands under the faucet filling them with cold water, leaning down I splashed the water over my face. Short startled breaths escaped my mouth at the frigid sensation. I repeated the process two more times before shutting off the water and drying my face on a hand towel.

I felt better, however nothing would replace a good night's rest. I tossed the towel on the vanity and got back to my task at hand.

My room is fairly *Spartan* in decor; I try not to clutter my life with meaningless materialistic things. The walls are painted stark white and the floors are oak, with a few area rugs placed symmetrically around to give the room some color. I have a queen-sized bed made from heavy, aged mahogany wood with matching nightstands and a dresser. A desk sits in the east corner of my room with an *iMac* computer resting on it. Next to that are my two five shelf bookcases, stacked full of books from authors like *Twain, Rowling, Sabatini, Wells, King, Poe, Haggard, Koontz and yes a few from Stephenie Meyers*. Hey, don't judge, I was curious as to what all the hoopla was about these books and movies. They may never become literary classics like *Moby Dick* or *To Kill a Mocking bird*, but they were entertaining. Whether you like the *Twilight* books or not women seem to love them. I think there's even a website where people write erotic stories involving all the characters. I'm pretty sure men aren't writing those sorts of stories or reading them for that matter. Well, unless the men are gay I suppose. But hey, whatever floats your boat. Besides the *Twilight* books can be a great conversation starter when you're out on a date.

I have only two things hanging on my walls. The first is a framed eight by ten black and white glossy of *Lt. Columbo* the greatest fictional detective ever in my opinion. Second, is a framed original *Avengers* cover, issue two ninety-six illustrated by comic book legend *John Buscema*. It's the cover that depicts the *She Hulk* knocking the crap out of the *Mighty Thor*. - No real significance there other than it was the first *Avengers* comic book that I ever read and I liked it. - Next to my dresser was an antique brass valet, which was heavily modified to meet my needs.

On it hung my plain black robe and armor that consisted of a unadorned brushed metal front and back breast plate, bracers for my wrists and forearms, a well worn thick black studded belt with shin guards that matched the breast plate. My robe and armor had magical enchantments, which helped absorb, deflect or redirect magical attacks, and they were also good at preventing things like swords or bullets from causing wounds as well. I'm glad I paid extra to have all that done when I had my things made. My advice to all of you that are thinking about becoming a Battle Wizard is to not skimp on the protection. One day when your magic or weapons fail you in battle the only thing between you and an eternal dirt nap will be whatever armor you happen to be wearing.

In a modified holder stood my Battle Staff - which concealed my thirty-two inch Wizard's Blade - and resting in a brass tray set into the base of the valet was my scarred and nicked eight inch oak wood wand about a half inch in diameter. The tip was capped with pure silver and had a core of twisted helix copper. Next to that was my bracelet, which was made out of long thick braids of silver and gold shaped into four swirled circles with enough of a gap to slip it onto my wrist. On the far wall facing east were two large windows that let in a lot of light, but I preferred a dark room when I sleep so I have thick blinds covering them. Across from the windows was my closet and that was my destination.

I exited the bathroom. I looked longingly at my bed as I walked past it. I was still pretty tired however I didn't have time for a five-minute power nap. I opened the door sliding some clothes down the rod giving me enough space to access the recessed wall safe at the back of my closet where I kept my valuables. I started to work the numbers on the combination when I heard the front door open.

"Do you need me to do anything for you Solomon?" I heard Mari call from the living room.

"No I think I can get things together for myself."

"OK,"

I heard her walk down the hallway past my open door to the room she shared with Barnabas. I opened the safe removing my two *Colts* and shoulder rig that also held a five-inch military style knife - none of which were exactly legal here in *Detroit*, but all of them had enchantments that rendered them invisible as long as they were in the shoulder rig. One of these days I should wear them to an airport to mess with the *T.S.A.* With my luck I'd end up receiving a painful deep body cavity search, not really something I'm itching to experience.

"May I help you Master!" Tilly said in an excited high-pitched voice.

I jumped he startled me so badly. Turning, I moved toward him, anger showing in my face and woven into my words.

"Don't sneak up on me like that!" I yelled towering over his tiny frame.

Tilly stood next to my bed shrinking away from me as his excited smile faded. He raised his hands holding them in front of himself the way a child might anticipating a punishment.

"I'm sorry, Master," he said in a small voice casting his eyes to the floor.

"What are you doing in my room anyway? I didn't ask you in here!"

"I... Uh... Barnabas," Tilly stammered

His eyes were as big as saucers and I didn't care. I felt bad for jumping on him, but goddamn it this is my room and despite what Barnabas thinks or says I can take care of my own packing.

"Get out!" I yelled.

Tilly flinched but didn't move. So I took him by the lapels in one hand leading him forcefully to my door pushing him out into the hallway.

"Get out and stay out!" I huffed out a breath and added, "You nosy little creep!"

He scrambled down the hall - his feet not appearing to make contact with the floor - out the front door not bothering to look back.

"What in God's name is wrong with you?" Mari asked in an angry tone.

I hadn't noticed her standing there; she was right next to me when I straightened. She was holding a few of Barnabas's clothes folded over her forearms.

"What?" I said defensively. "He came into my room uninvited. He has no business being in there, I didn't ask him…"

"You're acting like a selfish self-centered brat," Mari said cutting me off in a harsh reproving tone.

"You have no right treating him like that! He's been through too much in the last few hours and doesn't need to be mistreated by the likes of you!"

"Now hold on a minute..." I said as I felt my temper rising.

"No, I won't hold on a minute." She said interrupting.

"You weren't taught to act like this. You were taught manners and respect. You were a good boy growing up, a little whiney and selfish at times yes, but still a good boy at heart. Life dealt you a terrible beginning I know, but you're surrounded by lots of people that love and care for you and its high time you started thinking of others beside yourself for a change. You don't have that luxury any longer, you need to grow up and act like a man instead of a little spoiled child. You have a responsibility to see to Tilly's needs and be good to him and treat him with the respect he deserves, he is after all yours now."

"What?" I questioned thinking she must be off your rocker.

Mari leveled her half hooded eyes directly into mine. I watched the corners of her mouth curl up into a wry knowing smile. She shifted the clothes in her arms so she could poke me in the chest with her finger.

"He is yours," she said, emphasizing each and every word with a poke of her finger.

"I over heard Barney and Oswald talking... You know that braid of metal Tilly wears around his neck, it's called a "Ring of Shame" Only Elves that have disgraced themselves, and their families or their race are forced to wear those rings as a punishment. They are striped of all their possessions, rights, freedoms, and are essentially reduced to being slaves." She finished with a touch of sadness in her voice.

"Well, I'm sorry that he's a slave... How does that make him my responsibility?"

"When you found Tilly in the back of the store you touched the metal ring or pendant around his neck, didn't you," she asked.

"Maybe..." I said searching through my actions earlier. Did I touch that pendant? I couldn't remember.

"In doing so you became Tilly's new owner and will remain his owner until the day that you or Tilly died or if whoever placed the binding spell on him were to take it off,"

"Wait, Bialek was his last owner..." I trailed off because my brain finally caught up with the facts.

"Bialek died, which caused the binding curse to flow back into the iron ring around Tilly's neck and remain there until a thick headed moron like myself was stupid enough to unwittingly accept Tilly's services by touching the ring,"

"That's right," Mari said patting my cheek with her free hand.

"Welcome to the world of adult responsibility,"

Mari smiled up at me then turned on her heels, walked down the hall back into Barnabas's room. I stood there, just thinking. My life as I'd known it... Correction my "carefree" life had just gotten a tad more complicated. I found myself in a situation that I really hadn't been before. My life was possibly in danger with respect to Barnabas and his band of Arthur nerds. It was only a matter of time before I found out how all these cards will fall on that subject. What I knew for certain, was that there were four powerful objects hidden somewhere. OK, I knew the locations of two of them. Christ I'd inadvertently become the vessel for one of them and there was a group or groups of people that would do pretty much anything to get a hold of them.

Now if all that wasn't a kick in the teeth, I have my own personal slave, which needs to be taken care of and looked after. Ugh... It's like having a toy poodle that can talk. I need to figure a way out of this situation and fast. Oh and I was apparently a spoiled selfish brat. My shoulders sagged as I turned round heading back into my room to finish getting my gear together.

It took another twenty minutes to get ready. I chose to travel light for the crown drop off. I decided against taking my Battle Staff, if I were going to get into a fight it would be an ideal weapon, but I'd be lugging around a wooden box and a staff might prove awkward. Conversely, there were the looks I'd get when I would show up in public with my staff. Guys toting around a Wizard's Battle Staff aren't really popular with the ladies and quite frankly I'm tired of the *Lord of the Rings* jokes. I wore my shoulder harness, which held my two *Colt Defenders* and six spare magazines of ammo as well as my five-inch military style knife. I also carried my eight-inch Wizard's wand strapped to my right wrist. The wand was held in a device that would allow it to spring out when I flexed my hand in a certain way.

I also chose to wear my bracelet on my left wrist. The wand and bracelet were tools to help me focus my magic. They're sort of like the nozzles on a power washer. Without a nozzle on the tip of the wand you get a wide spray of water, however if you attach a nozzle with a smaller aperture you get a more focused, more powerful stream. Wizards like Barnabas and Oswald are very practiced in the art of hand gesture magic and can wield power effectively without any tools like wands or bracelets. Barnabas has been teaching me a bit of that form of magic, but it is extremely difficult and takes more concentration. I can manage some of the more basic spells like lighting candles or opening locks or even moving small objects. As for my attire, I kept it pretty simple. I wore a black t-shirt with the online game *City of Heroes* logo on the front, a pair of faded blue jeans, my steel toed construction boots along with my red and black *Bugaboo* winter jacket.

I made sure to grab a small leather pouch from the drawer of my nightstand before heading back down stairs. Barnabas was standing at the counter, a canvas army surplus medic's bag rested beside him. I assumed the wooden box containing the crown was inside. Oswald, Glum and the Vampire twins were conspicuously absent. Mari was I assume still upstairs and I saw no sign of Tilly. I walked over to Barnabas standing on the other side of the counter across from him.

"Where is everyone?" I asked curiously.

Barnabas looked up smiling.

"Everyone is doing what they have been assigned to do. Oswald and Glum are questioning our two Vampire guests in the basement, Mari and Tilly are packing what we will need when you get back and you of course are taking this…" he placed a hand on the medics bag. "…To a safe place."

"And where exactly will I be taking that?"

"You'll be going to Chicago, more specifically Stumpwater's. I want you to give this to Reb Ironbolt."

"The barkeep at The Laughing Goblin?" I asked, puzzled.

"He and his people will know how to protect a treasure of this nature, he is a Dwarf after all."

I nodded slowly in agreement. Dwarfs were miners, skilled craftsmen and tenacious fighters. Hell, Dwarves would protect treasure or anything that was given to them to guard to their dying breath. I think the urge was deeply imbedded into their genetic code or perhaps it was more of a precious metal fetish. Whatever the cause for the Dwarves fanatical devotion to gold, silver and precious stones, Reb wouldn't give the crown up without a fight. He'd probably give it to his brother Garse Ironbolt for safekeeping. Reb's brother Garse was one of the nine Dwarves that sat on the Strun Council that oversaw Morda the Dwarven gold horde. Barnabas made a good call there.

"Alright," I said.

Barnabas pushed the bag toward me.

"Have you seen Tilly?" I asked.

Barnabas shook his head in the negative, I turned calling for the little guy.

"Tilly, I'd like to have a talk with you if you please."

I waited a moment then heard an audible crack and felt the thrum of fading magic.

"Yes, Master," Tilly said timidly.

Tilly stood peaking around the side of the counter; the way a child might shyly peak around a parent's legs when confronted with a person unfamiliar to them. I saw where I'd grabbed his coat and led him from my room; the lapel was ripped almost completely off. Tilly had tried to mend it with a few pieces of *Scotch Tape*. Seeing that made me feel like a complete and utter dick. I got a sinking feeling that maybe Mari was right about me. Maybe I was a selfish bastard. I knelt down attempting not to appear intimidating. I beckoned him to come closer. He did and cautiously almost fearing I would lash out at him again. He stood about a foot away from me with his eyes focused on the floor as I continued.

"I owe you an apology Tilly. It was wrong of me to raise my voice and place my hands on you in the manner that I did. I wanted to say that I'm sorry for being a selfish person and ask for your forgiveness and my promise that it will never happen again."

I caught Barnabas's approving expression out of the corner of my eye as Tilly raised his eyes to meet mine. He gave me a happy yet apologetic smile.

"Oh no Master. The fault was all mine, I should not have entered your room without permission or startled you in the manner that I..."

"Tilly," I said in an even tone, interrupting him. "That is neither here nor there. I had no right or cause to treat you the way that I did and I'm sorry for that... Can you accept my apology?"

He grasped his hands nervously smiling a heart felt smile, nodding. If I had to guess I'd say that he'd rarely been apologized to, if ever.

"Thank you... Now since I'm your Master and if you're going to be seen outside these doors…" – I waved a hand at the front doors to the shop – "…in my company these clothes that you're wearing simply won't do."

Tilly looked over his clothes, his hands moving over them in a self-conscious manner, his cheeks reddening slightly. When his eyes met mine again there was a hint of embarrassment in them.

"I'm going on a errand and I'd like you to come with me," I said.

I reached into my coat pocket, removing the small leather pouch.

"I want you to take this," I said handing it to him. "What's in it is yours now and I want you to buy some new clothes and whatever you might need for the next few days."

Tilly opened the bag emptying the contents into his left hand. The bag contained nine gold coins and twenty-three silver coins, all of which were about the size of U.S. quarters. Along with the coins were six rubies roughly one half inch in diameter. Gold, silver and jewels were the preferred method of currency in the magical community. However since the world reached the twenty first century more and more Wizards, Dwarfs, Elves and creatures of every description have been moving to modern paper currency. I'll tell you the story a little later of how I got the leather pouch. It involves Goblins, a former girlfriend and an sick Bog Salamander. Anyway, the pouch had been in my nightstand for years, Tilly needed what was inside more than I did. Besides, I felt bad about treating him the way I did and this small gesture hopefully would be a good first step to correcting my selfish character flaws. Tilly carefully placed that money back in the pouch drawing the mouth of the bag closed with the leather straps. When he raised his head, I noticed tears welling up in his eyes as he spoke.

"Thank you Master," he said, emotion in his voice.

He reached into his back pocket removing an old tattered handkerchief, wiping his eyes and blowing his nose with it before returning it to the pocket.

"Are you ready to go?" I asked.

Tilly nodded, smiling without saying a word. I stood walking over to the counter. I picked up the medic's pack slinging the strap over my head and around my left shoulder. That way it'd be difficult for anyone to take it from me. I turned facing the door to the shop raising my right hand. I made a slow vertical up and down gesture with my open hand while uttering my destination.

"Stumpwater's,"

There was a crackle and a blue swirling portal opened about five feet in front of us. I looked down to Tilly bobbing my head in the direction of the portal.

"After you"

Tilly obeyed hurrying through the portal. I turned back to Barnabas who seemed nervous.

"Be careful," he said.

"I'll be back in a little while," I said, turning walking into the portal.

# Chapter 8

I stepped out of the portal onto a sidewalk at the corner of *Roosevelt and Campbell Road* with Tilly in front, about a hundred yards East of our destination. Magical defenses around the entrance to Stumpwater's made it impossible to open a portal any closer and the patrons of Stumpwater's like it that way. It kept the more darker elements of the magical world from causing trouble anywhere near the entrance or inside for that matter. Some scuffles have taken place over the years, but the security of Stumpwater's has proven more than up to the task for any troublemakers.

I scanned the area around us. There was a fenced in open lot behind where we stood, a blue trailer standing within the lot close to the street. On the West side of *Campbell* were newly built high priced homes on property that until recently housed a large moving and storage warehouse for over a quarter century. The

*Southside of Chicago* had seen something of a revival in the last few decades or so. Where there were once industrial sites and project housing now stood expensive homes, strip malls and fast food places. It was, for lack of a better cliché an up and coming place. Families and young single urban professionals were flocking back to the city in droves paying through the nose for a lifestyle purportedly filled with peace and prosperity. Appearances as they quite often are, were deceiving even with the new look; the *Southside* was still a pretty rough place during the day and especially at night.

The portal closed with an audible crackle. I notice an old man pushing a shopping cart with a loud squeaky wheel overflowing with crushed aluminum cans hurriedly moving away from us. Snow was piled up on both sides of the street making his retreat a bit more difficult. He must not have been accustomed to seeing this mode of transportation. I looked down at Tilly giving him a slight wink, which he returned with a bright smile.

I beckoned him with a nod to follow and we started walking toward Stumpwater's. Our frozen breath plumed from our nostrils and open mouths with every step we took. Tilly looked to be shivering from this brisk *Chicago* weather. We'd be inside Stumpwater's shortly. The entrance to this magical shopping mall is concealed with a powerful enchantment so that Normal's cannot stumble upon it accidentally. It's located under the railroad bridge on the north side of *Roosevelt Road* in *Chicago*. The door is protected by magical wards and defenses so even if someone or something wished to enter they couldn't do so unless the Doorman opened the door for them.

We were roughly twenty-five or thirty feet away from the door to Stumpwater's when a tall, imposing man built in the image of the *Incredible Hulk* stepped from the shadows under the railroad bridge. He was over seven feet tall and to say that he was huge would have been an understatement. His arms were as thick as my head. He was dressed in various shades of grays and black, his wardrobe consisting mostly of old cast off clothing. A deep hoodie was pulled up over his head, which obscured his features. He wore a long tattered overcoat over that. His name was Grim Jack and everyone in the magical world knew that he was the Doorman or outer guard of Stumpwater's. No one got in or out of the place without being scrutinized by him and his magical abilities.

If perhaps you decide to venture out one day looking for the bridge that I've described and you encounter Grim Jack, take my advice and just pass on by without speaking to him. It would be a much safer course of action. The reason being is that no one knew without any degree of certainty exactly what Grim Jack was. There was some speculation that he was a half Vampire, though there was no evidence to support that. While others claimed that he was some sort of hybrid Troll because he was always seen under a bridge. There were still others that believed Grim Jack was a Dragon that had taken human form for some reason or another. The fact of the matter was that all anyone knew for sure was that Grim Jack was mysterious and extremely powerful, he didn't talk much if at all and had absolutely no sense of humor.

Tilly's footsteps grew hesitant slowing as he fell into step directly behind me. I really couldn't blame him; I wanted to hide behind something as I drew near the towering figure before us. About six or seven feet away, Grim Jack raised his hand motioning me to stop. Apparently Tilly didn't see the gesture or perceived me stopping, because he bumped into the back of my legs pushing me forward a few inches. I turned glaring down at him.

"Sorry Master," he whispered in an apologetic tone.

I turned back to Grim Jack noticing he surveyed us with the demeanor and patience of a *DMV* employee indifferently helping with an address change on a driver's license. If any of you have been in a *DMV Office* for this purpose recently - especially in *Michigan* - you know of what I speak.

"What is your purpose here?" Grim Jack asked in a deep voice that sounded like stone rubbing against stone.

"To enter Stumpwater's. I have business with Reb Ironbolt," I replied calmly.

A few seconds ticked by after the last word had past my lips when Grim Jack's eyes abruptly flared with bright yellow light. Wispy tendrils of power undulated like a clutch of snakes coiling in a mass around the edges of the bright beams of light erupting into brilliance only to fade into nothingness seconds later. Two penetrating spotlight shone upon us scanning over our bodies from head to toe. When the beams hit the sidewalk the light disappeared, leaving dark spots pulsing in my vision.

Grim Jack raised his right arm to the side flexing his fingers open. A wall of translucent energy snapped into being encircling all three of us. The wall shimmered, writhing in slow swirls; it was almost like looking through a poorly made pane of window glass. It was a containment spell and a powerful one. He was probably having a problem with how I was armed today. His magic may have keyed on the fact that my guns were concealed with magical enchantments. I'd gone to Stumpwater's in the past wearing them and there wasn't a problem then. Maybe he was reacting to Tilly or maybe he was just having a bad day and I just happened to be the one he was going to take out his frustrations on. Regardless, we weren't going anywhere for a while. Grim Jack lowered his hand and spoke.

"Your power has grown tenfold since last we met Young Wizard, which is rather puzzling. You carry a powerful relic of antiquity thought lost centuries ago and you have as a companion, a bound Elf known to be the servant of Hans Bialek. Explain." He said bluntly.

Contained in Grim Jack's amiable question, was a command for me to tell him what the hell was going on. He knew about the crown, which meant the information he had at his disposal was considerable or he was very knowledgeable about a great many things and either of those lines of thought were very disconcerting. He had also keyed in on the power I'd absorbed from the crystal. I had a little more respect for his vision. Shit, Grim Jack could literally see into a person. Good thing I was wearing clean underwear.

OK, so now I had a major problem. Do I tell him what was going on and risk someone overhearing everything or take the chance that Grim Jack might decide to double cross me and take the crown for himself? I could also remain silent leaving myself to the mercy of Grim Jack, a powerful and mysterious magical being. I was screwed no matter which way I thought about it.

"What I may have to say could mean my life and the life of my companion. I will not risk revealing it without knowing the information is safe," I said, hoping my voice sounded steadier than I felt.

"Speak," Grim Jack said. "None shall hear your words, "

With that I gave a curt nod, then I told him everything. I didn't leave anything out either; there was no need to. I told him what I knew about Barnabas and King Arthur's relics, About the Albino and the Vampire twins, I told him about Tilly, how his master was slain and he ended up with me. I even told him about what we had for lunch. Not sure why I did that, but I think being nervous had a lot to do with it. Grim Jack listened to it all, never once interrupting and when I had finished my long and animated diatribe he just stared at me unmoving with his head cocked to one side, thinking.

After what felt like an eternity he finally straightened his head and spoke.

"The path that has been set before you young Wizard is a dangerous one. I do not envy your future that has yet to be revealed,"

He made a gesture with his hand and the curtain of energy that surrounded us faded away.

"I cannot help you once you enter Stumpwater's, but my advice to you is to seek out Baugrun and stay close to him. It is important for you to be ever watchful, evil tends to find you when you least expect it," he said with something that sounded like regret in his voice.

Grim Jack placed a dinner plate sized hand on my shoulder. He looked deeply into my eyes then spoke.

"Be well Young Solomon and should Baugrun have questions tell him to direct them to me,"

He removed his hand moving over to stand close to the old weathered cement wall that made one of the supports for the railroad tracks above. He placed his left hand over a small red spray painted interlocking S and W. Almost immediately the cement wall folded in on itself, cement ground against cement making an unpleasant sound as it formed into an arched doorway. A huff of warm air hit us in the face as Tilly and I moved to stand in front of the archway. We heard the distant sounds of what lay beneath and caught many pleasant scents that wafted up, but unfortunately there were a few foul ones mixed in that as well. The stone steps looked threatening for some reason. No, the more I thought about it they were not threatening, but foreboding. I'd walked down these stone steps more times than I can remember and they never made me hesitate like this.

Grim Jack gestured for us to enter, after a few short seconds of more hesitation I placed my foot on the top stair and began my decent down to Stumpwater's followed closely by Tilly.

The stairway down was so familiar to me I could've walked down it with my eyes closed. The stairs were roughly thirteen feet wide from stonewall to stonewall. The ceiling rose almost twenty feet high to accommodate the larger beings of the magical world. You'd be surprised at how many Trolls, Centaurs and Cyclops frequent Stumpwater's. The walls of the stairway were made of finely carved granite stone, so precisely honed that they fit together without any mortar. The stairs were made of the same opulent material. Every five feet or so on both sides of the walls and directly above on the ceiling forming a triangle pattern, were glowing yellow stones about the size of a professional sixteen inch softball which illuminated the way in rich soft yellow light.

There were eighty steps in all. You walk down ten steps, turn left walk down another ten steps and so on until you reached the bottom. At the bottom of the eighty steps another arched doorway greeted you. This one had magic runes carved into each of the stones forming the arch and was essentially the second line of defense for Stumpwater's, Grim Jack being the first. There was only the Main Entrance that served to let customers into Stumpwater's proper. Dozen's of egress points around the world however deposited patrons near the railroad bridge. Two ornately carved wooden doors about six inches thick gilded with gold were open during business hours. The carvings depicted various scenes from magical history or what Normals would call myth or fairytales. My most favorite carving was on the interior side of the open door. It's located on the lower right panel of the right door. It depicts a scene from one of the lesser-known *Grimm Brothers Fairytales*, entitled the *"Old man and his Grandson"*.

Tilly and I entered Stumpwater's. The place was a marvel of Dwarf craftsmanship and engineering. The space that Stumpwater's fit in was approximately two hundred and fifty thousand square feet with similar stone facing on the walls, floor and ceiling just like the stairwell. The ceiling rose thirty-five feet at its upper most point curving downward to about twenty feet. From the ceiling hung dozens of yellow crystal chandeliers about five feet in diameter, banded with braided black wrought iron and suspended from chains which hung down at varying lengths the longest being about ten feet. Each chandelier gave off enough light over the shops and streets to give the cavern more of a topside feel of late afternoon.

The Main Street cut right down the middle of the cavern. It was about twenty feet wide, which was intersected by another street at the middle forming a cross. The shops took up spaces on both sides of the street. There were shops you could buy potion ingredients, shops you could buy armor or arms, there were shops to get a bite to eat, - if you ever get the chance to visit Stumpwater's I recommend you try a Yuckberry Tart. They look horrible, but smell and taste heavenly. You can find them at Votes Bakery tell him I sent you. - Shops to buy animals and even a few taverns to stop in and get a drink. The shop facades were made of a variety of materials, such as stone, brick or finely carved woods. The architecture and style of each shop depended largely on the proprietor's culture or items being sold. Large wooden or metal sign shingles hung over each door denoting the name of each establishment. Much of Stumpwater's reminded me of a scene of old *London* described in a *Charles Dickens* novel entitled *Barnaby Rudge.*

Two Dwarfs dressed in full battle dress, long braided beards and sharpened battle axes stood at attention on both sides of the open doors, standing stoic like guards at *Buckingham Castle* in *England*. Stumpwater's was fairly busy today, the Main Street was crowded, however Tilly and I were able to navigate our way through unimpeded. The Laughing Goblin was at the far end of Stumpwater's so we needed to pass by quite a few shops before we got there. We passed by Pu

Yin's Oddity Shop, Stickney's Potions, Durum's Creature Depot and Spinnaker Votes Bakery. We were just about to pass by Craven's Tailor Shop when I felt a tug on the hem of my jacket. I stopped, turning. Tilly was gazing longingly at the display in the window. There was a handsome purple suit, which was just about Tilly's size. I knelt down.

"Would you like to do a bit of shopping while I deliver this to *The Laughing Goblin*?" I asked.

Tilly turned a little red, head bowed, never making eye contact with me. His fingers nervously picked at the straps on the leather bag.

"Yes Master... But I can wait until you have finished." He said.

I placed a hand on his shoulder smiling.

"I think I can manage the drop off. Why don't you go deck yourself out with a new suit of clothes and whatever else you will need,"

Tilly raised his eyes to mine returning the smile.

"Who knows, you might find a nice plump Elf woman to have a drink with." I said giving him a knowing wink.

Tilly's cheeks colored.

"Thank you Master!" he said in a jubilant tone.

He turned hurrying into Craven's past a pair of witches lugging a heavy cracked cauldron. I watched the door close. I stood, feeling the weight of the bag I carried over my shoulder. I felt utterly alone at that moment.

Another totally irrational feeling I know, but real nevertheless.

I turned heading for *The Laughing Goblin*. I hoped Reb was expecting me. I scanned nervously from left to right as I went. I felt eyes watching me though I never saw anyone looking in my direction. It's funny in a way in which people; left to their own thoughts can make themselves frightened over nothing. How a person can see Boogeyman around every corner or hear sounds that really aren't there. I'm usually not someone who panics or gets scared easily, I have a pretty rational mind for danger. There are really only two responses to have, fight or flight. Now that I think about it there are three. There are the two I already mentioned and there's also being scared stiff. Sometimes a person's wiring shorts out and they just don't react at all. I tend to fight more than I flee. Call it tenacity or just being plain stubborn. So whenever I venture out I always try to prepare for any situation I may encounter and there is absolutely nothing wrong with being cautious or over thinking things. Cleaning out Brood Worm tanks can sort of prepare you for situations that would make anyone afraid.

I walked a casual yet brisk pace attempting not to draw attention to myself. I still couldn't shake this feeling that I was being watched. I guess I'll have to chock this up to a healthy case of paranoia. I made my way past the two witches struggling to get their cauldron through the door at Tebron's Blacksmith Shop. In the reflection of Tebron's storefront window, I saw a man of average height, stocky, dressed in a leather jacket with black wavy hair walking along with me on the opposite side of the street observing me intently. I stopped abruptly turning to confront the man so interested in me. I had a spell ready and a hand on one of my *Colt* pistols incase his intentions were less than cordial. When my eyes came to the spot where I thought he was standing, there was nothing. He was gone. I looked up and down the street not seeing him in either direction. I had to get to the *Laughing Goblin* and give this crown to Reb Ironbolt.

I turned heading for Reb's place, moving faster now. I was about fifteen feet away from the cross streets when a large stone disc rolled out of a small alley between two shops ahead of me on the left side. The disk was a little bit bigger than a manhole cover, three inches thick with what looked like complex designs chiseled into the stone. The disk was moving too fast for me to determine what the markings were, given how my day had gone so far I knew this couldn't be good. The disc's progress slowed as it intersected my position. I watched the damned thing stupidly instead of running away like a normal sane person. It came to a stop teetered for a moment then fell backward down onto the cobblestone surface with a deafening stone on stone thud.

Great, I thought, *Round Two* has just begun. If things like this keep up I'm going to have to invest in a good cutman.

131

# Chapter 9

I retreated a few steps, not exactly sure what to make of it. A green bolt of lightning shot down from one of the chandeliers striking the stone disc dead center. I perceived around me that the street had quickly and quietly cleared. I could feel many sets of eyes, which were peering out at me from the safety of the now closed shops. I think I even heard locks being turned and bolts being slid into place. There was an eardrum-bursting crack of sound and then the lightning bolt was gone. In front of me on the stone disk stood a figure well over six feet tall dressed in black flowing robes which moved without the assistance of any wind. The black cloth flowed around him like motes of dark smoke. The figure's face was concealed by a silver *Janus Mask* made to represent a drawn angry tragic face. In the figure's hand rested a gnarled Wizard's staff. From the alley that the stone disc rolled emerged four pale figures dressed in plain unremarkable dark suits, dark glasses covering their eyes. If I had to guess I'd say these four were Vampires and the guy holding the staff was a Wizard. Where's *Captain Obvious* when you need him? I really need to start listening to my paranoia.

The four Vampires filed in behind the tall Wizard spreading out two on each side. My left hand disappeared inside my coat withdrawing one of the *Colt* pistols. I flexed my right hand. My six-inch wand popped out on a spring mechanism, my hand closing around it. Behind me I heard the scuff of shoes on the stone street. I glanced to my rear spying three more individuals looking almost exactly like the other four suit-clad men. I added up the numbers arrayed against me, seven Vampires and one Wizard. I turned my body slightly so that should they attack, I could let loose at least two spells before I got the hell out of the way. I kept my eye on the tall Wizard.

"Give me what you carry boy and you will leave this place alive," the tall Wizard said hissing his words.

My heart beat faster now steadily moving up into my throat. I needed something to drink, my tongue stuck to the roof of my mouth and my throat was dry. - Why is it you get thirsty when you get into a scary situation? Makes no sense to me. - If I kept him talking long enough the Dwarf guards or Baugrun might get here in the next few seconds. The place wasn't that big so I had a good chance of getting some help.

"I'm sorry to disappoint you, but if I don't deliver this box in the next thirty minutes or less I won't get paid and I really need the money. Do you know how much a delivery boy like me makes?"

The tall Wizard raised his staff, smiting the end on the stone street. At the place his staff hit the ground a wave of energy surged out from that point spreading into a wide cone under the cobblestone causing the stones to fly up a few inches as though there were something traveling under them. On instinct, I raised my right hand making a horizontal slash at the street a foot or two in front of the wave heading toward me. A large gash appeared in the street ten feet long and six-inches wide. The cone of energy hit my line of defense creating a minor explosion, which caused stone fragments to fly everywhere, striking the stores, the ceiling and a few even hit a chandelier or two. The blast was directed up and away from me, which surprised me and I think the look on my face may have reflected that. My spells aren't normally as focused as that. They're solid yet crude, Barnabas always said my control would come to me as I practiced and got older. The spell was only meant to counter the power sent at me and not to deflect any solid objects.

I heard the three Vampires behind me rush headlong toward me. Turning my attention to them, I raised my *Colt* leveling it at the nearest one firing two shots rapidly. The Vampire bobbed and weaved eluding the bullets. Overhead I saw movement. Dark shapes hurdling down on top of the Vampires from the shop rooftops. Three large Wolves the size of small horses,

135

two dark brown in color and one a silver gray collided with the oncoming Vampires tearing into them as they slammed the bloodsuckers into the ground. The attack was swift and a complete surprise. It was a gruesome struggle and the Vampires gave as good as they got, however the Werewolves and their ability to heal were too much for them to over come and were losing the fight and their lives.

I turned back to the tall Wizard and the other four Vampires, figuring that my rear was covered - go ahead, you can make a joke if you'd like – I saw two more Werewolves plowing into the two Vampires on the left side of the street dragging them down. The tall Wizard's attention was fixed on me; he dipped his head casting a spell. The two remaining Vampires were nearly upon me. From the side street at my right a huge black and grey creature barreled into my oncoming attackers closing its massive jaws around the torso of one and knocking the other into a stone bench fifteen feet away. The beast thrashed its massive head violently from left to right. The head and arms of the Vampire went flying in one direction and his legs went flying in another. The part remaining in the creature's mouth was swallowed in one gulp. The beast turned heading for the Vampire that he knocked into the bench.

It was Naga Baugrun's pet Gog. For those of you unfamiliar with a Gog, they're a reptilian-like creature, which are twice the size of a Siberian tiger. Gogs have thick powerful bodies and walk on four equally powerful legs, balanced by a thick muscular tail about five feet long. The head of a Gog is long and quite large, almost like an animal straight from the Jurassic era and filled with two rows of long sharp dagger-like teeth. Naga's sudden appearance startled the tall Wizard. He didn't see Baugrun, the Watcher rushing in from behind, his sword raised high above his head. He used a small wooden cart laden with fruits and vegetables as a springboard vaulting in the air, leaping toward the tall Wizard's back, his sword cleaving down in a two handed attack.

At the last second the tall Wizard whirled round bringing his staff up defensively. Baugrun's sword struck a mighty blow on the staff; white dazzling sparks erupted from both wood and steel. The tall Wizard turned in a half circle pulling an eight-inch blade from a hidden pocket in his robes thrusting it at Baugrun's rib cage. The Watcher deflected the blade's thrust with his steel wrist bracer. Following through the movement, Baugrun grasped the tall man's wrist twisting it until the blade fell harmlessly to the street. The tall Wizard shrieked in pain, kicking at Baugrun's chest causing him to release his wrist. The Watcher retreated a few feet. This gave the tall Wizard an opportunity that he may have been hoping for, because Baugrun seemed to be more than a match for him in physical combat. The tall Wizard smote the end of his staff on the street; using that end he drew a circle around himself roughly forty-eight inches in diameter. Wherever the end of the staff touched it erupted into a line of white-hot fire encircling him. When the circle was closed, a column of fire exploded upward from within engulfing the tall Wizard in flames that felt as hot as a blast furnace. The column of fire rose up from the street. I lifted my arm shielding my face. I followed it up rising to the ceiling passing right through the stone. The fire continued until it had entirely passed out of sight. All that remained was a glowing spot of red-hot stone in the street. My eyes returned to the scene around me. Baugrun knelt beside the stone disk examining it by prodding the disk with the tip of his sword. After a few short moments it seemed he was completely satisfied with his investigation. Baugrun lifted his sword bringing the heavy handle end down onto the center of the stone breaking it into three pieces. There was a small pop of an explosion when the spell had been broken.

    I holstered my pistol getting to my feet. Baugrun stood sauntering over to me wiping blood from his sword. Baugrun stood about my height, but was more muscular. He wore form fitting dark green leather pants and coat. Worn over those were his plain black mail and armor. His dark brown hair fell to his shoulders and he had a short well-groomed beard and mustache. Baugrun is a confident and rugged individual sort of like a Medieval Marlboro Man. He gave me a wide smile as he sheathed his sword. Baugrun stopped a short distance away from me.

    "Greetings Solomon are you unharmed," he asked in a deep baritone voice.

    "Yes," I replied. "No worse for ware."

"That is well,"

I looked around the carnage then back to Baugrun.

"What happened to the Dwarf security?" I asked.

Baugrun's smile faded.

"Killed by these Vampire scum. Those at the Main Door took three of them before they were overwhelmed," he answered in a somber tone. "They were all good fighters and good friends. It's fortunate we had Werewolves in such numbers here today otherwise the day would've been lost, don't you think?" He asked.

It's very unusual for Werewolves especially five of them to be in Stumpwater's at the same time, a rare sight to say the least. When werewolves get together in larger numbers a contest for dominance always breaks out, it's only a matter of time. So the Werewolves adhered to a strict policy of keeping their numbers to no more than two or three at a time when in Stumpwater's. The fact that five were here at one time meant only a few things. One, there was a rogue pack that didn't care about the rules. Two, the Wolves knew something was going to happen and the Vampires were likely to be behind it and Werewolves couldn't pass up a chance to kill their mortal enemies. Or the third option, which meant that five Werewolves showed up here coincidentally taking advantage of the fact that at least seven Vampires were inside Stumpwater's doing a bit more than shopping.

Yeah, I don't believe the third option either.

"How did the Vampires and that Wizard get in here past the arches?" I asked.

Baugrun pondered the question. It may have been my imagination, but it appeared as though he was considering my role in this attack and if I could be trusted with whatever information he told me. After a short pause he spoke.

"I am not sure Solomon... Vampires cannot enter Stumpwater's without help. Just before the attacks happened I was called to the storerooms. Three Elves were found dead beside a stone similar to that one," he said gesturing to the now broken disk.

"They are called hopping stones and they are the work of Dark Elves."

"Dark Elves," I asked.

I honestly didn't know much about them. They were something Barnabas never touched on in my studies. I've heard stories, mostly rumors about them over the years. What I knew wasn't encouraging. Where the High and Wood Elves were good and kind the Dark Elves were evil and hate filled. Dark Elves have appeared in small groups through out history, by small groups I mean no more that five or ten. Man hasn't seen them in great numbers for a hundred or so years and no one has sought them out. Some say they can be found in swamps where most of the unpleasant things of the world seem to live and thrive. You hear stories on occasion of people disappearing in swamps. How many times have you heard the phrase, *"The swamp just swallowed them up."* If the Dark Elves decided to make an appearance now that didn't bode well for humanity. Imagine the plague of the *Black Death* and *World War Two* combined.

When I came out of my musings Baugrun's eyes were fixed on me in a way that might suggest I were under suspicion. I didn't want to be thought of as a co-conspirator with the Vampires, however this wasn't the time or the place to be telling him everything. There was really only one thing that I could say that would ease Baugrun's mind. After all, these Vampires were after the crown and my being here was possibly the reason those brave Dwarves lost their lives. I owed it to them and Baugrun not to keep secrets.

"Sir Baugrun," I began.

"I haven't the time nor is this the place to tell you of my involvement regarding the events that have happened here today. Know that I wasn't part of their scheme, but the victim. Grim Jack knows all and should you have any questions I would ask him."

At that Baugrun's eyes shot up in surprise. The Watcher nodded in understanding. Naga lumbered over to me, dark blood stained his teeth and muzzle. Given the fullness of his belly it looked as though he'd cleaned up his messes and then some. His massive body collided with mine nearly knocking me on my ass rubbing up against me affectionately. I smiled patting his rough scaly back and sides. He let out a deep chested rumble that would've made a passable "purr" if Naga happened to have been an idling *Peterbilt* truck.

"He remembers you Solomon," Baugrun said gratified.

"Few carry such favor with Naga, you should feel honored."

"Believe me Sir Baugrun I do,"

Right then something occurred to me. I searched around the area finding what I was looking for, one of the Vampire bodies. Bobum said that he; Tish and Earl found a mark on one of the Familiars casing the Magic Shop. I had a hunch that one or if not all these Vampires were marked. There were very few "Independent" Vampires running around these days.

I walked over to one of the Vampire bodies that hadn't been completely ravaged by either the Werewolves or Naga. The one I chose was pretty badly chewed by one of the Werewolves, but what I wanted to examine appeared to be still intact. Baugrun and Naga decided to move over to where I stood, curious as to what I could be up to. I knelt beside the body; I would have to move it in order to check out the tattoo. The back of the neck was the usual place for the mark. Occasionally some would be marked on the wrist or ankle. I was betting that this particular Vamp was a traditionalist. I placed my hands on the Vamps head turning it; suddenly the Vampire's head was wrenched from my grasp. I stood quickly to see that one of the legs of the Vampire inside Naga's cavernous mouth. He was flailing the body about proudly as though it were his favorite stuffed animal.

"Don't eat it," I yelled lifting my hands in a placating gesture trying to get him to release the body before he shook it apart.

Baugrun enjoyed the way I was making a fool out of myself based on all his chuckling, which was the extent of his helpfulness. After the novelty of bungling wore off he said to Naga in a commanding tone.

"Naga, Drop it,"

Naga stopped his proud display of his newfound item of interest - the body - yet he didn't drop it as he was instructed. He looked at Baugrun with the animal equivalent expression of *"you must be joking,"* Baugrun placed his balled fists firmly against his hips displaying disapproval with his Gog. He repeated the command, more forcefully this time.

"Naga, I said drop it,"

Naga let out a frustrated guttural huff of air making a movement with his body that looked to me like a dissatisfied shrug. He opened his mouth letting go of the leg sulking away ten or fifteen feet. I moved to the body thankful for what I was seeing. Naga's playful display - if you want to call it that, yuck - had shifted the body in such a way that the tattoo was clearly visible. The mark was of the triple "X" design, the one Bobum had drawn for Barnabas with the *French* fry. There wasn't enough left of the other Vampires to make certain that they all had the same triple "X" mark; I was going to assume they did. It was standard practice for Familiars to be marked when they're still human, once they'd gone through the death and rebirth process of becoming a Vampire, it's next to impossible to mark the skin of an immortal. I pulled out my *iPhone* taking a picture of it.

"What interest does that mark hold for you Solomon," Baugrun asked curiously.

I placed my phone back in my pocket standing.

"Not entirely sure, but a lot of weird things have happened today and I wouldn't want to return to Barnabas without having at least looked over the scene for clues as to who or what is causing this trouble."

The doors of the shops opened here and there, various people and creatures timidly filing out surveying the destruction and carnage. Naga moved over to Baugrun sitting down next to him. His long tongue licking at the blood on his face and neck. Behind me to my left I heard a set of small newly shoed feet hurrying up to me. I turned to see Tilly decked out in a new dark brown suit and shoes. His arms were laden down with four large packages wrapped in brown paper and tied with coarse string. He also carried a few matching bags in each hand. He stopped a foot or two away from me out of breath, a concerned look on his face.

"Where were you," I asked.

"I was being measured for my new suit of clothes when the fighting broke out Master and the shopkeeper closed the door… I wasn't able to get out to help you… So I finished shopping," he said in a guilty tone.

"He's correct Solomon," Baugrun said.

My eyes rising to meet his.

"Each of the shops have wards on the doors and windows preventing anything from entering when invoked, but they also prevent those inside from exiting."

I nodded slowly taking in the information. I turned my attention back to Tilly, his eyes on the ground shifting his weight from one foot to the other. He looked scared and very guilty.

"I hope you got some new handkerchiefs to replace that old tattered one in your pocket," I said finally in an even voice.

A smile washed over Tilly's face, his eyes rising to meet mine.

"Yes Master, I did. I got new shirts, socks, I ordered two pairs of shoes and a pair of boots as well, but those won't be ready till next week. I bought a new sleeping gown and hat along with a new belt..." He said excitedly.

"That's very good Tilly, you can show me all your things when we get back to the magic shop," I said cutting him off. Trying my best not to dampen his enthusiasm.

Human shaped forms appeared from shadows lurking between the buildings. Naga let out a threatening deep chested growl. Baugrun's hand went reflexively to the hilt of his sword. It looked as though things might not be finished yet.

# Chapter 10

Five Werewolves now in human form approached Baugrun and me, shrugging on various articles of clothing or wiping their mouths clean of pieces of flesh and blood. All of them I recognized, three I knew however by faces alone. Most werewolves aren't the talkative types tending to be quiet loners. One of them pulled on a well-worn black leather biker's jacket. Race, he was the one I'd seen in the reflection of the store window. The man walking to his left finished pulling a black t-shirt over his head tucking it into his tight blue jeans, I'd seen this man's face more times than I could remember. It was Abner Dempke, leader of the Wolf Pack Barnabas and I frequently helped over the years. Abner was tall and skinny. When I say he was skinny I'm in no way implying that he was weak, far from it. You wouldn't know it by looking at him, but

Abner is made of wiry bands of muscle, which he developed over the years working as a garbage man. Even without being a Werewolf I'm sure he'd be a handful as a normal human if someone ever decided to pick a fight with him. Abner's gray hair was cut short which he kept meticulously trimmed never letting grow out too long. He had a kind handsome face that was marred by three long scars, which started from under his hairline on the left side of his face, ending at his chin.

Baugrun turned to face the Werewolves. They stopped a respectful distance away from both he and Naga. There were few around that wanted to tangle with that pair. Of course there were always those misguided individuals that got it in their heads to test Baugrun's skill with a sword or the sharpness of Naga's teeth.

Abner inclined his head in a gesture of respect to Baugrun, the others of his pack mirroring his example. The Watcher returned the gesture, though perhaps not as respectfully.

"Greetings Abner, what brings you and your pack to Stumpwater's today?"

"We're here at the request of a very old friend that has helped me and my pack... We're just returning the favor," Abner replied.

Wait a second. *"A request from a very old friend."* That sneaky bastard, he knew something was going to happen here. He knew all along and didn't tell me. That's what Zeg meant when he said someone would be there. Barnabas sent Zeg to Abner and the Werewolves with a message asking them to look out for me. *Goddammit* he knew. Barnabas used me as bait to draw Lord knows who out into the open to see what they'd do. He didn't want me to get hurt so he sent the Werewolves to shadow me once I got here. The question I kept asking myself was how did he know they'd try and get the crown from me here in Stumpwater's? No one outside of Barnabas, Oswald, Mari, Glum and me knew what was said in the shop. Well, there were the Vampire twins, but they were bound and asleep through the whole thing. They weren't able to get a message to anyone. Barnabas even placed a spell over Blackmane's while we talked and I'm relatively certain that none of us had time to contact anyone. The more I thought the more questions were raised. If I kept this up I'd burn out a few brain cells. I needed answers, badly. When I saw Barnabas again he and I needed to have a talk.

"By old friend I assume you are talking about Barnabas?" I asked interrupting.

"Who else would I be talking about Sol? We've never known a friend like Barnabas Blackmane. He takes care of our sick, makes sure we have food, clothes and a place to sleep... We owe him more than we could possibly repay." Abner said with a fiercely proud tone in his voice.

"When he asked us to keep an eye on you and make sure you didn't get hurt, we didn't hesitate. You've been a friend to our kind Sol and we won't forget that,"

I glared at him. Am I the only one that sees something wrong with using someone like a pawn in dangerous games that is more than likely to get that person killed, which in this case was me. The Bible is full of people that *God* used as instruments of his will and most of the time things didn't turn out so well for those individuals. Even in our favorite stories we see the manipulation of main characters by mentors that have their best interests at heart. I screw up my life well enough on my own; I don't need someone like Barnabas helping me along that road.

"Well whatever the reason for your presence, it's greatly welcomed today." Said Baugrun.

I felt a gentle nudge at the back of my leg.

"Master," Tilly said in a whisper.

I turned glaring down at him. He took a step or two back. I assumed my face still showed a reflection of my anger mulling over Barnabas's actions regarding my life. It took a moment to soften the hard scowl I had going, but I managed it. I knelt down on one knee in front of Tilly.

"What can I do for you Tilly?" I asked.

Feeling a little more comfortable he took a step in my direction leaning close.

"Master," Tilly began. "Don't you think it would be prudent to make the delivery while things are somewhat quiet at the moment?"

With all that's been happening, I completely forgot I had the crown still slung over my shoulder. It's always good to have someone else around thinking with a clear head to help get you back on track. Tilly was right. That's what Barnabas asked me to do, deliver the crown to Reb Ironbolt and then return to the magic shop. The fact that he'd arranged extra security - Abner and his Werewolves - speaks volumes for how much he cares for me. The cynical and skeptical part of my brain however was screaming,

*IT WASN'T BECAUSE HE CARES ABOUT YOU; IT WAS BECAUSE HE DIDN'T WANT YOU TO LOSE THE CROWN!*

I think it might be best for me to concentrate on the latter, but keep the former in the back of my mind.

I stood facing Baugrun.

"We have to get to the Laughing Goblin, that's why I'm here. I have something very important to give to Reb."

Baugrun nodded thoughtfully surveying me and the others with a suspicious eye. He patted Naga on the side; the Gog turned his head nudging Baugrun affectionately.

"Naga and I have work to do," he said glancing at the ceiling. "I trust Abner and his pack can escort you the rest of the way to Reb's safely?"

Abner spoke no words he just acknowledging the subtle order given by Baugrun with a nod.

"And Solomon, when your intrigue is over," he started to say then amended his statement with. "That is if you survive it of course... you and I should get together to talk about all this." Baugrun said. Then he added. "Over a nice pint of ale,"

I nodded thoughtfully.

"I'll buy the first round," I said.

Baugrun and Naga turned, walking toward the Main Door. He waved a hand without turning back, in a loud booming voice he said.

"Until then!"

I beckoned everyone to follow me.

"Let's go," I said.

Abner and his Wolves fanned out around me like the *President's Secret Service* detail while we walked to Reb's place. The streets were coming alive with activity. Dwarf craftsmen and engineers were already at work clearing away debris, measuring holes in the stone street and examining the storefront facades and windows for any damage. Cob Elves were hard at work cleaning up the remains of the Vampires, while patrons filed past all this orderly chaos bustling in and out of the shops once again. It was a truly amazing site to see how fast they got to the repairs. Dwarfs are fastidious in their work and absolutely hated it when things are broken or dirty.

We made it to the Laughing Goblin with no incidents. Looking at the old place I felt at ease, I'd spent many nights eating good food, drinking ale or just losing money playing cards. It was one of my few frequent hangouts and I know that what I'm about to say might sound silly, but I actually felt like I belonged there. The dark heather green facade with large gold gilded letters above the wide paned glass windows and shutters spelling out the name "The Laughing Goblin" looked the same now as it did the day I first laid eyes on it nearly fourteen years ago.

We filed into The Laughing Goblin; I noticed that the "CLOSED" sign was still in the window. I paid it little attention as our noses were assaulted by some delicious smelling food, which caused my stomach to growl. When you first walk into The Laughing Goblin Maura, Reb's wife greets you. She collected coats, cloaks and your weapons. Reb doesn't allow weapons in his place; he says it's hard on the furniture. Today for whatever reason, Maura was absent. Every time I've come here she's always met me at the door. It was a weird feeling not hearing her tell me to please deposit my weapons in the nearest empty cubby hole.

I led the way into Reb's place. It was conspicuously empty, which was unusual because the Laughing Goblin was a happening place in the magical community. I've never had an easy time getting a table. Even the bar was so crowded at times you had to elbow your way through to order a pint. The place was dark, however the bar was lighted with a few candles. Even though the light was sparse I could see the inside of the Laughing Goblin well. It was similar in style to an old world Irish pub, wall-to-wall dark hardwoods and brass adornments. There was a large mirror built into the wall behind the bar, bottles of all manner of spirits stood on recessed shelves in front of it. A large mantled fireplace was on the right side of the bar; above it hung the mounted head of a Club-tailed Dragon. Speaking of the dragon's head, Reb claimed he'd killed it on a hunting trip to Mid-Realm. I however have always suspected that story was nothing more than malarkey. It was my firm opinion that Reb purchased the head in a resale or oddities shop and the story came later because of all the attention the head garnered. Heavy chairs were stacked on the tables, which were arranged symmetrically around the bar. The curious thing was that the chairs hadn't been placed down on the floor after last night's cleanup for the afternoon rush. Something was rotten in *Denmark*.

Reb stood behind the bar wiping a stack of bar glasses one by one with the whitest towel I have ever seen, the thing practically glowed. Reb was a Dwarf and a fairly standard specimen of the species. He stood around forty inches high and was stocky. He had a long red beard, which was tucked under a white apron he always wore. His eyes were bright blue and a jolly smile could always be seen on his face. Today however, the smile was absent, replaced by a hard line. His eyes were red and puffy under a set of deeply knitted brows. Something was wrong here and after the day I've had thus far this wasn't good. As we got closer to Reb a few of the Werewolves fanned out weaving their way between the tables positioning themselves around the tavern just in case something were to happen.

"Hello Reb," I said in a friendly tone.

"Solomon," he replied.

Abner and Race took up positions behind me. Tilly stayed behind us, standing by the door. I placed my boot on the brass footrest leaning on the bar.

"Bit dead in here. Did the commotion outside scare everyone off?" I asked.

"Things like that are bad for business nary a man nor beast likes to eat or drink around them that fight. It upsets the appetite and closes money pouches. Bad for business."

Reb wouldn't make eye contact, his eyes stayed focused on the glass he was cleaning. Though the light in the tavern was almost nonexistent I noticed a few things. The first thing I noticed was that Reb had a large nasty bruise forming on his right cheek. The second thing I noticed was that the heavy door leading to the kitchen and winery was closed. I could see fresh gouges and scrapes in the wood where someone forced it closed. Reb noticed my roving eyes and started cleaning another glass more vigorously.

"Can I help you," Reb asked nervously. I could see beads of sweat forming on forehead. I leaned in close to him.

"I was about to ask you the same thing," I said in a whisper. Reb's eyes opened wide, he nearly dropped the glass.

"I don't need no help," He said quickly. Any non-interested observer might have said a little too quickly.

"Uh Huh," I said pausing for a moment in thought then asked. "Reb, where's Maura? Why isn't she here today?"

He slammed the glass down hard onto the bar.

"Her and me ain't been seein' eye to eye lately so she toddled off to her sister's." He replied in a tight voice.

"That where you got the bruise on your right cheek?"

"Aren't you the observant one," He slung the white bar towel over his shoulder gesturing to the bruise.

"Nah sonny, this here was cause by piece of rock that hit me when I stuck my head outside my door to take a peek at what all the fuss was about. Good thing for me I wasn't an inch or two shorter. That piece of stone might have cost me my eye," he said.

"Where are all the servers today?" I asked. "They couldn't have toddled off with Maura to her sister's."

In the mirror behind Reb I noticed Abner and Race were inhaling deeply. They moved slowly around the tavern sniffing the air searching for the source of the smell. They were on to a scent and by the bristling of their hair I'd have to guess they didn't like it all that much.

"Ain't any customers here, so there ain't no reason to keep em round. I done sent them all home," he said in a angry tone.

Reb picked up another glass then slammed it back on the bar agitated.

"You're supposed to be givin' me somethin' from Barnabas and not asking questions that ain't none of your business."

Reb noticed the way the Werewolves were sniffing the air as well and I could see more drops of sweat forming on his brow. Something was definitely wrong here and it was my hunch that Reb's wife Maura was in danger. Hell for all I knew she was being held behind that closed door. I had to keep Reb talking for a little while longer. I didn't have a clue of what I was going to do, but talking seemed the right thing at the moment.

"If you got somethin' for me," he continued. "Lay it right down on the bar and go... If you got nothing then just bugger off! I wasted too much time with you already."

I nodded considering his words, finally I asked.

"Sure, I have something to give you from Barnabas. This might sound a bit off subject, but can I get a pint of Rothgar's Ale first?" I asked, pulling a gold coin from my coat pocket, slapping it down on the bar then pushing it toward Reb.

"What?" Reb asked and then shook his head. "No, Bars closed."

"Come on, I'm parched. You could practically strike a match on my tongue, see."

I stuck out my tongue so he could examine it more closely.

"Can I just have a pint of Rothgar for old times sake?" I asked as persuasively as I could. I got a little smile from him that seemed to ease his tension slightly.

"Yeah, alright. One pint comin' right up," Reb said moving over to the cask of Rothgar ale and away from the door.

Truth be told I was thirsty and could've used a drink. As far as ale goes I'm a Pinhurst man. Rothgar ale is horrible. It's thick, it's heavy and has a pungent smell with a bitter after taste. Rothgar Ale is almost like drinking a *Pastrami* sandwich, a drink in my opinion that's only fit for Trolls or Goblins. The only reason I wanted a mug of that horrible ale was because it was the farthest cask away from that door. I needed Reb out of the line of fire for what I was about to do. The Werewolf near the fireplace cautiously made his way to the bar sniffing the air just like Abner and Race. He stopped, standing to the right of the closed door. I glanced first at Abner then to Race getting their attention. I made a movement with my head indicating the door hoping that they'd understand my meaning. They did, they backed away from me fanning out. I flexed my hand. Making the wand spring out from the mechanism attached to my wrist. My fingers closing around it, I leveled the wand at the door. A mote of red light glowed at the tip. I gave my wand a flourish speaking the words of the spell in a loud clear voice.

"Patefacio Ianua!"

Reb turned just in time to see the door explode outward off its hinges landing with a loud crash of wood against wood on two or three of the bar tables behind me.

"Maura!" Reb yelled.

Three dark forms darted from the now open storeroom. A blur of color and motion was all that I could perceive. They were fast. The Werewolves however were much faster. Abner and his pack fell on the three forms - without changing form I might add - bringing two of them down immediately leaping over the bar. The third form was taken down by Race a few feet short of the window. I rushed around the bar heading for the storeroom. Reb had beaten me there. I found him kneeling beside Maura removing her gag and bonds, tears streaming down his face thankful that she was unharmed. The Laughing Goblin's six employees were struggling in their bonds looking no worse for wear. I helped Reb untie all the Dwarves and then headed back out to the bar to discover exactly who we were dealing with. Abner met me by the door as I emerged from the storeroom.

"Are they alright?" He asked concern-hanging heavy in his voice.

"Yeah," I replied. "They didn't seem to be injured just tied up. I think Reb got the worst of it."

"Thank heaven."

I paused staring at him then said.

"Thank heaven? I never pegged you as a man of God."

Abner chuckled.

"God may not have the interest in this world as he once did, but that doesn't mean he isn't there. Besides my father, who's a devout *Catholic* once told me there are no atheists in foxholes." He said with a huge smile punctuated with a wink.

I gave a little chuckle of my own.

"That's very true." I offered, my attention turning to our captives.

Abner noticed my eyes drifting to the two over by the bar. He moved silently in their direction, taking up a position beside them. They were definitely Vampires; they had the same look as the others we fought in the street not a half hour ago. Whoever we were up against they wanted this crown badly. What was most troubling about the whole thing was that they knew all our plans. More questions for Barnabas when I saw him again. I regarded the two Vampires on the floor, two of the Werewolves were holding them down and the Vampires didn't seem to waste energy struggling. I noticed off to my left that Tilly had taken refuge by the cloakroom door. He gave me a shaky smile disappearing off into the small room. At least he was somewhere safe and out of the way.

"Release me you filthy freaks!" said an insane sounding high-pitched voice. "My Lord will kill you all for treating his faithful Rabeck in this manner. He will boil your flesh from your bones and feast on your marrow!"

I turned my attention to the one that nearly escaped. He was struggling violently. Race and another Werewolf were having a difficult time keeping him restrained. The creature I saw made my blood run cold. I'd never seen a being quite like him before, this Rabeck. He was short and thin almost to the point of being emaciated. He wore patchwork leather clothes of varying shades of brown sewn together with thick rough stitching. He had shoulder length coal black hair, light gray skin and black eyes. There were no whites to his eyes or irises and his teeth... His teeth were black and pointed like you'd find in a Mako or Goblin shark's mouth.

"Stop struggling and you won't get hurt asshole," Race grunted through clenched teeth.

Rabeck let out a shriek sounding more mind numbing than nails dragging against a chalkboard. I moved toward the struggling Rabeck light shining through the window illuminated my form. He looked so unusual, so very strange that I took my iPhone from my back pocket snapping a few quick pictures for future reference. Rabeck saw the movement causing him to look in my direction. When his eyes fell upon mine he froze. A slow reverent smile moved across his face.

"Master," he said in the kind of voice you would reserve for Popes or Kings. "You've come to save Rabeck from these wretches."

Master?

I hoped to *God* I didn't just mess up again and got stuck with another slave. One was bad enough. It was more than likely I reminded him of someone. Was he a slave to another Master as Tilly was to me or was Rabeck a devoted follower of some leader of a supernatural cult? The deeper I got into this business of Barnabas's and Oswald's the more questions were raised and the more terrifying and dangerous this path I was becoming. I moved a few steps closer to him. His breathing slowed as he stared up at me waiting, for what I had no idea, but he had a fanatical glint in his eye. Race and the other Werewolf got a better hold on him. I needed some information from him and I didn't think he'd be helpful revealing anything to me, but he might just reveal something to his Master. I had to go about this the right way and since my only real experience or knowledge of an overlord came from watching the *Star Wars* movies I decided to channel my inner *Darth Vader*. A bit off the wall I know, but I was taught to use what you got.

I lowered my voice and did a passable *James Earl Jones* impression, taking care not to add the patented *Darth Vader* breathing sound at the start of every sentence.

"You have failed me for the last time Rabeck."

For added effect I flicked my wand casting an illumination spell creating small spheres of light that swirled all around me, making my appearance more menacing than it actually was.

"No! Master! No! It wasn't me. It was those dirty Vampires and that Wizard," he said in a frightened accusing voice, hatred building with every word.

I already knew there was a Wizard mixed up in all of this. Well, two actually, Whitey and the tall man in black. The burning question was why. Wizards and Vampires just didn't get along. In fact, not many beings in the world of magic got along with Vampires or associated with them very often if at all. Besides their need for blood, Vampires craved power and would throw anyone under a bus to attain it. There are legendary stories of Vampires double-crossing humans throughout history. Even though they may have never been mentioned by name, Vampires have been behind many of the more notable events in history. Ever hear of *Joan of Arc*? *King Charles the First*? *The Romanov Family of Russia*? How about the *Third Reich*? I know it sounds like I'm giving Vampires a bad rap and you'd be right, I am. To be fair there are those very few Vampires that are honorable, but they are as rare as four leaf clovers or politicians that have morals.

"I held my ground waiting for the boy to deliver the box," his head moved in quick jerks, his eyes fixing on each Werewolf in turn.

"These filthy freaks prevented me from obtaining it for you Master," his breathing grew earnest. "Kill them Master... Kill them all as a favor to me, your faithful Rabeck."

"I do not tolerate failure Rabeck, I should tell them to rip you from nape to naval and eat your liver." I said actually impressed at my ability to imitate *James Earl Jones*.

Rabeck's eyes went wide, he said in a pleading voice.

"No Master! Don't let them hurt me. Give Rabeck just one more chance... Just one more." Black sweat ran down his forehead into his eyes.

"I will keep them at bay faithful Rabeck," I said turning to my left looking at him obliquely.

"But I require information from you to make sure you understand your mission and your place."

"Oh... Yes Master, anything," he said. Joy replacing the dejected harried look.

"Ask Rabeck and he will answer... Ask."

"Why are you trying to get the box from the young Wizard?" I asked hoping he didn't hear the nervous quiver in my voice.

Rabeck tried to rise up on his elbows, Race and the other Werewolf kept him in place. Rabeck's smile faltered realizing he was still being restrained, it returned however when his eyes met mine again.

"It was part of the bargain you struck with that mortal Wizard... The one that craves life and power now, the one you helped turn."

"Very good Rabeck," I said turning my back on him chewing on my lip.

The one I helped turn? What did he mean by that? His answer was somewhat vague and woefully unhelpful. I needed more information from him and I had to get it.

"What was the Wizard's name Rabeck?" I asked in a low distant tone.

I heard a sound behind me, a very strange sound. A sound that made the bones of my spine vibrate like a xylophone. It took me a few moments to realize that Rabeck was laughing. His laugh sounded like a cough from a four pack a day smoker that started at the age of eight, a deep and raspy sound.

"You know his name Master, you know it better than Rabeck ever could."

I wheeled around on him.

"Tell me his name," I spat in a harsh booming voice leveling my wand directly at the center of his chest.

I wanted to wring the truth out of him, but I knew I couldn't do that. If I did the Black Guard would be looking to question me afterwards. So I decided on a spell that I could control even after I cast it. The spell I chose to use was a spell Barnabas taught me. One he said that he learned from the Wood Elves. Where Dark Elves use hatred, death and pain to fuel their magic Wood Elves use life, love and nature. I truly didn't want to hurt him, however I needed answers and this spell should help me get them.

# Chapter 11

Rabeck recoiled in terror. The vice-like grip the Werewolves were applying kept him stationary. I cast the spell in a loud clear voice, "Textus Redimio."

Luminous tendrils of energy erupted from the tip of my wand creeping through the distance between us like fast growing vines. Rabeck let out a whimper as the energy hit him square in the chest.

And nothing…

Absolutely nothing happened. The spell simply spread over his chest dissipating into nothingness. He was immune to my magic. My spell was about as effective as using a leaf blower or throwing a glass of water on him. I think the surprise of the spell not working showed clearly on my face because Rabeck's expression turned murderous. He renewed his attempts to throw the Werewolves off him.

"LIAR! IMPOSTER!" He shrieked, black froth erupting from the corners of his mouth. "You will pay for your deception!"

It was my turn to look scared. I took a few steps back from the flailing Rabeck. The two Vampires took a cue from their leader and resisted as well, one actually managed to get to his feet. Abner was there in an instant to help. My magic didn't seem to work on Rabeck and the Werewolves were having a tough time keeping these three under control. Something needed to be done quickly. In my moment of indecision Reb, the barkeep hurdled over the bar like he was in an Olympic event. A gleaming weapon raised in his hands and a look of revenge on his face, a roar of hatred and anger bellowing from him. He landed two feet away from the closest Vampire bringing the weapon down in a streak of silver. The battle-axe bit two inches into the wooden floor. I saw the head of the Vampire roll away up under a bar table. Without pausing Reb had the axe extracted from the wood turning in a tight half circle bringing the butt end of the axe handle in contact with the standing Vampires rib cage just to the right of the sternum.

The Vampire crumpled to the floor coughing up black blood; his breathing became erratic and raspy. I think Reb punctured the Vampire's left lung. Reb straightened turning toward Rabeck shifting the battle-axe in his grip. Rabeck chuckled. It was a creepy sound.

"The Master will deal with you all in time and I will be there to see him wring the life from each of your worthless carcasses,"

Rabeck continued to chuckle for a few seconds longer then he bit down hard on something in his mouth and swallowed. His eyes rolled back into his skull, small lines of black blood or saliva formed at the corners of his mouth. Rabeck convulsed, his skin bubbled, the tissues underneath undulated. Race and the other Werewolf released Rabeck's arms jumping to their feet getting as far away from him as they could. He looked like he was going to pop like a zit. I thought quickly casting a spell around Rabeck that would enclose him in a protective shield circle. Luckily for all of us I did, no sooner had the shield gone up, his body burst like an overfilled water balloon. His body and skeleton turned into some sort of dark gelatinous liquid, which continued to boil and bubble as we watched. Finally his remains evaporated into a discoloration on the hardwood floor. I stared at the spot Rabeck lay a few seconds before. It was Abner that broke the silence.

"I think you need to get back to Blackmane's Solomon and us wolves need to disappear," Abner said in a calm commanding voice.

"I think you're right," I said my eyes still fixed at the spot on the floor.

"Yeah, you lot clear out," Reb said looking down at the injured Vampire.

"I'll take care of this mess."

I turned toward him placing my wand back up my sleeve. I considered my options. There was no way I was going to give Reb the box after everything that happened and I think Reb knew not giving it to him was the right thing to do. Plus he'd make the Vampires disappear and quite frankly I didn't want to deal with that or the questions I knew I would have to sit for once Baugrun got wind of what happened in here. The best thing to do was leave.

"Master, I think we should be leaving now," Tilly said in a small voice.

I turned, Tilly stood by the door looking very pale and nervous.

"You've been there the whole time and couldn't lend us a hand?" I said, disappointment in my voice.

"Well," he began. "I was holding all these packages and to be honest I am quite timid by nature."

The Werewolves and even Reb chuckled.

"We'll talk later about how you should react when a fight breaks out. In the mean time let's get back to the shop."

Tilly moved over to stand by my side as Abner turned to me.

"Tell Barnabas that we're always at his service. Race will accompany you back to Blackmane's just as a precaution."

"I will and thank you for keeping me out of trouble," I replied.

Abner nodded.

"I think the rest of us need to go help clean up some of this mess, after all we're responsible for quite a bit of it,"

Abner smiled turning for the door, the other three werewolves followed him out of The Laughing Goblin. Reb walked over to the bar placing his bloodstained battle-axe down on it. He picked up an old battered pewter mug filling it with ale from one of the casks.

"I should've figured out what you were up too when you ordered a pint of Rothgar. He snorted empting the mug in one long pull. Reb placed the mug down on the bar next to his axe letting out a loud wall-shaking belch - it's bad manners when in the company of *Dwarves* not to belch when you're drinking and eating. It's a sign that you enjoyed what was being served, so take my advice and don't be offended, just respect your Dwarf hosts and belch to your hearts content - Reb turned to me holding out his hand.

"I want to thank ye for saving my Maura and my people Solomon... I owe you a debt," he said in a grateful tone.

I took his hand and nodded.

"I accept this debt should the time and need of your repayment present itself. Until then it will not be spoken of," I replied in the traditional Dwarf way.

"Are Maura and the others OK?"

His smile was dark and clouded.

"She's fine, one of those Vampire bastards fed on her."

Now I understood why he wanted to clean up the mess. I didn't envy or pity the Vampire because I knew what Reb had in store for him wouldn't be pleasant. I placed my hand on his shoulder giving it a gentle squeeze. I never really knew what to say or how to react in situations like this, but I knew Reb would understand the sentiment.

"We need to be on our way," I said.

Reb nodded. Race, Tilly and I turned heading for the door."

"Solomon," Reb called after me.

I turned back to find him rummaging around in his coin bag. Reb removed a small coin.

"Barnabas said to give it to you when our business was complete, that you would know what to do with it."

I moved over to Reb's, he held out his hand dropping the little coin into mine. I examined it. Realizing what it was, a little smile crept onto my face. The coin wasn't a coin, but an old *Detroit Bus Token*. It was a gift an Elf Lord had presented to Barnabas. The token had been enchanted to take the person that held it anywhere that he or she wanted to go. It even worked here inside Stumpwater's.

"When did Barnabas give you this?" I asked.

"An hour or so before you arrived and maybe a half hour before these vermin..."

He turned fixing his eyes on the wounded Vampire lying on the floor.

"It wasn't Barnabas that actually gave me the coin, Oswald and his Troll dropped it by." Reb continued.

I nodded thoughtfully, more questions for Barnabas. I took the token in my thumb and forefinger.

"Thanks again Reb."

He nodded then picked up his battle-axe from off the bar. I extended my arm and said in a clear loud voice.

"Blackmane's Magic shop!"

A red swirling mass of energy opened up a few feet in front of me. I jerked my head in its direction beckoning Tilly and Race to follow. I stepped through the doorway.

We found ourselves back at Blackmane's. The front of the store was empty, no one was around. I really didn't expect there to be anyone waiting, Barnabas and the others were probably off gathering their things or scheming, one or the other I thought. The clock above the carving indicated that it was ten to three. The doorway closed behind us with a muted crackle, we were back safe and sound at home once again. I walked over to the glass counter where we kept a few of our more rare items placing the medical bag and the *Detroit Bus Token* upon it.

"I'm kind of starving, do you think I could get something to eat," Race said rubbing his stomach.

Tilly's new shoes squeaked and clicked over the hardwood floor as he placed his boxes and bags on a stool slightly taller than he was, standing on tiptoe to place the last bag on the stack.

"I'll fetch him something to eat Master," Tilly said in a helpful tone. "Do I have your permission to enter the upper floors of the apartment Master?"

"Yes Tilly, you do," I answered without turning.

"May I get something for you to eat Master?"

I was still tired from last night's events. Tired from this mornings events and tired from what went on at Stumpwater's. I was just plain tired physically, emotionally and mentally. My thoughts whirled around in my mind. I needed to talk to Barnabas in order to make sense of them before everything made me too angry to talk rationally.

"No Tilly," I said finally. "Thanks for the offer, just see to Race's needs for the moment."

"Very good Master," He said visibly crestfallen, he turned to Race.

"If you would please follow me Sir." Tilly beckoned heading for the stairs, Race following.

I placed my hands on the counter, bowed my head letting out a deep calming breath. I tilted my head first to the left side then to the right, cracking the tension out of my neck.

"You know, if you keep doing that you'll have arthritis in your neck by the time your a hundred," a familiar voice said from the center aisle of ingredients.

"You set me up... You knew what was going to happen when I showed up at Stumpwater's didn't you," I asked in a flat voice, too tired to muster the effort to inject anger into my tone.

Barnabas walked toward me carrying a new backpack and some winter gear. Which he placed on the floor by one of the shelves containing books on Levitation, Time and Space Manipulation and Transmogrification. I noticed he was fully clad in his battle armor.

"Not precisely, I knew that something might happen but was not sure exactly what. That's why I asked Abner and his people to be there... I didn't want you to come to harm." He said moving over to stand behind the counter directly in front of me.

"You could have at least let me in on what was going on you know." I said raising my head just enough so that I could glare at him from under my knitted brows.

"No I couldn't, I didn't want them to know we had anticipated their move." Barnabas replied.

I rolled my eyes as I stood to face him.

"Can you tell me now what all this was about? Can you tell me why you set me up and used me like bait to flush whoever it is out into the open?" I asked my voice raising an octave or two as I finished.

Barnabas remained silent just looking into my eyes mulling over his answer.

"As I've said before... These relics," he said resting his hand on the medical bag. "Are very powerful and if all four were to be brought together by the wrong person millions of innocent people could die. My decision to use you as bait was a calculated risk,"

"Calculated," I began, but was briskly cut off.

"That is why there were eight members in the Octagon and two Wizards assigned to watch over each of the relics," "It was a fail safe set up by Merlin himself." "Someone might be able to get their hands on one or even two, but not all four." "That's why I sent you to Reb with this box." "That's why I risked your safety, don't you realize how dangerous all of this could potentially become,"

He paused letting that last point sink in, then he said.

"If something were to happen as it already has, all eight of us knew the contingency plans of the other's. We would know what each pair would do to make each of our relics safe." "The eight of us in the Order knew about Oswald's and my plan to give Reb the crown for safekeeping and now six are left."

I started at that, realization flooding into my brain.

"You needed to know if you were being betrayed by someone on the inside, one of the members of the Order," I said as facts congealed in my brain.

Barnabas nodded.

"I know that Oswald and I haven't betrayed our oath, nor has Greybeak or Thrum... Neither of them have the mind for such treachery... We know from Tilly that Hans Bialek is dead along with his apprentice Olivia, her being dead, however is speculation until we can get to Bialek's compound,"

Barnabas scratched at his chin.

"I know for a fact Orm is dead, while you were at Stumpwater's I went to his cottage,"

Barnabas paused before continuing and then he locked his eyes on mine.

"I found his body drained of blood and his cottage ransacked,"

He trailed off, a pained expression overcoming him.

"What about James his apprentice," I asked not wanting to hear the answer.

"There was no sign of him if he were behind this, which I doubt, Orm would've dealt with him severely, that unfortunately leaves Victor Felderbach and Rodfar Groakus as possible suspects, I have doubts that either of them could have betrayed the Order"

"Treachery is usually committed by someone that you least expect," I mused.

Barnabas's face scrunched up distastefully at my words.

"I suppose the two of them could've worked together and figured out a way to get past the secrecy spells. I simply can't see how that would be possible... The spells were design to keep the eight of us silent when it came to the Order's secrets... They would've been incapacitated with excruciating pain had they tried to remove the spells," Barnabas trailed off in that line of thought.

He shook his head in a way that indicated that he couldn't believe where his line of thinking led him. As an afterthought he opened the medical bag removing the box from within.

"Could it have been one of the other apprentices or could the information be extracted from their minds by another Wizard?" I asked. "Your apprentice showing up was a sudden turn of events you have to admit."

"Yes, I believe someone either summoned him by accident or was specifically searching for him. Rahm was not after the crown, I am sure of that. At the time I was convinced that he knew nothing of the Order or its inner workings but it would seem that I was mistaken regarding him. Rahm trailed Tilly here and may have been surprised at his destination that led to the altercation between all of you. Who he's working with or for remains an infuriating mystery. As you know the information that each of us carry is protected deep in our minds by powerful spells and the information cannot be communicated in anyway unless all of the members of the octagon are present. It would take four of us together or only in the event of one of our deaths for the spells on each of us to be removed." Barnabas said.

"So it sounds like you have two traitors instead of just one." I supplied.

"Yes... It would seem so." Barnabas answered.

He placed the box on the glass counter stuffing the medical bag in a shelf behind him.

"At least they didn't get the crown," I offered.

Barnabas smiled opening the box. Turning it so that I could look inside. The box was empty. The crown wasn't inside.

Son of a bitch, I was the diversion. I think my mouth dropped open hitting the counter because Barnabas regarded me with an amused expression. Finally I said.

"You're an asshole you know that."

"Now, now... No need for profane name calling. You knew very well that we couldn't risk the crown falling into our enemy's hands. Oswald and I had to take precautions. The crown disappeared the moment you walked through the doors to Stumpwater's. That by the way was Oswald's contribution to this little charade and leaving the bus token should you need to return here quickly,"

"So you left me in the dark about what was going on and risked my life over an empty box." I said, my anger building.

Barnabas replied, "Not entirely empty."

Barnabas lifted a corner of the blue silk fabric removing a small gold foil wrapped piece of candy. It was one of Madame Rue's double chocolate covered toffees, coated with a layer of cherry liqueur flavored white chocolate.

"Asshole," I muttered.

He unwrapped it, popping the decadent chocolate into his mouth.

"Now don't you feel better that you saved such a delicious piece of confectionary from the forces of darkness?"

"Oh yes, that makes me feel so much better," I replied with as much sarcasm as I could weave into my words.

It was getting hot standing there talking to Barnabas whether it was the heat in the shop or my anger I took off my jacket tossing it on the glass case next to the empty box.

"It had to be done Solomon," Barnabas said with heartfelt remorse in his tone.

"If I had another option at the time I'd have used it. All that I can say is that I'm sorry for putting you into that situation and I am grateful that you returned unharmed."

There he goes with logic again. Why is it when you're pissed at someone they can always throw logic in your face to diffuse the situation. I sighed a deep surrendering sigh, which was really all I could do. Yes, he put me in harms way. Yes, he withheld information that might have gotten me captured or killed and yes he took precautions to make sure I was all right. So why was I pissed? I was pissed because he used me like a puppet. He didn't trust me enough with the information he had and that the goddamn box was empty. I risked my life over an empty box.

AN EMPTY DAMN BOX PEOPLE!

"I want you to know," I began. "I really don't like you at the moment."

"Obviously," Barnabas replied with a bit of snark in his words.

"In the future," I continued. "Could you at least let me make my own decision about where and how I am to risk my life? I'm not a child anymore Barnabas."

Barnabas thought for a bit and I thought I saw his eyes tear up. He cleared his throat and the misty eyes vanished.

"No my son, you're not a child any longer and in the future, I'll treat you as the adult you've become. Now, tell me everything that happened at Stumpwater's," He said inquisitively.

I told him everything I could remember about the events that happened and in as much detail as possible not skipping over anything. I told him about the tall Wizard and Vampires that tried to help him. I told Barnabas about what Baugrun had said about the hopping stones and how he thought they got into Stumpwater's undetected. I told him about the mark on the neck of one of the Vampires, which he found most interesting. I also told him about what happened at the Laughing Goblin and the two Vampires we encountered there as well. I told him about Rabeck, Barnabas seemed to be extremely interested in him. He asked me to describe him, remembering that I had a few pictures of him I pulled my *iPhone* from my back pocket and handed it to Barnabas. I watched his brows rise in surprise, the color left his face and he gasp. My *iPhone* dropped from his fingers clattering on the glass. Barnabas backed away from it.

"Get rid of that photo," he commanded.

"Why?" I asked.

"Do it," he said curtly. "Do it now,"

I picked up my *iPhone* deleting all the images of Rabeck. I looked to Barnabas; his eyes were focused on a point behind me. I didn't think Barnabas even realized I was still in front of him.

"What is it? Do you know this Rabeck?"

Barnabas didn't speak for a good five minutes. When he finally did regain his faculties he ran a hand over his forehead wiping sweat away.

"No. I've never seen him before, but I know his kind... That creature in the picture is a Dark Elf..."

"A Dark Elf, I asked?"

"Yes, cruel vicious beings that feed upon the pain and the suffering of others. They make appearances ever so often and when they do famine, war, pestilence and death follow in their wake. This Rabeck is a lesser Dark Elf, but still very dangerous."

"Lesser Dark Elf?"

"The Dark Elf society is divided into three casts... The first and most powerful is the Mystic cast; they're born with great power and wield it as easily as humans breathe. The second most powerful cast is the Warrior cast. Weaponry, strength, military tactics and strategy are the skills, which they practice to deadly effect. The third and most numerous of the Dark Elf society is the Worker cast. They are smaller in stature than the other two casts and are the craftsmen, iron masters and war smiths. They are responsible for forging weapons, architecture of their cities and feeding the populace. Rabeck is a member of the Worker cast, that I'm quite certain of,"

"Why did you want me to delete the pictures of him off my phone," I asked.

"Dark Elves can use images of themselves to listen or spy on the person that holds the picture and in some instances use it as a doorway allowing them into the person's home. Dark Elves and their magic are extremely dangerous and should never be underestimated. It sounds as though this Rabeck used an egress potion of some sort, so it will take some time for him to put himself back together,"

Barnabas trailed off in thought.

"When I had this Rabeck cornered in The Laughing Goblin I used the Wood Elf spell you taught me, it didn't work on him. It just bled away without any effect," I said in the silence.

Barnabas looked up at me, giving me a sympathetic smile.

"What have I told you about spells practiced by nonhuman beings," he asked.

I remained quiet because as usual when I get questions like these the answers tend to be elusive. Barnabas patted my forearm.

"Spells used by Wood Elves derive their power from nature, the world around us, the heart and soul of the individual and the belief in oneself and the magic being employed," he said.

"It didn't work because you didn't put something of yourself into it. You just cast the spell because you thought it would work,"

"What do you mean put something of myself into the spell," I asked completely clueless to his meaning.

Barnabas smiled patiently.

"The best way to describe it is when an artist creates a work of art, they must put something of themselves such as love, passion, sorrow, joy, envy or anger into their work. More importantly however, they must believe in themselves and their craft as well as their medium in order to convey what their mind's eye compels them to create,"

I nodded in understanding even though I only grasp a portion of what he was trying to convey.

"So... what you're saying, its sort of like creating toons I use in the games I play online. It started out as just a character, but now it has sort of a life of its own, with it's own look, it's own bio and own way of acting and playing in the online world even though I'm the one controlling it. Because I sort of put something of myself into my toon," I said trailing off.

I think I finally understood what he meant. Barnabas gazed at me uncertainty evident in his expression. He didn't have a clue to what I was talking about.

"If you say so," he finally managed humoring me.

Don't you just love it when people don't understand you?

Barnabas turned, realization evident on his face.

"Vampires... Vampires are the key to all this." He said finally.

Barnabas straightened leveling his eyes on mine; he picked up his subway token placing it in the pocket of his cloak.

"Get your battle gear on, we must speak with Adrianna Thorne before we go to Bialek's to investigate."

"Adrianna Thorne?" I asked in a somewhat stunned voice. "The head of the largest Vampire Clan in the *United States*? That Adrianna Thorne?"

"The same," he replied.

Barnabas turned to the door that led to the basement and his laboratory, where he did most if not all of his potion making and creation of our magical implements.

"I thought I'd never be the voice of reason, but ARE YOU INSANE?" My question sounded less a question and more a statement of fact.

Barnabas turned to me for an instant flashing a trusting smile.

"Quite probably." He said turning back to the basement.

"Why on earth are we going there," I asked, frustrated.

He stopped glancing back to me, frustration of his own showing in his expression.

"Because the twins that took such a liking to you have the Thorne family crest tattooed on the backs of their necks, so making a visit to the house of Thorne is as good a place to start as any,"

Then he said.

"If you wouldn't mind on your way up to change please ask Race if he'd like to join us for as long as we might need him and that I'll make it worth his while."

Barnabas raised his hand rubbing his thumb against his index and middle fingers in the universal gesture for money. I must've just stood there dumbfounded, because his eyebrows knitted together in a look of impatience then he said.

"Well, what are you standing around for we need to get moving! We've lost too much time already with me thinking like an idle schoolboy!"

Startled, I turned heading for the stairs that led up to the apartment. What is that old expression? Out of the frying pan into the fire. I hoped Barnabas knew what he was doing going to see Adrianna Thorne. Disturbing or disrespecting a Vampire of Adrianna's age and power usually ended one of two ways. Dead or just dead. Given that we were literally heading into the center of her place of power I really didn't like our chances of returning home alive.

# Chapter 12

A loud crack rang in my ears and my stomach felt like it was still at the magic shop or least that was the sensation I was dealing with at that moment. I wasn't sure what Barnabas had done, but this didn't feel like how I'd traveled by the "bus token" before. We found ourselves standing on the fortieth floor of the *Thorne Building* in what looked like a waiting room. The building itself was located on *Canal Street* situated next to the *Chicago River*. It was spacious and tastefully decorated with cream leather couches on both sides of the room, two large ficus plants stood beside each. In front of us was a receptionist's counter made of highly polished rust colored marble. Glass doors coated with smoke colored privacy tint stood respectively on the right and left sides of the counter. Behind the counter sat a cute young woman with long curly bright red hair done up into a loose bun. Her eyes were down presumably writing on a piece of paper or perhaps typing away on some sort of smart phone. Directly behind her mounted on the wall was a large gold metal logo of a circle with an off center block capital "T" situated in the lower right, under that were the words "*THORNE ENTERPRISES, INC.*" in black block letters.

"One moment," she said without looking up.
Barnabas placed the enchanted *Detroit Bus* token into his cloak pocket. – I've got to get me one of those little beauties, it'd definitely save a lot of travel time and opening of portals - I watched the receptionist lift her left hand to touch something just in front of her on the counter. A few moments later the tinted glass doors on both sides of the desk swung open. Two tall and dangerous looking men dressed in dark suits emerged from what I assumed was the office, letting the doors swing shut behind them. They positioned themselves in front of the doors, blocking the entrance.

Behind us two similar looking men entered the main doors of the office assuming postures not unlike their associates. I could see bulges under their jackets, which could only mean that they were armed. All four were wearing dark sunglasses so it was difficult to get a good look at their eyes. That really didn't sit well with me. You see the eyes as they say, "*Are windows into one's soul*". In many respects that's true. You can tell a lot about a person through body language, but some people can learn to train their body to fool a person's observation skills. That's not the case with someone's eyes. No matter how hard a person tries, the eyes will always give you away. Which is why quite a few people in the business of security and law enforcement wear sunglasses. Of course they'll say that the glasses are for protection or for looking cool, but in reality I think they know the eyes are unreliable and wear them to prevent someone from getting a good read on their state of mind.

I smiled a toothy grin; you really had to admire this red head behind the counter. It took a lot of discipline to sit there calm and collected. The Vampires seemed to take choosing their employees seriously and invested the time in training them properly to deal with the unusual. If she were scared or startled she didn't show it. The sight that she was presented with should've at least caused her to arch an eyebrow.

But it didn't.

Barnabas and I stood before her in full Wizard battle gear, staves held confidently, ends resting on the floor. Race to my right slightly behind, holding the two Vampire twins bound, gagged and one held over each shoulder, their rears presenting forward. He wasn't even inconvenienced by the added weight. Werewolves are powerful beings. When in human form they have heightened strength, senses and recovery from injury. It's not until they transform into the wolf that their true power is revealed. Most normal people would have pissed their pants when a group of people dressed like us just appeared out of a swirling red door of magical energy. It seemed as though she's had seen it all before and we were only boring her. That sort of hurt my feelings. Here we were all dressed up to impress, all magical, all imposing and bam!

Nothing.

Barnabas and I glanced sideways at one another waiting. The red head put down whatever she was working on raising her head. She was cute. Full pouty lips, oval face, bright round blue eyes framed with long dark eyelashes and her cleavage. I could stare at that all day. In all honesty I was doing just that. She cleared her throat in an amused yet charming fashion. My eyes connected with hers and she gave me a patient-reproving smile.

"Good afternoon gentlemen. Is there anything that I can help you with today," she asked politely?

"Good afternoon young lady," Barnabas replied.

"My associates and I seek a meeting with Ms. Adrianna Thorne, if of course that wouldn't conflict with her busy schedule."

Before she could answer the door behind her to the right opened and a short, thin man in a black suit stepped into the waiting room. He moved with purpose. His face was long and thin. Which complimented his baldhead. The only hair I could see anywhere on his face was a little soup patch on his lower lip and his eyebrows. A pair of thin silver oval shaped glasses rested on his hawkish nose. Everything about him screamed obsessive-compulsive disorder. His appearance was meticulously honed and crafted, nothing seemed out of place. Except for his expensive shoes. There were beads of water on the highly polished black leather. Given his manner and appearance it'd be difficult for me to believe that he'd have accidentally dribbled water on them without removing his shoes and re-polishing them. He moved between the receptionist's counter and us. He stopped a few feet away going completely still. I mean statue still. I couldn't even see him breathing. His eyes were a shade of deep green. This man was a Vampire.

I was sure of it.

After a short moment he turned his head to the left, never taking his eyes off us speaking to the young woman.

"Morgan," He said. "Could you excuse us,"

Morgan didn't reply she stood immediately without question. She picked up a smart phone off her desk heading for the door this man had entered. I know this might be a bit crass, but a man has to appreciate beauty when it comes his way. I'm stuck in a little storefront surrounded by magical tools, supplies and other oddities. How often do you think I get to see someone like her? Not very often would be the answer. You know this is one of those key moments that I've read about so often. If I let it slip away I'll be kicking myself in the ass for years to come for not saying anything. I thought to myself what the hell.

"Hey Morgan," I called to her as calmly and with as much cool as I could gather from my deep well of nerd.

She paused turning toward me.

"If you're not doing anything later, I mean when we're done talking with your boss, would you be interested in grabbing a cup of coffee... With me?" I asked hoping I wasn't sounding too much like a dork or at the very least, desperate. I could see Barnabas turn toward me in my peripherals scowling. He huffed out an impatient breath, turning his attention back to the bald guy. Behind me I heard a mocking laugh.

"Really Sol? You're trying to get a date now?" Race said amused.

Race simply didn't understand. How often does a guy like me get the opportunity to meet a woman like Morgan let alone have the time or the courage to ask someone like her out. Life is too short to just wait around for next time. Everyone says *"I'll do it tomorrow or I don't feel like it right now,"* Screw that. What's the worst that could happen? I look like a fool or she tells me no? I weighed the risks and I went with looking foolish on taking a chance.

Morgan's cheeks colored, her lips stretched into a flattered smile, she glanced nervously over to baldy.

"I'll think about it." She said amused.

Morgan bit her lip looking me over and then turned exiting through the door. Once the door swung shut it got quiet. Pin drop quiet, then baldy spoke again.

"Well gentlemen, Ms. Thorne's schedule is quite full today, so I must insist that you all turn around and exit our office," Baldy commanded in a voice void of threat or emotion.

I attempted to open my big mouth and ask him "*Who the hell he was,*" Barnabas's free hand flew up covering it. So it sounded like a clipped muffle.

"Please forgive my ignorance, but whom might I be addressing?" Asked Barnabas.

Baldy leveled his gaze at Barnabas, still no emotion in his expression. This guy was good at giving absolutely nothing away.

"I'm called Bartholomew, I'm Ms. Thorne's personal assistant and bodyguard."

Behind Barnabas and me came a deep-throated belly laugh. Race was laughing at Bart's employment credentials. Bart leveled his gaze upon Race narrowing his eyes. Then Race spoke while laughing.

"You're her bodyguard? You? This is a joke right? You look more like her interior decorator or fashion shoe guru. When she has you fetch her coffee do you do it with a spring in your step? Or maybe when she's out of the office do you try on her shoes?"

I didn't see Bart move, one moment he was there standing in front of us, the next he had Race by the front of his shirt, a five inch double edged knife pressed against the left side of his neck. I could see an indentation on Race's skin. Race simply stood there looking calm and unperturbed, staring down at Bart with

193

the most cocksure shit-eating grin on his face. He was trying to get a rise out of Bart and he got one.

"I guess I struck a nerve, huh leech?" Race said contempt in his voice, his smile never wavering.

As I've said before Vampires and Werewolves hate one another deeply and will go out of their way to kill each other if they get the chance. This blood feud has been going on for centuries and no one knows the exact root cause for it. I've learned to just stay out of the whole thing. Looking at the two of them in their pose of utter hatred for the other, I realized a few things. First, Bart's speed surprised the crap out of me, he moved so fast. There are some very talented and fast people in the world, but this guy was lightening fast. The other thing that surprised the hell out of me was the fact that Barnabas had his sword unsheathed and the sharp point pressed against the base of Bart's skull, right where the neck meets the head. I looked around the waiting room, the other security guards should've been pouncing on us or at the very least had their guns drawn commanding us to put down our weapons or something. Instead, all the security guards were hunched over fumbling with their pants, which were down around their ankles. Their firearms were on the ground in pieces. They'd simply fallen apart. It appeared that during Bart's attack Barnabas magically pantsed all of them and disabled their weapons.

That was so freaking cool!

Do you realize the level of skill, concentration and spell control something like that takes to accomplish against one opponent let alone four? This is one of the many reasons I loved being a Wizard! I'd like to see *David Copperfield* try that one.

"It would be wise for you to remove that blade from my friends neck. I'm reluctant to spill your blood and spoil this rather beautiful and I assume expensive carpet but I'm not averse to it." Barnabas said in an icy tone.

"I am not afraid of you Wizard or your kind. I'm only obliged to show you respect given that both our peoples have signed a nonaggression pact. This filth however, has no such protection under that agreement and I'm well within my rights to rid this world of one more abomination." Bart said, hate and loathing woven into his words.

Barnabas raised his free hand opening it palm out leveling it in the direction of the nearest guard. He closed his hand into a fist abruptly and all four security guards were slammed backwards against the walls behind them. Barnabas raised his fist a few inches. All four guards lifted off the floor a good two feet held motionless.

"I'll repeat myself one last time," Barnabas said calmly, steel in his voice. "Remove the blade from my friends throat, now."

"Or what Wizard?" Bart said through gritted teeth.

Barnabas didn't answer in reply he increased the pressure of the sword point against Bart's neck cutting into the skin. A trickle of dark crimson blood oozed from the cut. There was going to be a fight and someone was going to get hurt or perhaps worse. The thought that kept jumping around in my head begging to be noticed was the fact that I'd done absolutely nothing to create this situation, which for me was a huge accomplishment. Behind me, to my right I heard a glass door swing open. I turned to see Morgan standing there, a bewildered look on her face. She scanned the scene before her. I immediately eased into my suave debonair sex magnet stance, bobbed my head in her direction and very eloquently said.

"Sup."

The side of Morgan's mouth quirked up into an amused grin. She slowly shook her head biting her lip and then spoke.

"Mr. Hollander I'm sorry to bother you while you're... working. Ms. Thorne has instructed me to tell you to please escort these gentlemen into meeting room three at your earliest convenience. She's concerned that the time and effort spent remodeling the office might be wasted should this situation get out of hand."

I turned to Bart and Barnabas. I could see a perceptible relaxation in Bart's posture. Reluctantly he lifted the dagger from Race's neck, wiping the blade on the werewolf's t-shirt before it disappeared up inside Bart's coat sleeve. I noticed a cut on Race's neck about a half inch long at the jaw line. I watched as a tiny drop of blood dripped from the wound. Within the time it took for that drop of blood to travel to the collar of his t-shirt the cut had healed itself. Only a dark red mark remained. Werewolves as I've said before can heal quickly. That's why it's not a good idea to provoke one. If you ever get into a fight with a Werewolf, you'd have to do a lot of damage to even put one out of commission. Silver of course being the only sure way of killing a Werewolf or immobilizing one. Fire can hurt them and possibly destroy a Werewolf, but if there are cells left alive within the remains they can regenerate the body over time. Barnabas removed the point of the sword blade from the base of Bart's neck returning it to the sheath inside his battle staff.

"It would appear that there is an opening in Ms. Thorne's schedule today after all gentlemen." Bart said through clinched teeth, obvious anger in his tone.

"But in the future I would suggest Wizard that you muzzle this dog in the presence of Vampires, before his mouth gets him killed."

"What's the matter leech? Afraid that I..."

Barnabas raised a silencing hand.

Race is known for his loud abrupt manner and it was unusual for me to see him acquiesce so readily to a hand gesture.

"Out of respect for your Mistress I will honor her wishes and not spill blood this day."

Barnabas took a step forward until he was almost nose-to-nose with Bart. A difficult task seeing that Bart was a foot shorter than Barnabas.

"But if you insult my friend again," Barnabas continued in a lowered level tone. "I'll let him tear you into a bloody mess, your Mistress's wishes be damned. Do I make myself clear Vampire?"

Bart considered his response for the slightest moment before answering. His eyes shifted to Race's, the Werewolf grinning happily, standing behind Barnabas.

"Perfectly." Bart answered, no fear in his voice.

Barnabas acknowledged him with a curt nod then walked past Bart heading for the door Morgan held open.

"Wizard." Bart called after Barnabas.

Barnabas paused, turning back to Bart.

"Release my men." Bart gestured to his four security guards held fast against the walls.

Barnabas rolled his eyes in an absentminded manner.

"Where is my head these days," Barnabas said as he raised his left hand snapping his fingers.

The four men dropped to the floor like curtains falling off a rod. They weren't expecting the sudden removal of their magical bonds and Barnabas didn't offer any warning either. They hit the floor with a thud. A slight smile of mischief creeping into Barnabas's face as he turned back to Morgan. I leaned close to my mentor asking in a whisper.

"You enjoyed that didn't you?"

He leaned toward me and replied confidentially.

"Most certainly!"

After a moment of amazed wonder, Morgan's warm inviting smile returned she leveled her gaze at me then Barnabas.

"If you gentlemen will follow me I'll take you to meeting room three."

Morgan turned, walking in front of us gesturing to follow her. Barnabas moved first followed by me with Race and the twins bringing up the rear. We entered the main office area of Thorne enterprises. The layout was not unlike any other high-rise office I've ever been in, except the atmosphere in this place. It felt cold and I'm not talking about the temperature, which was comfortable even in my battle gear. You know how you can walk into a home or restaurant and feel a welcoming vibe like there is life, not only in the people that frequent these places or the delicious food and drink that is consumed there but in the building itself. Here there was no life, just a feeling of stagnation and danger. I couldn't explain it, it felt cloying. Sure the place looked nice but death felt like it leached from every corner.

Morgan was like a flower pushing up through a crack in the sidewalk reaching for the warming rays of the sun in this place. She was human, in that I had no doubt at all. There were quite a few of the others that I saw darting in and out of offices that lined the wide hallway that were human as well. Most were not paying us any attention; they were going about their day-to-day business as usual, talking on phones, having meetings or just typing away on computer keyboards. But here and there spread around the office like weeds invading a well-kept lawn, I could see faces far too beautiful and far too pale to be human. Predatory eyes tracked our every movement. It struck me that they were not unlike wolves disguised amongst the sheep waiting for their chance to attack.

# Chapter 13

**M**organ opened a set of wide double doors gilded with gold in intricate patterns directing us into a spacious conference room off the main office area. The room was at least twenty five hundred square feet and decorated in a style not unlike the waiting room. The room was rectangular in shape with an impressive glass and metal table situated in the center of the room with ten rather comfortable looking yet expensive chairs symmetrically placed on either side. One single imposing chair rested at the head of the table, presumably for the boss, Ms. Thorne. Above the table mounted on metal swivel arms were seven, forty-inch flat screen monitors. All were turned on and the THORNE Enterprise logo appeared and disappeared randomly in different spots on the monitors as the screensaver. On either side of the table against the walls were two long buffet cabinets with sliding glass doors matching the style and material of the conference table. Each buffet had four glass water pitchers filled with ice water and six matching tumbler glasses placed in a loose half circle around them. At the far end of the room was a window that spanned the width as well as the breadth of that side of the room. You could see a great part of the city's skyline even from our vantage point.

Morgan led us to the far end of the conference table where the lone foreboding chair rested. Bart and a few of his men remained near the conference room doors glaring at us. I really couldn't begrudge him his scowl. He and his men were just shown up on their home turf and Bart seemed to be the sort of person that wouldn't let that slide without enacting some measure of revenge. Morgan gestured to the chairs on the left side of the table then spoke.

"If you all would have a seat Ms. Thorne will be with you momentarily. Can I get you gentlemen anything while you wait?"

"Yes," I said... "Your phone number would be nice."

I felt the end of Barnabas's battle staff thump against my breastplate and saw his disapproving glance in my direction. Morgan smiled a very adorable smile of consideration then replied.

"You're very sweet, but I'm afraid I'm going to have to say no. Is there anything else I can get you?"

She glanced around to each of us in turn. We all smiled shaking our heads in the negative, remaining silent as we did. I think that her answer would qualify as strike three just in case any of you were keeping score. The *Mighty Casey* just struck out, again.

"Well then, if you gentlemen will excuse me I have a few things to do before I leave for the day."

Morgan turned to head out of the room, but paused. Her eyes fixed on a point behind me to my left. She flashed a huge grin and an interested wink before she turned exiting the conference room. I glanced behind me to my left; I watched Race's eyes follow her out. Bart closed the door behind her, leaving us to wait. When the door finished closing Race turned back catching me eyeing him. He shot me an arrogant smile.

"Can I help it if she has a weakness for bad boys Sol?"

I turned away; a surly crestfallen curtain had descended upon me. Here I thought I was the one that she'd been making the eyes at in the waiting room in reality however Race, the "dog boy" had caught her eye. If I could've sagged onto the floor in a depressed heap I would have.

Typical.

A short stocky Werewolf that looked an awful lot like a young *Hugh Jackman* walks into a place carrying two-bound leather clad Vampires over his shoulders and the women go weak in the knees. I needed to work out more.

203

The double doors opened, a tall and extremely attractive woman strode into the conference room flanked by four other people. Bart and his men however didn't accompany her into the room. When my eyes fell upon this woman I felt a subtle wave of sexual energy flowing over and around me. The feeling was not unlike walking from an air-conditioned home out into a sultry summer day around sundown, however this was infinitely more pleasurable. The air in the room seemed to just part like a curtain as she approached. This was I presumed Adrianna Thorne and by her bearing and confidence it couldn't be anyone but her.

She was a tall statuesque woman, five eight or five nine, the four inch heels she was wearing put her over six foot. Her outfit was tailored to fit her every line and accentuate her every curve, which would've put any well-known supermodel living or dead to shame. Adrianna looked to be twenty-five or twenty six years old judging by her nearly flawless skin. Though pale as is the accustomed hue of any Vampire, her skin still retained a remnant of what I assumed to be a *Mediterranean* cast. Her long thick mane of deep mahogany hair fell just over her shoulders moving like spiders silk on a light breeze. I noticed a tiny mole just above the right corner of her mouth. Her eyes were the color of pale jade - the eye color that all Vampires share - and looked as though they contained countless centuries of experience and knowledge. Something else resided in those captivating eyes, I saw dominating absolute power.

Adrianna flanked by her retinue walked around to the opposite side of the conference table. They stood across from us keeping the table as a barrier between our two parties. There was a slight pause as she surveyed the situation; a wide businesslike smile appearing on her face then she spoke.

"Good afternoon gentlemen, to what do I owe this visit to my place of business today," she said in a polite yet commanding tone.

Her voice, like her outward appearance was beautiful. I detected a slight hint of an accent, Greek or maybe Italian, I wasn't sure which, even after the hundreds of years she's been alive her accent though subtle was still noticeable.

Barnabas moved forward bowing, never taking his eyes off her.

"Ms. Thorne," Barnabas began. "My apologies for the rudeness in which it was necessary to gain an audience with you. We meant no disrespect, it was necessary however because my associates and I have a matter of the utmost importance to discuss with you."

Adrianna remained impassive to his apology.

"That much I gathered. There are few in this world that would've dared to be this bold risking the severe consequences if the matter were not of importance Mr. Blackmane. Had it been anyone other than you," She paused considering her next words. "Well let's just say they wouldn't have gotten so far."

205

Barnabas smiled, inclining his head to the amount of respect, which he was being shown. I was a bit surprised that Adrianna Thorne knew Barnabas. It sounded like they had known each other or more precisely knew about one another through some past dealings. The expression on my face probably reflected my surprise, because Adrianna's eyes swept to mine, she regarded me for what seemed like a very long span of time, but in reality it was only for a few seconds. Then she turned her attention back to Barnabas.

"How may I help you and your associates today Barnabas Blackmane?" she asked.

"First, Ms, Thorne, I'd like to return a few things that I think belong to you." Said Barnabas.

Barnabas turned to Race still keeping his eyes on Adrianna.

"Race" he continued. "If you please."

Race being Race smiled, and then forcefully hurled the hooded Vampire twins one after the other on the floor at the head of the table, knocking over the big chair with a crash. Race is a Werewolf as I've mentioned before and has absolutely no love for Vampires, I really don't think that he intended to knock the chair over out of spite.

Honest.

The twins bounced and skidded a few feet huffing out muffled breaths coming to rest against the conference room windows, the big chair lying upon them.

Adrianna glanced to a tall wiry looking Vampire with long shaggy brown hair standing to her left. Their eyes met and he walked over to the twins. He righted the chair placing it back at the head of the table before raising them both to a sitting position. He leaned them against the window, pulled their hoods off revealing the Vampire twins faces, mouths still gagged with pieces from Glum's hanky. They looked over to our side of the room pure hatred for us lurked in their eyes. Then they looked over to Adrianna, hatred and murder burned in their gazes for her.

"Zoe and Isabel, I might have known," she said, disappointment in her voice. "Still causing problems I see."

Adrianna turned her attention back to Barnabas.

"I'd offer you my apologies for their behavior Barnabas, sadly these two are no longer part of my house... I expelled them over six months ago for joining a group of anarchists called the Pure Bloods. I will however do you a favor and get rid of them for you if that is your wish."

I could see the wheels working in his mind as Barnabas pondered her words, then he said.

"I've heard of the Pure Bloods,"
Barnabas reached into his cloak. Adrianna's bodyguards tensed visibly reaching for concealed weapons under their jackets. Barnabas's hand halted its progress he eyed the bodyguards.

"Relax gentleman," Barnabas said calmly. "Had I wished to harm Ms. Thorne there'd be nothing you could do to prevent it,"

Adrianna glanced at her bodyguards. Their hands were once again at their sides. Barnabas produced a folded piece of paper.

"I was wondering if you'd be so kind as to tell me about this," he said unfolding the paper, placing it on the table then sliding it to Adrianna.

On the paper drawn in thick pencil lines was the mark that Bobum had drawn in the smear of ketchup. The triple "X" mark. She glanced at the image without picking it up. Her eyes widened perceptibly returning to their normal impassive size. She was familiar with the mark though it remained to be seen if she'd share any information with us.

"How did you come by that," she asked flatly.

Barnabas smiled genially.

"Where I got it is not as important as what you can tell me about it Ms. Thorne... I must confess that my sources have limited information regarding this mark. It's my belief however that you and the other houses might be interested in the knowledge I possess. After all our people may have a common enemy, the Pure Bloods are a group of rogue Vampires bent on ruling humanity which are causing unrest in both our worlds... It might benefit us both if you'd tell me about them?"

Adrianna's body assumed a thoughtful posture bordering on sultry as she pondered Barnabas's proposal. After a pause long enough where you would've been able to sing the entire song of *"Happy Birthday"* and a few bars of *"For He's a Jolly Good Fellow"*, the corners of her mouth twisted up into a wry smile and Adrianna said.

"Barnabas, Barnabas, Barnabas, you know very well that question carries with it information that might prove harmful to myself and my people and therefore is a very valuable commodity. What do you have to barter with?"

"How much do you think is a fair price Ms. Thorne?"

Adrianna giggled. The sound was so charming you couldn't help but smile at hearing it.

"I don't want money, I have enough of that already." She said crossing her arms and tapping an index finger thoughtfully on her chin.

"It's been such a long time that I've had an adequate diversion, one that has kept my attention for more than a few hours that is," a wistful tone in her voice.

Her eyes rested on me, she seductively nibbled on a long well manicured thumbnail through a roguish smile.

"What about either of these two young men" She said regarding me occasionally glancing in Race's direction. "They look fit with plenty of energy."

She scrunched up her nose looking Race over.

"The Werewolf is far too savage and hairy for what I need. But, he'd make a suitable pet... Is he paper trained," She asked off handed her eyes locking onto mine. "But this one would make for an excellent, distraction."

She turned back to Barnabas.

"Would you consider parting with either of them or both if you have grown tired of them."

Barnabas was about to say something but was cut off abruptly by Race.

"Fuck you leech, I ain't nobody's pet!"

I watched as Race's hair bristled, anger building inside him, the seams of his clothes strained as his body puffed up. He was going to blow his stack and I was in close proximity to the eruption. Adrianna turned her head lazily in his direction hooding her sultry green eyes. It took me a second or two to realize she was using her glamour.

"Hush little puppy," she said in a smoky tone reserved only for the bedroom.

I felt a wave of potent sexual energy released in our direction. It flowed, eddying around us, not unlike water flowing around a large stone in the middle of a gently moving stream. Except this sensation was warm and inviting, laced with an inescapable compulsion to kneel and worship at Adrianna's feet. There was also a need, a desire to do quite a few other acts with her that would require at least an *NC-17* rating. The affect on Race was intense and immediate. He stalked toward her, a low lust filled rumbling echoed deep in his chest. He tore frantically at his clothes ripping them off his body. He reached the table crawling over it to get to her, his libido fueling his urges. Race's progress abruptly stopped midway over the table. He didn't move a muscle; he was simply frozen in place. I heard Adrianna giggling like a little girl that just got tickets to have breakfast with the *Disney Princesses* for *Christmas*. Glancing in Barnabas's direction I realized he had his right hand extended, subtle magic swirling around his outstretched hand. I was sure he was using the same spell to immobilize Race he and Oswald used back at the magic shop.

I turned my attention back to Adrianna. I was surprised to see a shocked expression, her eyes resting on me. After a short moment I realized something. I hadn't been affected by her glamour the way that Race had been. Don't get me wrong I was experiencing stirrings in.

Well...

You know...

The place where my other brain resides making poor decisions from time to time. My "*Love Rocket*" was, for lack of a better expression standing at attention and that was it. I wasn't experiencing anywhere near the mind haze Race had been hit with. A Vampire's glamour is very powerful. Years ago it was used mainly for hunting as a way to draw prey closer to them. Nowadays, they still use it for hunting however amusement has become its main use. Being a Vampire over a millennia old, I should've been a misshapen blob of goo at Adrianna's feet yet I wasn't. Given her expression I just became the new flavor of the month.

Her lips parted.

"Intriguing," She said thoughtfully in a distant whisper.

"Adrianna," Barnabas said. "Stop this now."

She mockingly stamped her foot like a spoiled child.

"Oh very well," she replied reluctantly.

And with that the lust filled glint in Race's eyes disappeared, he returned to his normal self, albeit slowly. Barnabas didn't release him though; he was giving Race an opportunity to cool off his temper.

"You were going to tell us about the Pure Bloods," Barnabas encouraged.

"Yes of course," Adrianna responded. "May I suggest a mutual exchange of information regarding this subject?"

"Agreed,"

Adrianna leaned over touching the glass surface of the conference table. A bright touch screen keyboard activated blinking into operation under her fingertips. Her fingers glided over the keys at a rapid eye crossing pace as she began to speak.

"Our information is incomplete at best," Adrianna began.

The monitors above our heads flickered to life. Images along with text flashed on and off the screen so fast I didn't think I could keep up with her furious typing pace.

"Over the last few years all the Vampire houses have reported members of their families going missing," "Even in my own house, ten have left never to be seen again."

Adrianna paused glancing at the twins.

"Eight now thanks to you," she said continuing.

"An insignificant number at first however the exodus is becoming a problem we can no longer hide. The frightening thing is that new vampires bearing this mark have turned up recently."

An image froze on all the monitor screens in the room. The image was of a simple design, the triple "X" that was on the paper Barnabas had given to Adrianna. The same mark I found on one of the Vampires that attacked me at Stumpwater's

"Yes, the Elder Council is familiar with this mark," interjected Barnabas.

"We've yet to determine the Pure Blood's leadership," she continued straightening. What we do know however is that they're gaining power and influence along with amassing large sums of money." "Our conservative estimates put their financial resources close to five hundred million dollars."

I whistled reflexively. That was a lot of money.

"That's far more than the Elder council has estimated." Barnabas said thoughtfully.

"Unfortunately I think both our peoples were far too slow to realize this threat and it is a threat Barnabas," she said bitterly.

"High ranking Vampires have been attacked and some killed in what looks like attacks from Wizards. The only thing that's kept the peace on our side are the old ones. They see these attacks for what they are, an attempt to cause a rift between our two peoples... The younger ones are the problem however... they want war," she finished.

"Yes, Wizards too have been attacked by what appears to be Vampires, the Elder Council has come to the same conclusion... So far they have been able to keep our people in line, but I don't know for how long... Tempers are strained on both sides,"

I didn't notice the shadows passing in front of the conference room windows until it was almost too late. Adrianna's glamour distracted me, however I had the presence of mind to get my defensive spells ready. Barnabas's teachings and repeated practice had prepared me for at least that much.

It was a trap I thought, about to spring on us. We'd been foolish and stupid. We marched right into the serpent's lair only to get ourselves captured or killed. Adrianna's glamour was just a sinister way of getting our attention off the situation at hand and off our ability to defend ourselves so her people could take us down unawares. Have you ever felt like a complete and utter dumb ass? Well, if you haven't, good for you. But if you have I think we can both feel for one another, because I was feeling like the stupidest person on the face of the earth at that moment.

In the split seconds I had to look over the situation I noticed a few things. First, Adrianna's people were reacting by pulling their weapons and brandishing them as they looked to the window. The second thing I noticed was that Adrianna's playful smile had vanished, replaced instead with surprise and anger. She had no idea that this was coming, which meant they weren't her people and we were all in for a world of hurt in the next few moments.

Barnabas had already turned his attention to the window as well. Race was still in a daze. I reacted by throwing myself over the glass table in a baseball player's slide attempting to put myself between Adrianna and the window. Don't ask me what compelled me to do so; I just felt I had to do it. Maybe her glamour affected me more than I realized or maybe it was because she was a woman and I thought she needed to be protected - male chauvinism at its worst, I know - or maybe just maybe if I didn't try to save her, they - meaning the Vampire clans - would think this attack was our idea and quite frankly we didn't need that sort of aggravation when this attack was over.

My feet landed on the floor inches away from her. I turned leveling my staff, a spell to call my defensive shield into being on the tip of my tongue when the conference room window exploded inward. I was too late, shards of glass about the thickness of my pinky rocketed throughout the room. I raised my arms ducking my head in an attempt to keep the glass from striking her. Barnabas's shield was up deflecting glass back toward the open window. Glass cut through Race's clothes and skin. I saw blood trickling from hundreds of open wounds only to close up just as fast. Two of Adrianna's people were on the floor, daggers protruding from their throats. Luckily my cloak protected us from the ricocheting glass, having an enchanted cloak that could stop most projectiles was extremely handy. Yet something didn't feel right, my balance waivered. I felt heat and the unmistakable sensation of a warm substance running down my right shoulder. Dizziness took hold of my senses and I had to lean on my battle staff to keep from dropping to the floor. Adrianna took me into her protective arms, holding me for a moment then I felt a sharp jab of pain as she pulled something from my back. She produced a dagger about eight inches long and coated with blood...

My blood.

The dagger pierced the defenses woven into my cloak and armor impaling me in the back near my shoulder. Had it struck me five inches to the left, it would've possibly severed my spine. That was a sobering thought. I'd taken the dagger that was meant for Adrianna. The dagger in her hand was specifically created to kill Vampires. It was called an Ash Dagger. When a Vampire dies by sunlight - and many older immortals choose this way to go simply from becoming bored - nothing is left of them but ash. During the forging process Vampire ash is added to the metal before it's hardened. When the dagger has been tempered the ash leaves a distinctive pattern of dots on the blade. Hence the name, it also makes the blade nearly indestructible and immune to most magical spells, however it's also lethal to all Vampires no matter how old or strong they are. The Vampire ash acts like a poison and a violent agonizing death results when it's introduced into the body. I'd just saved Adrianna from an assassination attempt.

Adrianna met my eyes and she smiled.

"Thank you," she mouthed looking back to the open window.

Sunlight and gusts of what felt like twenty mile an hour winds poured into the room. The glass must've been coated with some sort of sun blocking material, which protected the room and possibly the building from the rays of the sun. Adrianna and her people were showing no signs of pain or discomfort, nor was their skin reddening. It was possible they were all wearing sun block and special *UV* blocking contact lenses. Sun block research, for all of you who were wondering and of course the budding conspiracy theorists out there who needed information on the existence of Vampires, was funded by Vampire shell companies in order to create something that would help them to hunt in daylight hours. Being confined to the night was such an inconvenience for so many of the older Vampires and frankly it was impractical for them to walk around in the daytime hours covered in heavy fabrics. Sun block worked so well that the formula was diluted and sold to other companies for us mortals to use and the Vampires made a fortune with it. Remember *Amber-Vision Glasses* that came out onto the market decades ago? Vampires were behind that too.

My eyes adjusted to the brightness of the sun as I looked to the shattered window. Eight figures clad in black glossy form fitting suits swarmed into the room, crawling on the walls and ceilings like nightmarish spiders. Dark face hugging goggles covered their eyes and each one of them wore crossed bandoliers over their chests with six daggers just like the one Adrianna was holding. Two of the attackers grabbed the twins, pulling them out of the window like rag dolls carrying them out of sight. The other six rushed at us.

Barnabas knocked two down with a magical strike then unsheathed his sword. Race had regained his senses. He'd changed form, his clothes ripped and tattered fragments lying on the table around him. He pulled one of the attackers off the ceiling, taking a monitor or two with it pinning the attacker down on the glass table where he began to rend and tear at the attacker's head and throat. For my part I leveled my battle staff at one of the attackers letting loose a white-hot lance of fire. It missed, but it was at least able to throw him off balance. He slammed into the wall leaving a huge depression in it. The remaining two of Adrianna's Vampire entourage leapt at the dazed assailant. Adrianna kicked off her heels, literally in the direction of the two remaining attackers, striking them one in the chest and one in the face. Though they did no damage they did give her a few seconds to react. She grabbed me gently spinning me down into her chair.

"Stay put," she said forcefully with a little hint of what I assumed was concern.

The conference room doors burst open; Bart along with five of his human security detail took up firing positions around the doorway just inside the room. They fired accurate and precise controlled three round bursts from their short-barreled *AR-15s* at the attackers. I didn't think it would've been a stretch of the imagination to assume that some of these guys were retire *Special Forces*. The rounds however appeared to have little effect. I watched Bart level his *AR-15* at Race placing a few well-aimed rounds into the big wolf's backside. Race whirled around growling and baring his teeth at the spiteful Vampire. In response Bart shrugged his shoulders in a "*Whoops*" sort of fashion. If he wasn't careful Race was going see what a bald rump roast tasted like.

I turned to Adrianna and she was gone. Well, not gone exactly per say, just difficult to see. Have you ever watched *Kung Fu* movies? The speed, skill and choreographed grace in which the martial arts masters move, if you haven't, I recommend you take in a *Jackie Chan or Jet Li* movie so you can appreciate what I'm describing. Neither of those *Kung Fu* masters however had anything on Adrianna. She was a blur of motion and color. The only time I saw her somewhat clearly was when she slowed down just enough for one of her fists, elbows, knees or feet to make contact with certain parts of her attackers bodies. Even then she looked like an out of focus movie. One of the attackers dropped to the floor out of the swirling tornado of motion. Convulsing uncontrollably like a bug that just got a full body spray of bug killer. He tore at the right side of his rib cage where Adrianna stabbed him with an Ash Dagger, the one I assumed she pulled from my shoulder. All I could see was about a half inch of the handle.

Race killed and dismembered his attacker then he moved to assist Barnabas. The attacker that Adrianna's two remaining people went after killed one of the pretty boy Vamps by ripping off his head. The other he picked up by the heels lifting him over his head slamming the Vampire down hard onto the floor. That attacker then surveyed the situation, realizing he and his remaining people were in a no win situation, let out a high pitched shriek, somewhere between a hawk's hunting call and a pissed off tomcat. The attackers that were still in one piece fled upon hearing the call escaping out the window. They disappeared as fast as they had appeared.

The room was a complete wreck. I only hoped that Adrianna had enough coverage for this kind of destruction. In any event she'd be remodeling this part of her building after this incursion. Vampires hate it when you throw down in their places of power or the places they go to blow off steam. Bart and his security team moved cautiously into the room filing down both sides of the conference room table toward us. Barnabas sheathed his sword then took out a cloth that he always carried inside his glove holding it against his cheek. He must've gotten a wound from one of his attackers or one of the few thousand shards of flying glass. Race stood watch unmoving in the direction of the smashed window. Droplets of dark blood dripped from his muzzle in slow continuous droplets. The pretty boy Vampire that got body slammed twitched; a low agonized sigh of pain escaped his lips, sounding not unlike bagpipes deflating. It'd be quite a few hours before his Vampire body repaired itself completely from the injuries. The other Vampire that lost his head wouldn't be coming back. Once a Vampire loses his or her head it's over, no regeneration. They're dead. Sunlight, Fire, decapitation and an ash dagger are the only ways to truly kill a Vampire.

The attacker Race had killed still lay on the glass table. The remains were bubbling and blistering, in some other places smoldering, which could only mean one thing, what was lying there was a Vampire. Vampires had strict codes of conduct that were designed to help keep the bloodshed between individuals and the Houses to a minimum. Vampires could challenge each other to a duel, but the Heads of the Houses had to give permission for it to take place. If a Vampire attempted, let's say to kill another Vampire without approval they wouldn't be around for very long. There were long lists of laws and stiff penalties that covered any sort of infraction. So, the fact that a team of Vampires possibly had just tried to take out Adrianna Thorne meant that all was not well in the world of the Vampires. That also meant, that the Heads of the Houses probably didn't know about this attack either. They were all predictable creatures of habit. They wouldn't blow their noses unless they looked up how to do it in those Vampire laws first.

The other Vampire attacker managed to turn himself over onto his stomach, slowly crawling toward the open window, his fingertips making holes and gashes in the carpet as he pulled himself along. Adrianna stalked a few paces behind him. Her coat was torn and ripped in places, as were her skirt and hose. The buttons on her blouse simply weren't designed to handle the variety of movements she displayed and had given way at some point during the fighting. Her open shirt flapped gently in the late winter breeze revealing a bra covering her ample bosom made of delicate lacey fabric.

Very alluring.

Adrianna moved to the attackers left. Taking her right foot she placed it under him, deftly flipping him over onto his back. He let out a cry of pain raising his hands in supplication. Adrianna knelt down beside him removing all of the daggers from his bandoliers, tossing them a side. Bart moved in stopping a few feet behind her. Adrianna stared at the Vampire like a cat deciding on what to do with a cornered mouse.

"Who sent you?" She asked in a low monotone voice.

I could tell she was struggling to hold back her rage. Though the full mask and goggles covering the Vampire's face made him impossible to read, he managed to look contemptuously up at her. Adrianna balled her hand into a tight fist bringing it down hard on the handle of the protruding Ash Dagger, driving it deeper into his chest. The masked Vampire let out a blood-curdling scream of horrific pain. The jolt of pain must've given him a dose of adrenaline because he scurried away from Adrianna on his hands and feet like a spider heading for some place dark and safe. He got to within a foot of the window when Race leapt on the Vampire's chest driving him once again to the floor in a huff of expelled air. Adrianna stood moving toward the Vampire.

"Where are you going," She asked, no hint of a question in her tone. "We have so much more to discuss... I asked who sent you," she said emphasizing the last three words,

Off in the distance, but getting closer were the unmistakable sounds of *Chicago Fire and Police* vehicles heading for the Thorne building. I think we all paused listening except for the Vampire. He tore off his dark mask and goggles. The sight we were presented with was unsettling. The Vampire was completely hairless with high pointed ears. His skin was pale white and translucent. You could actually see the muscles and skull under his skin. His eyes were obsidian black with no whites to them whatsoever. His teeth were discolored like they had been soaked in blood and his fangs appeared to be longer than the average Vampire He looked completely alien and creepy.

None of us realized what he was doing until it was too late. He was lying in the sunlight without the protection of his mask. His head began to smolder then burst into bright red flames. Race backed off the Vampire's chest away from the blaze. It was almost as though someone doused his head with kerosene and set a match to it. He was apparently committing suicide rather than being questioned. He was dead already with that dagger stuck in his chest, that death was only a matter of time and he knew it. He wanted to die knowing he hadn't violated his code of honor, if he indeed had one. He never even made a sound; his body only convulsed violently then went still. It took only a half a minute for the fire to consume the skin and muscle. Only a scorched skull with smoke billowing from the eye sockets attached to an unburned body remained. I stared dumbfounded at the unmoving body.

"Avery... Morris," Adrianna said breaking the silence.

Two of her security detail stepped toward her.

"Yes, Ms. Thorne?" They both said in chorus.

"I want you to take Jerrod down to the lower levels and place him in one of the holding cells. Start an I.V. of blood, I don't want him waking up and going on a human killing spree to sate his thirst."

Both men nodded in assent, slinging their weapons over their shoulders. They moved over to Jerrod, one man at his head, the other at his feet. They bent down getting a solid hold on the unconscious, unmoving Vampire lifting him with little effort hurrying out of the room.

Adrianna walked over to the buffet on the right side of the room. She bend over sliding a panel out of the way producing two bottles of what looked like *Woodford Reserve* or some other top shelf bourbon. She placed them on top of the buffet opening the bottles. What, was she going to have a celebratory drink after kicking some ass? After she opened both bottles she left them on the buffet turning to another of her people.

"Gauge," she said.

Another of her security force stepped forward.

"Yes, Ms. Thorne?"

"Find Abbey, have her get in touch with our contacts at the *Mayor's office, City Hall*, the *C.P.D. Superintendent* and the *C.F.D. Fire Marshal*." "We're going to need their help in containing and burying this mess." Also have her talk to our contacts at the local News stations and print media, she'll know what to tell them."

"Yes, Ms. Thorne," he said turning rushing out of the room.

Adrianna picked up both bottles walking first over to the headless Vampire. She poured the bourbon liberally over his head and body. She then moved over to the two Vampires that had ash daggers protruding for their necks pouring bourbon over them. When that bottle was empty she dropped it.

"Bartholomew?" She said as she continued pouring bourbon over the dismembered Vampire lying on the glass table. "Please take these gentlemen to my office." "Give them refreshments and tend to their needs."

She turned her head in Race's direction.

"Matters might go more smoothly if you change back to your human form."

Race cocked his head quizzically the way only a dog could manage. He complied with Adrianna's request and within a few moments he was standing there, in his human form completely naked. A smirk blossomed on Adrianna's face, her eyebrows rose in a playful expression as she regarded the particular region of his body slightly below the belly button.

"Bartholomew, would you be so kind as to provide this very excited young man with suitable clothing?"

Race looked down at his midsection realizing that he was at... Let's go with "*Full attention.*" He smiled shrugging his shoulders.

"Sorry," he said completely unapologetic.

"Don't be," said Adrianna. "I like your enthusiasm."

She moved over to the Vampire with the toasted head pouring some bourbon on him as well. Bart gestured for us to please move out of the room, which we did in great haste. None of us wanted to remain.

# Chapter 14

Adrianna poured a line of bourbon from the body over to where we were all standing. She even had the presence of mind to pick up her high heels on her way out. When the second bottle was empty she tossed it carelessly back inside the room. Adrianna lazily held out a hand palm up in front of Bart. He reached inside his coat producing a plain silver *Zippo* lighter, which he placed in her hand. She flipped the top open.

"If you'd be so kind Bartholomew as to get in touch with our insurance company."

She flicked the lighter, a bright reddish orange flame danced hungrily upon it.

"I think we are going to have to file a claim for fire damage."

She tossed the lighter onto the line of bourbon. The alcohol caught fire after a few seconds slowly creeping its way toward the bodies igniting carpet and whatever else it came in contact with as Bart closed the doors. Adrianna led the way as we filed in behind her. I became aware of something almost immediately. The atmosphere in the office had changed. It didn't feel right to me. It was as though the life force of the place had been replaced with utter silence, the silence of a tomb. It wasn't until I took about twenty steps that I realized the office was completely empty. It was devoid of the sounds that I'd heard when we first walked through the place and the watching eyes that tracked our every move.

"Where is everyone," I asked, my curiosity peaked.

Adrianna glanced back in my direction.

"What's your name," she asked.

"Solomon, Solomon Drake," I replied.

"Well Sol," she continued. "Do you mind if I call you Sol?"

"No"

"OK Sol, I really didn't know how our meeting would end and quite frankly I didn't want any witnesses in the event our meeting happened to go poorly... So I made everyone, except for a few key people leave early for the day... As it turned out, it was the smart thing to do."

I nodded thoughtfully then asked.

"Shouldn't we get out of here before the fire spreads through the whole office?"

Adrianna laughed another of her charming whimsical giggles.

"Have no fear Sol the fire isn't going to spread." She didn't elaborate any further. I assumed because she thought I knew the reason why, which I didn't so I left it alone.

Bartholomew hurried past everyone getting ahead of Adrianna. She turned a corner to her left heading for another pair of etched gold leaf double doors that I assumed was her office. It appeared given the layout of this side of the building that Adrianna's office took up a large corner of the fortieth floor. Bart opened the doors letting everyone file inside. Adrianna's office was huge, definitely an office befitting her power and station in the two worlds she straddled, the world of business and the world of Vampires. Two sides of the triangular shaped room were glass windows revealing a great view of the *Chicago River*.

There was a desk; the base was made of a dark grey marble topped with a thick sheet of curved grey glass standing near the apex of the triangle near the windows. A dark grey high backed leather chair stood behind the desk with two smaller matching ones arranged on the opposite side. To the right and left as you entered the room appeared to be two fairly good-sized rooms. I had no idea what was in each of the rooms, because the doors were closed. Two couches matching the style and color of her office chair were placed diagonally along the wall. Behind each of them placed upon pedestals were white marble busts of two men. There was a personal flavor to this office that the rest of the floor didn't possess. A person - under the right circumstances - could feel at home in this room.

As I thought about it, I felt like I began to understand Adrianna. It seemed to me that work was all that she had. Vampires didn't sleep; they didn't have to because they're immortal. Immortal beings like Vampires didn't need to renew themselves the way humans did through sleep. They did that through drinking blood, so there was no need for her to have a bed or a home for that matter. Then again I was assuming that she had neither. For all I knew she had homes in every major city around the world. However, right now being here in her office I guessed in many ways *Thorne Enterprises* was her home. I wondered what it'd be like for me not having someone as an equal to share eternity with. That was a depressing thought. I knew Adrianna was over a thousand years old and in that time how many people had come along that she considered a friend, confidant or even a lover. I started to feel sad for her as I thought about how lonely her existence must actually be.

Adrianna walked behind her large desk placing her blood stained shoes down beside the phone. Barnabas stood a foot or two behind one of the chairs in front of Adrianna's desk holding a handkerchief to his cheek. I stood slightly behind him to his right bent in pain leaning on my battle staff from the dagger wound in my shoulder. Race for his part had picked up a pillow off one of the couches holding it in front of his midsection. Bart glanced in Race's direction rolling his eyes disapprovingly. He turned heading out of the room. Adrianna leaned over her desk showing more of her ample cleavage. She lingered that way for a good long moment then pressed a button on the telephone keypad. A male voice came over the speaker.

"Executive Kitchen"

"Henry, this is Adrianna Thorne would you be a dear and send up an assortment of deli sandwiches, chips and ice cold drinks for our guests."

"Sent to your office Ms. Thorne?"

"Please," she replied.

"We'll have it for you in about twenty minutes. Do you require anything else?" Asked Henry.

She looked up from her desk in our direction studying us and then she added.

"And a first aid kit,"

"Right away Ms. Thorne."

"Thank you Henry."

Adrianna pressed another button on her phone hanging up. She turned to the windows behind her, raising her arms above her head stretching. Then she turned back to her desk, a look of concern mixed with realization showing in her expression. She moved a file folder revealing a small touch screen pad near the left edge of her desk. Adrianna swiped her finger from left to right and a keypad lit up with three colored buttons, she touched the red button. The sound of powerful electric motors firing up in concert with metal gears and chains clanked to life. Thick heavy metal shutters descended from the ceiling in front of each window sealing us off from the awesome view of *Chicago* and a possible escape route. The shutters, I realized would offer us some protection should the Vampires attempt to attack again.

Adrianna raised her eyes in our direction once more straightening, placing a hand on her hip.

"Please make yourself comfortable gentlemen, we're quite safe here. Don't worry about ruining the furniture."

Barnabas relaxed his posture leaning his staff against Adrianna's desk, settling into one of the comfortable looking seats that stood in front of him. He let out a pained muffled grunt leaning back taking the bloodstained handkerchief from his cheek. The bleeding had stopped revealing a five-inch diagonal cut from his ear to his jaw line. I watched Barnabas remove a shard of glass roughly an inch long from the wound wrapping it up in his handkerchief.

Adrianna gave an approving smile as she moved around her desk removing her torn blouse as she went. My eyes, head and upper body followed her graceful movements. I didn't feel like a complete voyeur because I noticed Barnabas and Race's eyes following her movements as well. She opened a closed door on the right of her office turning on a light then stepping inside. I realized that she'd entered her private bathroom, after hearing the distinct sound of a shower being turned on.

Bart reentered Adrianna's office, clothes draped over his right forearm carrying a pair of white expensive looking *Nike* high top sneakers in his left hand. He walked over to Race dumping the clothes and shoes unceremoniously down onto the cushions of the couch next to him then turned in Race's direction coming to stiff attention.

"Compliments of Ms. Thorne beast," he said bitterly inclining his head in a mocking disrespectful show of respect.

"Thank you," Race replied with an equal amount of gratitude, flipping him the bird.

Bart scowled turning as he looked for Adrianna.

"Douche bag," Race muttered under his breath.

Race dropped the pillow on the couch where he'd gotten it. He picked up the clothes dressing hurriedly. The clothes seemed to fit him well. They consisted of a pair of blue jeans, a white "T" and a *Chicago Bears Hoodie*. Bart noticed the door to the bathroom was open and I'm sure he heard the sound of running water. He glared at all of us in a *"You should all be ashamed at yourselves"* look, then walked over to the door crossing his arms positioning himself in front of it, daring us to look in that direction.

Barnabas reached into a small leather pouch hanging from the belt around his waist. He searched in it for a bit removing a small clear glass jar, about the size of a *CARMEX* lip balm container filled with a brownish salve. He unscrewed the cap and I knew immediately what it was, just by the smell. It was Elder Root salve which worked well for sword cuts, dragon bites and hexes, though the last two claims have yet to be tested. The main ingredients in the salve were Elder Root sap, Tiger snail mucus, dried Granite moss, salt from the *Dead Sea and* extraction of Sea snake venom. All of which were mixed together then boiled down into that foul smelling yet very useful salve. He applied a liberal amount of salve to the cut on his cheek with a perceptible wince - did I neglect to mention that it hurts like the dickens - which began to bubble almost in the same manner peroxide reacts when pouring it on a cut. Barnabas stood eyeing me, which was never a good sign.

"Come over here and let mc look at your wound," Barnabas said in a concerned fatherly tone.

I raised my hands displaying them in a *"No Thank You"* gesture.

"I'm good," I said trying to placate his doctoring instincts.

There was no way in hell I was letting him put that crap on me. Barnabas leveled his gaze at me in a way that always meant business. It was the look he'd given me when I was younger around that age most boys didn't want to take baths. I was a stubborn kid - OK I still am - and no matter what I refused to do, in the end Barnabas always made sure I did. I took a step away from him.

"We can do this the easy way or I can wait till Ms. Thorne comes out of the bathroom and I can show her how much of a cowardly prat you can be," Barnabas said, his last word ending in a devilish smile.

I heard Race chuckling somewhere behind me.

Damn! He never plays fair. Even though Adrianna's a Vampire, there was no way in hell I was going to look like a frightened little weakling in front of her and Barnabas knew I'd do anything not to be embarrassed. He was acting like a parent pulling out those none too flattering photos of you when you were a kid. You know the photos I'm referring to don't you? A picture of you laying face down in your *Spaghetti O's* asleep in your high chair. A picture of you seated upon the potty with your hands raised in triumphant accomplishment or my absolute favorite a picture of a little boy wearing his mother's high heels clopping through the house. – Not that I've ever done that myself - Having been an orphan I sort of missed the boat on all those embarrassing photographic memories. Barnabas has managed to make up for them with situations like this over the years. I sighed turning around pulling off my cloak. Barnabas moved behind me examining my wound.

"The dagger struck the gap between your back plate and shoulder pad I'm afraid, you should've been wearing your chainmail,"

I rolled my eyes.

"Yeah... Yeah... Hindsight is 20/20, is it still bleeding?" I asked.

"It appears to have stopped,"

I felt his fingers probing the cut. A few thoughtful sounds escaped his lips. Barnabas let out a puzzled sound.

"What," I asked, my concern growing. "What's wrong?"

Barnabas didn't say anything for a long moment then he said in a confidential tone.

"The wound. It's completely healed. There's nothing here now but some dried blood and what looks like a scar that is a number of weeks old, strange."

"How can that be," I asked.

"I'm not sure," he replied in a tone that indicated he had no answer.

"But I may have a good idea,"

He wiped his hands on my cloak. Which wasn't cool at all, but what was I going to say. It was then that I heard an annoying squeaking sound heading into the office. I turned with Barnabas to see a craft service cart laden with a large covered platter. Beside that were two metal champagne buckets filled with ice, cans of soda, and some bottles of water. A small plastic first aid kit was tucked between the platter and one of the buckets. I didn't see any chips. Oh well, you can't have everything. A young man dressed in a black chef's uniform pushed the cart. The sight of this impending banquet caused us both to forget about my wound. My mouth however watered and my stomach commenced growling at the sight. Race was already at the cart. He lifted the cover from the platter revealing a variety of delicious looking sandwiches I'd ever seen or had the pleasure of smelling. Race handed the cover to the young man snatching up two thick ham sandwiches on onion rolls and a can of *Coke* for himself before settling on one of the couches. Barnabas and I took a little longer in choosing our food. I leaned my battle staff against the cart going for a roast beef sandwich on marbled rye and a *Coke*. - No *Dr. Pepper* to my dismay - Barnabas went for salami on a Kaiser roll and a bottle of water.

The young man bowed with a smile, first to Bart, then over to Race. He left the room carrying the cover to the platter, closing the door behind him. Barnabas and I settled into the two chairs in front of Adrianna's desk wolfing down our food in the most civilized manner that our hunger would allow. The sandwich was delicious; it was like heaven on two slices of bread, thick slices of roast beef, pepper jack cheese, crisp lettuce and just enough spicy mustard to not kill the flavor.

Yum.

"Ah. I see your refreshments have arrived," said Adrianna's sultry voice. "I hope they meet with your approval."

My head turned in the direction of her voice, but not before I bit off another large mouthful of delicious sandwich. In retrospect I shouldn't have done that because I nearly choked when I caught sight of her or more accurately, what she was wearing. Adrianna wore a silk champagne colored robe that fell mid-thigh leaving next to nothing to the imagination. As she toweled off her hair, I noticed that it was either chilly in her office or she was doing a bit more in the shower than getting clean, because her erect nipples were showing quite clearly under the delicate fabric. She smiled impishly walking over to her desk standing behind it. Bart took up a position to her left clasping his hands in front of him glaring at us for dramatic effect.

"The food is excellent Ms. Thorne, Thank you," Barnabas said standing, coming to attention.

I rose as well. One of the things Barnabas was adamant about when I was growing up was teaching me respect and etiquette where the opposite sex was concerned. Not many men today open doors or pull out chairs or stand when a lady enters the room. I know the concept seems outdated, but in my mind a woman should be treated like a woman.

"Please gentlemen, don't stand on ceremony. Sit, sit, and finish your meal. It's the least I could do."

"Thank you," we both said settling back into our chairs.

Adrianna finished toweling off her long hair, flipping it to one side then placing the towel around her neck. Adrianna used her fingers to put her damp hair in a more manageable state. She swiveled her chair toward her then sat down at her desk. I didn't know the act of sitting down could be so, exhilarating. She picked up a small stack of stapled papers from the left side of her desk then leaned back in her chair and began meticulously scrutinizing each page. I glanced at her unobtrusively between bites of sandwich and sips of *Coke*. I don't know about you, but I hate awkward silences, they're uncomfortable and make me feel uneasy especially when I'm eating and someone else is not, it just doesn't feel right to me.

"Is that a good read?" I asked.

"Not really," she replied not taking her eyes off the page.

I also don't like it when people don't give me their full attention. It makes me try that much harder. Am I a brat? Yes, I think I am. Behind me I heard a muffled belch and the distinct sound of Race going back to the cart.

"So, whatcha reading," I asked in a slow drawn out somewhat annoying manner. "Short story? Stereo instructions? The cliff notes for the Kama Sutra,"

Her mouth quirked up into a tiny smile, yet she kept her eyes focused on reading. Bart fixed his eyes on me letting out an annoyed growl.

"No, Nothing so interesting. I'm reading a boring contract that deals with buying some property on the *Southside of Chicago*,"

Barnabas finished his meal rising from his seat, scanning about for somewhere to throw out his bottle and napkin. Adrianna looked up from her papers reaching under her desk.

"Here you are Barnabas," she said handing him a small wire wastepaper basket. "You may put your trash in here." Barnabas discarded his rubbish and Adrianna replaced the can back under her desk.

"Thank you," Barnabas said.

He walked over to the cart picking up the first aid kit turning back to face Adrianna.

"Might I be able to use your facilities for a moment?" Barnabas asked gesturing to the wound on his face.

"Of course... Be my guest."

Barnabas disappeared into the bathroom turning on the light then closing the door behind him.

I finished my sandwich and the few remaining sips of *Coke*. - My garbage meeting the same fate as Barnabas's. - I was still hungry, so I got up heading back to the cart. Discovering that there were no sandwiches left on the platter. Race was seated on the couch finishing off what I assumed to be the last one. There were eight sandwiches on that platter by my count and he ate six all by himself. I slumped my shoulders disappointed grabbing another *Coke* from the champagne bucket popping the top then swigging down a nice long drink. I meandered around Adrianna's office checking things out taking a better look at her statues, two Picasso's on the walls, which I hadn't noticed when we entered and they appeared to be originals. On the other side of the room, in front of another closed door I noticed a subtle lump under the carpet. At first I thought it was an imperfection of the floor itself, but on further inspection I realized it was a pressure switch of some sort after running the toe of my boot over it. I thought of calling Race over to step on it to see what would happen. I made my way to the metal shutters placing my hand on the beveled interlocking surface. The metal wasn't steel though it could've been titanium or perhaps some sort of composite material.

"What is your opinion of Vampires, Wizard," Bart asked in a passionless voice.

I turned toward him with an amiable smile planted on my face discarding my empty can where the first one ended up. I placed my hands into my pockets.

"To be honest I've never really given Vampires much thought until today."

Bart smiled a cocky smile then said.

"That isn't an answer to my question,"

"I know it isn't an answer to your question," I said cutting him off. "Truthfully I haven't had much contact with Vampires. None at all really, so I don't have a good or a bad opinion about your kind."

Bart snorted folding his arms.

"Yes, I can see that you spend quite a lot of time around Werewolves. Perhaps they've helped shape your opinion about us," Bart replied, disgust in his voice.

Race stood, looking pissed off. I removed a hand from my pocket holding it up in a *"take it easy I've got this"* gesture. He gave a slight nod settling back down onto the couch.

"It's true, I have a lot of experience with Werewolves, I don't deny that because Race's pack came to Barnabas for help and he gave it without question. Vampires on the other hand have never come to our shop for any reason. Until today of course, now it would be irresponsible for me to form an opinion about Vampires based solely on that one interaction or on anything that I've heard or read. I'd hope that after everything Barnabas has taught me over the years I'd have an open mind about things and not letting others influence me."

Bart glared incredulously in my direction. He was probably used to oaths and insults from just about everyone when it came to his kind and my answer wouldn't be believed. After all I was nothing more than a dirty human with magical abilities, two very disgusting things in Bart's prejudiced eyes.

"Well said," Adrianna said through an approving smile.

Barnabas exited the bathroom placing the first aid kit back onto the cart, four butterfly strip band-aids visible on his cheek to help keep his cut closed. He walked over to Adrianna's desk.

"Ms. Thorne I wish to thank you for your hospitality and understanding, I think we all have much to discuss and time is growing short."

Adrianna tossed the packet back onto her desk leaning back in her chair.

"Yes Barnabas, you were about to say something before we were rudely interrupted in the conference room," Adrianna replied.

Barnabas nodded, turning he walked a few paces away from her then turned back.

"What is said here cannot go any further than the five of us in this room, is that understood Ms. Thorne?" Barnabas said gravely.

I moved over to stand behind Barnabas; Race came to stand next to me. Adrianna studied all three of us for a minute or two then glanced up to Bart regarding him. It seemed that something passed between them because he inclined his head; they both turned their attention back to us.

"I can give you my assurances that what is said here will not be disclosed to anyone else, but can you be sure of your associate?" She said looking into Races eyes. I noticed his hair was standing up perceptibly.

"I too can give my assurances that none will utter anything that is discussed here and I will personally take anyone to task that believes otherwise," Barnabas replied looking squarely at Bart. It was sad, but at that moment I had the urge to start yelling Fight! Fight!

"Proceed," Adrianna said with a satisfied nod of her head.

"Within the last twenty four hours events have led me to believe that someone is trying to destabilize the tenuous peace between our people. It is also my belief that a small group of Wizards and Vampires are working together to achieve this end," Barnabas said gravely.

"And what evidence do you present to support your suspicions?" Adrianna asked skepticism woven in her tone.

"I have yet to confer with the Elder Council if there have been any other recent casualties other than the two that I can confirm independently, because frankly I am not certain whom I can trust with this information."

"You say that there are two Wizards that have been killed by Vampires. How do you know this?" Asked Adrianna.

Barnabas hedged. I knew he didn't want to reveal the inner workings of the Octagon to a Vampire, but he'd have to tell her something if he wanted information from her in return.

"Eyewitness testimony from a Cob Elf named Tillander Duggins, and my own. I saw the body of my friend Orm and evidence at his home pointed to Vampires,"

Adrianna sat in thought thinking on Barnabas's words. He continued.

"They were killed not just by Vampires Ms. Thorne, but with the help of Wizards. There was no other way anyone could've gotten into their protected places,"

"What lies! You mean to stand before my Mistress trying to make her believe your false words! No Vampire would ever help a Wizard!" Bart said cutting Barnabas off.

"Bartholomew brings up a good point Barnabas, what would the motivation be for Vampires and Wizards to work together?" She paused then added. "Recent events notwithstanding."

Barnabas took a deep breath considering his next words. I was just as interested as everyone else in the room to learn the motivation behind this possible dark alliance. What Barnabas was saying if true was a frightening prospect for the entire magical world. Few if any would be able to withstand the might of our two worlds united in a common goal.

"As of this moment I cannot devise the motivation of these rogues, what can be obviously seen is their blatant attempt to begin a war. What's more, there is also evidence that Dark Elves might be involved in all this somehow and that's a far more frightening prospect than all out war between the Vampire families and the magical world," Barnabas said.

"Dark Elves? That's absurd! Dark Elves haven't made an appearance in decades! You'll have to come up with a better lie than that," Bart spat in a raised voice.

"It's true," I chimed in. "Earlier today Race and I fought with one."

"Yeah, the little bastard was strong too, we barely managed to hold him down," Race added.

Bart lifted an accusing finger at Race and myself.

"You see! Wizards and Werewolves working together creating this lie!"

Adrianna reached out placing a hand on Bart's arm. He jerked his head in her direction. After a moment he seemed to calm down as she gently lowered it for him.

"You'll have to forgive Bartholomew's difficulty in believing your story, there's been many centuries of bad blood between our peoples. I am inclined to at least believe there is more here than meets the eye. I've received reports that four high-ranking members of the Mordin family have been killed and there is evidence that a wielder of magic is to blame. You say that two Wizards that you know of are dead and that Vampires are to blame. Is that right Barnabas?"

"Yes, however I don't believe Vampires alone killed them. This very afternoon a Wizard accompanied by the twins we brought with us here, entered my shop and attempted to kill my apprentice," Barnabas said gesturing to me.

A sly smile crept onto Adrianna's face. It was the kind of smile lawyers often get when they find a flaw in a witnesses testimony.

"They attempted to kill him?" Adrianna asked skeptically, indicating me with a look. "Forgive me for being rather blunt, but your apprentice doesn't strike me as being much of a Wizard. I doubt they mistook him for you,"

"No offense to your abilities Sol," She added quickly glancing in my direction.

"None taken," I replied.

Barnabas was at a loss for words. I think this may have been a first; I wondered how he was going to talk his way out of this one. Adrianna let him ponder for a few moments before she continued.

"You ask me to trust you, yet you don't trust me... I know the mistrust between our people is not easy to get past, however let's cut through all the pretenses shall we. You and I are far too old to be playing these games of deception,"

Adrianna leaned back in her chair with a confident air about her.

"Barnabas, I know you belong to a secret group of Wizards. I know there were eight of you in this group and I also know that you and the rest of your lot are protecting something. What I don't know is exactly what you're protecting, but from what you've told me it must be very valuable for two Vampires and a Wizard to show up at your shop attempting to recover it," Adrianna said. "I also know that the Black Guard has added quite a few recruits of late and to me and my people that is rather alarming. Is there a threat to the Elder Council that has yet to be seen or are your people preparing for a possible conflict that may break out in the near future," she asked.

Barnabas surprised by her statement, grinned.

"My compliments on your information gathering Ms. Thorne," Barnabas remarked impressed.

Adrianna inclined her head at the compliment.

"Since we are dispelling with pretenses," Barnabas said continuing, "I'll concede that I do belong to such a group and I will also concede that what we protect is valuable and the Wizards that have been killed belonged to the very same group. It is also true that the Black Guard has been adding to their ranks of late. What I think

247

you'll find most interesting in our exchange of information is that we've noticed more blood farms than usual have been popping up in every major city around the world and that the Vampire population has increased approximately fifty percent in the last two years. Many on the Elder Council see this as a possible prelude to war, so you can see our concern regarding recent actions coming from the Vampire families. With people on both sides dying violently by each other's hands it is only a matter of time before the powers that be decide to call for blood. If whoever is behind these turn of events obtains what we protect, many will die and the world will be plunged into chaos and darkness. You know very well that I don't give in to hyperbole,"

It was Adrianna's turn to look stunned at the amount of information that Barnabas had on the Vampires as well as their movements. It appeared as though both sides took a close interest in the other. She thought for a long moment then sat up straight in her chair.

"My God, we're pawns on a chess board," she said finally.

"That's precisely the conclusion that I'd arrived at, but we are a few moves behind in the game and will quite possibly lose if we don't catch up. The Ashari were sent here to kill you Ms. Thorne,"

Barnabas reached into the pocket of his cloak producing an Ash Dagger. He dropped it carelessly on her desk. The dagger made a tinny clatter of finality coming to rest in front of her.

"If they'd succeeded in removing you from the head of the largest Vampire family in *North America* our two people's would be preparing for war this very moment. You know as well as I that the Ashari will try again to kill you, so the safest place for you to be is with me and my people as we attempt to get to the bottom of this," Barnabas said.

For those of you unfamiliar with Vampires, the Ashari are a group of highly trained assassins that drink the blood of other Vampires. Vampire blood makes the Ashari stronger and faster, but at a price. They live in almost complete darkness. Even the light from a common flashlight can blister their skin. After a moment of silence Adrianna asked.

"Where will you be taking us Barnabas?"

"Mistress I must protest this course of action..."

Adrianna raised her hand cutting him off.

"I'd suggest that you dress for a much cooler climate." Barnabas replied.

Adrianna looked in my direction, steepling her fingers, elbows resting on the chair arms. Our eyes met. I could see a slight upturn of the corners of her mouth.

"Would you gentlemen be so kind as to give me a moment alone with Solomon," she said.

Bart looked mortified by her words. Perhaps they were having a difficult time penetrating the heavy bowling ball shine of his baldhead. He composed himself before the words poised on the tip of his tongue spilled out. He reluctantly obeyed her request bowing before following Race and Barnabas who'd already made their exit without any objections. When the doors to her office closed she said.

"I am quite curious about something Sol,"

"And what is that," I asked.

She let my words hang between us as her eyes appraised me. I was certain that she was able to peer into my body and see out the other side.

"You could've let that dagger kill me and there would've been no shame or dishonor for you or Barnabas. So that leaves me with a very perplexing question as to why you Sol, a mortal Wizard would save a Vampire's life," she asked.

It was my turn to let the words hang between us as I pondered her question. Why did I save her life? Yes, I came up with a few reasons while I was in the thick of battle to explain my actions at the time. Now as I stood before her I really didn't know why I did it. Impulse perhaps. None of my reasons made sense now.

Well, of course they did and yet they didn't. Let's be honest, a gazelle wouldn't throw itself in front of a bullet to save a lion. The gazelle knows the lion is a danger and would never buddy up to one. The lion, being a lion, would just eat the well-meaning gazelle afterwards anyway. There would be no thank you, no mournful thought or even one shed tear as the poor gazelle's life bled away. There'd be just a slight pause as the lion tucked a napkin under its chin, produced a knife and fork to begin eating its meal. Yes, I know I watched far too many cartoons when I was a kid.

So sue me.

Why did I save her life? Come on brain help me out. Finally I shrugged then said.

"Your blouse was very pretty and looked expensive, I didn't want to see it ruined,"

Adrianna unsteepled her fingers, she stood making her way around the desk.

"You are a coy man Solomon Drake," she said. "There are not many men that can resist my charms. In point of fact you're the first that's done so. Most men react in one way or another just like your Werewolf friend," she said glancing in the direction of her office door.

"But we're still left with my initial question as to why you saved my life," she asked again curiosity laced in her words.

She leaned against the edge of her glass desk. The movement quite possibly would've garnered an "R" rating had it been viewed by the *Motion Picture Association of America.*

I shrugged again.

"Even I don't understand half the things I do at times,"

She smiled at that.

"Did you save me because you were trying to curry favor with me,"

"No,"

"Did you save me because you wanted me in your debt,"

"No," I said defensively.

She pushed away from the desk stalking toward me. I stood my ground as not to look weak, praying that the sound of my quaking knees couldn't be heard.

"Did you step in front of that dagger because you're a big strong man and you had to save weak defenseless little old me," she said mockingly in a *Scarlett O'Hara* southern accent.

"You're not old… Technically," I answered with a nervous shrug.

She cocked her head arching a sexy eyebrow. The action gave a disbelieving aspect to her attitude.

"No," I said finally.

She halted her advance inches away from me looking up searchingly into my eyes. I stood five or six inches taller than her when she wasn't wearing heels. She no longer possessed the confident presence she exhibited earlier, before events took an unforeseen turn. The delicate silk robe caressed her skin as her body made subtle movements. The sound was hypnotic, acting like a siren's call to my libido. Her hair still had a damp sheen from the shower and I found myself longing to run my fingers through her thick locks. Taking a fist full of it, gently pulling back her head exposing her neck to rain soft kisses over it. I was either going mad with desire or she placed a powerful glamour on me, which I didn't think was the case. This mind fog was all my own. The delicate fragrances of the soaps and lotions she used during and after the shower made it even more difficult to concentrate. Given her close proximity to me I had an excellent vantage point to peer down at her ample cleavage. There were advantages to being six foot four.

"Did you step in front of that dagger because you fancied me," she asked finally in an intimate whisper.

I felt a stirring in my loins as my traitorous penis began to ache, pulsing to life. Blood emptied rapidly from my head. The seconds ticked by and I found the mind fog growing denser. Obviously my loins were throwing a party and my brain cells weren't invited. She moved away from me glancing down at the now visible bulge in my pants. Adrianna looked back into my eyes now framed by an embarrassed hue of deep red.

"I think I have my answer," she said with a pleased smile.

I remained silent. There was really nothing for me to say because my penis was doing all the talking. Adrianna moved closer rising up on the tips of her toes closing the distance between our lips. Hers brushed seductively against mine. Her breath, which came in long needful exhales was chilly against my lips. The sensation stoked the fire rising in my soul. I caught a whiff of her breath, the unmistakable scent of strawberries and cream.

"I haven't been with a man in such a long time," she said in a passionate whisper.

"Neither have I," I replied then wanted to kick myself for saying such a boneheaded thing.

Adrianna's lips broadened into a smile. She pulled back a few inches to gaze into my eyes. I'd be lying if I said I hadn't been mesmerized by the green hue of hers. I was frozen like a deer staring into the oncoming headlights of a car.

"You have the bluest eyes that I have ever seen. Has a woman ever told you that," she asked.

"Not that I can remember," I replied in an unsteady voice.

"You seem nervous,"

"I am," I said and I was. My experience in the bedroom with a woman was woefully nonexistent. I didn't want to, "disappoint" should this go any further. Sadly, I was hoping that it would. I needed sex badly like a drowning man needed a lifesaver, the flotation device, not the candy.

"Do you like that I make you nervous," she asked.

"Yes," I said.

She bit her bottom lip through a sensual, pleased smile exposing her sharp canines. Her hands roved over my chest, down my stomach and around to my ass. Where they lingered for quite a long time.

"Your ass is so firm," she said happily surprised groping my cheeks with her soft probing hands.

"Thanks," I said self-consciously. "I do a lot of squats."

It was a lie of course. The closest thing I did that even resembled a squat was sitting at my desk to play computer games, but who was going to tell, right?

The anticipation of tasting her lips was unbearable. She'd gotten me completely worked up and my libido was in overdrive. I couldn't wait any longer I had to know what her lips felt like. What they tasted like. I leaned closer to her full luscious lips for a long overdue kiss. She didn't pull away. She moved to meet mine. One of her hands, the left one I think, moved up cupping the back of my neck. Her fingers stroked the fine short-cropped hair on my head. Our lips were so close; I could feel the chill of her intoxicating Vampire lips against the smoldering passion of mine. Her tongue flicked out tracing my bottom lip ever so lightly, then her teeth nibbled it before drawing away a fraction of an inch. My eyes closed enjoying the sensations. Warm shivers flowed up my spine; goose flesh erupted over the length of my body. My tongue moved to meet her's.

So close now.

So very close.

Her other hand cupped my right buttocks as she pressed her body into mine. It was a glorious sensation. I couldn't take it any longer. I wanted her here and I wanted her now. Up until this point I held her gently. I was afraid that I'd hurt her. It was insanity talking that I thought I could hurt her in anyway. It was more than a little likely that Adrianna could injure me if she chose. Not listening to reason, my arms pulled her into a desperate longing embrace. This was going to happen, I wanted it to happen. My need for her was great and the opportunity was now. Just as I thought I was going to taste her delicious lips, she pinched my ass.

Hard.

Which was a startling turn of events as you might imagine, I rubbed at the spot on my behind as she walked by me. I hoped there wouldn't be a bruise. She had pinched me with the force of a pair of vice grips and may have possibly used her nails.

"I'm sorry Sol, but we don't have time for anything else at the moment," she said amused; however I detected a subtle hint of longing disappointment in her tone.

She turned to face me and then she said.

"You have my attention Solomon Drake. I hope I have yours,"

I nodded pathetically.

"Yes, you do," I said. "But did you have to mistreat my tush,"

Her lips curled up into a satisfied smile.

"Consider my behavior with you a promise of things yet to come," she said turning on her heels heading for the door next to the bathroom.

# Chapter 15

We arrived back at the magic shop by portal an hour later than expected. Adrianna took a fair amount of time picking the right winter wear for our excursion to Bialek's compound. Being the time of year that it was - winter - it'd be fairly cold there now. Adrianna wanted her outfit to be functional yet stylish.

She ultimately settled upon an all white form fitting ski suit ensemble, the hood trimmed with gray fur. A slender white belt accented with what looked like a brushed nickel buckle and studs rode low on her hips. Her shoes, I kid you not, she wore a pair of five inch heeled winter boots that hugged her calves. They were also trimmed to the ankles with the same gray fur as her coat. Her hair was done up in a long stylish ponytail with a few well-placed strands of hair to give her that alluring appearance. A pair of black and red metallic *Bobster*

*Fuel* ski goggles rode on her forehead. She looked like a statuesque *Bond Girl*; of course I'd never seen a *Bond Girl* as gorgeous as Adrianna.

Bart on the other hand went for functional. His attire consisted of a black and red ski suit with matching boots. Even though he was Adrianna's bodyguard, he apparently would be doubling as a pack mule for this excursion. Slung over his right shoulder was a heavy backpack that matched the color and style of Adrianna's getup. Given his expression that looked somewhere between eating a lemon and being constipated, I didn't think he approved of his Mistress's choice of outfits. I must also mention that Adrianna generously provided Race with some winter gear as well. It just goes to show that even though there was bad blood between Vampires and Werewolves a common interest helped dull the bad feeling if only for a short time. Barnabas and I still had to gather our winter gear before we headed out. Which was the only reason we came back to the shop. Adrianna's eyes drifted around appraising her surroundings.

"What a charming place you have here Barnabas,"

"Thank you. It's not much but we like it," Barnabas said grinning placing a hand on my shoulder.

The portal closed behind us and it felt good being home. I was still tired from this morning's excitement and the intense spell casting didn't help matters either. I spied our backpacks, snowshoes and other snow related gear resting neatly on the front counter. I then heard the clopping of Tilly's heavy soled shoes on the hardwood floor as he hurried up to us.

"Master," he said in unbridled exuberance. "You've returned! I have your backpack all packed and have laid out your winter..."

Tilly's words trailed off as he caught sight of Adrianna and Bartholomew. Without a word or even a warning Tilly raised his right hand. Power swirling around it, he sent shards of ice hurdling toward them. I lifted my battle staff slicing the air in an up and down motion casting a fire shield spell.

"*Incendia Contego*," I yelled in a loud hurried tone.

A swirling disk of red orange fire roared into existence a foot in front of Adrianna and Bart. The ice shards struck my shield with a hiss evaporating on contact. I whirled to face Tilly.

"Tilly," I yelled. "These are our guests and you will treat them with respect!"

Barnabas shook his head in obvious disapproval, yet he remained silent. I knew by the working of his closed lips he was doing his best not to level a severe admonishment to Tilly for his actions. He appeared to be satisfied that I was handling the situation as well as it could've been handled so he headed for the stairs to the apartment. I snapped my fingers and the fire shield disappeared as quickly as I had summoned it. Tilly just stared at me simply stunned.

"But Master," Tilly said in a - *just between you and me sort of tone* - "They are Vampires..."

"Vampires," exclaimed a tiny muffled surprised voice. Or at least that's what I thought I heard. It sounded more like. "Mampires!" The voice came from the direction of the backpacks.

Just then Earl, our rotund Guarding Gnome's head popped out of a pocket flap on my back pack. A strip of *Teriyaki Beef Jerky* clutched in each of his hands, Earl's cheeks were filled to bursting with what I could only imagine was the same snack food. He looked like a chipmunk that just found a full tin of assorted nuts. His attention was divided between finishing his culinary conquest and doing battle with a dangerous foe. Ultimately he made his decision, which could plainly be seen in his expression. He regarded the beef jerky affectionately for a moment, gently placing both strips down on my pack before he drew his maced club then hurled himself at Bartholomew with the ferocity of a shopper at a *Walmart Black Friday Sale*.

Bart's eyes grew wide in an - *OH SHIT* - sort of expression right before Earl's mace connected with his forehead. The shop echoed with an ear splitting metal on bone sound that would've made your skin crawl if you heard it. Bart's hands flew up to his face in pain. Earl's momentum nearly carried his bulk over Bart's shoulder, but the little Gnome reached out a big right hand grabbing the hood of Bart's coat staggering the Vampire with the movement. Earl clambered up onto Bart's left shoulder grasping his mace in both hands, he wound up into a textbook batter's stance then cracked Bart on the back of the head with a swing that would've made *Pete Rose* proud.

"Argh," Bart exclaimed in surprise or perhaps pain, I couldn't be sure.

Race by this point had dropped his pack and was laughing uncontrollably. He sounded like a mule jonesing for an apple. While all this nonsense was happening, the regal Adrianna looked on with quiet grace. Much the same way I'm sure *Queen Elizabeth* might react if her prized Corgi took a dump on a two-hundred year old rug at *Buckingham Palace* directly in front of the *French Ambassador* during a gathering of state. Shock followed by mortification, laced with a well-masked hint of satisfaction and humor.

I'll admit that I was slow to react because the whole scene was comical and absurd. When I finally made it into motion Bart had Earl clutched in both hands attempting to wring the life out of him. Earl, never one to be taken so easily, clamped his jaws down on the fleshy part of Bart's right hand between the thumb and forefinger. After another exclamation of pain a higher octave than the last, Bart in a fit of rage hurled the Gnome at one of the heavy wooden ingredient cases behind the counter. Earl smacked into the side of the case with a loud thud. He lingered there for a moment before slowly peeling down off the wood falling to the floor like a limp noodle. I looked on with a stunned expression hanging on my face.

"You shouldn't have done that," I finally said to Bart. "Now he's going to take it personally."

I craned my neck inching closer to the counter hoping Earl was all right. Tilly let out a concerned gasp hurrying around behind the counter to check on Earl's condition. Two seconds hadn't ticked off the clock before Tilly tore up the hardwood floor scurrying in the opposite direction from where Earl had landed. We waited a moment in quiet anticipation. The silence was broken a second or two later by a triumphant resounding "Ah. Ha!" Then the head of my other *Louisville Slugger* baseball bat appeared above the level of the counter. The bat moved erratically, bobbing and swaying like a caber being carried by a six inch *Scotsman*. - Did I mention that Guarding Gnomes have the same strength and lifting capacity as a full-grown human being? Food for thought if any of you were thinking of making fun of their diminutive size –

Earl rounded the counter, his feet padding heavily under a full head of steam. The bat grasped firmly in both hands leaning against his right shoulder, a look of vengeful resolve on his face. Bart backed away unsure of what to do, ultimately he raised his hands defensively awaiting the attack. I moved in between them, once Earl got started it was difficult to get him calmed down. I braced myself for the knock on the head I was about to receive, when Mari walked out from between the bookshelves on our left. An edition entitled *"Magic and You - A Normal's Guide to Coping with Mystical Power"* clutched in her hand. She grabbed the end of the bat with her free hand - without looking up from the page - lifting it and Earl off the floor, his chubby little Gnome legs still pumping. Mari held the bat so that Earl was hovering a few inches above the surface of the counter. I heard muffled titters coming from Race and Adrianna as I moved over trying to placate Earl.

"Hey," I said in a loud sharp yell. "Calm down!"

In answer Earl let out a growl redoubling his efforts to get to Bart, even though his feet weren't making contact with anything.

"If you want him to calm down you have to get his mind off his anger," Mari said in a *"we've been down this road before"* sort of tone.

Thinking quickly I reached over to my backpack picking up the two discarded strips of beef jerky. I waved them before his eyes.

"Hey Earl, want some jerky?" I asked. "Yum."

Earl's eyes began to lose their focus on Bart. A hypnotic rhythm settled into the movement of his head. His eyes and head tracked the magically floating jerky, the way a cobra sways to the music of a snake charmer. Earl's eyes hooded, a blissful smile formed on his face. His grip faltered, slipping off the bat. Earl landed on the counter with a plop raising his arms lunging greedily toward the strips of jerky. I moved the strips out of his reach placing an index finger on his chest halting his progress. A look of disappointment appeared on his face, he vacantly stared between my finger and the jerky.

"Ah. Ah. Ah," I said. "You can't have the jerky until you promise to be good and not try to kill our guests."

Earl rolled his eyes pushing my finger away from his chest. He then crossed his arms in disgust turning his body partly away from me.

"Come on now. Do it for me,"

He turned a little more away showing me more of his back.

"Tell you what, I'll throw in another strip of jerky."

He turned back a fraction of an inch quirking an eyebrow in obvious interest.

"Four strips," I said finally. "That's my final offer."

He faced me arms still folded considering, then he nodded once. Earl glared in Bart's direction as I fished out two more pieces of jerky from my pack. Earl lifted his hand extending his middle and index finger gesturing them at his eyes then turning his hand around pointing one chubby digit directly at Bart in a universal *"I'm watching you"* gesture. I presented four pieces of jerky to Earl, our agreed upon price which he roughly yanked out of my hand biting a nice big chunk from one of the strips. He stalked petulantly to the edge of the counter, hopping off, disappearing from sight.

"You and Barnabas have some amusing friends and acquaintances," Adrianna said finally through a wide smile.

"Yes. Very," Bart retorted in a haughty tone.

I smiled apologetically, not knowing exactly how to respond. I nodded a few times then shrugged. *Shakespeare,* eat your heart out.

"Come on boy," Barnabas said yelling from the stairwell to the apartments. "Stop trying to impress Adrianna, get yourself up here and get ready!"

My shoulders tightened and my cheek's flushed with color. I want you all to read back a few paragraphs making your own determination, was I trying to impress Adrianna or was I trying to keep Earl from kicking Bart's ass? I knew full well that I wasn't trying to catch her eye. Is she gorgeous and would I love to get into her pants? Yes and yes. The reason however that was stopping me from even attempting to make a fool out of myself over her was the fact that she was a Vampire. I was more interested in her sucking something else instead of my blood. I stood there, head dropping into a sulk. There was no way that I was not going to be teased about this moment. I could already see Race's mental gears turning stockpiling insults and one-liners.

"Go on upstairs," Mari said as she laid her book and the *Louisville Slugger* down on the counter. "I'll take care of things down here."

"Thanks," I said half-heartedly.

Mari walked around the counter making her way over to Adrianna and Bart. She first held out her hand to Bart, a caring friendly smile showing on her lovely face.

"My name is Mari I'm a friend of Barnabas and you are," she asked, milk and honey in her voice.

Taken aback by Mari's forward manner, Bart tried to plaster something on his face that almost resembled a smile.

"You will forgive me, but I do not shake hands," Bart said as he casually clasp his hands behind his back. "As for who I am, Bartholomew is my name and I am Ms. Thorne's personal assistant and bodyguard,"

"It's true," I said. "Bart's a secretary,"

The look he gave me could've melted an iceberg. Too bad he wasn't on the deck of the *Titanic* the night it sank. Mari unfazed by the lack of Bart's manners smiled curtly moving over to Adrianna extending her hand once again. Adrianna took it without hesitation.

"I must apologize for Bart," she began. "He takes my safety a bit too seriously at times… I'm Adrianna Thorne. Pleasure to meet you, Mari was it?" Adrianna asked.

Mari fixed her caramel colored eyes on Adrianna.

"Yours is a lonely heart, but still good deep down, your darker half hasn't completely taken over," Mari said finally after a long pause.

"What are you some kind of gypsy fortune teller?" I asked.

I've always believed that Mari had some sort of gift or power. She's good at reading people, telling the good from the bad. If she hadn't decided to become a nun in her youth, I believe she would have made an excellent cop. Mari turned to me.

"Aren't you supposed to be getting ready? Go!"

She turned back to Adrianna. Exasperated, I made my way upstairs.

"No wonder Solomon likes you," Mari said conspiratorially to Adrianna.

I groaned loud enough for all to hear.

"I love your snowsuit," I heard Mari say.

"Thank you," replied Adrianna.

"I'm curious though, did you realize the tight fitting coat would make your breasts appear larger or were you going for a more promiscuous look when you bought it? I personally would have chosen something a little more practical," asked Mari.

My shoulder muscles tensed into a tight ball as the last few words passed through my ears. Between Barnabas and Mari I didn't know whom I wanted to kill first. The sad thing was that I didn't have a shovel or bag of lye after I'd finished the deed. Had I been a *Boy Scout* I'd have been prepared for instances such as this. I sighed; I needed to get a place of my own.

I was able to put my clothes on faster than *Superman* took his off when there was a phone booth nearby. Tilly's organizational skills were incredible. Everything had been laid out and ready for me. I did make a few changes to my wardrobe however. Tilly's intuition for picking out the things he thought I would need was impressive. He had no idea however regarding what weapons or gear I wanted to take along, which was fine. After a little thought about where we were going and what I'd be wearing, I opted for my battle staff in lieu of my wand. It would've been impractical to keep fishing the darn thing out of a pocket and my wrist rig would be useless because of gloves and the *Velcro* sleeves on my coat. I decided - after much deliberation - on a drop leg holster for one of my *Colts* along with four magazines of ammo. I'd loved to bring along both pistols, but I had to economize. I also decided to wear my bracelet, placing it on my left wrist and as an afterthought I wore my titanium chainmail shirt under my winter coat. The mail wouldn't stop bullets or arrows, but it would protect me against claws and blades, which were more of a concern given that the Ashari were on the prowl. After finishing getting dressed I examined my appearance in a full-length mirror that hung on the backside of my door. I looked quite ruggedly dashing. My attire not to far removed from what *Han Solo* wore in the movie, *The Empire Strikes Back*. A comparison I hoped anyone that caught sight of me might make, though I looked nothing like *Harrison Ford* in real life.

Satisfied with my appearance I made sure to check around two or three more times just in case I forgot anything. I looked through my bookshelf grabbing three books to read not really knowing how long we'd be gone, then I made my way downstairs to the others.

Nearly everyone was assembled around the counter. Adrianna and Mari were still talking - I guess Mari's comment about Adrianna's attire wasn't taken as an insult - Bart stood off to the side by the front door brooding. Race and Barnabas were engaged in a conversation about employment opportunities for Werewolves and Tilly hovered beside Mari. I noticed he was dressed in a green calf length coat trimmed with white fur. A pack bursting at the seams rode on his back and he carried a slender wood staff a little shorter than he was. Everyone turned in my direction when I entered.

"Well now we can get going. I see that you've finished your preening," Barnabas said jokingly.

Snickers filled the room as Adrianna excused herself from Mari strolling over to me. I lifted a fist brandishing it at Barnabas in a *"To The Moon"* gesture, any fan of the *Honeymooners* would appreciate. She admired my winter wear stopping close to me - and by close I mean you couldn't have slid a playing card between us - Adrianna ran a gloved hand over the fur of my hood as though she were caressing the fine pelt of a mink or some other animal used in the furrier trade. Her eyes had a smoky, sultry quality to them and when she spoke my heart melted.

"I think he looks handsome,"

Her finger traced the line of my jaw, which sent ripples through my body as she gave me a wink.

"I. Uh. Thank you," I replied.

She bit her bottom lip turning away walking over to stand by Bart.

"Alright," Barnabas said. We need to get moving."

Barnabas took up his battle staff, which leaned against the edge of the counter. He made his way around it to stand in a circle design that was set in the floor.

"If everyone could please gather around me."

I grabbed my pack and snowshoes from the counter, shrugged into it as I went to stand with the others. Juggling the snowshoes and staff was another chore entirely. The circle was made of various metals including gold, silver, copper and a little platinum. The design was roughly one hundred and twenty inches in diameter set flush into the floor. It was made up of three interlocking circles in the center forming a triangle. Around the three circles were various arcane occult symbols and designs. I'd spent many nights on my hands and knees polishing the metal with metal cleaner keeping the design free of tarnish, so I was pretty familiar with how it looked.

"Everyone within the circle if you please, we don't want to leave pieces of you here when we go," he said soberly.

As if that sort of thing happened all too often. I wasn't sure if he was being serious or having a laugh at our expense. We'd know shortly one way or the other.

We did as he instructed. It was difficult to remain within the circle while wearing our backpacks, but we somehow managed it.

"Now there's a snowstorm raging where we're going please make sure you have yourselves bundled up,"

With that, we pulled on our hats, put up our hoods, slipped on or gloves and ski goggles. We appeared to be a bunch of hapless mountaineers ready to tackle *Pikes*

*Peak.* I looked around at each of us and began to get an unsettling feeling. Up until now it hadn't occurred to me, how much could we really trust Adrianna and Bart? So far we had all be playing nice for the common good. Given an opportunity would they betray us? I've remained alive this long mainly being suspicious of others and staying as far away from trouble as I could, granted I've been wrong from time to time in my ability to read others. Barnabas seemed to trust them, I just wondered if his trust was misplaced or misguided this time. Having Race along might be his way of evening the odds. Werewolves were formidable creatures and on their best day four Vampires would have a hard time taking one out. I was never good at sleeping with one eye open - mainly because I was addicted to sleep and got so little of it - but I had a feeling by the time that this was all over I'd be an expert at it.

"I want to take this opportunity to warn you first timers that the effects of this may seem uncomfortable and disorienting, I assure you however that affects will be temporary and the cold air will help set you right in no time," Barnabas said in a disinterested flight attendants voice explaining how your cushion could be used as a floatation device.

I thought I heard an audible gulp from everyone assembled, I couldn't be sure so I chalked it up to nerves.

"Barney," Mari said hurrying up to him. "Be careful and come back to me."

271

Barnabas smiled handing his staff off to me, which I expertly juggled even though my hands were full of my own crap - that last statement was figurative and not literal, just in case you were wondering - he took her into his arms.

"My dear, the devil himself couldn't keep me from you," Barnabas said in a tone filled with love and devotion.

Then he did something that I had rarely seen him do; Barnabas leaned down planting a movie like kiss on Mari's waiting lips. I think we all let out an "Awe." - except for Bart, his heart had to be made of stone - Their cheeks flushed a bit, but our heartfelt expression went unnoticed as their kiss went on for some time. After the first few seconds it started to get a tad uncomfortable. We all had the good sense and respect to look away concentrating on other things around the shop. I decided to gaze into a mirror directly behind Adrianna, the vantage point gave me a wonderful view of her shapely behind. Out of the corner of my eye I saw their kiss end when Barnabas straighten. He had a nice shade of black cherry lips stick in the shape of Mari's lips on his. She smiled apologetically, reaching into her sweater pocket producing a handkerchief, which she folded over her index finger wiping the lipstick from Barnabas's lips. He flashed her a devil may care smile then cleared his throat as he took back his staff.

"Right," Barnabas said. "Now we can go."

He gave a wink to Mari then elbowed me in the ribs. I think it had something to do with the fish lips thing I was doing with my mouth.

"Remember to activate the defenses as soon as we leave, Bobum and his people will take care of the outside."

"Yes, yes," Mari said in a mildly annoyed tone stepping out of the circle. "I'll remember."

Barnabas took the end of his staff placing it on a circle near the outer ring. He pressed his staff down causing a little mechanical clicking sound of metal on metal. A wall of pulsating yellow energy swirled into existence around us. The energy moved at an ever-increasing rate of speed expanding inward toward us. Energy flowed over and around us like water. When the energy finished filling the center of the circle there was a brief flash of white-hot light and we were no longer standing in the magic shop.

# Chapter 16

I've never really thought about or even considered what it would've felt like to be a washcloth getting rung out. An uncomfortable disorientating feeling of being squeezed tightly for every last bit of moisture remaining in the cotton fibers, an off the wall thing to be thinking about I know. After this trip however, I could definitely appreciate that feeling. I decided then and there, that I wanted no part of this type of travel in the future. When the swirling circle of magical energy dissipated and our senses returned to normal, we found ourselves standing in the middle of a raging snowstorm with a deep biting cold nipping at everything the elements could get to. I took in our surroundings, my vision still spinning like I'd just gotten off a *"Tilt A Whirl"* carnival ride.

In the distance before us I viewed a wide mountain range that stretched for miles. A thick covering of clouds obscured the peaks and most of their size couldn't be determined. I was surprised that given the amount of snow falling visibility wasn't as poor as it could've been. A dense suffocating forest of trees dusted with thick layers of snow surrounded us. Their dark trunks stood out starkly against the unmarred whiteness of the snow. Like pillars from some unholy cathedral.

Somewhere off to our left - I had no idea of the distance - I thought I heard what sounded like the flowing water of a slow moving river. As I made a slow turning circle, I got the distinct impression that not many human beings had trudged this way before if at all. Wherever we were it was remote and isolated. After a moment or two of getting my bearings, I realized we were standing in a circle roughly the same size as the portal we'd left. The force of the energy had cleared snow as we appeared in the space. The design of this circle was uncannily similar to the one at the magic shop save one major difference. This one was chiseled into a type of obsidian shimmering quartz stone rather than set in wood. Snow was piled around us a good three feet high. We were going to have a hell of a time making our way through that even with snowshoes. I worried more about Tilly. The little guy would never make it through that. One of us would have to carry him.

I turned back to the others in time to see Race shrugging out of the last of his clothing. He squatted down stuffing them into his pack. Now free of his confining clothes steam rose off his body in steady plumes. After fastening his pack he stood, handing it off to Tilly. Race flashed a cocky smile followed by a wink right before his form shimmered, transforming into the large black wolf that I'd seen him change into earlier that day. Race let out two deep-chested barks before lying down in front of Tilly. The little Elf flung Race's pack up onto the wolf's back then scrambled up himself. Settling onto Race's back behind the shoulders, he wedged the pack under him grabbing two handfuls of fur as Race got to his feet.

Adrianna moved over to Barnabas as my adoptive father knelt down to put on his snowshoes.

"Where exactly are we," she asked in a raised voice to be heard over the background noise.

"*Siberia*, near the *Ob River*," he said in a similar tone. "About five miles from our destination."

Adrianna nodded turning to Bart giving a curt nod. He inclined his head then gracefully leapt up onto the rim of snow piled around the circle peering around us in a searching pattern.

I turned to Adrianna and asked.

"What's he doing?"

"He's scouting for us. Bartholomew has excellent eyesight and hearing," she replied.

It was possible that I had a suspicious look on my face or my body exuded mistrust because Adrianna smiled patiently like a reproving schoolteacher then said.

"Don't worry Sol, Bartholomew and I have given our word to Barnabas and we will honor it. He's dealt honorably with us and even put his life in danger to warn us of his suspicions and we'll not forget that."

I nodded as she finished. Her words making me feel more at ease. A devious smile appeared on her face. I watched her take out a smart phone holding it in front of her turning one way then another as though she were checking reception.

"Besides, there's no chance of getting a signal in this remote area and absolutely no way of calling my people to help us kill you if that were our intention."

I chuckled. Nervously.

She placed her phone back inside her coat patting me gently on the cheek. I'd be lying if I said I hadn't been frightened by her words and the cold chill running down my spine was because of the weather. Even though she was joking - at least I thought she was joking - it was still a scary proposition that her people were only a phone call away. I looked to Bartholomew; though his face was only in profile I could see a satisfied grin on his face. Vampires it seemed were completely sadistic.

Adrianna joined Bart at the rim of the circle as Barnabas stood. He elbowed me gently in the small of my back getting my attention. He pointed to my snowshoes dangling limply in my right hand. I nodded absently then knelt to put them on. Barnabas trudged up to the Vampires. Race barked an annoyed bark - which was probably meant for me - then plowed into the snow. I was left to put on my snowshoes with shaking hands, that weren't a result of the cold weather and reflected on whether or not I would make it back home. You want to know the funny thing that was running through my mind? It had nothing to do with my predicament or impending unseen fate. The thought that my mind was fixated on at the moment was that I, the crazed irresponsible person that I am, was becoming attracted to Adrianna.

A Vampire. I know, crazy right?

Granted the more I thought about it, the more I thought that I had a snowball's chance in hell of her even thinking twice about me. I mean come on. To her I was nothing. I had no money, no political standing, my sexual experience was inadequate at best and I had no place of my own to take her back too even if I wanted to try and put the moves on her. There was a bright side however, she was flirting with me after all and I didn't see any flirtation directed at Race or even Barnabas. Maybe there was something there. Maybe she saw something in me that she liked.

OK, other than my blood.

Or maybe I was just being stupid and my heart was going pitter pat because she showed a little interest and kindness toward me. You can probably tell that my experience with women is non-existent. I could count on one hand how many dates and girlfriends I've had over the years. The last girl I dated was about four years ago. Lori Simms was her name. We met as fate would have it at a gas station. Lori had somehow locked her keys inside her car. Me being the gentleman that I am was kind enough to unlock her door. One of the other gas station patrons had a coat hanger in their trunk.

I made a great show of bending the hanger to a useable shape, inserting it into the gap between the window and the door on the driver's side. Then when no one was watching, I unlocked it with a simple magical spell. I looked like such a rock star that she invited me out to dinner to thank me. That relationship lasted nearly two months and then as what usually happened, tragedy struck. I made the mistake of bringing Lori home, to the magic shop. To be fair I really should've called first to check to see what Barnabas was doing. Lori and I were in the area and on the spur of the moment I asked her if she wanted to meet the man I called dad. How the hell was I supposed to know that Barnabas was helping a pair of grief stricken Goblins nurse their Bog Salamander back to health in the back room of the shop. I know what you might be thinking,

*"What's so bad about a Bog Salamander?"*

First off, they aren't the cute little spotted amphibians kids fish out of ponds all across the country. Bog Salamanders grow to about eight feet long with huge shovel shaped heads, thick bodies and are often mistaken for alligators in the wild. They also secrete a green colored mucus that's highly prized in the potion brewing industry. The mucus is used as a catalyst in many of the more complicated potions. An ounce of the stuff could fetch ten gold pieces easy.

Lori handled the Goblins all right, I have to give her that. She obviously was uneasy about the whole situation, but she acted like a little trooper. Lori even looked on with good humor as Barnabas doctored the salamander. She completely and utterly freaked however when the damn thing spat a basketball sized glob of mucus onto her face and chest. The Goblins produced glass vials from their frock coats then proceeded to industriously collect the mucus from off Lori. Needless to say the Goblins pursued her when she bolted like a scared rabbit, all the while believing that she was absconding with their valuable property. I caught up to them and persuaded Lori to allow the Goblins to collect as much of the mucus as they could or they wouldn't leave her alone.

Reluctantly she did so with as much grace and courage as the situation warranted. When they were finished with their harvest, they gratefully thrust a leather bag into her hand, bowing respectfully then hurried back to the shop. The next few moments didn't go so well for me. I received a hard slap on the face followed by a harsh warning never to call her again. To make her point even clearer, she threw the bag – which I found out later was filled with gold and jewels - forcefully at my chest then stormed off crying.

I shook my head standing, the last buckle fastened on my snowshoes and a feeling of melancholy settling over me. I took in a breath, exhaling a deep sigh. Maybe I should just start accepting the fact that I'm destined to be alone. There were very few Wizards that had any luck what so ever meeting someone or even settling down. Being a Wizard is an exceptionally cool job. The forces of nature are yours to command yet with all that power a guy still can't get a girl to go out with him. Oh well, a subject best to be brooded over another time. Right now I had to keep my mind focused and ready for what might lay ahead. Though, I really didn't know much about that either.

I shambled up the snowdrift to join the others. Barnabas consulted a map and compass getting his bearings before we set off. Five miles would be quite a hike in this storm. The last thing we'd want to do is get ourselves lost right at the start. Race prowled around doing what dogs do, sniffing the snow relentlessly. I half expected him to sidle up to a tree and hike his leg on it. I watched him prowl around; I became acutely aware of how actually cold it was. The hole blunted most of the effects from the storm, but now standing in the full force of the biting arctic gale mixed with swirling snow I shivered uncontrollably longing for my nice warm bed and convenience of an adjustable thermostat.

"We have to trek through the forest to our right in order to avoid some of Bialek's defenses," Barnabas said in a raised voice for all of us to hear.

"Will we get to our destination in a more timely manner?" Adrianna asked, her voice rose as well. "I'm concerned about the Elf, I'm not sure how much exposure to the elements he can tolerate."

Barnabas and I looked over to Tilly. Even with the added heat from Race's wolf form his teeth chattered together with the rapidity of a jackhammer. Barnabas nodded in agreement.

"We may need to stop and set up camp along the way," Barnabas said. "Night will be upon us with in a few hours."

"Then I suggest we get moving Barnabas," Adrianna replied.

"Stay together and in visual range, with the intensity of this storm we could lose track of one another quickly."

Barnabas turned to Bart handing him the map and compass.

"Adrianna has confidence in your abilities, as do I… I would deem it a favor if you would lead us to our destination," Barnabas said. "We are indicated as these red dots here."

He pointed them out with a gloved finger.

"The blue dots are the defenses we have to navigate through and our destination is the black square."

Bart's attitude became suspicious he glared at Barnabas.

"Why do you want me to lead you Wizard," He asked in a guarded tone.

Barnabas smiled.

"Should weather conditions worsen, we may need to separate, only Adrianna, Race and yourself would be able to get Tilly to Bialek's quickly." Barnabas said in a grave tone. "Solomon and I would only slow you down."

Bart nodded, understanding evident in his features.

"I'll lead you to your destination Wizard. But this in no way makes us friends," Bart said indicating the map and compass in his hand.

"I'll return them to you as soon as we get to our destination."

On that note Barnabas turned gesturing for Bart to get in front of us. Which he did, after consulting the map and compass. We set off for our destination, Bart in the lead followed by Race with Tilly, then Adrianna. Next followed Barnabas, then myself six or seven paces behind. Walking around wearing snowshoes isn't fun by any stretch of the imagination. Especially if a person hasn't worn them in a while or isn't use to walking around with large tennis rackets on your feet. OK, they really aren't shaped like tennis rackets, however the same odd shape applies. First, you have to get accustomed to large cumbersome ovals on your feet made from hard plastic, aluminum and *Velcro* strips. When you walk in snowshoes however, you must widen your stance so that you don't step on the other shoe. To be fair snowshoes aren't impossible to master or difficult to use, it just takes time and practice. I've never really liked devoting time in learning how to use them, because I hate snow and everything that has to do with cold weather. But that's another story.

Our intrepid group moved at a fairly good pace, though I was falling behind, as usual. Race moved through the snow easily bounding from one spot to another. I wondered if Tilly was getting motion sickness. Barnabas had absolutely no difficulty moving in the snow. He appeared to be on a power walk, every step sure and confident. I on the other hand looked completely uncoordinated, like a duck that lost it's waddle. As for the Vampires their progress wasn't impeded by the elements or terrain. It was as though they each weighed no more than a feather barely disturbing the snow as they moved resolutely on.

We'd gone approximately a mile in roughly an hour and a half. The sun continued to dip down in the West, which meant we'd be out of daylight in a few hours. I was hoping that Barnabas was going to set up camp and we'd get to Bialek's place in the morning. Sadly he was notoriously stubborn and wouldn't stop till one of us dropped from exhaustion. My body ached from the top of my head to the tips of my toes, which were so cold I could no longer feel them. My clothes on the other hand clung to my body like a cellophane wrapper on a piece of *American* cheese. Sweat pooled under my winter clothes as I attempted to keep pace with the others. The frigid wind swirled around me biting through to my skin. I just couldn't get warm. My teeth chattered like a pair of novelty teeth and my body shivered uncontrollably. To make the situation worse, my throat was as dry as straw. I couldn't quench my thirst because my bottle of water had frozen. I ended up resorting to eating the snow around me - I made sure I got it from places Race had not been so don't worry, I didn't eat any yellow snow - which helped my thirst, but made my already cold body shiver even more.

We made our way through a dense part of the forest filled with trees that had grown near a ridge with a steep incline. The forest floor hadn't been blanketed with the drifting layers of thick snow like the open expanses, but that didn't mean we were free of obstacles. The forest floor was littered with fallen twigs and branches lying only a few inches below the snow. I managed to get my snowshoes hung up twice. I couldn't complain all that much, the trees being so close together helped with the wind immensely, I didn't feel as cold as I did before.

The storm continued to rage unrelenting around us with no sign of abating anytime soon, this was one of those occasions that weren't fit for man or beast. Much to his credit, Bart found a clearing among the trees that shielded us from the wind. The canopy above our heads afforded us enough cover to help keep the snow at bay. We rested for about fifteen minutes. I took the opportunity to eat something. Easier said than done. The jerky was frozen hard as were the two *Baby Ruth Bars* I'd packed. The only thing that was somewhat thawed out was a chocolate chip granola bar. I guess you'd call it luck that one of the chemical heat packs I carried activated in my pack keeping the darn thing from freezing. Granola bars aren't my favorite snack food to eat. I only bring them along because Barnabas tells me too. If I could figure out a way to keep an *Italian Beef Sandwich with Chili Fries* warm on a camping trip I'd have that to eat.

I didn't feel at all satisfied with the short rest period or inadequate snack, but our taskmasters; Bart and Barnabas wanted to press on. I got up from the rock that'd been my makeshift place to park my behind. Getting up however was difficult. My ass felt like a frozen pot roast right out of the deep freeze. My joints were stiff and my leg muscles rebelled against my insistence that they help get me to my feet. Instead, they were on the verge of cramping.

My body felt tired, worn out and for the first time in my adult life I felt old, really old. Like pass the false teeth Mildred so I can eat old. As I have said before I'm in my mid-twenties, by far the youngest person on this little expedition. Race would be the next youngest at just over one hundred and twelve. I had no idea how old Bart was, but he had the air of being from the mid to late seventeen hundreds. Barnabas was over seven hundred years old and I knew Adrianna had to be at least a thousand. I was the proverbial baby of this particular bunch, but I'd wager a million bucks that I felt the oldest right at this moment. It didn't matter at all that three of our party were supernatural beings, two of which were Vampires. Adrianna and Bart were immortal and would not change in physical appearance or succumb to fatigue, ever. The other, Race though long lived was not immortal. He'd remain as he was until the day he died. Not a gray hair, not a wrinkle or middle-aged potbelly would ever tarnish his appearance. I let out a deep depressed sigh. Not at the thought of being old or how unfair it was that I didn't have any of those cool powers that the others possessed.

No.

Those powers came at a price. A price I wasn't willing to pay. The depressed sigh was in response to the thought of having to hike the three and a half miles to Bialek's place and there wasn't any guarantee I'd be getting any warmer along the way or when we arrived.

# Chapter 17

We continued on our march, my spirits far lower than they were twenty minutes before. We emerged from the protection of the tree line that served as our wall against the snow. The storm appeared to have gotten stronger. Winds had increased in intensity gusting so forcefully staying upright was difficult. Don't get me started on the snowflakes; they had increased in size falling with greater rapidity. The cynical side of my brain immediately began thinking that this was all a conspiracy perpetrated by *Mother Nature* to punish me for all my complaining. Why couldn't she teach me a lesson by raising the temperature twenty or thirty degrees? That'd sure put me in my place. Bart led us in a wide arc around, what appeared to be nothing. There was a drop off forty feet or so to our left, however there wasn't anything that I could see that would prevent us from traveling in a straight line. It just didn't make any sense to me; then again I wasn't the one holding the map.

My right foot felt heavy almost to the point of dragging. I paused taking a glance down discovering my snowshoe hung loosely by a strap, which was torn nearly in two. It collected snow as I walked making my progress sluggish. Great, the strap must've gotten cut on a sharp branch somewhere along our hike. I shrugged out of my pack placing it on the ground in front of me. I knelt down in an attempt to repair my snowshoe. I rummaged around in my pack taking out a couple of thin bungee cords roughly eight inches long. I managed to reinforce the damaged strap by creating an "X" around my boot using the bungee cords to hold everything in place. I stood moving around in a circle discovering that the bungee cords worked well. Satisfied with my jury-rigging, I closed my pack struggling back into the darn thing. Man it was heavy. My pack felt like Tilly had packed Mari's entire kitchen into it. Along with a *Weber Grill* and a full bottle of propane. I know I'm exaggerating but come on already. Putting on a fully loaded pack is difficult to begin with. Add in snow gear along with the conditions that I currently found myself in and you have a recipe for complaining.

After I got myself situated I looked around discovering that I was alone. Everyone had continued on without noticing that I'd stopped. Dammit! I'd been so stupid. I hadn't called out indicating I had an issue, which is what you're supposed to do while hiking so things like this didn't occur. I'd chide myself later about my lack of hiking etiquette; right now I had to catch up to the others. I could see far enough ahead where their tracks disappeared around a large rock about forty or fifty yards away. If I hurried I could catch up to them. I learned a while back in math class that the shortest distance between any two points is a straight line. So using that logic I set off at a brisk lope in the direction of where the tracks disappeared.

Remember when I was talking about all the blowing snow and deep drifts? Well, I realized far too late why Bart had led us around in a wide arc. He was avoiding a cliff covered with an overhang of snow that made the actual cliff appear to be twenty feet wider than it actually was. I got maybe ten or fifteen steps out onto the overhang before the darn thing gave way under me. A few tons of heavily packed snow broke loose cascading down carrying me along with it. The whole heap rolled and tumbled into the valley forty or fifty feet below. The fall was anything but pleasant. My limbs slammed into chunks of ice concealed within the snow, I tumbled head over tail five or six times. My face planting in the snow just as many times forcing cold icy matter down the front and back of my coat. Even more collected inside my boots.

When the mass of snow finally came to rest, I found myself buried in a dark icy tomb. I was alive and I didn't think anything was broken, which was a good thing. My hand still gripped tightly around the shaft of my staff. I took a few seconds to calm down, my heart rate was beating at a rapid pace to the point I could feel a hell of a headache rising on the inside of my skull. I moved the hand holding my staff in an up and down movement. Making a pocket of space large enough to begin to dig my way out. I slowly moved my body with purpose packing the snow around me into a small tunnel as I went. The snow covering me was only a foot and a half deep which made it easier to get out of the predicament I was in. My head broke the surface of the snow and I gulped air like a scuba diver whose air tank had gone empty. Using my staff as an anchor, I pulled myself up and out of the icy pit, collapsing onto my back just lying there in the snow.

    I felt numb yet my body was still able to radiate pain. The collection of snow inside my coat wouldn't let me forget the sensation of being a *Popsicle* however, I ultimately forced myself up into a sitting position and it was a painful exertion. I tugged off my wet gloves, pulled down my hood followed by my goggles then went about digging the snow from off my face and out of my coat. The last few handfuls ended up being formed into a nice sized snowball, that I hurled at a nearby tree, missing it by a good three feet. I guess the *Detroit Tigers* wouldn't be calling me to pitch for them anytime soon.

    I ran a bare hand over my damp hair mantled with a thin layer of snow, then pulled my hood back up over my head. I did my best to wipe the goggles free of snow before placing them back over my eyes. I took off my pack again remembering I'd packed a spare set of winter gloves in a *Ziploc* bag. After replacing the wet gloves with dry ones I sighed happily. Wearing damp gloves in this weather would not have been a good thing to do. I crammed everything back into my pack zipping it up. I picked up a handful of snow eating it a bit like a flavorless snow cone, letting it melt to gain a measure of relief from thirst. My teeth ached from the frozen sensation, I was thirsty and there wasn't another way to get water into me. As I took up a second handful I noticed that I had lost a snowshoe and the other was badly damaged. I sighed. My walk just got a lot harder. I still had my pack and my battle staff. I felt the comforting weight of the *Colt* still strapped to my thigh, so I wasn't too badly off. Still, I didn't relish the idea of trudging through this mess without the help of my snowshoes.

Barnabas was the outdoorsman, not me. He'd buy all sorts of gear such as fly-fishing equipment, cross country skis, mountain bikes and these snowshoes so he and I could enjoy the outdoors together. Now don't get me wrong I do like some outdoor activities, just not all. Especially where cold weather is concerned. I hate anything to do with winter or just cold climate in general. I think my aversion to the cold stems from my first few winters I endured in *Detroit* growing up in a drafty orphanage. Sister Mari did her best with the money she had to work with, but it was cheaper to keep the heat low. Sweaters and blankets were a necessity in that old drafty building. There was nothing worse - to me anyway - than being cold and not able to get warm. I was glad when I'd heard that the orphanage had been condemned and demolished, no longer would kids have to suffer in that rat hole.

I put my pack back on as I pushed myself to my feet then promptly sank to my ankles in the snow. I sighed a long-suffering sigh. I had two options before me. The first was to find a way back up the ridge hopefully running into the others or second and most attractive to me was to find some shelter, build a fire in order to wait out the storm then find them in the morning. I didn't think they'd gotten far and with any luck they'd have noticed that I wasn't with them hopefully deciding on a similar course of action. My mind made up, I cast the bent snowshoe aside then started trudging my way through the storm looking for a place to hunker down for the night.

The deeper I moved into the forest the more strangely familiar the surroundings became to me. Though I'd never been here before somehow I knew where I was and where I was going. Every rock, every tree and every drift of snow had an eerie déjà vu quality about them. A thought nagged at me. A thought that floated at the fringes of my memory yet I wasn't able to grab hold of it bringing it back into the light. It wasn't until I made my way into a large clearing through the thick line of trees that the memory crystallized and I could see it more clearly. This clearing was in my dream.

I was here. I dreamt about this place. There are times, though not all that often I have precognitive dreams. I can literally see glimpses of things to come. I once won two hundred dollars at a casino in *Tunica, Mississippi*. I'd dreamt a few nights before that a coin had been left in the tray of a slot machine next to a bank of six ATM machines. Normally when I go to a casino I stay near the *Blackjack* tables because I detest slot machines with a passion.

Anyway, I had gone through my *Blackjack* money – one hundred dollars - finding myself wandering through the casino. I stumbled upon the area in the casino next to the ATM's I'd dreamt about spying a machine called "*Break Your Cherry*". Inside the tray rested a twenty-five cent token and the rest you know. Though now I realized my dream about this place was more than a glimpse it was a frigging double matinee and there would be danger here. My hand went instinctively to the *Colt* on my thigh. I drew it out of the holster pointing the barrel at the ground, my finger resting upon the trigger guard. I gripped my battle staff tighter rubbernecking around scanning for danger.

I cautiously made my way into the clearing figuring being out in the open would give me an edge I'd need against the creatures that might be lurking around this place. I heard a twig snap to my right. I jerked my head bringing the pistol to bear on the sound. I tensed ready to fire stopping short of pulling the trigger. Before me stood seven huge Caribou, their backs coated with a light dusting of snow, one of which had a magnificent set of antlers on its majestic head. They scuffed their hooves at the snow uncovering the frozen grass that lay beneath. The buck - I assumed because of the rack - raised its head leveling his gaze directly at me. My heart pumped a furious rhythm as the buck's ears flicked this way then that, searching for danger chewing on a mouthful of frozen grass or twigs. Satisfied there was no danger - I mean to the buck, a cold, tired Wizard holding a gun obviously wasn't - he went back to scuffing the snow with the others.

I inched around the herd giving them a wide berth as to not agitate that big fellow with the antlers. I was averse to having my skinny ass impaled by them. I took my eyes off the Caribou, adjusting my course heading for a gap in the trees. When I turned back the caribou were gone. The only evidence of their exit was swaying branches marking the path of their egress.

There was no sound or warning of the danger until it presented itself. Five huge, hairy white ape creatures charged toward me from a concealed spot among the trees a few feet to the right where the caribou stood. A sixth creature emerged a few moments later from the trees a pace or two behind the others. In my dream there were only three of these creatures, now I had six to contend with. How lucky can a guy be, right? I faced them aiming my pistol at the lead creature. I fired three rounds in quick succession. The first went wide missing completely, the second hit the creature in the shoulder staggering it's furious pace, the third hit it's left thigh. The lead ape which was badly injured by my shots, hit the ground in a tumbling heap tripping up two of the others following closely behind. I adjusted my aim firing off the four remaining shots in the magazine at the two that hadn't been tripped up.

I missed.

I holstered my weapon turning to flee, something strange happened however. My body acted of its own accord. I wanted to run like hell. I even recall my mind screaming out for that action, but my body felt rooted in place as though I had no control over my actions. My left hand transferred the battle staff to my right. Then raising the arm holding the staff I involuntarily smote the end down into the snow striking frozen ground. My arm pushed the staff forward like the bottom was part of a fulcrum. Inside my head I heard an unfamiliar voice utter.

" Undo of terra quod navitas,"

A wave of energy lashed out from the end of my staff in a cone shape spreading wider as it went. Snow mixed with frozen soil churned up ten feet into the air forcing the creatures back thirty-five feet or more. The tidal wave of power left a two and a half foot gouge in the ground wherever the magic spell touched. I was in complete shock. I felt my eyes had grown to the size of saucers because they hurt behind the protection of my goggles. The debris cloud dissipated and I perceived the ape creatures getting groggily to their feet. In my head I literally felt the force of someone slapping me across the face - my cheek actually hurt - as well as the same voice that cast the spell yelling at me,

"Run you fool! Run!"

I popped the clips on my pack shrugging out of it as I turned heading clumsily in the opposite direction away from the creatures that wanted to end my life. I didn't need the extra weight to contend with and would try to come back later for it. I knew it was a stupid thing to do, leaving all my stuff here, but it wouldn't do me any good if they caught and killed me.

A blur of white motion swept past my eyes barely missing the bridge of my nose. I perceived for the briefest of moments my staff sailing end over end away from me disappearing completely into a deep snowdrift. A creature I hadn't seen grabbed my coat, lifting me off my feet then slammed me violently to the frozen ground. Pain coursed through my body, stars drunkenly danced around in my field of vision. The creature lifted me again hurling me twenty-five feet away. I bounced a few times skidding to a halt. My upper body and my waist were buried in a thick layer of freshly disturbed snow. I think a groan of pain or a whimper escaped from my lips as my ability to breathe returned. I just laid there in agony; some part of my brain began prodding an urgent thought out from the shadows.

If I didn't move or do something now I was surely dead. A fact I knew already even before my brain started trying to tell me the obvious. I was in pain, hurting, close to blacking out and my body just didn't want to move. I willed my shaking hands to brush the snow from my head and off my goggles. As an afterthought I removed them, discarding them. Then with a little more exertion I propped myself up on my right elbow to view the situation. The movement churned the contents in my stomach. I wanted to throw up, but I forced my stomach to calm down.

The ape creature that attacked me had gone over to check on his comrade's injuries. That was bad, for me at least. These apparently weren't mindless violent creatures. They had feelings and compassion for their kind. I may have killed one of them and perhaps injured two others, which meant there might be some hurtful payback coming my way soon.

"Stop thinking and move!" Were the only words the little voice in my head began shouting in a loud anxious tone. How could I argue with my conscience? I rolled over onto my knees. It was a slow process with my joints popping painfully when my weight settled on them. I could feel the ground trembling behind me. I knew that the ape creatures were coming for me. I didn't bother to look, my heart pumped with new cowardly adrenalin. I pushed myself up into a gangly four-legged gate. Using my feet and my hands was difficult and awkward to say the least. I probably looked like a Giraffe taking its first wobbly steps. I felt a heavy tremor behind me that above all else got me moving faster. My momentum kept me from getting into a two-legged gate so I kept scrambling along on all fours like some sort of crab that was missing most of its genetic code. I got maybe another ten feet further before I felt a powerful blow strike my hip sending me airborne twisting and turning like a limp rag doll until I came to rest on my back roughly a dozen odd feet away.

Instinct took over or maybe it was a healthy dose of self-preservation, but I wasted no time. I slogged myself backward using my arms and legs not daring to turn over trying to crawl. I moved pretty well keeping a good distance away from the three sets of grasping hands, which were clawing at me for any piece of my body that they could get a hold on. I hadn't any idea where this newfound energy originated from and I really didn't care. I bobbed left, then right, ducking my head avoiding a fist that would have put a huge dent in my thinking abilities. I dropped to my back kicking my legs over my head, rolling away from them. They kept missing me. At one point I darted between one of the beast's legs. A fist meant for me landed in the family jewels of the other beast. That helped put one of them out of action for a few moments at least.

This little game went on for a minute or two more until that fateful moment when I banged my head against a fallen tree buried in the snow. I got cocky knocking myself senseless. I watched through bleary-eyed pain, as two white ape creatures moved toward me, murderous hate in their eyes. The only sounds I could hear were the crunching of the snow under the weight of their massive bodies, their animalistic breathing and the beating of my heart as it tried to pound its way out of my rib cage. It was difficult to focus on anything. I felt as though I was losing consciousness. All the pain in my body that I'd somehow suppressed came flooding back in earnest. My stomach churned and I couldn't help but lean to one side vomiting onto the snow. The creatures were about five feet or so away. One of them vindictively flicked snow into my face; the other inched closer with a huge outstretched hand. The unsettling thing about this situation was that I was at peace. I know that sounds dumb, but in a way I sort of knew what to expect. In my dream I died and I wasn't afraid of the dark any longer. I struggled to stay awake, it was difficult, but I managed it for a few more seconds at least. I even drifted into a state of delusion because I could've sworn that my imagination was getting the best of me.

I heard a leonine roar, deep and deafening in volume drowning out all other sounds. The ape creatures looked startled. Had they heard the sound too or was I just imagining this as well? Then an odd thing occurred - well, it was odd to me in any case - a huge dark furry mass blurred into my field of vision rocketing over my head tackling the stunned ape creature closest to me, driving my attacker to the ground. With a huge balled fist the dark furry creature drove it down onto my attackers chest with bone breaking force. The sound of the impact made my stomach lurch once again. Blood choked from the creature's mouth while the dark furry creature held it down. The ape creature gasped deep gurgles thrashing feebly for a few moments then went still.

The dark furry creature rose to its feet quicker than a flash of lightening. It turned vaulting, landing beside the other startled creature. In seconds it had a massive fur covered arm around the other beasts neck. The two struggled viciously jerking each other one way then the other, the second attacker trying desperately to escape. At one point the struggling ape creature sunk his massive jaws into the forearm of what I had hoped was my savior. The bite didn't even make the latter flinch. The dark furry creature arched back in a quick jerking motion pulling the ape creature off its feet. Pivoting to its left I heard the ape's neck snap. The dark furry creature loosened its grip on the ape and its body fell boneless to the ground.

Wisps of steam signifying its last breath escaped its mouth. I watched in stunned horror, as a third ape creature leapt onto the back of the dark furry creature pulling him into a tight bear hug sinking its large canine teeth repeatedly into the dark furry creatures neck. Thrashing and bucking in erratic circles the dark furry creature tried in vain to throw its attacker off. The ape's arms must've been made of coiled steel because it didn't budge an inch. The dark furry creature turned locking eyes on a large tree fifteen feet or so away. It turned running backwards in the direction of the tree. There was no time for the ape creature to react. Both of their massive bodies slammed into the heavy tree trunk. Snow knocked from bare branches fell in icy clumps on top of them. Knocked senseless, the ape creature's eyes rolled back in its head and its lower jaw relaxed. Its grip however remained firmly around its foe.

The dark furry creature walked five or so feet forward then hit the tree again. It repeated this three more times until the ape slid off limply from the back of the dark furry creature. I thought I heard a deep reverberating crack pin balling off every surface around me. I didn't know if the sound came from deep inside the tree trunk or the ape's now lifeless body. I slipped further into unconscious as I watched the dark furry creature turn in my direction making his way with purpose over to me. It knelt in front of me peering into my dimming eyes. I was still unsure if this was a male or a female and I was in no shape to ask. Two points of fire blazed where its eyes should've been, the rest of its face was an unidentifiable form. It raised a huge hand blocking my field of vision, I couldn't fight to stay awake any longer so I gave in to sleep and everything went blissfully black.

# Chapter 18

I stood at the edge of a small pool rimmed by dark oddly shaped stones. I had a strange feeling that *Tim Burton* designed the pool because it looked like something he might have had in one of his movies. The pool itself was filled with a gently rippling silver liquid. *Quicksilver*, if I wasn't mistaken.

Light shone down upon me from a source I couldn't see. The light reminded me of the bright orange glow you'd sometimes get in *Detroit,* as dawn would break in the waning days of summer. The light though brilliant was not uncomfortable. Tiny motes of dust swirled lazily through the cylinder of ethereal illumination catching my attention for the briefest of moments. I leaned over the edge of the pool to gaze into the metallic liquid. What I found there startled me.

The reflection appeared to be of me, but at the same time it wasn't. The face looked uncannily like my own, with subtle differences however. Long and angular in shape with high cheek bones. The nose was thinner than mine. It had a hawkish quality with flared nostrils. The hair - white as snow in color - fell to below the shoulders. The ears were pointed almost like an Elf's.

No.

Exactly like an Elf's. The feature of this face that startled me the most was the eyes. My eyes are the color of a Topaz sky on a clear spring day, where this man's eyes were light brown almost caramel in color they exuded a malice that terrified me. His eyes had the look of a top predator, like a *Great White Shark* or *Komodo dragon*, soulless, devoid of humanity. The animals I just mentioned stalked and killed their prey for survival, this man's motivation however appeared to go beyond that. Though all this was an uninformed observation I could see the orgasmic love of killing lurking there in those eyes.

I shivered as I straightened. I had no idea who that man was, but I knew I didn't want to meet him. The fact I resembled him made me wonder, who was he and why am I just now seeing his likeness. Hell, for all I knew I was dead and this was the first part of some weird entrance exam to get into Heaven or Hell depending on how my tests were graded. It'd be my luck to fail out of Heaven and have to repeat life. I hoped that whoever was in charge graded on a curve.

"The shroud of death has yet to be pulled over your eyes young Wizard," a strong powerful voice neither male nor female, but a mixture of both said from beyond the cylinder of light.

I jerked my head in the direction of the crisp voice, thick with a cultured old world British accent. Had the voice started spewing out a torrent of vile sexually profane language I do believe anyone within earshot would have found it charming.

A blurry form stood appraising me. The form never really took on any kind of shape, instead it blurred from one out of focus image to another. Almost as though there were multiple images fighting to be seen at the same time. Somehow I knew the form I was looking at was a person. The only thing I could really make out, were colors. Lots of blues and white mixed with a little hint of gold.

"Who are you," I asked. "And what is this place?"

The blurred form regarded me and then said.

"You are careless and dull witted as a child not yet weaned from its mother's teat young Wizard."

"Am not," I shot back. The king of witty comebacks, that's me.

"You didn't answer my questions," I continued.

"How observant," the form said in an arrogant tone. "Perhaps if you chose to ask more intelligent questions I would choose to answer them."

I sighed. I never get a straight answer and have to work for the crappy ones I always tended to get. Why do people with knowledge have to make up dumb ass ways of getting you to answer the questions they ask? I moved closer to the blurry form walking right into the cylinder of light. Which had a similar effect of walking into a sliding glass door and as it turned out it hurt just as much. The light acted as a barrier preventing me from leaving the illuminated circle as well as I presumed keeping the blurry form away from me. I probably looked a lot like a mime with my hands pressed against the invisible wall.

"Perhaps it was a mistake to bring you here," the form said disappointed. "You are much too young and not ready for the knowledge I possess."

"Now wait a minute," I said agitated. "You are the one who decided to be all mysterious not me. If you want to talk, then talk. Don't be a prick about the whole thing."

The blurry form said nothing for almost a minute then a low throaty laugh echoed around me. It was the kind of infectious heartfelt laugh that made me want to join in, but I didn't.

"Very well young Wizard, we will proceed in your manner of your generation… Judging by your knowledge and experience I will endeavor to keep my words and answers simplistic in scope."

The blurry form satisfied with its insult, turned gliding slowly to the left. It was difficult keeping my eyes from crossing as he moved, sort of like dealing with a bad headache.

"Ask your questions," said the blurry form.

I hesitated gathering my thoughts not wanting to waste my questions on dumb ones. Who knows when this person was going to decide to clam up?

"Well, let's start with the most important question. Am I alive or is this the waiting room of the afterlife?" I asked curiously.

"You have an odd sense of what is and what is not important. However, since that is your question, yes you are yet alive and resting this very moment in a place of safety," it replied.

"So I survived the ape attack?"

"Obviously," the blurry form replied sarcastically.

"So this place we are in... is it a real place or is it an image created by you?"

The blurry form hesitated.

"The simplest answer young Wizard is yes," it said pausing once again then continuing. "This place is contained within the walls of your mind.. I created it so that we might converse. You are also correct that this place though a conjured reality is quite real... If I were to pierce your flesh here the wound would appear in the same place on your body in the conscious world."

It was my turn to be silent.

"And this pool of quicksilver?" I asked jerking my head in the direction of the pool.

The blurry form stopped abruptly saying nothing for a long moment.

"He knows not what the murky waters of the past keeps hidden from his eyes?" The blurry form said to know one in particular.

"What are you talking about?"

The blurry form gazed at me as if seeing me for the first time then it said.

"The pool is many things, a repository of knowledge, a mirror into your very being, an aid for learning magic. It can also reveal such things contained in your mind not yet realized or things forgotten long ago. Thoughts, memories and even lessons that you have learned which have yet to take hold. By your look of utter bewilderment you have many I would surmise,"

I raised my right hand giving the blurry form the finger. Either it didn't know what the finger meant or it didn't see the gesture because the blurry form just kept right on speaking unperturbed.

"When you find yourself in a deep dreamless slumber as you are now, or in a conscious state where your thoughts need order, you can will yourself to this place to speak to me or gaze into the pool to look upon yourself."

"So what you're saying is that the pool behind me is sort of like a replay button for my brain?" I asked.

The blurry form regarded me silently, possibly perplexed by my use of words. Like flipping the bird, it was probably unfamiliar with the gesture as well as what a replay button was.

"Never mind," I said finally. "I get the idea."

I looked around then asked.

"Why did you bring me here?"

"To show you this place and take my measure of you." The form said seriously.

"I thought you already did that, you called me careless and dull witted if I recall correctly."

"I am still making my determination about you, but my mind is leaning closer to village idiot,"

I threw up my hands letting out a groan of frustration stomping around the pool.

"*Jesus Christ* on a *Popsicle* stick!" I began. "I get this kind of crap from Barnabas all the time! It's like having an asshole Wizard in the real world and one floating around in my head."

I trailed off as a thought occurred to me, an unsettling thought. I turned pensively back to the blurry form. I know I've never been accused of being stupid, - present company excluded of course - it just takes me a little while to connect the dots. I'm a bit thick headed about many subjects - women being the most obvious – however, I knew who this person was. A knowing smile shown on my face as the curtains in my mind opened. I said.

"You're Merlin, aren't you?"

The form remained silent for a long moment and then it flickered. A subtle pulse of energy emanated from the middle of the blurry form then all the images fighting to be seen merged together into a tall older male figure.

"Very good young Sir. Though my opinion of you is still tarnished. You have found the answer and for that I am pleased." He said giving me a respectful incline of his head.

"So the power that I absorbed from the crystal also contained a copy of who you were in life?" I asked.

"Not a copy young Sir, all that I was or would ever become along with my power resided within that crystal."

My hand instinctively went to the almost healed ash dagger wound on my shoulder. Merlin smiled.

"You healed the injury I got from the Ashari assassin," I asked.

"To be more precise your body did the healing, I simply instructed your mind and body on how to accomplish the process more quickly along with minimal pain," he said diffidently.

"So when I get hurt I heal faster now," awed excitement in my question.

"Yes young Sir, but be warned you are not in possession of godlike powers, you are still mortal though you now have knowledge to be slightly more than mortal," caution in his tone. "I merely removed the restrictions that nature hath placed upon that process nothing more."

I nodded thoughtfully. How cool was this development! I could heal quicker. No more of Barnabas's witch doctor salves or cures. All I needed now were *Adamantium* claws and I could be friggin

*Wolverine*. Then my mind drifted back to what this spirit initially said. Then I asked.

"Wait, you mean you're the actual Merlin," I asked. "I mean his ghost...Spirit," I amended. "Your spirit," I finished awkwardly.

"Precisely," he said soberly. "I am Merlin," "Author, poet, artist, Wizard and the sole keeper of the knowledge of *Prometheus*,"

He went silent reflecting on a thought or memory.

"I foresaw the death of my King," he said.

"Such wonderful times," he continued. "I also saw my eventual imprisonment in that piece of stone that every Wizard from here to *Peking* worships."

"*Beijing*," I said interrupting.

"Beg pardon?" Merlin asked.

"*Peking* was renamed *Beijing*."

Merlin sighed. "I've been asleep far too long. I've missed entirely too much. The last time I was employed a young *Queen Elizabeth* sat upon the throne of *England*."

"Wait, your last host was *Queen Elizabeth*?" I asked skeptically.

"Indeed," Merlin replied absently.

"As I recall she was vindictive and bloodthirsty."

"Yes, she was," he said in a mournful tone.

"You made her into what she was?" I asked, then an icy chill ran down my spine as realization dawned. I was Merlin's current host. I could only imagine what he had in store for me.

313

"Heavens no!" He said defensively. "Her bloodlust came from her father *Henry the Eighth*. He was a murderous, philandering bastard." Merlin said, vile anger in his tone.

Merlin went quiet for a good two minutes. He stood there, shaking his head from time to time, remembering I assumed, and then he said.

"*England* was beset with enemies on all sides, the crystal was given to her at a time when there was the most need. Once I discovered her true self, the one that lurked deep inside her heart I remained dormant not assisting her in any way. Sadly I bore witness to her vengeful hatred and malice."

His eyes met mine and then he smiled.

"You young Sir however have a good strong heart where kindness has an honored place. You think only of yourself at times, but make up for it by your deeds. You need only apply yourself and you could become great." He said in an uplifting tone then added. "Perhaps not as great as myself, but a lesser great nevertheless,"

I said nothing. Mainly because I was just a little embarrassed. Not many people have said that I could become great. - That included Barnabas - It was good to hear that someone thought I would amount to something if I only applied myself. Granted the words of inspiration came from the spirit of the most powerful Wizard that ever lived, which now resided inside my head, I think I'll file this under the glass half full heading. Almost as an afterthought, something began to gnaw at me. Now that he was inside my head, how much influence might Merlin actually have over my thoughts and actions. Would he be able to manipulate me the way a skilled puppeteer can manipulate marionettes?

"You're the one who's been making my magic stronger," I asked finally.

Merlin quirked an amused smile.

"In matter of fact Young Wizard, the power which was exhibited in your spells resided within you already. Your teacher, Barnabas has been instructing you in the use of weaker spells."

"Weaker spells?" I asked.

"Yes," Merlin replied. "You have a rare gift for harnessing enormous quantities of raw power from the world around you releasing it at your will. Most wizards never achieve such levels of power even if they live to be one thousand years old."

I glanced at my hands.

"You can influence my thoughts and actions, right? You're inside my head I mean, you have access to everything that makes me... Well me," I said not looking at Merlin.

"I can, yet again I cannot. I have the ability to take control of your body, which includes your magic if I wish; you however can dispel my influence with your own will. It is not my intent to take over your mind, body and soul for my own purposes, our minds are separate and I wish to keep it that way. My purpose is only to guide and help you to hone your abilities. I can advise you, help teach you spells and magical control other Wizards have only dreamt of."

I placed my hand on the invisible barrier glancing at my surroundings.

"Is that what this is?" I asked. "This circle is a barrier between your mind and mine?"

"Yes, I have seen far too many occasions where the effect of direct influence on a host can be destructive. It was necessary to keep our two minds separate." Merlin said.

Something else occurred to me. When it did, I think I may have blushed a deep red, but I had to know.

"Did you help me resist Adrianna's glamour at her office,"

Merlin chuckled heartily.

"No young Sir, you did that all on your own… You have surprising control over your libido,"

I may have blushed even more.

"Her glamour had no effect on you whatsoever," I asked.

"I would be telling you a falsehood if I said it did not, I had hoped you would embrace the forward manner of her advances, but fate was not on my side nor yours as it turns out,"

That was gross and creepy on so many levels, Merlin riding shotgun in my head wanting me to score with Adrianna, talk about voyeurism.

"So you can experience emotions as well as sensations through me," I asked.

Then he paused for just a moment offering me a grin.

"Of course, I am able to hear, smell, see, feel, along with taste everything that you eat," He broke off suddenly lifting his head sniffing the air, a pleased smile on his face.

"In fact I smell a delicious beef stew cooking and you haven't eaten in quite a while. Besides, I haven't tasted stew in years. I think you should wake up now."

Merlin raised a hand. I raised mine in protest

"No wait," I pleaded.

I saw a flash of bright light then darkness once more.

# Chapter 19

I awoke, lazily coming back to consciousness the way you'd rouse yourself on a brisk autumn morning. Knowing that the chilly air awaited that moment you threw off the covers to chill you to the bone. Instead you lingered beneath the deliciously cozy blankets for those brief few minutes longer, like reluctantly leaving the embrace of a lover.

OK, maybe the reality wasn't as romantic as I described, but I was comfortable and didn't want to get up. It felt like it did back in my high school years, cocooned under my covers in a darkened room with Barnabas standing at my door commanding me to get up for school. He eventually won those battles - with magic - but not before I got a few extra minutes of bliss.

Sleep drifted away drowsily much the way I felt and I became aware of the scents drifting around my nostrils. They were by no means unpleasant, there were however too many to process. Pine was the first thing I smelled, followed by a fragrant vanilla tobacco. Then the familiar scent of wood smoke wafting its way to my nose behind that was the mouth watering stew Merlin had mentioned. Leather, I definitely smelled newly tanned leather along with a whole bunch of smells I couldn't identify. That stew made my mouth water, it felt like I hadn't eaten in days, which I probably hadn't

I reluctantly opened my eyes, not wanting to wake. I'd assumed that when I finally woke I'd be in some sort of dank frozen cave with a huge hairy beast looming over me sharpening a rusty nicked cleaver on a jagged rock as it hummed the *Chili's "Baby Back Rib"* tune. The sight that met my adjusting eyes was surprising.

I was lying in a large bed nestled beneath a handmade patchwork quilt. The bed was situated in one corner of a modest cabin. The walls looked as though they were finished in knotty pine. The cabin appeared to be clean and well kept. My left arm was bandaged and resting outside the quilt. I let my eyes scan about my unfamiliar surroundings. The cabin, one room in its entirety, roughly comprised the size of a large two-car garage with high ceilings. The cabin was functional yet devoid of many personal touches, no photos or paintings or knick-knacks of any kind. There wasn't even a calendar hanging anywhere that I could see.

Next to the bed stood a dresser with an attached oval mirror. A pitcher and bowl sat upon it with a red and white checked towel folded neatly beside them. Beyond the foot of the bed I spied a small kitchen area, a potbelly stove stood at the far end of the room, it's sides glowing a faint red. Atop the stove sat a large steaming pot, which I realized was the source of the delicious smell of stew.

Situated in front of the stove was a plain looking table and four chairs. My now empty backpack hung from one of the backs of the chairs, its contents were placed neatly upon the table. On the back of another chair hung my chainmail shirt along with my clothes neatly folded over it. I checked under the blanket thankful to see that I still wore a t-shirt and briefs. I hadn't yet become the victim of a *"Deliverance-like"* experience. A stone fireplace was built into the side of the cabin opposite the table and potbelly stove. A warm inviting fire crackled in its hearth. To the left of the stone hearth hanging on a series of wooden pegs hung a long black fur coat with matching gloves and boots. It appeared that my rescuer wasn't a beast after all. Situated in front of the fireplace stood an enormous faded and worn brown leather chair. In it sat a man that could've been *Paul Bunyan's* little brother.

My eyes did a double take. Which hurt. Though he was seated, I judged he could've easily been Glum's height. The man though large and husky appeared not to have any fat on him. His skin was a burnt orange in color. The sort of hue you'd get if you frequented tanning salons more often than was medically advisable. I also spied numerous faint jagged white scars on the exposed skin of his head and hands. His attire was plain and unremarkable. He must order his clothes from the "*Farm Hands, Cowboys and Amish*" catalog. Thick jet-black hair fell below the level of the man's shoulders framing his aquiline face. Held in his left hand was a tiny book. After a moment of squinting I realized he was reading one of the paperbacks that I'd brought with me. The other two rested on an end table beside his chair. A pair of lit candles next to the books provided light for reading. By the looks of the book spines, he'd read them a number of times. I was taught long ago not to stare, the calluses on my knuckles from Sister Mari's wooden ruler were proof I had difficulty learning that lesson. However, he was focused intently on the book and I didn't want to interrupt him as he read. He possessed the expression of a man that had found a coveted pot of Leprechaun gold and was meticulously counting every coin.

To hell with it, I thought. I needed a few answers and I was hungry. If I had to smell that delicious stew any longer my stomach was going to escape through my belly button to eat that entire pot by itself.

"Hello," I said, the words coming out raspy, weaker than I felt.

He gave no indication that he'd heard me. When his eyes arrived at the bottom of the page he dog eared it then regarded me.

"Hello, I trust you are feeling better?" he replied in a thick *German* accent.

"Yes," I said adding a bit of a smile. - It hurt to smile - "Thank you for saving me from those ape creatures."

"Yeti's," He said soberly. "Yeti's attacked you,"

He placed the book on the end table getting to his feet. - My God he was tall -

"Though I have never seen them in such numbers before, nine in all. Most unusual," he continued moving over beside the bed examining my arm.

"Your arm is healing nicely, it was broken when I found you,"

He regarded me suspiciously for a moment.

"You carry the staff of a Wizard… are you a Wizard then," he asked.

"Yes, I'm still an apprentice though,"

"Human,"

I hesitated not understanding his question, then I realized Merlin's healing factor had to be making him wary of who or more importantly what I was.

"Yes, I'm just employing a spell to speed along my recovery,"

He nodded thoughtfully.

Not exactly a lie, but not exactly the truth either.

"How did you know they were out there?" I asked. "The Yeti's I mean, with the storm and all?"

He hooked a powerful looking thumb at the oval mirror on the dresser.

"A gift from an old friend," he said. "I can see trespassers miles away in any sort of weather day or night."

A disturbing thought jumped into my mind. I attempted to get myself to a sitting position, what I managed to do instead was give myself a pounding headache as well as a bloody nose.

"The others," I blurted out through the pain. "Are they OK?"

One of his huge hands rested upon my chest, gently forcing me back down onto the bed. He took up the pitcher on the dresser pouring some water into the bowl. He then wet the towel wiping the blood from my face and nose. The towel felt icy against my skin, which was a welcomed easing sensation. I relaxed as he helped stopped the bleeding. The pain from the headache was a different story however.

"Your people are fine. They are camped about three miles northeast of here." He said in a calming voice. "When you have rested and have eaten I will point you in their direction when the storm abates."

I stared blankly up at him, trying to process the words I'd heard. Making certain they were in fact what he actually said. I hesitated before asking.

"Point me in their direction? You won't be taking me to them yourself? What if there are more Yeti's out there waiting to finish up on me," I asked, a hint of anxiety bubbling up in my tone.

He remained unmoved by my pleas, wiping the last of the blood away.

"There is no danger to you young man."

"Solomon, my name is Solomon," I said interrupting.

"I know what your name is young man, I did after all go through your things. As I said there is no danger so you will make the journey unmolested. You must excuse me however for not escorting you myself, you see I don't like being around other people. That's why I live in this remote place by myself."

He straightened moving quickly into the kitchen area. He placed the bowl along with the blood stained towel on a well-used chopping block that sat under a small window.

"Are you hungry," he asked.

I nodded without speaking. My stomach however made a growling noise reminiscent of a seal begging for a fish from its keeper. He returned the nod with a hint of a smile as he bustled around his little kitchen. The first thing he did was to move over to the potbellied stove. He took the lid off the cast iron pot, billows of steam wafted up from the contents inside. The smell was incredible. He ladled some stew into a pair of oversized bowls, replacing the lid on the pot then he rummaged around under a small cupboard producing a bed tray with fold down legs.

He set up the bed tray arranging a bowl of stew, a spoon, a good sized crust of bread, a cloth napkin and a mug filled with what looked like strong tea neatly on the tray then brought it over to me. I scooted back against the headboard arranging the pillows so that I could sit up. Just moving that little bit made my muscles and joints cry out in pain the way your body would protest after working out for four hours straight when you hadn't done anything strenuous like that in a long while. I was proud of myself though, I whimpered only once. He placed the tray over my legs, which made me feel like a little kid. The tray was larger than a normal bed tray; it literally came up to my chest. Regardless of that inconvenience, I grabbed up the spoon with my good hand hell bent on digging into that stew. The motion was abruptly arrested however with a gentle rap on the back of my hand, I lowered the spoon back to the tray looking up at him a little crestfallen and still hungry.

"We must say grace," he said in a hushed respectful tone.

He turned grabbing one of the chairs from around the table dragging it scratching over the wood floor up beside the bed. He went over to the counter placing a piece of bread in his bowl picked up a spoon and a mug of tea for himself, then walked back to the bed seating himself into the chair placing his food on a small nightstand next to him. He leaned forward grasping his hands in prayer bowing his head, as an afterthought he looked up at into my eyes encouraging me with a nod of his head to mimic his actions. I complied. I mean he saved me after all and was going to feed me. He bowed his head once again then began to pray.

"*Heavenly Fath*er, though I am not worthy I humbly ask you to bless this meal we are about to receive. Thank you for providing us with thy bounty to keep your servants healthy and strong and *Heavenly Father* please watch over Solomon keeping him safe from harm. Amen,"

I couldn't help regarding him for a moment, there was something more about this man then meets the eye. Not in a bad way mind you, but there was something else he wasn't telling me. He lived in this remote place away from civilization and other people. That alone was a bit strange, however not uncommon for people to shy away from others, like the *Unabomber* for instance. It was the first line of his prayer that got me thinking, *"Though I am not worthy"*. I couldn't put my finger on it, but for some reason I knew that line meant more than just a devout *Catholic* praying to *The Lord.* - Granted, I was only assuming that he was *Catholic* - He lifted his head and I said in a thoughtful voice.

"Amen,"

He turned picking up his bowl of stew along with his spoon.

"I know this isn't much, but it fills the belly," he said apologetically.

I smiled as I picked up my own spoon dipping it into the stew.

"It smells delicious,"

I lifted the spoon to my lips blowing a cooling breath of air onto the hot stew. The spoon like the bowl was a bit on the largish size which was a tad disconcerting. I opened my mouth shoveling the stew greedily into it. I froze savoring the mouthful of stew as the various flavors collided with my palette. The meat wasn't beef, probably some other game animal that lived in this area, but it was tender and the taste was indescribable. My taste buds were assailed with the flavors of roasted onions, garlic, mushrooms, carrots, ground black pepper, a little salt and the faintest hint of sage. All the ingredients masterfully combined into the best stew I ever tasted. I noticed out of the corner of my eye my host watching me. I assumed as with any cook he tried gauging my like or dislike for his dish. I turned my head in his direction eyes locking on his. A few moments of uncomfortable silence hung between us until he broke it.

"Is the stew not good?" He asked in a hopeful fishing tone.

"No," I said, watching his shoulders droop perceptibly, and then I continued. "This is the best stew I've ever tasted," I proclaimed plunging my spoon back in the stew for another mouthful.

A wide approving smile shone on his face as he dug into his stew almost as hungrily as me. Deciding to not stand on ceremony I ate like a pig, I even sopped up the remains of the stew with the last of the crust of bread which I have been told is very anti-*Emily Post*.

"If you still have room," he said standing, "I made strudel earlier today."

"Strudel?" I asked, wiping my mouth and hands with a napkin. "I like strudel"

He smiled happily placing his dishes on the bed tray, and then picking it up he carried it into the kitchen area. I settled back into the bed letting the stew digest. I'd have gone for another bowl, but once he had mentioned it, I really wanted something sweet and that strudel sounded awesome. I watched him moving around putting things back in their places. My stomach gave another growl when he opened a small breadbox producing a pan of strudel then proceeded to drizzle icing all over the pastry from a copper cup.

"What's your name," I asked inquisitively. "You know mine, but we have yet to be properly introduced."

The question elicited a change in my host's manner. He stood stone still possibly contemplating the question or me. The last of the icing dripped languidly from the lip of the cup as the silence stretched on. Over the years I've found that if it takes a person more than a few seconds to answer a question they're either reluctant to answer the question for reasons known only to that person or they are searching for a plausible lie to tell you because the truth might make you think differently about them. I was hoping that neither were the case here; he seemed on the surface to be a nice person. Of course if villains all wore black and twirled a pencil thin mustache between their thumb and forefinger whilst they did their evil deeds life would be a whole lot simpler. We would avoid the evil people in the world because we'd know them by their look. Unfortunately, we don't live in a world painted from the palette of black and white. Our world is a muddled canvas covered in many shades of gray. Sadly, the evil people blend in far too well and are difficult to spot. Everyone thought *John Wayne Gacy* was just a normal guy that enjoyed dressing up as a quirky clown called *Pogo* until the authorities started finding the bodies, which I believe totaled thirty-five in all. That's how it is with the truly evil people in the world; you don't know they're evil until it's too late.

He put the now empty copper cup on the block next to the pan of strudel. Taking a deep breath he straightened considering me with a half-hearted smile.

"My name is Wilmar, but I haven't been known by that for many years," he said somewhat reluctantly.

His hand lifted fingers roving over his face.

"This face is not the face that I was born with."

That was an odd statement to make. What, did he get a facelift or something?

"I'm sorry," I said in reply. "But I don't understand what you're talking about."

He slammed his hand frustrated down on the cutting block. The force of the blow toppled the copper cup and made the pan of strudel hop a good inch in the air. My only thought was not for my safety, but for the safety of the strudel. - If that doesn't prove I'm insane nothing will - I watched him wearily, hoping he didn't go all *Annie Wilkes* on me. He sighed deeply, shoulders drooping. He moved sulkily over to a tiny bookshelf that I hadn't seen before. On it were what looked like a dozen or so books. He pulled a thin book from the shelf before walking over to the bed presenting it to me. I took it from him examining the cover.

The book appeared to be an old edition. I had no idea of its age; the faded worn hardbound book pages had yellowed over time. If I had to guess by the outdated method of raised letter printing I'd have to say the book was at least one hundred years old. The title of the book was familiar to me, though in *German* I could read it - *Frankenstein or The Modern Prometheus by Mary Shelley* - I'd read the *English* version of this particular book in high school. It was the first book that helped foster my love of reading and a paperback copy of it rested in the shelves of my own modest library at home.

When my eyes sought out his, I found he'd returned to the pan of strudel, calculating eyes watching me. I lifted the book waggling it absently as I began to speak.

"If I understand your meaning by giving me this book, you believe yourself to be *Frankenstein's* creation," I asked skeptically.

Wilmar stared in my direction, a puzzled expression on his face, I rested the book in my lap waiting, the puzzled expression however remained. Did he expect me to scream in terror or bust through the door trailing blankets in my wake? He didn't understand that I grew up watching movies like *Night of the Living Dead* on late night television or had nightmares about *Freddie Kruger, Michael Meyers* and *Jason Voorhees*. It wasn't until Barnabas introduced me to the world I was destined to become apart of that I truly knew fright for the first time.

"You mean wretch, monster or murderer don't you?" He replied bitterly. "

"No," I said unapologetically. "I meant creation."

I lifted the book showing the cover to Wilmar briefly before returning it to resting upon my lap.

"I've read this book many times and if you are who you say you are then I don't think of you as any of those things that you mentioned."

His puzzlement deepened.

"But I killed all those people," he said remorsefully.

"Yes, I know. I don't agree with what you did, but you were obviously driven to it."

Wilmar looked absolutely dumbfounded.

"This is what I know," I continued. "And please correct me if I'm wrong. You were created by an ego maniac scientist from various parts of dead people and then were subjected to a means of resurrection that is still unknown to this day. After his glorious moment of creating life, *Victor Frankenstein* shunned you as an abomination. Now as you've said your name Wilmar doesn't go with your face. That must've been a terrifying shock. Dying with one face, then waking with an entirely different one completely alien to your memories. You were vilified by the people of your day because of your unusual appearance, and when you asked your creator for a companion he refused. Then you embarked on a revengeful killing spree to rob *Victor* of all he held dear. When he was driven mad with guilt, you and *Victor* set out on an odyssey to destroy one another which led you both up here to the top of the world in which your creator died as a result of his own stupidity. Then you paddled off in hopes of destroying yourself on a funeral pyre."

I finished watching Wilmar's reaction. He remained perplex and I believed that he really didn't know how to react or respond. I again hoped he wouldn't turn into a murderous lunatic. Since I obviously had an insane streak in me a mile wide I pressed on.

"But something happened, didn't it Wilmar? Something happened that prevented you from killing yourself."

His head lowered and I thought I saw a tear trail down his cheek, but upon reflection the candlelight may have cast shadows giving that appearance.

"I tried. I came ashore many miles north of this place. There was not much in the way of wood to build my fire and that fact alone compelled me to trek inland. After a few weeks I made my way to a place that had suitable fuel for what I needed to do. I set to work building my funeral pyre in the manner of the *Viking* funeral rites." "Log upon log I cut and stacked, then when all was ready, I climbed atop the logs with a lighted torch setting the whole thing a flame. The fire raged for hours even burning the clothes from my body yet, I did not die."

He bowed his head shaking it regretfully.

"When the fire had burned down to glowing embers, I crawled from the smoldering ashes hungry and dying of thirst."

He raised his eyes searching for mine.

"I had not been killed. I had no burns upon my body. I failed trying to end my miserable life. It was as though death no longer had a hold on my mortality. As I lay there in the snow I thought that *God* was mocking me, as he has always done even before *Victor Frankenstein* made me into this," He spat bitterly.

I nodded sympathetically remaining silent as he spoke. I'm sure he's had this all bottled up inside him for more years than I could count. He like everyone else on this planet needed someone to talk too. Even though I'm somewhat childish at times and selfish, I'm a good listener knowing when to keep quiet. I figured this was one of those times. I watched him sigh then quirk up one corner of his mouth into a smile.

"By and by I overcame my hatred of *The Lord* eventually I got up from where I lay cold, wet and hungry resolving to take another chance at life."

"Wait," I said interrupting. "How long did you just lie in the snow?"

He snorted an embarrassed little laugh.

"Perhaps a week maybe longer, I am not certain. But after coming to terms with my immortality I decided the best thing for me to do was make a home here so that I would not menace humanity any longer and for over a hundred years I have,"

He smiled; relieved I think that someone actually listened to his story.

"My fur suit," - He pointed a finger to the drying furs by the fire – "Scares off everyone that comes my way which are rare occurrences. In your case though I could not in good conscious leave you to die in the snow,"

He paused thinking for a moment then a wide wry smile came to his face.

"Had I done that," he continued. "I would have deprived myself of your company and your wonderful books."

I laughed which made my ribs hurt, but I didn't care. It felt good to laugh.

"You don't get many books out this way, huh?" I asked.

"No," he said, depressed. "Being isolated from humanity has many drawbacks as well as its advantages."

He glanced in the direction of his modest library. His expression turned thoughtful however as he looked back to me.

"It's amusing," he continued. "I was worried that you would have acted like all the others so many years ago. That you would look upon me with horror shrinking away afraid and terrified."

He grew silent turning away from me.

"The only thing that I am afraid of is that you won't be letting me have any of that wonderfully smelling strudel," I replied, smiling.

Then for added effect I tucked the bed sheet into my t-shirt under my chin. Wilmar turned back letting out a deep belly laugh as he returned to the pan of strudel serving it out on two metal plates. In no time he was beside me again handing me one of the plates settling into the seat beside the bed. We tore into our pastry as though these were the only two pieces of strudel left in the world. I've never been fond of strudel, - chocolate of any kind being my favorite sweets - this was very good and I told him so. There was a berry flavor I didn't recognize, but it tasted an awful lot like raspberry.

"My mother was a wonderful baker, she taught me everything I know," His face brightened at some remembrance.

"She taught me to read and write three languages as well," a melancholy settled over him.

"She was taken far too young, perhaps if she had lived a bit longer I would have not come to this,"

His shoulders sagging again then I said.

"You do realize that things have changed in the world and now a days you wouldn't create the sensation that you would have so many years ago"

He raised his eyes to mine. This time I saw tears in his eyes.

"Really?" He asked, hope in his tone.

"Yes," I said chuckling though not in a mean way. "By today's standards you're tame when it comes to things that scare people. More people are afraid of the tax man than you."

He remained silent, yet interested as I pressed on, feeling glad that my foot hadn't found its usual resting place, my mouth.

"Even your size wouldn't cause people to take a second look. The world is made up of people of all shapes and sizes with wild hair color, piercings and tattoos. This world is vastly different than the one you knew. Information is at one's fingertips and technology, you'd marvel at what the world has accomplished."

Keying in on my words his eyes lit up. Wilmar stood moving to the table where my belongings were neatly placed. He picked up something then hurried back over to me. He took his seat once again opening his hand. I smiled when I saw what he had gotten.

"Would you tell me what this is," he asked eagerly. "I thought it might have been some sort of mirror or cigarette case."

"This," I said taking the item from his hand. "Is an *iPod Touch*,"

I pressed the top button, turning the screen to him. The little *Apple icon* appeared, his eyes growing wide with fascination. When it finished booting up I slid the "locked" bar revealing the home screen.

"It plays music,"

I pressed the music icon then scrolled down the play list selecting something at random. *"Don't answer me,"* by *The Alan Parsons Project* began playing through the speaker. The volume was low because I mainly use my ear buds, so I turned it up.

He listened with childlike awe, I wasn't entirely sure he appreciated retro eighties music.

"It plays movies," I continued.

"What are movies," Wilmar asked intrigued.

I smiled backing out of the music app selecting the movie one instead. I pressed the first movie I saw, *Jaws*. I turned the screen lengthwise so the movie would appear in wide screen. The movie was queued to the part where *Sheriff Brody* backs into the cabin of the *Orca* while staring fixedly out the window at a shark fin approaching the boat in the distance. Without looking at *Quint* - who is working on a fishing reel - *Sheriff Brody*, played by *Roy Scheider* delivered the now famous line, *"You're gonna need a bigger boat,"* Wilmar's eyes grew even larger as a giddy sound of delight passed his lips.

"And you can even read books,"

I backed out of the movie app and clicked on one of the three reading apps I use off and on. The book I'd been reading - *the Hitchhiker's Guide to the Galaxy by Douglas Adams* - popped up and I began leafing through the pages by way of swiping across the screen with my finger.

"See," I said.

Wilmar's childlike curiosity got the best of him. He placed his plate of strudel on the dresser, gently taking the *iPod* from my hands. I looked on with satisfaction that I was able to at least repay him in some small measure for his kindness. The *iPod* looked tiny in his large hands that he took great care not to damage.

"How many books are contained within this device," he asked excitedly.

"Well," I began. "It's got quite a bit of space - I stayed clear of technical specs figuring it would be lost on him - so you could store roughly a few hundred books. More if you dumped your music and movies I suppose."

"How do I find the book selection," he asked pressing the display like an inquisitive kid.

I briefly explained the *iPod's* functions, which he picked up quickly going through the list of novels. It wasn't a huge library only a few dozen books but there were enough to give Wilmar hours of enjoyment.

"The glass face is so tiny," he said unperturbed.

"Yes it is," I replied. "If you come back with us to *Detroit* my *iPad* would be more suited to the size of your hands."

Wilmar halted, his eyes deliberately meeting mine. He considered my words for the minutest of moments and then reluctantly handed the *iPod* back to me.

"I cannot return to the world of men."

"It was only a suggestion," I sighed as I pushed the *iPod* back into his hands. "I give this to you as a gift for your generosity and help, it is the least I could do."

He took it gratefully, like I'd given him a bar of gold, though I detected a tinge of suspicion lurking in his eyes.

"Thank you,"

"You're welcome," I replied. "You don't need to worry about charging it as long as you leave it in the case. It has a charm upon it that keeps the battery charged."

Sleep rapped upon my door of consciousness again. It was probably a result of the great food coupled with the exertion of talking or it could've been my body's way of combating the headache I could feel rising behind my eyes. The pain, a dull achy throb, grew more painful the longer I sat up. I closed my eyes resting my head back on the pillow. I felt Wilmar's eye searching, trying to get a read on me. After a few moments he broke the silence in a soft voice.

"I appreciate what you are offering me and it is a very tempting thought... But it is better for everyone if I stay here away from man."

I regarded him with half opened eyes. He stood placing the *iPod* inside a shirt pocket then collected the plates from dessert. His eyes fell on mine once again.

"Rest now... You need to gather your strength for when you are ready to return to your friends."

He turned heading into the kitchen area. My heavy eyes closed as the haze of sleep approached. No thoughts were in my head, which was unusual for me, I was just numb, tired. Sleep finally took me and I was happy that it did.

# Chapter 20

I didn't know how long I'd slept this time, the only thing I knew for certain was that I hadn't dreamt at all. Merlin hadn't visited me either. I half expected him to dispense more of his *Yoda-like* Wizard advice. Maybe he was resting as well. Perhaps the stew put him into a long overdue food coma. Did Merlin even need to sleep? He was a spirit after all; did spirits have earthly needs like sleep? That was definitely a question for another time; right at that moment I didn't want to think about anything thought provoking. My head was pain free, I felt tempting fate was a horrible idea. My eyes lazily scanned the room.

I was still in bed though, today - whatever day it happened to be - the cabin seemed quite and lonely. I heard none of the sounds from the previous night. No crackling fire. No wind buffeting the exterior of the cabin. No simmering pot of stew. My things were gone from the table. I spied my backpack neatly packed waiting near the front door, my chainmail draped over it. Light spilled in from tiny windows on three sides of the cabin, which looked somehow smaller in the daylight. The cabin however didn't lose any of its homey feel. The fire in the hearth had burned down to smoldering red embers. The temperature had plummeted considerably within the cabin, judging by the chill I felt pressing against my exposed neck and cheeks; it had to be around fifty degrees. I didn't see Wilmar anywhere. The place was far too small to have a place to hide. It was just a box with no closets or other doors to speak of. I assumed he'd be reading something on the *iPod* or rereading one of the three books I had with me. He however was nowhere to be seen and I noticed the furs were gone.

    I sat up, - tried to at any rate - my body wasting no time in reminding me that I got my ass kicked by a bunch of Yeti's. Pain moved through me like a jolt of electricity, but the pain itself was far less sharp, almost like I had been resting a few weeks instead of a few days. At least I thought I'd been here only a few days, I wasn't sure. I may have been here a month for all I knew. I would have to ask Wilmar when he appeared again. A feeling of unease settled upon me realizing my host was absent. My mind began thinking of irrational unpleasant possibilities. For instance, Wilmar outside this very minute digging a shallow grave in the frozen earth for one maimed Wizard. Then again there's the possibility that there's a shed near the cabin where my host was in the process of selecting a suitable gardening implement in which to kill me, I've always had a vivid imagination. On more than one occasion I've let my imagined terrors get the best of me, scaring the living crap out of me.

Just then, right in the midst of my silly musings almost as if he'd heard my thoughts, the cabin door opened and in walked Wilmar. Dressed in his furs, lugging an armful of freshly split wood for the fire. He glanced in my direction giving me a stone-faced smile.

"You're awake I see," he said mechanically. "Good, you will be able to make an early start for your friends encampment."

He moved to the fireplace, opening a worn wooden box with squeaky hinges to the right of the hearth. He dropped the armload of wood into the box with an echoing thud. He fed the fire a few logs before dropping the lid back down removing his coat. I got the distinct feeling all was not well today,

"Is there something wrong Wilmar," I asked cautiously. "Is there anything that I can do?"

"Yes, you could leave," he said curtly hanging up his furs.

That was fairly direct and to the point. Given the fact he could probably crush me like an empty beer can, this was a great opportunity for me to make myself ready and get out of his hair.

"OK," I said, pulling the covers off me.

I can't convey to you the intense unpleasant sensation that met my exposed skin, but it was flipping cold in that cabin. Goose flesh erupted on my skin and my teeth began chattering almost immediately. As I wrapped my arms about me in a vain attempt to coax heat into my body I noticed that my bandaged arm was no longer bandaged. I moved it around testing the tenderness of it. My arm may not have been broken any longer, but it felt like I'd been through a rigorous game of punch buggy at the *Volkswagen* assembly plant.

"I do not wish to be unfriendly toward you young man but this is how it must be," he continued. "Our talk last night awakened desires in me I have not experienced in ages and should I return to the world of man, I have no doubt that what has already happened to me will happen again. The world will never accept a monster despite your assurances."

I nodded not sure exactly what to say, then looking in his direction I simply said.

"I understand."

I turned my attention to my clothes, which were cleaned as well as neatly folded on the seat of a wooden chair Wilmar had pulled up beside me while I was sleeping. I kicked my legs off the side of the high bed dangling them over the edge. My feet weren't able to touch the floor. Resolved in my desire to get the day started I slid off the bed, my rear facing outward. I was surprised when my feet hit the floor; the bed rose to my waist. I actually smiled. I felt like a child getting out of the orphanage bed I slept in for many years. The beds in the orphanage were made for adults; there was no such thing as kid sized beds for the poor when I was growing up. Sister Mari took what she received in donations as well as cast off items people would give to her making good use of whatever it was. I credit my agility to that orphanage bed. In order to get into it, I'd have to make a running start then vault like a gymnast. That way was much easier and a hell of a lot more fun.

Oh, did I mention that the wood floor felt like a sheet of frozen lake ice under my bare feet? I reached for my clothes stiffly pulling them on, my body shivering uncontrollably. I watched Wilmar take up a metal poker coaxing the fire back to life. I glanced over to the pot bellied stove relieved to see that the metal still glowed a faint orange. I grabbed my things moving over to that oasis of heat in order to put on my remaining clothes. I became acutely aware of my aches and pains as I went through the simple motions of getting dressed. The beginning twinges of a headache I'd hoped to avoid pulsed faintly at my temples. My exertions coupled with my shivering weren't helping matters either.

I pulled on my heavy sweater, after a few moments began to feel the shivering subside. Wilmar watched me obliquely as I looked searchingly around the cabin, my heart sunk as I realized there wasn't one.

"I have to go outside don't I," I asked in a deflated tone.

The faintest of smiles played on his face as he gave a curt nod.

"You may use the chamber pot under the bed," he said gesturing to my aforementioned resting place. "You are not accustomed to this rustic life are you?" He added.

That idea didn't appeal to me either. I didn't want him watching as I did my business. I think my expression spoke volumes because Wilmar chuckled as he stood placing the poker back in its holder. If I had to go only number one it wouldn't have been an issue. Sighing, I resigned myself to what I had to do. I moved over snatching my coat off the peg, shrugging into it. I turned back to Wilmar.

"How far from the cabin is the out house," I asked.

"About twenty five yards around back," He replied, then added. "There is a path freshly cleared this morning that will lead you right to it."

I nodded squatting next to my pack. I brushed the chainmail to one side; it made a slithering metallic sound as it hit the wood floor. Opening my pack I picked up my protective shirt thrusting it into the bag. I searched for the item I would desperately need for what I needed to do, a roll of two-ply toilet paper. I stood feeling a tad dizzy, too much blood rushing to my head. I needed to eat something. I turned thrusting open the door, cold air hit me like a two by four to the bridge of the nose. I inhaled a deep frigid steadying breath, hoping to God that my privates survived the experience. Pulling the hood up over my head I set out to do my business.

I don't think many people realize what an awful experience it is going to the bathroom out in nature, far away from the comforts of our modern society. My idea of camping or roughing it is a lodge with electricity, an almost endless supply of hot running water and of course room service. There are some who'd argue what I described wasn't camping at all, which I would have to staunchly disagree with. The lodge would be out in a forest, which is the main ingredient in camping. What's wrong with having the comforts of home when you're roughing it? Birds have their nests, bears have their dens and beavers have their dams. Why can't I have my eggs, bacon and hash browns served in a climate controlled hotel room? Am I spoiled to the modern way of life? Hell yes and proud of it too!

I returned to the cabin finding Wilmar seated at the table eating something from a bowl with a spoon. My teeth chattered so rapidly they sounded like someone feverishly pecking away at an old electric *Smith Corona Typewriter*. I tossed the roll of toilet paper onto my pack, stiffly shuffling over to stand in front of the fireplace. I thought to myself, a nice shot of bourbon or whiskey would've helped my situation. Unfortunately, I didn't have either in my pack. I was also fairly certain Wilmar wasn't a drinking man, so there wouldn't be any spirits in the cabin.

"There is porridge on the stove if you are hungry," I heard Wilmar say behind me.

I turned obliquely in his direction giving a stiff nod. I didn't dare open my mouth for fear my chattering teeth would shear off the tip of my tongue. I contemplated my situation as my body shook off the chill. I'd eventually have to brave the cold once again. Not a thought I was happy thinking, then another thought occurred to me as thoughts often do when I tried to avoid unpleasant situations or tasks. Why did I have to go to them? Why couldn't they make the trip to me? It was a good idea that'd buy me a few hours of warmth at least. I knew Wilmar didn't like visitors, going to great lengths to preserve his privacy. In this instance however I felt there was an outside chance that he might go for the idea if I pose it correctly.

"Barnabas should've figured out where I was with a spell by now," I said to no one in particular through chattering teeth, hoping Wilmar was listening, which I was certain he was.

"I'm surprised he hasn't come to find me yet."

"He cannot locate you with magical or mortal means, not here at any rate," Wilmar answered confidently.

My body warmed sufficiently enough the chattering of my teeth had subsided for me to speak more clearly without fear of amputation. I turned facing Wilmar, not really to answer him, but more importantly to warm my backside. It'd taken the brunt of the cold weather while doing my duty - no pun intended -

"What do you mean," I asked.

"There are stone pillars that resemble trees encircling this place. They create a shield and masking barrier that prevents anyone or anything from venturing too close. If anyone does find their way through the barrier, the magic spells gently compel them to move on never knowing this place was even here." He said, raising his left arm.

The bracelet was a simple flat braided ring of gold that fit snugly around Wilmar's wrist.

"This bracelet allows me to pass through the barrier at will and anything that is with me is protected," he continued lowering his arm and then went back to eating his porridge.

That sounded like some strong magic he had working here. He wasn't a Wizard, I was sure of that, so that could mean only one of two things. First that this barrier was here when he came to this place long ago, which I admit could've been possible. Unusual things get found all the time, but in this case however that scenario was highly unlikely. Wilmar needed a bracelet in order to use the barrier field thingy. He may have found the barrier, but finding the bracelet and knowing how to employ it was a long shot at best. What I felt was more plausible, was that someone helped him create it. The only burning question was who? I knew that Bialek was in the area; he was possibly the Wizard who created it. Bialek was after all just as powerful as Barnabas, this barrier sounded like something he would've been able to accomplish. Defensive magic was Bialek's specialty.

Bialek helped Barnabas with complex defensive spells on a regular basis. I was fairly certain that everyone in the Wizarding Community of consequence knew of Bialek's talents and that he was a recluse that liked privacy. If it wasn't Bialek that made it, then who?

"That sounds like a pretty useful thing," I said impressed.

"Who helped you make it," I asked uneasily.

Wilmar straightened in his chair puffing out his chest, in a proud unwavering tone he answered.

"My Wizard friend that lives just over the ridge a few miles from here, he created it. I helped put the pillars in place."

A deep spine-freezing chill ran through me despite the heat from the fire warming my behind. Wilmar didn't know. He didn't know that Bialek, his good wizard friend was dead. Christ, this was one of those key moments that had to be handled delicately. I've never been any good at dealing with emotional moments, deaths, births, infidelity, bad news about a medical diagnosis, sick or dead pets. I never learned or never wanted to learn how to tell people unpleasant things. I grew up orphaned. I never knew my parents, nor have I ever mourned for the death of my mother or dwelt on the fact that my father left her when she was pregnant with me. I'm great at burying my feelings deep down inside myself. I suppose you could make the argument that I am emotionally stunted, but I bet there isn't any one reading this that wouldn't rather take a pointy stick to the eye than tell someone that his or her good friend has just died. My body tensed before I spoke. It's always best to beat a hasty retreat instead of being pounded into a red mushy stain on the hardwood floor.

"Would your friend happen to be named Hans Bialek?"

Wilmar smiled broadly.

"Yes," he said. "That is his name."

He dug into his porridge once more, lowering his head to take the mouthful, then paused. He raised his head, his eyes meeting mine. I watched as the smile faded.

"How do you know his name?" He asked as I watched a bit of porridge drip from the spoon back into the bowl.

"He is why my friends and I are here in this forest. I hate to have to tell you this, but your friend Hans Bialek is dead... He was murdered." I answered uneasily ready to bolt from the cabin through one of the walls.

I couldn't read any emotion in him; he just sat unmoving, not doing anything except breathing. After what seemed like an eternity, tears welled up in his dark brown eyes. He sobbed only once. Wilmar place the spoon into the bowl then pulled a red handkerchief from his pants pocket. He dabbed tears from his eyes, honking his nose into it before returning it to his pocket. Without warning he raised his hand clenching it into a fist bringing it down violently onto the surface of the table. The force of the blow was so great that the table split in the center about an inch or two wide. His bowl of porridge rose above the table five to six inches into the air before clattering back down into an overturned mess. It may have been my imagination, but I kid you not I felt the force of the blow travel through the hardwood floor under my feet.

Wilmar pushed back his chair noisily on the wood floor standing. His eyes met mine with something resembling absolute resolve in them. Then asked.

"Do you know who is responsible for this?"

"Not yet," I replied. "That's why all of us have come here to determined how and why it happened."

He gave a nod.

"His apprentice the young girl, Olivia... Is she safe?" He asked earnestly. If I didn't know any better I'd swear that he had feelings for her.

"We don't know if she is alive or dead,"

He pressed his lips into a thin line. His brows knitting deep furrows into his forehead, then the expression was gone.

"And what of the little Elf servant, Tillander?" He asked concerned.

"He's alright, a little beat up but alright." I said and then added. "He is safe and with us."

"Thank The Lord," he replied.

His hand moved to his chest clutching something under his shirt. A crucifix was my first thought. His eyes closed as his lips moved in a silent prayer. After a few seconds Wilmar moved over to the dresser removing the pitcher filled with water from the basin. He stalked over to the fireplace kneeling. Wilmar emptied the entire pitcher onto the fire drowning the flames. Billows of gray smoke issued from the popping logs as the fire snuffed reluctantly out. Wilmar stood placing the pitcher on the mantle facing me.

"I will be coming with you. Get your things," he said in a curt tone.

I didn't have to be told twice, I did as he said and did it quickly.

# Chapter 21

Wilmar and I trekked for nearly an hour and a half heading toward the spot where the others were encamped. That included the time it took to get our things together before we left his cabin. The route we were taking was far from direct, which sort of sucked, but it had the virtue of presenting me with a great view of some of the most beautiful scenery that I ever saw. The sun shone through a wide column of patchwork clouds moving lazily to the east. The sky was a brilliant topaz blue; it had the appearance of a calm sea inviting a person to dive in for a swim. I think the snow however was probably the most beautiful thing I had experienced so far that morning. I know I've said on multiple occasions how I hate snow with a passion, but even the most hating heart would've stopped for this breathtaking site. Snow covered the ground in uneven drifts; tree branches strained under the weight of a heavy mantling yet everything glittered like a king's ransom of diamonds. Wherever I looked it was as though mirages resembling piles of those precious stones were conjured by some mischievous winter sprite to fool me into filling my empty pockets. I was glad however that I had my ski goggles down over my eyes; otherwise I believe the continued exposure to such a sight would've caused me to go blind.

    Wilmar led the way cutting a path through the deep snow. Drifts of the fine powder rose to thigh height on him, for me however they were nearly waist high. His long pondering strides bulldozed through the snow making it far easier to follow in his wake without snowshoes. Mine had succumbed to an untimely end a day or so ago as I may have already said, so I appreciated his efforts immensely. Wilmar, dressed in his dark furs with his own pair of antique ski goggles riding on his forehead seemed to not be affected by nature's glaring wonder. He'd lived up here for so many years that I assumed his eyes had become acclimated to the blinding brilliance of the snow. The goggles may have been for show or some misunderstood *Steam Punk* fashion statement. He had the appearance of a great grizzly bear trudging through the snow on two legs. I wondered how many hunters had taken pot shots at him over the years mistaking him for that formidable predator. Then again, anyone who coveted his or her privacy as much as Wilmar knew how to stay out of sight. We traveled roughly two miles or maybe a little more, the walk however didn't tire me in the least, it just made me bored. For me, being bored ultimately leads to the smart assed side of my personality becoming more prominent than it normally would. All the mental guards residing in my head take a nap or something leaving smartass guy free to roam making life more interesting.

"Are we there yet," I asked in a whiny exasperated tone.

Silence.

Obviously Wilmar wasn't familiar with the etiquette of this particular game. He'd missed the introduction of the automobile along with the subsequent lifestyle and culture that had sprung up around that particular invention. No drive-in movies, no drive-thru fast food joints, no car washes, no arguing over a parking space. He's probably never stopped at a truck-stop to eat unhealthy greasy food or used a bathroom that reeked of urine after decades of use and poor cleaning. All of this meant I needed to help familiarize him with such things. It was my duty after all.

"I'm cold and hungry and I have to pee really bad," I said in a more exaggerated annoying tone.

Silence again. He did turn back in my direction however, glaring.

"How much longer do we have to walk out here? Can you carry me? I don't think I can go much farther, my legs feel like boiled spaghetti." I said in the same tone as before, but ended the statement with a mock pleading sob. I will concede that "smart assed guy" was more "annoying guy" right now.

Wilmar wheeled around grabbing the front of my coat lifting my pack laden form off the ground a good three feet. Fabric and zippers strained under the force exerted by his meaty fist. If I hadn't been prepared for some sort of response I may have soiled my snow pants. Thank the Lord for my strong bowel and prostate control. He pulled me close until we were literally nose-to-nose. The scowl on his face said everything; he was in no way interested in my little game. Wilmar held me in his unwavering grip until he felt that his point had been made and then he huffed out a growl putting me down.

I waved a hand in front of my face pretending to waft away his bad breath. Adding a cough or two to add drama to my performance. Wilmar simply turned continuing his way toward the encampment.

"I guess you've never heard of *Tic Tacs* so far out in a place like this," I said falling in step behind him once again.

"Now that you are on the mend and have found your voice again, I find you quite annoying," Wilmar said peering obliquely back in my direction.

I couldn't help but smile. I'm a cut up by nature or smartass if you wish to judge me for my actions thus far. Perhaps my carefree cynical manner is precisely why Barnabas is a harsh disciplinarian. Well there's that and he's British. I absolutely hate somber situations or grumpy people or anyone that doesn't want to talk. I like to engage people in conversation and if possible make a person smile or laugh. I enjoy seeing people happy. It warms my heart making me feel good in the process. Before you start pointing out the obvious or lecture me that annoying someone isn't the best way to get someone to smile or laugh I'd like to say in my defense that I completely agree with that assessment. You're forgetting one important aspect of my personality. I have a mischievous streak about a mile wide. Besides, Wilmar made me get up out of a nice warm toasty bed to take this hike in the frigid air, seriously he had this coming.

"Wait until you get to know me," I answered. "I'll show you levels of annoyance that you never thought possible."

"I would rather be stricken with an incapacitating case of the Palsy." He said through what sounded like a wide smile.

"That's harsh," I replied. "I might actually be a good friend if you only got to know me."

Wilmar turned abruptly, confronting me.

"I already had a good friend and from what you're telling me he's dead! I don't need another, especially a friend like you!" He bellowed emphasizing each clipped word.

I had no words to respond to his heated torrent. When they finally came Wilmar didn't give me the chance to say them. Something caught his attention. He placed a big hand over my mouth silencing me as he moved closer, hunching over me in a protective stance.

"Be silent," he whispered.

His head darted around scanning quickly in different directions. Without warning Wilmar forced me to the ground. A black blur the size of a small horse slammed into him. Whatever hit Wilmar sent both he and the form itself tumbling away from me. It wasn't until I was able to get to a kneeling position to survey the situation that I realized a huge black wolf had attacked Wilmar. It took my mind only a few seconds more to realize the wolf was Race and the Werewolf was putting up a terrific fight. He had pinned Wilmar face down savagely biting at his neck. When the big man moved to get an arm around Race, the Werewolf slithered out of the hold reversing direction then darting back in for a bite at Wilmar's arm or hand.

I spied another form emerging from the tree line to my left, moving fast. This new form raced headlong toward Wilmar struggling to get to his feet. A glint of something metallic in each of its hands, the form leapt a car's length away from the big man landing on Wilmar's back. It was Bart. His arms and hands blurred repeatedly in lightning fast strikes. His knives cut deep into the back of Wilmar's fur coat, tufts of hair flew up with every vicious stroke. Race it appeared was the distraction. I felt more than heard the growl of anger that came from Wilmar. Snow actually fell from the tree branches as the echo boomed away from the battle. Wilmar threw Bart off his back getting to his feet. He then pivoted out of the way of Race's attack. Wilmar was extremely quick and agile for someone of his size and bulk. Using his right hand, he grabbed the Werewolf by the scruff of his neck. He whirled Race around in a wide circle over his head like a wrestler ready to body slam his opponent into the mat. He'd struck Bart in the process however, who'd rushed in for another swipe at Wilmar. The blow struck Bart square in the chest sending both he and Race rocketing into a snowdrift thirty feet away. A yelp of agonized pain came from Race as he landed hard on the frozen ground. He and Race flailed drunkenly attempting to get to their feet. Wilmar turned with a murderous look in his eyes to the direction of a nearby cluster of trees.

I looked on dumbfounded; I became acutely aware that I wasn't alone. I glanced to my right; there the beautiful form of Adrianna knelt beside me. She watched the scene as well. She quirked a smile then looked into my eyes.

"Too bad we don't have any popcorn, this is a really good show." She said in a whimsical tone. "Much better than the rubbish they put on television these days."

She placed a hand on my shoulder inching closer to me.

"Are you alright... Can you walk?" She asked concern in her voice.

Her hand moved to the side of my face. Her thumb affectionately stroked the skin of my cheek. For a second there I was distracted as my eyes regarded hers. I came back quickly to the situation at hand however.

"Yes, but what are they doing?" I asked scrambling to my feet.

Her hand dropped to her side.

"Saving you of course," she replied puzzled.

"They're going to get themselves killed," I yelled hurriedly as I plodded heavily through the snow moving to get between Wilmar and my two misguided rescuers. Adrianna jogged effortlessly at my side, backwards.

Show off.

"We must get you away from this creature," she said. "He seems to be extremely formidable and dangerous."

"He's not a creature," I said, heat in my voice. "He's only dangerous because they attacked him! You're all making a terrible mistake!"

Adrianna regarded me shaking her head skeptically then fell into step at my side running forward this time. It was difficult enough keeping my footing in this snow. I couldn't count how many times I nearly slipped, tripped or skidded. Luckily Adrianna was there to keep me from looking awkward or uncoordinated. Wilmar wrapped his powerful arms around the trunk of a tree about the thickness of a telephone pole. He braced himself giving his upper body a quick brutal jerk snapping off the thirty-foot tree four feet from the ground. He turned shifting the massive tree in his grip lifting it above his head like a power weightlifter. Wilmar lunged forward hurling the massive tree in the direction of Race and Bart. My breath caught as I tracked the trees arc falling short of its target by six feet.

"My God," Adrianna gasp.

Adrianna changed course heading for Race and Bart fumbling around in the snow. They moved like two drunks trying to find a car in an empty parking lot. It appeared that Wilmar rang their bells worse than I thought. Shaking the cobwebs from their minds was proving to be a difficult task. Race was in his human form, which meant he didn't have enough sense to keep his wolf shape. I moved to intercept Wilmar. His rage had blinded his reason. Missing his targets may have stoked his anger because he was now stalking toward Race and Bart. I didn't even know if Wilmar saw me standing in front of him. I searched the ground for something, anything to help me get Wilmar to change his focus off them.

At first I thought of just pelting him with snowballs, but decided against that idea mainly because there was no sense in making him angrier. The closer he plodded toward me the faster my heart pumped. Then an idea came to me, I had my *Colt* pistol holstered to my leg. I could fire off a few rounds in his direction possibly drawing his attention, but if I missed I could hit him and a bullet wound out here might prove life threatening. Then again since Wilmar was fire proof I had to assume that he was also bullet proof. If I shot him there's no telling how he'd react. Imagine a rhinoceros getting stung by an *African* bee, not an encouraging picture. It was then that I realized I was still holding my battle staff.

With hastily mustered resolve I planted my feet raising my staff high, then driving the end of it into the snow striking the frozen ground beneath while uttering a simple yet effective attention getting spell called *Thunder Crack*.

The spell does exactly what the name implies. When a Wizard - such as myself - utters the spell then slams the end of his staff down on any solid surface a loud echoing wall of sound is produced getting everyone's attention. It's a great trick for parties and compelling a room full of squabbling Wizards to shut the hell up. On this particular occasion I put too much force in the spell because it bowled Wilmar off his feet.

I turned back observing Adrianna getting to her feet, a deep-rooted scowl casting daggers in my direction. My spell apparently knocked her off her feet getting snow in her expensive boots. I shrugged apologetically turning back to Wilmar. He was on his feet again; anger that had been directed at Race and Bart was now fixed upon me. A balled fist the size of a cantaloupe was drawn back for a punch destined to flatten my face like a pancake... Oh, did I mention he was less than an arm's length away?

I brought my staff up defensively as I closed my eyes. I didn't want to be witness to the hurt Wilmar was going to lay on me. I'd rather it happen quickly knocking me senseless. No pain, just out cold. The pain I could deal with if and when I woke up. It was at that moment I heard a spell uttered deep in the recesses of my mind, feeling a pressure in the front of my head, a pressure similar to an intense sinus headache. I wasn't able to hear the words of the spell being uttered, but I could feel magic welling up inside my body then being channeled through my right arm into my staff. A long slow creep of something warm dripped from my right nostril.

The pressure in my head became so great pain erupted behind my eyes and I collapsed to my hands and knees dropping my staff. My eyes, clinched tight in pain reluctantly opened to the sight of blood patting onto the snow dripping freely from both nostrils. The contrast of my red steaming blood against the stark white of the snow was striking.

Merlin, I thought.

It was the only logical explanation for what was happening. Being essentially a spirit he could use my body and magic freely. All he'd have to do is supplant my consciousness for his own or what is more commonly known as possession. Except, I was aware of myself still having control over my body and it's actions. So whatever he was doing was something entirely new to me. It was an effort to turn my eyes up but I forced myself to do it. What I saw gave me a new sense of respect for the ancient spirit that resided in my head. A clear quivering sphere of energy not unlike a droplet of water only more massive hovered a few inches off the ground. Inside the sphere, Wilmar with a surprised look on his face was frozen in time. Not even an eyelash moved. My head felt heavy. I could no longer hold it up at that angle. The next thing I knew was that I was staring blankly at the snow beneath me.

Deep in my mind I heard a satisfied "humph" followed by "Pray, one day hence thou might be as skilled as I," in a thick *Shakespearean* accent.

"Show off," I muttered incoherently unimpressed.

I could sense Merlin's grin at my wise-ass remark. Then - as though they were never there - the pressure and pain in my head simply vanished.

"It would be wise my young friend to eat something," Merlin said. Then he added, "It will help with the effects of my intrusion into your conscious mind."

The bleeding slowed to a few droplets then stopped all together. Crunching snow under heavy footfalls sounded as someone came near to me. I felt a large hand that could only have been Wilmar's resting gently on my back as he knelt beside me.

"Are you alright Solomon," he asked concerned?

I nodded, not knowing whether I would vomit if I had opened my mouth to speak. My head spun with an unpleasant dizzying sensation. I had to keep my mind focused on anything other than that feeling.

"Get away from him," Adrianna growled closing the distance with Wilmar at a high rate of speed.

Without turning in her direction I raised my hand in a staying gesture. Wilmar's hand tensed on my back in anticipation of her attack. Luckily Adrianna understood my meaning slowing her approach finally stopping about ten feet away from Wilmar and I.

"He's a friend," I said in a dazed raspy voice. "And I really don't want to get this started up again."

I forced my head to turn so I could look up into Wilmar's eyes.

"Are you alright," I asked warily glancing over to the tree lying in the snow.

Wilmar's eyes followed the direction of mine. A subtle hint of shame entered into his bearing, then his eyes sought out mine once again.

"Yes," he said after a silence. "The anger is gone." "One of God's messengers came to me. He told me that you all are friends and that I should stop this foolishness."

He finished by making the sign of the cross reverently bowing his head then placing his hand on the lump under his shirt. I on the other hand blinked skeptically.

"One of God's messengers," I asked.

"An angel," he replied, "One of our Father's messengers,"

"What did he look like?"

Adrianna inched closer to us intrigued no doubt by the topic of conversation.

"He had a long white beard tucked into a golden sash round his middle. He was dressed all in blue carrying a long wooden staff."

"A long white beard?" I said aloud as realization dawned.

"Yes," Wilmar continued.

Merlin not only stopped Wilmar's attack but he also projected his image into his head to calm him down. That took a huge amount of skill and effort with magic to accomplish that. I was fairly certain that Barnabas couldn't have done that and he is one of the more powerful Wizards I know. Merlin had not only been a big help to me in recent days, he has effectively saved my life twice.

"Thank you for your help," I thought as respectfully as I could. In reply I heard a satisfied, "You are welcome."

Wilmar and Adrianna helped me onto my unsteady legs. Race and Bart were up moving albeit slowly over to where we stood. Wilmar pulled a cloth from his coat pocket pressing it to my nose.

"Thank you," I said gratefully.

I glanced over to Adrianna.

"This blood isn't bothering you is it," I asked.

She shifted her weight onto one hip obviously insulted by my question.

"I'm over a thousand years old Sol, it'd take significantly more than a few drops of blood from you to send me into a feeding frenzy. If that were the case I would have sucked you dry in my office," She said in a wry tone.

It didn't take long for that childish side of my brain to key in on the more important words she'd said. Which caused a smile to erupt on my face. However, I decided to keep my childish sexual innuendos to myself.

I cleared my throat letting the smile fade, as my eyes moved to my would-be rescuers. They looked more focused now, both glaring petulantly in Wilmar's direction. He appeared to be completely unfazed by the daggers they were casting in his direction. He did after all take a measure of them both, finding them wanting.

"Guys I would suggest you just calm down," I said admonishingly.

"I'd like for you all to meet Wilmar," I said gesturing at the man in question.

"I don't know if he's a friend just yet, but he is at least an ally and he saved my life. So I want you to show him the respect that you would show me." Then I added.

"Otherwise, I'm going to sit down over there on that uprooted tree trunk and watch him kick your asses,"

Bart and Race glanced over to the place I indicated, a sobering expression shown on their faces as Wilmar shot them both a smug yet confident look clenching his hands into tight fists for added effect. His rough powerful hands making a well oiled leathery creaking sound further punctuating the threat.

Bart was the first to speak.

"I am Bartholomew, Miss Thorne's personal assistant," he said.

"You are both Vampires are you not," Wilmar asked curiously.

"We are," Adrianna chimed in. "Is that a problem for you giant?"

Wilmar shook his head then said.

"No Miss Thorne, but I will pray for your souls."

Wilmar looked in Races direction.

"And you are a Werewolf, yes?" Wilmar asked.

"Yep, Race is the name, howling is my game,"

Race looked Wilmar over, smiling.

"You look like a big old *Sherman Tank*... Mind if I call you Tank?"

"No, my name is Wilmar," Wilmar said flatly.

Race's amiable smile faded as quickly as it had appeared.

Wilmar leaned down close to me placing a hand to the side of his mouth whispering.

"What is a tank," he asked.

I grinned as I replied. "I'll tell you later."

I handed Wilmar back his hanky now stained with a bit of my blood. He took it stuffing it in one of his pockets then he removed his coat. Bart moved toward him. Wilmar turned his coat around to survey the damage Bart's blades had done to it. His coat probably looked like the arm of an expensive couch right after a cantankerous cat got finished sharpening its claws on it.

"My apologies about your coat, I didn't know at the time you were an ally." Bart said, no emotions of regret or apology in his tone.

"Your blades it would seem, need to be sharpened," Wilmar replied turning the coat for all to see.

His coat didn't have a mark on it. No slashes or cuts of any kind even though Bart went to town on it, viciously slicing into it with his twin blades. I turned back to the spot Bart had attacked Wilmar. There were still tufts of fur evident dancing on a light breeze over the well-trodden snow. Bart's expression was comprised of disbelief with a hint of puzzlement; in fact we all had that sort of expression on our faces. In the midst of the silence that followed I caught a distant echo of pompous laughter. I looked from each person in turn realizing it didn't originate from any of them. Then the peel of laughter grew louder.

Merlin.

Not only did he stop Wilmar's attack, calming him down with the angel appearing illusion, he also repaired the big man's coat, a minor yet impressive feat. It would seem that all the stories I'd read about the person so many people referred to as the First Wizard were true or at least based in fact. Merlin cast three complicated spells in as many seconds and he didn't even break a sweat. OK... Yes technically I agree that because Merlin was now a spirit residing inside my brain he was incapable of breaking a sweat, but you know what I mean. It took next to no effort to pull those spells off. It occurred to me that Merlin just might be the equivalent of what *Mozart* was to music or what *Michael Jordan* was to basketball.

"God works in mysterious ways," Wilmar said through a wide knowing smile.

I didn't have the heart to tell him what actually happened. That's one thing I couldn't do to him or anyone for that matter. Which was to place doubt in their belief structure. *God* may have had a hand in what was going on; then again he may have not. I live in the supernatural world. A world filled with dangerous magical creatures, strange places, peculiar objects and powerful immortal beings that defy description. A world well over ninety-five percent of this planet's population doesn't even know exists. I've ridden dragons, dueled other Wizards, danced with Elves, arm wrestled Trolls, haggled with Goblins, played tug of war with Werewolves and most recently I've been tempted by a Vampire. However, in my twenty plus years I have yet to meet an Angel. That in no way means they don't exist, nor does it mean their boss doesn't either. It's always good to err on the side of caution. So I believe in everything until it is proven not to be true. I was beginning to feel the cold deep inside my bones once again and wanted to find someplace warm.

"Which way to the camp," I asked Adrianna.

"We'll take you there now," she replied. "Tilly has been beside himself since you've gotten yourself lost, he'll be glad to see you."

I smiled faintly. I actually missed the little guy. I turned to Race.

"Are you going to change back into a wolf or just let it all hang out," I said gesturing in the general area of his... Nakedness.

He glanced down at himself.

"It ain't like it's something you never seen before," he said unashamed of his appearance.

I rolled my eyes as Race's form shimmered and a large black wolf stood in his place. Race the wolf let out a huff shaking his head. He bounded fifteen feet away from us, barked a few times and then headed off into the trees.

"I guess he wants us to follow him," I said to Wilmar. "Just watch where you step, don't want to be tracking his steamers all over the forest." I added chuckling to myself.

We all turned following Race as he led us to the camp.

# Chapter 22

We approached the cave in which Barnabas and the rest of our party had made camp. The cave itself was screened from sight by a line of trees that obscured the entrance from any passersby. Barnabas or Tilly had placed a heavy curtain over the outside of the entrance, which I assumed was to help keep out the elements. Race bounded up to stand five or six feet away from the cave's entrance giving a few quick high-pitched barks. After a moment, the flap opened with Barnabas emerging from within, a relieved expression on his face. Which was then marred by the look of sudden surprise as Tilly, my Cob Elf pushed his way between Barnabas's legs galumphing toward me.

"Master," he shrilled excitedly. "You're alive!"

Wilmar sidestepped Tilly's mad rush as he collided with my legs nearly toppling me over. Luckily, I had Adrianna there to help hold me steady. I placed my free hand on his back, giving it a few quick friendly pats followed by a nice strong hug.

"I'm glad to see you too," I said through a wide smile.

"Well, I see you managed not to get yourself killed," Barnabas said walking up to us.

That was his way of saying "Nice to see that you're all right." If Barnabas ever showed any genuine emotion toward me I wouldn't know what to do. Take up drinking or hard drugs I suppose. Perhaps both.

"I missed you too," I said as Tilly released me.

Tilly turned to Wilmar extending a hand.

"Wilmar!" He exclaimed. "So nice to see you again,"

Wilmar stooped deeply to take the Cob Elf's offered hand. He did it with a gentleness and grace I thought not possible for a man his size.

"Tilander Duggins, I am glad to see that you are all right," Wilmar replied.

Tilly let go of Wilmar's hand moving up beside me. Barnabas turned to Wilmar extending his hand.

"How did you end up babysitting my apprentice," He asked gesturing in my direction.

Wilmar took his hand giving it a friendly shake before he released his grip.

"It is a long story, had I know that he was your apprentice, I would have instructed him in the art of remaining quiet" Wilmar said glancing in my direction cracking his knuckles.

I simply shrugged; there was no argument to be made there.

"We'll have to see about that... Anyway, come inside and let's hear it. I'm sure you have many questions yourself." Barnabas said turning back to the cave.

He opened the flap with his left hand beckoning us all inside with his right. Adrianna held my arm as the others filed into the cave past Barnabas. Tilly lingered questioningly at the opening beside my mentor.

"Are you two coming," Barnabas asked.

"We'll be along in a moment, I need to speak with Solomon,"

Barnabas shrugged entering, pushing past my worried Cob Elf. When the cave flap closed shutting prying eyes off from our interlude, Adrianna turned to me.

"What did you want to talk to me about," I asked dubiously.

Her eyes regarded mine as though she were searching for something deep inside them. She said.

"I haven't acted this way toward a man since I was a young woman,"

An embarrassed smile touched her lips.

"You had me worried when we found you were no longer with us... If you only knew the thoughts that raced through my head of what I imagined may have happened to you,"

Taken by complete surprise as to the nature of this conversation, I moved closer, pressing my hand against her cheek.

"I'm fine," I said, my voice shaking.

For added reassurance I stepped back letting my staff fall to the ground as I made a slow revealing circle giving her a complete unobstructed view of my uninjured body.

"See, no cuts or holes, I still have my arms and legs as well as all my fingers,"

Holding up both hands with palms facing me, I purposely kept one finger bent in a way that may make someone believe that I had lost that portion of my digit. With a mock gasp mixed with a feigned look of surprise I fanned out my fingers giving them a sly waggling.

She smiled, which made some of the worry for me bleed away from her expression. Adrianna closed the short distance between us taking my hands into hers.

"I don't know what it is about you Solomon Drake but you make me feel young with a deep sense of happiness I haven't felt in ages,"

"I'd be lying if I said that being around you didn't make me feel almost the same way... Other than the young part... I mean... The age thing between us... You being so much older and all... I stammered, my words trailing off into an awkward silence.

She quirked an irritated, yet patient eyebrow as her smile faltered minutely. My yapping it seemed was endangering this wonderful moment. Score one for the male intellect. No worries. Time to implement plan "B" to salvage the situation. Then I said.

"I'm just going to stop talking now,"

"Thank you," she replied.

She let go of my left hand; her hand rising to my face with her middle and index fingers extended. They caressed long looping circles over my bottom lip.

"I never thanked you properly for saving my life Solomon… In all my years, no man has done so selfless an act for me,"

I think I may have blushed at that point. I was by no means a hero nor did I consider myself one. I did what I did on instinct because she was in danger, we all were. I probably would've thrown myself in front of anyone to protect him or her and if I were in a similar situation in the future I'd do it again without hesitation. I'm more creature of habit than hero, however before I could respond disputing those kind words, her hand was behind my head guiding my lips to hers for an unexpected yet welcomed kiss. I wish I could say that I composed myself as many of my favorite leading actors from the golden age of movies. Actors like *Cary Grant* or *Clark Gable*. They'd take control of a kiss, imposing their strength and will on the female lead or at least that's how it would play out on the silver screen. In reality I melted into the kiss like a bar of chocolate left in the sun.

My eyes languidly falling closed to the sensation as my arms encircled her delicate frame. Adrianna's lips, warmer than the air around us were still chilly against mine. They felt like the first delightfully frozen taste of a cherry flavored *Popsicle*. Her silky lips felt deliciously soft against mine, moving at a leisurely electrifying pace. Be it from the act of kissing Adrianna or the effects of her Vampire venom, my lips tingled with unbridled delight. Her lips pressed tighter against mine with her urgent need. I thought I'd lose the tenuous control over my body when I felt her searching tongue part my lips. When mine met hers the smoldering embers of my passion I'd been successfully holding in check up to that point ignited into a roaring fire of lust and desire. My arms desperately pulling her closer to me holding her tighter as her arms did the same. Whatever this was between us, be it want, love, need, lust or passion both of us now were entwined in its ever tightening coils. I didn't know how long we were like that. Two people caught in a riptide of heated passion. Not thinking, just letting go of constricting inhibitions allowing instinct to take over.

It was glorious.

Nothing this good lasts forever and I felt Adrianna's desperate needful want ebb. There was a distinct reluctance on her part at breaking our kiss. Breaking our embrace. I didn't want it to end either, but she pulled gradually away. Her eyes were closed as she nibbled at her lower lip when I opened mine. Perhaps she'd kept them closed to linger in the moment just a bit longer before reality had to be let back in. When her eyes finally opened they had a content satisfied quality to them. She then smiled apologetically as her fingers went to my lips gently wiping at them.

"Lipstick, sorry,"

I shook my head dazedly as though the effects of an anesthesia were wearing off, leaving me in a blissful euphoria.

"I'm not, does the color look good on me," I asked humorously.

She scrunched up her nose disapproving at my suggestion, though there was playfulness in her response.

"No," she replied seriously. "Peach Parfait would go better with your complexion than Plum Velour,"

"I didn't realize there was such an extensive palette of lipstick colors,"

"You have no idea," she said as I lost myself in those green eyes.

"You know where I come from a handshake more often than not will suffice as a thank you," I said, and then added. "But I think I like your kind of thank you far better,"

She grinned, her eyes lingering on mine as our lips moved casually closer for another kiss. The cave flap opened abruptly, Bart poked his head out from within. The daggers he had aimed in our direction were palpable.

"Ms. Thorne may I remind you that time may be of the essence, how long will you indulge this fascination of yours," Bart piped.

Her expression faltered replaced with one of simmering anger. She let out a frustrated huff then said.

"We better join the others,"

She turned heading into the cave, I scooped up my staff following a few paces behind. Adrianna fixed Bart with such a piercing glare that he averted his eyes as she passed. I caught the look only from her peripherals, which made me want to slink away. As I passed, Bart's hand caught my arm in a vice like grip halting me in place and then he whispered.

"When this is over mortal she will cast you aside as nothing more than a fleeting infatuation,"

He released my arm pushing past me into the cave heading to stand over by Adrianna, who had by now returned to her reserved aloof manner, hopefully directed more toward Bart than myself.

Tilly hurried up to me, relieving the burden of my pack and staff, giving Adrianna a suspicious glance as he moved to a bench to stow my things.

Wilmar lingered near the entrance of the cave gawking excitedly about the interior.

"May I offer you some refreshments," Barnabas asked Wilmar in a patient tone.

Wilmar slowly bobbed his head in assent. His eyes roving with childlike wonder around the cave. I haven't a clue how long he may have been standing there - I was busy with other important matters - but it appeared he'd been wonderstruck for a while.

"Coffee, tea, carbonated beverage, hot cocoa or water," Barnabas continued.

"Cocoa if you please," he responded distractedly.

I'm only guessing mind you, but I think it may have been the fifteen hundred square feet within the cave that made Wilmar speechless or possibly the fine rugs and tapestries that gave it a more homey feeling. Then again it may have been the antique oak dining table with eight chairs placed around it flanked by a matching credenza filled with fine china and silverware. It may have also been the round fireplace made from roughly chiseled stone encircled by comfortable red velvet chairs with matching ottomans. But if I were a betting man, I would've said it was the six large book cases filled with first editions of hard bound books that caught his attention the most, mainly because his eye lingered on them the longest. The cave looked less like a cave and more like a finely decorated vacation home.

"May I take your things for you Sir," Tilly asked Wilmar.

"No," Wilmar said coming back to himself. "No Tilander, I will keep them... Thank you."

"Very good, Sir. I'll have your cocoa in a moment," Tilly said turning, bustling away.

Barnabas moved to the chair at the head of the previously described table. He drew out his chair as he beckoned Wilmar to have a seat at the table.

"Please have a seat so that we may discuss recent events," Barnabas said cordially.

Wilmar hesitated.

"You will forgive me for not sitting down, but I do not believe that my weight will be good for your delicate chairs." He said, a slightly embarrassed tone in his voice.

"Pish Tosh," Barnabas said. "Why, I'll have you know that the Grand Ogre Ferg Ravenchoker sat at this table in that very chair," He said indicating the chair in question. "And he didn't have any issues with my delicate furniture."

The corners of Wilmar's mouth turned up in an indulgent grin. The big man inclined his head pulling off his long fur coat, draping it over one of the red velvet chairs as he made his way over to sit in the chair across from Barnabas. Wilmar settled his formidable weight onto the delicately crafted chair. He hovered for a moment before committing his entire bulk to the operation. Satisfied that he was in no danger of ruining one of the finely matched dining room chairs he relaxed.

Adrianna moved closer to the table but didn't sit down. Bart followed her movements, however he stood a respectable distance away. Race had changed back into his human form strutting around like a prized rooster surveying a barnyard for babe hens without any regard for the rest of us having to view his more naked bits. He moved nonchalantly over to one of the comfortable chairs by the fireplace. He was just about to hop over the back of it when Barnabas's voice rang out in rebuke.

"Race," he said without looking at the Werewolf, an edge to his tone. "Go put some clothes on before you sit on my furniture!" "We are all quite impressed with your abilities and physical attributes, that being said I want you clothed when you are not in wolf form."

Dejected, Race's cocky expression faltered replaced with one somewhere between eating an entire bag of lemons and inhaling the decaying earthy scent of raw sewage. He turned stalking for the sleeping area of the cave grumbling under his breath every step of the way. Satisfied a genial smile once again appeared on Barnabas's face as he gave Wilmar his full attention.

"My apologies for the outburst Wilmar, but I detest sitting in a place where an unclothed sweaty backside has been." Barnabas said distastefully. "It is one of my pet peeves as the younger generation says."

Wilmar raised his hand in an understanding placating gesture.

"I understand Heir Barnabas, I too have had to deal with my share of unpleasant behavior,"

He glanced in my direction.

"For example, your apprentice thinks that he's amusing,"

Well, that's a hurtful thing to say to someone. Wilmar's in the cave less than, what ten or fifteen minute's tops and this is the first meaningful thing he says. Not "Hey nice cave." or "Love the tapestries." or "Mind if I peruse the library," No, he has to go right to insulting the hot looking Wizard guy. Now, I don't normally go around referring to myself as a "hot Wizard" in matter of fact this is the first time. I don't do so now out of vanity or pride, but with the knowledge that at least one woman, Adrianna - Vampire though she may be - finds something "hot" about me.

Barnabas glanced in my direction before turning his gaze back to Wilmar.

"Yes, sadly he does," Barnabas, agreed. "No matter how often others tell Solomon that his humor is far from being amusing, he continues to maintain the opposite opinion."

"That's only because you two grouches don't appreciate my comic genius and timing," I replied smiling.

"I agree with Barnabas and Wilmar," Adrianna piped in. "You're not that funny."

I gave a long-suffering glance to Adrianna that she answered with a playful wink. After the chuckles died down Barnabas said.

"I think Solomon has endured enough of our ribbing. Please Wilmar, tell us what you know,"

Wilmar began his tale without any preamble. The first thing he told us about was his enchanted mirror alerting him to the presence of Mid-Realm creatures in the woods. Then he spoke about how he found me nearly unconscious as well as badly beaten at the hands of a group of rampaging Yetis. He also mentioned their unusually large numbers along with the strangeness of them being in this area. Normally they wouldn't venture far from the doorway between our two worlds. He spoke of treating my wounds, feeding me, going through all the stuff in my pack, which spurred more questions from

Wilmar. Barnabas finally had to stop him, bringing him back to the matter at hand. Answers about the times in which we lived and the wonderful gadgets that dominated our modern lives would have to wait for another time.

After a pause, Wilmar said.

"I would like to hear of what happened to my friend..." Wilmar checked then added. "Our friend Heir Bialek."

"Where should I begin," asked Barnabas.

Tilly came scampering out of the kitchen area carrying a small silver tray, a pair of tall ornately painted white china mugs rested upon on it. Cocoa topped with a generous dollop of whip cream sprinkled with nutmeg sloshed gently in the mugs. Tilly deposited the first mug next to Wilmar then he presented me with the other, a wide contented smile lighting his face.

As he passed by me he noticed Wilmar's fur coat slung over the back of one of the red velvet chairs. He scurried over to it making a disapproving "clucking" sound with his tongue. To his credit the little Elf took the heavy fur coat awkwardly in both arms while still balancing the silver tray, then he walked it over to the spindle coat rack hanging it up before heading back to the kitchen area.

"At whichever point you feel I should know about whatever has happened," Wilmar said.

I gratefully sipped the cocoa. It was hot, almost to the point of burning my tongue, but delightfully good.

The cocoa was thick with a rich flavor like drinking a bar of milk chocolate. This was not made from instant powder packs. Tilly had made a drink that was worthy of the Gods taste buds from scratch. I was in heaven. I held the mug in both hands savoring each sip as I listened to the conversation.

Barnabas inclined his head then began. He told Wilmar about Whitey tracking Tilly to the magic shop after he murdered Hans Bialek. A slight pang of sorrow could be detected in the big man's face as Barnabas presented the details. He told Wilmar about my encounter with the Vampires and the tall Wizard at Stumpwater's. It took Barnabas a little explaining for Wilmar to understand what Stumpwater's actually was, seeing that Wilmar had never been there before. Barnabus spoke at length about traveling to Adrianna's building, where we stumbled into an assassination attempt that nearly succeeded in taking her life.

Barnabas also told Wilmar about the relics of King Arthur in great detail as he had relayed them to Adrianna, but wisely left out information about the exact whereabouts as well as the specific nature of the protections surrounding each relic. The last thing he said was that he'd received a message from Oswald twelve hours ago. Apparently he and Glum had taken the crown to prevent Whitey or the tall Wizard from getting it.

"A moving target's harder to find," Barnabas said.

Which I guess is true if you're a non-magical person, but infinitely more difficult if you're a Wizard.

Spells and charms must be employed to mask whomever or whatever you are trying to hide. Stationary spells are easier to maintain because they are located in one place drawing power from the surroundings to concentrate the veil. Spells that require a person to be mobile however, masking their whereabouts is next to impossible. The spell must continuously be cast as you're on the move, only an experienced wizard with absolute concentration can pull it off. In this case, I was hoping that Oswald was just such a Wizard.

Barnabas raised a hand extending it palm out at a point beyond the fireplace. An obsidian stone sphere roughly the size of a sixteen-inch softball rose up from its brass base atop one of the bookshelves flying gracefully toward him. The sphere hovered to the middle of the table between the two men then began to rotate, slowly at first, then faster with each rotation. As the speed increased a swirling pattern of white energy pulsed to life at the spheres inky center. In a few seconds the swirling energy, which resembled water going down a sink drain grew to about fifty inches in diameter eclipsing the obsidian sphere. Dark shapes began to coalesce into recognizable images as Oswald's voice became audible as though it was being tuned in on an old time radio.

"Barnabas, are you there," Oswald asked as his image came into sharper focus.

"I'm here," Barnabas's voice replied though we never saw him.

"We're still on the move just as planned, but I fear that someone is close on our trail," Oswald said.

I was more than a bit surprised at Oswald's haggard appearance. He took absolute pride in the way he looked. He was an extremely vain man spending far too much time at the salon or in front of a mirror. To see him in this disheveled state was distressing.

"Are you safe,"

"For now yes," Oswald replied. "But I don't know for how long."

"Have you identified who is following you?" Asked Barnabas, concern in his voice.

"No," Oswald replied. "But I know they're close, I can sense their presence as can Glum." "He has been rather edgy of late."

Suddenly, Oswald let out a huff of surprise, then was forced out of view to be replaced by Glum's bald troll head. He gave a crooked toothy troll smile.

"Hi Barnabas," Glum said in his deep raspy voice. "Where Solomon?"

"Hello Glum," Barnabas said in a voice very reminiscent of a parent speaking to a child that has just found a frog and wanted to bring it in the house. "He's not here at the moment."

"Oh," Glum said disappointed. I didn't know he cared for me that much. Trolls aren't known for expressing their emotions. Well, I guess anger and hate are emotions but they aren't the important ones.

Oswald did his best to force Glum out of view, but it was a hopeless effort. He had the body density and weight of a granite boulder that was just as immovable.

"Now see here," Oswald squeaked in an exasperated tone, pushing against Glum on every syllable. "Mind your manners."

Glum slowly moved to the left ceding Oswald more of the mystic camera's eye.

"Glum Hungry," Glum said as his head disappeared from view.

"Yes I know," Oswald affectionately patting Glum's cheek. "I am too, we will get something to eat soon,"

"Glum want Hamburgers," Glum said excitedly from somewhere out of view.

"We'll see, now behave yourself,"

Oswald adjusted his jacket then smoothed back his messed hair as he once again looked toward us in the recording.

"We'll do our best to stay ahead of anyone following us," Oswald said.

The image flickered for just a moment right at the end of his sentence, almost like losing reception on a vintage television set with rabbit ears. Then a black blur moved across Oswald's field of vision directly in front of him. Whatever it was darted quickly from right to left obscuring Oswald from the camera's eye. Out of view Glum's angry growl rose threateningly in volume as a look of panic entered into Oswald's expression.

"I will contact you soon if we are able,"

Then the message abruptly ended.

Silence dominated the atmosphere of the cave as we stared at the diminishing orb of white light. After a moment the obsidian sphere rotated silently in front of us, then gradually moved back to the shelf settling once again on its cradle.

"We're going to help them right?" I asked. "We can't just leave them alone and defenseless."

"No," Barnabas replied in a pained voice "We cannot risk it."

My anger inched higher. Oswald was Barnabas's best friend and colleague. No, he was more than that. Oswald was family. He may have had his eccentricities, but he was a kind man always treating me with love and respect. I couldn't sit here doing nothing to help, leaving him to whomever or whatever might be pursuing them. Barnabas must've been reading my expression like a book because he added just as I opened my mouth to argue.

"Oswald and Glum knew the danger when they took up this responsibility... They volunteered for it my boy and if the thought hasn't crossed your mind..."

Barnabas paused looking at each of us in turn.

"We are in as much danger if not more," he continued. "Because we are running straight at the danger while they're fleeing from it."

A long silence fell upon those gathered around the table.

"Oswald and Glum are your friends. Our family. How can you not do anything to help? If your places were reversed, Oswald wouldn't hesitate, he'd be doing what he could to help you," the words spilling from my lips like an open faucet.

I felt ashamed for my adoptive father. His pained expression didn't move me in the least. I wanted my words to sting him. Sting his pride and arrogance. I didn't care about hearing any of his rational or strategy. They needed our help, I wanted to grab my things and rush to their aid,

"Much more is at stake than any of us realize Solomon," Wilmar said.

His eyes caught mine as he continued.

"Barnabas is not being cautious for himself or for us but for what we must protect. It isn't enough to rush in where angels fear to tread, we must be intelligent, cunning as well as strong... I've known Barnabas for many years now and I can tell you he cares deeply for Oswald and Glum as you do and would help them if he could,"

Wilmar fell silent. After a short pause he added.

"I cannot speak for the rest of you but I also accept this danger and by the grace of God I will not shrink from it," Wilmar said, his words filled with resolve. Turning to Barnabas he said.

"I will fight alongside you if you wish me to,"

"As do we," Adrianna piped up. Though Bart didn't look as enthused about being a part of the little group.

"I'm not sure who or what is behind any of this, but those responsible for killing your friends, as well as those that planned the attack on me which killed some of my people must be found and dealt with."

Race came out from behind a dressing screen pulling a tight fitting t-shirt down over his sculpted abs. He moved over to one of the chairs around the fireplace, pausing he looked right at Barnabas. A contemptuous look plastered on his face, he vaulted over the back of the chair landing hard in a sitting position with a spring clanging thud, his feet resting comfortably on the ottoman.

"I'm indifferent about the whole thing man," he said. "But I'll stick around just for these plush digs."

He nestled his shoulders deeper into the comfortable cushions of the chair, his toes waggling at the warmth from the crackling fire.

I felt a gentle tugging on the hem of my shirt. I glanced down to see Tilly, his puppy dog eyes looking expectantly up at me, waiting for me to throw in with the rest of this lot.

"Yeah... OK," I said finally, "Tilly and I are in too."

Tilly gleefully hopped in place clapping like a kid finding out he was going to *Disneyland*. Barnabas looked around the cave to each of us. His eyes lingered on mine a little longer than the rest. After a moment he rose from the table.

"Since everyone is in agreement then we must make preparations," he said. Then added. "We will be leaving in twenty minutes."

"Awwww..." Tilly groaned. "But Master Barnabas Sir, I've just taken three large pans of *Sheppard's Pie* out of the oven. I would hate for it to go to waste."

Barnabas's mouth quirked up into a relenting smile.

"Yes, that would be a waste."

He pulled out his pocket watch flipping open the cover.

"Shall we say forty five minutes until our departure? That should give us ample time to fill our bellies with Tilly's *Sheppard's Pie* before we go."

Barnabas turned to Adrianna and Bart as he tucked his pocket watch back from whence it came.

"Our guests may have use of anything in the cave as we dine unless you wish to sit with us of course."

Adrianna inclined her head in an acknowledgement of thanks.

"We'd be delighted to join you," Adrianna replied diplomatically, then added. "We no longer have a need to eat human food, conversation however, appeals to me far more at the moment,"

Bart's expression remained impassive, I was thinking that he was rolling his eyes on the inside and giving us each the finger mentally.

"Please, everyone have a seat while I get everything ready," said Tilly.

We obeyed Tilly taking our places around the table, Barnabas at the head, with Wilmar at the opposite end. Bart was seated beside Race, judging by their expressions they both were simply loving the seating arrangement.

Sarcasm.

Tilly, be it a flash of inspiration or insanity seated Adrianna next to me. I didn't know whether to thank him or brain him with a serving spoon. The feelings that stirred in my being earlier were still lurking within me. I wanted her badly. Though I wasn't sure if I could control myself, but I was going to do my best. With our interlude outside the tent cut short, I felt there was some unfinished business between Adrianna and I. Perhaps Tilly picked up on that. Regardless of his motivations I'm glad he placed us together. It gave me an opportunity to be close to her once again, even if it was only for a little while. During dinner our hands found each other's under the table. Her small yet powerful hand in mine, our fingers entwined. It was a little slice of heaven and I found myself not wanting it to end.

# Chapter 23

**W**alking, from everything that I've read is without question one of the best exercises a person can engage in to stay healthy and fit. While that might in fact be true, I was wishing for a fast snowmobile or an eight-team dog sled as we hiked the three miles to Hans Bialek's compound. Our progress hampered by knee high snow and bitter cold.

Given my continual lamentations regarding the climate we found ourselves in, I can almost hear the mocking complaints of you the reader as it relates to my courage, my fortitude and my manhood. Such things like,

*"Stop your bitching already its not that bad,"* or *"Aren't you a freaking Wizard?"*

*"Don't you have the ability to wield the powers of the heavens and the earth?"*

*"Why can't you just wave your magic wand, recite a spell zapping your whiny self there, so we don't have to*

*hear you complain about how cold it is or how long it takes to walk from place to place."*

The answers to these well thought out queries are quite simple. First off, I don't bitch. Complain? Perhaps, but I like to think that I point out obvious flaws in certain situations as they relate to my well being thereby giving voice to them.

Secondly, magic - incase you haven't realized - is incredibly cool to use, but it's also governed by the rules of physics and therefore has limitations like all things in the universe. Rules, that modern science strictly adheres to regarding what we know today to be true and the rules yet to be realized by scientific formula in the future. When a Wizard employs a fire spell, or an ice spell or makes objects or even creatures of every description appear for example, they just don't come from thin air or out of a monkey's butt. - Though that would be funny, a magical monkey butt - Everything, and I do mean everything that a Wizard creates must come from somewhere.

In the television series *Star Trek* they have these wonderful devices called "replicators." These devices can make food, clothing, elements both basic and complex, and various other devices, ship components and a myriad of things that are far too numerous to list here. They can do all of these things based on a simple principle and that is that matter and energy are the same. By that I mean, it takes matter to create energy and energy to create matter. Everything in the universe was created by a huge release of energy (*The Big Bang*) most of the basic elements we know today originated from that explosion. We humans also use many of those elements to create other more complex elements by combining them in various ways. During the process of creating these new elements energy is released.

Magic is more or less the same. Now, I'm not going to waste more words along with blank pages to explain the magical arts. That'd take up more time, which we don't have and would possibly be extremely boring to you the reader. Probably more boring than this book is possibly all ready. If you diehards are interested in learning about the magical arts they'll be covered in later editions of this narrative. All you really need to know now is that a Wizard is someone wired at the genetic level to manipulate the energy within our universe, which contains a lot of it. Wizards can accumulate the energy that exists around us storing it like a battery then use it as needed. Most of the time people that have a bit of magic ability in them don't absorb energy consciously it just happens naturally like breathing. They take in small amounts without knowing it. Others like myself are true Wizards; we can absorb more energy using it in more complex ways.

There are varying degrees of people in the world with this ability. Just like there are a few great baseball players out there, like *Babe Ruth* or *Roberto Clemente*. When you get the chance to watch them play ball you're in awe that they're that good at what they do. Then there are the other players that play on the same teams with these all stars that suck to varying degrees, which is painful to watch at times. A trained Wizard in the magical arts can take the energy that he or she has absorbed releasing it in a manner that depends largely on the spell employed. Our minds visualize, shaping the desired spell we wish to unleash and having a vivid imagination, concentration, knowledge about a variety of subjects as well as a determined will are the key. The words that a Wizard says or thinks binds the mind and energy together, but we need an object to focus that power, otherwise the energy dissipates becoming useless. A wooden staff was the first focus item used in magic or that is what many magic scholars believe. Staffs are still widely used today. Certain woods are better to utilize than others. Then one day long ago, a lazy Wizard that got tired of lugging a heavy piece of wood around decided to use just a tiny branch discovering it worked almost as well as the staff. He or she called it a "wand" just to be different. Then over the years Wizards found that certain metals worked even better, which led to a larger variety of focuses to be created. Some Wizards use canes, bracelets or rings as their "wands".

As I may have said already, most everyone in the world has some sort of latent magical ability. Just look around. There are people that are good at gambling, some are good at business, a few are good at sports or can find lost objects, and some can see things about to happen or cook fabulous meals. The list of minor magical abilities goes on, but it's a rare thing indeed to find someone that can actually wave a wand and make something happen. It'd probably surprise you that out of the world's population today less than a few hundred thousand people scattered around the inhabited continents can actually wield magic to a devastating degree. Now having said all of that, I can "zap" or shift myself from one place to another with ease.

What you may or may not have realized or taken into consideration is that the location we're in has magical spells and defensive wards laid down all over the place. All of them specifically to prevent Normal's, from stumbling into the valley or to keep Wizards with less than honorable intentions from popping in unannounced. The only reason we were able to shift here in the first place was the tethered circles. The first circle located inside Blackmane's Magic Shoppe, the other being the snow covered stone glyph that we shifted onto when we arrived. So that means my faithful, yet occasional surly reader, we have to walk through the knee-high snow, in the cold.

The spiral path that led to Bialek's compound wound its way up to the top of a heavily wooded hill roughly three hundred feet in height. One had to be careful because there were false paths, pitfalls and magical defenses every step of the way. Luckily for our group, Barnabas knew where many of the defenses were, because he helped create them. Otherwise, our group would've been minus one Werewolf named Race, who enjoyed "marking" things.

For those defenses Barnabas didn't know, he was able to reveal or detect them with a magic spell although with a few it took some time to figure out the correct disarming spell. As we reached the summit, Bialek's compound lay roughly fifty yards ahead of us concealed by a first class wall of magical energy, invisible to the naked eye yet very powerful. The bad thing about it, if there were a downside to such a cool display of magic was that the wall masked everything behind it. All an observer could see was the surrounding forest, there wasn't any indication that a human had made their mark on this place nor were there any signs that a disturbance had taken place.

We remained outside the wall for nearly three hours waiting for Barnabas to disengage it so that we could proceed. This particular defensive spell stumped him blunting all his attempts to take it down. To say that he was not in a good mood would've been an understatement. Tilly sat next to me on his pack fidgeting with a button sewn to his coat. I sat on my pack eating some beef jerky. Race lay curled up in a ball under a nearby tree recovering from his "accident". Wilmar rested on a log reading one of the books he'd gotten from me, *Captain Blood by Rafael Sabatini* I think. Bart was breaking logs in half with an index finger. I'd wager watching the intensity at how he dispatched those defenseless logs that he pulled the wings off of flies in his youth, behavior many experts believe leads to the wearing and or eating of human skin and body parts. Adrianna sat cross-legged on a large flat rock in the shade of a group of dense trees. Her eyes closed, a smile of serene contentment shown upon her face as if in deep meditation. Being a curious young man and a Wizard, I wondered what thoughts might be on her mind.

Now, I've never been one to buy into the myth that Vampires read minds, but a curious thing happened. Adrianna languidly opened one eye focusing it in my direction the corners of her mouth quirking up into an amused smile. That doesn't prove anything I know, she could've just had a reaction similar to a predator prey response. I'm not in any way saying that I'm a predator, but everyone's had that feeling they're being watched at least once in their lives if not more often. She puckered her lips sending me a kiss over the distance between us closing her eye once more. Tilly touched my arm getting my attention as well as drawing my eyes away from Adrianna.

"Master," he said in a hushed voice.

"Hmmm," I said chewing a mouthful of jerky sounding a bit put off.

"Would Master Barnabas be cross with me if I offered some assistance?"

As if on cue, a ball of white-hot fire issued forth from Barnabas's open palm incinerating three large trees to his right.

"Jumping Butterballs!!! Save me from Kings and Idiots!" Barnabas yelled in frustration.

Barnabas doesn't say any of the good profane words. That list of specific words that get your mouth washed out with a bar of soap for using. He chooses instead to use such vulgar disdainful language that was in constant practice roughly a little over a century ago when *Teddy Roosevelt* was President.

"No not at all," I said around a mouthful of jerky, a smile on my face.

Tilly cringed moving closer to me, shifting away from Barnabas for protection.

"Look," I said finally after swallowing. "If you know something that'll help us get to the compound then tell him. He won't be upset with you, only with himself because he cannot figure it out."

Tilly looked up at me then over to Barnabas giving a quick nod, obviously deciding his course of action. The little Elf got up, brushed off his pants then trudged over to a very old, very upset Wizard.

"Master Barnabas," Tilly said timidly.

Barnabas closed his eyes taking a deep calming breath as he turned to look down at Tilly.

"What is it Tilly," he asked, obvious frustration in his voice.

Tilly cringed at Barnabas's tone and glowering expression, but I have to give the little guy credit, he stood his ground pressing on.

"Well Sir," he began. "My Master... that is my former Master, made a pass key of sorts in order for me to move through the defensive wall should the need arise, because as you may or may not have realized there is no way to take down the wall unless Master Bialek deactivates it himself..." His words caught on something he was going to say; instead a pained expression appeared on his face before he continued.

"We know he can no longer do that." Tilly finished his voice cracking.

Barnabas stared down at the Cob Elf for a long silent moment and then he knelt in front of him placing an understanding hand gently on Tilly's shoulder.

"Where is this passkey?" Barnabas asked.

Tilly gestured at the area of his neck.

"Since this will be attached to me for the foreseeable future, Master Bialek enchanted it for the purpose of being a passkey." Tilly said in a just between us tone even though we could all hear him.

Barnabas pondered this revelation carefully then asked.

"I assume that only you might be able to pass through the barrier,"

Tilly nodded enthusiastically,

Barnabas gave a thankful though disappointed pat to Tilly's shoulder.

"I'm sorry Tilly, unless we can bring down the wall so that all of us may pass through the barrier, the passkey unfortunately is of no use to us,"

Barnabas gave Tilly a reassuring squeeze of his shoulder.

"Thank you Tilly."

Then he stood turning back to ponder the wall.

"Master Barnabas," Tilly said tentatively.

Barnabas continued to ponder vexed at the wall.

"I was also shown how to take down the wall should I need to return with help."

At that revelation I think I perked up considerably. Though I was fairly surprised that it took as long as it did for Tilly's words to register in Barnabas's brain. He must've had a serious case of tunnel vision going on there

Barnabas's head turned in the direction of Tilly like an old great horned owl's zeroing in on its prey.

"Well, why the devil didn't you say so in the first place," he said, frustration giving way to exhalation. "Right, off you go!"

Barnabas hooked a finger in the direction of the invisible wall.

Tilly started in a way that might lead an observer to believe he wasn't too keen on the idea or that he hadn't thought completely about helping or factoring in the consequences of such a rash decision. His hand rose to his face absentmindedly, fingertips resting on his lips in a contemplative gesture.

We got to our feet gathering up our belongings. I grabbed Tilly's backpack, astounded at how much such a tiny thing weighed. It was only a third of the size of mine. What did he have in this thing, bricks? Then it dawned on me, I hadn't seen Race's backpack since we arrived. Tilly's pack must be some sort of Ambry Bag. An Ambry bag is an enchanted bag for storing things. The bags can open to accommodate large objects or a large number of larger objects. The bag's storage space is limited by the type of spell it has upon it. I've heard from various individuals that Cob Elves utilized Ambry bags more than anyone in the magical community. This however was the first time I think that I've ever seen one up close.

Barnabas gazed down at Tilly, his right eyebrow cocked in a disapproving arch.

"Well," he said, restraint in his voice.

Tilly started nervously at Barnabas's tone. Turning, he rushed headlong into the wall of energy without thinking twice about whatever might be on the other side. I wasn't sure if he was more scared of the unknown or Barnabas's angry temper. Over the years I've learned to loathe Barnbas's temper. Given the choice between a sternly worded lecture from Barnabas or being eaten by a rock scaled dragon known to be the meanest and most vicious breed of that species, I would take the lecture. Come on, do you honestly think that I would willingly be eaten by a dragon?

Tilly passed through the barrier easily. All that happened was a rippling effect appearing at the place where he entered, like a pebble tossed into a still pond. The wait for him to shut off the wall of energy took a minute maybe two, but it felt like an eternity. I think I could've spoken for everyone present - except Bart of course - that we were all worried about Tilly with varying degrees of concern. The thought he may have confronted something dangerous crossed my mind a few times. Ultimately Tilly accomplished his task. What was revealed to us when the wall vanished like a wisp of smoke made me shudder.

Tilly stood fifteen or so yards away and about as many yards to the left from the point he entered the barrier, his hand pressed loosely against a tree that had been sheared off three feet from the ground. In fact, all the trees had been violently culled in the same manner. As though a great explosion had occurred in the center of the protective shield leveling everything in its destructive path. Bialek's stone compound which he called home for hundreds of years simply wasn't there, stone debris encircling a blackened crater fifteen feet deep were all that remained.

Judging by the amount of debris it was a good-sized structure. Two twelve foot wooden pikes stood on either side of a mostly snow covered stone path that led to what was until recently the entrance to the compound, bodies rode on the sharpened points like mangled insects on display in a gruesome menagerie. Scattered around the area of destruction were some body parts from creatures I couldn't identify, though there were a few bubbling remains I did recognize, those of Vampires. I was amazed that the Vampire remains were still here and that the suns rays hadn't obliterated them. Perhaps the wall of energy somehow preserved them. Whatever the reason, the battle that took place here was ferocious and bloody. Bialek had apparently taken many of his attackers with him.

Barnabas moved carefully over to Tilly following the path the little guy made in the snow. I followed Barnabas's lead not wanting to blunder into any booby traps. Barnabas knelt beside Tilly, placing a hand on the Elf's left shoulder consolingly. Tilly's reaction to Barnabas's gesture was slow. He reluctantly tore his eyes away from the scene of destruction focusing his numb disbelieving gaze on Barnabas's eyes. Tears streamed down his face. He opened his mouth in a vain attempt to say something, but the emotions he was experiencing choked them off. He closed his mouth as his eyes returned to the destruction.

I approached Tilly from the other side kneeling next to him just as Barnabas had done. I was about to place a reassuring hand on his shoulder when he turned burying his face in the soft material of my coat sobbing uncontrollably. I patted his back gently attempting to console him. The others moved in around us tense and wary. Wilmar along with Barnabas moved over to a blackened blob of what until recently was some sort of living creature.

Barnabas poked at the blob with the inquisitive nature of a cat using the end of his staff. Wilmar knelt close to the blob thrust two fingers into the mass, rubbing the substance between his thumb and forefingers, before - and this is disgusting - he smelled and tasted it. I nearly vomited up the beef jerky watching.

"Mid-Realm beast," Wilmar said, disgust in his tone. "I'd stake my life on it."

"Yes," Barnabas said agreeing with Wilmar's assessment. "The question is, which beast. Judging by the number of remains..." He trailed off considering. "There were many such creatures."

Wilmar stood scanning about as Adrianna and Bart began examining the Vampire corpses or rather what remained of them. Race moved silently around investigating the outer area of the carnage.

"There were at least fifty of these Mid-Realm creatures along with twenty vampires by my count," Wilmar said moving to the corpse Adrianna was examining.

"This Vampire was from the Alverez clan," Adrianna said standing.

She moved to the next pile of Vampire remains that was about ten yards away kneeling beside them.

"Alverez Clan," She said standing, moving to the next.

She paused on these remains, pain mixed with betrayal filling her expression. When she spoke she choked back what sounded like tears or anger, I simply wasn't sure.

"Thorne clan... This one was one of my family."

She stood glaring at the remains, her expression unreadable. She moved over to an uprooted tree sitting down upon the trunk.

"These over here are Menconi and Thorne," Bart said.

Tilly composed himself removing his face from the newly formed saucer sized tear stained wet spot on my coat. I stood observing Adrianna as Tilly took out one of his fancy handkerchiefs to dab away the tears under his swollen eyes. I placed his pack beside him before making my way over to Adrianna. I had no idea what she was feeling. Betrayal is an ugly thing to experience. It gnaws at you like no other feeling can, because it involves both love and trust. I'm a firm believer you can't give someone your trust without first loving them. In my short life I'd yet to feel betrayal anywhere near the level that Adrianna was experiencing it at the moment. I'd been hurt sure, but I've never had my trust violently ripped from me. My trust has been bruised somewhat over the years - this little adventure being the worst in that regard - just like most people in the world at one time or another.

Her people, her clan was of her blood, literally. The blood that coursed within their veins came directly from her. For lack of a better phrase, all the Vampires she created were essentially her children. Just like human infants after someone is turned they need to be cared for as well as protected until they're strong enough. The newly turned are also taught how to be a Vampire. There are some though, familiars that are educated in becoming a Vampire long before they are turned. Sort of a Vampire in training if you will. Adrianna and her people invest time, patience, resources and yes even love in rearing their Vampire children.

One of the most sacred laws in the Vampire world that carries automatic death should it be violated is that no Vampire except for the head of the clan or a designated Turner can create a Vampire. That's the main deterrent to ensure that the world isn't overrun by huge numbers of Vampires, which in turn allows them to maintain a low profile in the human world. I've learned there're a few Vampire malcontents that would like nothing more than to put humans in the place. These "Outlaw" Vampires normally aren't part of any clan though many are branded with family marks. It wouldn't surprise me that that many in the Vampire world identify with their beliefs. "Outlaws" believe we humans are nothing more than a food source or prey to be hunted.

Adrianna along with many of the older Vampires kept to the old way. Their words and honor still mattered to them. Core beliefs ingrained into Vampire society over the centuries. So for some of her people - the younger ones to be sure - to blatantly disregard her orders, carelessly cast her love and support aside along with the hard fought truce between the Vampire world and the world of Wizards was possibly a tremendous blow to her pride as well as honor. Blood would be the only offering that would restore balance. I stood next to her awkwardly glancing obliquely in her direction trying to think of something to say. Nothing came to mind of substance. Oh sure, amusing anecdotes were the first things my mind went to. Sadly, this was not the time for such things, even though a few were actually quite funny. After grasping at thought threads in my mind of the right course of action, my instincts spoke to me. I simply sat beside her giving her the space she required, but more importantly so she'd know that I was there and concerned about her. Aside from the lust I felt for her, I really didn't want to see her in pain, which was the truth. Adrianna remained silent for a good five or ten minutes. I kept quiet not breaking the silence even though I wanted too.

"Thank you for not speaking Solomon," She said sorrow in her tone. "Sometimes words are not needed."

"Is there anything that I can do for you," I asked, uncertain.

I could tell she was thinking about my offer, because a smile appeared. It wasn't a mechanical indulgent smile, but one of genuine joy and dare I say hope.

"You're such a sweet man," She said through her smile placing a gloved hand on my cheek. "Sadly, this is something that I have to deal with on my own, but I thank you for the offer."

Her eyes searched the depths of mine once again, though somehow this time was decidedly different. Her questioning glance had changed to one of glad

415

affirmation. Her hand moved behind my head as I felt the gentle urging force of her pulling me closer. Her eyes burned with the hunger that I'd seen and experienced outside Barnabas's tent. My mind felt this wasn't the time for such things, but my body felt differently about it. Who am I to argue? Her eyes closed as the gentle force slackened. I could sense an internal struggle happening behind her eyelids. Her hand dropped from behind my neck moving to her lap. When her eyes opened she stood, her controlled businesslike air returning.

"Do you have any idea what you're doing to me Solomon," she asked turning back to me.

The movement accentuating her curves even though they were concealed beneath her winter gear. I inadvertently glanced down at my lap then back up to her. Did she have any idea what she was doing to me? I remained silent and seated.

"You've awakened thoughts and desires I haven't experienced in centuries,"

She closed her eyes once more giving her head a mind-clearing shake. I could literally feel the lust radiating from her. When her eyes opened they were fixed squarely on me.

"You and I have much to discuss when this is over, but one question gnaws at me,"

"What is that," I asked. Surprised that I could talk.

Her smile returned, and then was gone.

"The question is, would you be able to keep up with me," she asked playfully.

Adrianna hooded her eyes then sensuously licked her lips in a way that promised a night of pelvis bruising animalistic charged sex as she turned away making her way over to Wilmar and Barnabas.

That wasn't fair on so many levels. Don't get me wrong it was nice, but so unfair. A woman showing any sort of sexual interest toward me is a rare occurrence. I'm not accustomed to it or the effect it has on my body. A good effect though it may be. "Give it to me now!" Is what my body was saying, while my mind was saying, "You do realize she's not serious about you right?" Now it's a matter of whom to listen too, my logical mind or my other mind that was hardening as I thought about Adrianna tracing her tongue over her ruby red lips. I stood hunching in an attempt to hide my "thoughts" from the rest of the group, when out of the corner of my eye I spied Bart. He was intently watching Adrianna with a look of utter disgust. He must've overheard what she'd said to me not liking it at all. Of course this is supposition, but either he's sweet on her or he thinks the way the hardcore Vampires think. Such as believing interacting with humans is wrong.

After the cursory examinations of various remains, Barnabas and Wilmar made their way to what until recently was Bialek's compound. The rest of us followed. I of course brought up the rear whereas Race decided to pause in order to relieve himself on a few of the Vampire remains. Much to my amazement, he was able to flash a doggie grin along with what sounded like a rough chuckle after each tinkle.

The closer I got to the proximity of the gruesome sight of bodies on pikes the more the bile wanted to rise in my throat. I could clearly see the horrific things that'd been done to them. There was something else as well, something lurking behind the scene of carnage. A creepy feeling I couldn't shake. My skin erupted in goose flesh with every crunch of snow under foot. Barnabas and Wilmar stood fifteen feet from the bodies. Adrianna, Bart and Tilly, with Race and myself approaching from the left, flanked them. The bodies were of an older man and a young woman, Bialek and Olivia was my guess. The naked bodies were torn and gashed in hundreds of places. Flesh hung in thick strips on their chests and abdomens fluttering in the gentle breeze like ragged torn cloth. Blood covered most of their bodies, but their faces were mostly untouched. There was no longer any doubt of Olivia's fate, she was dead and our list of suspects grew shorter.

"Be on your guard young Wizard," Merlin said in a concerned whisper. "Dark magic is at work."

"Could you be a bit more specific?" I asked thinking the question. If I began speaking out loud to what appeared to be myself, people would think I was crazy. All right, slightly more crazy than I already was.

"Can you not feel the dark magic in this place?" Merlin asked. "The feeling of cloying closeness as though a malevolent spirit was pressing in upon you."

I did feel something, though I couldn't put a name to it. Merlin picked up on the creepy vibe I was getting or he got the vibe funneling it to my mind and body. Regardless, there was something more here than any of us could see. I was almost certain Barnabas felt exactly what Merlin and I were feeling.

"Thank you," I replied. "I'll warn the others and be on my guard."

"You are most welcome young Wizard," Merlin answered back. "If you should meet an untimely end there is no telling where I may end up and I am quite intrigued regarding this time I find myself in."

"So this is all about self preservation for you?" I thought.

"Of course young Wizard."

I could respect that. He'd been cooped up in that crystal for hundreds of years in isolation. No books, no television, no board games or crossword puzzles, just his own thoughts to keep him company. Man, that was a depressing thought. I'd hate like hell to have to be trapped inside another vessel after being out for a short time. In matter of fact I personally wouldn't go back into a little crystal without a fight.

"Fair enough," I replied.

"Are these your friends," asked Adrianna compassionately.

"Yes, Hans Bialek and his apprentice Olivia," Barnabas replied pondering the situation. "The body of James, Orm's apprentice doesn't appear to be anywhere around either,"

Wilmar dazedly looked between the two pikes his eyes coming to rest on Olivia. The pain in his expression made me want to cry. I felt for him, I really did. Then he composed himself.

"Perhaps his body was obliterated in the explosion or carried off by the attackers," Wilmar offered.

"Perhaps, but I doubt it. If that were the case why did they leave their bodies behind," he reluctantly agreed.

Wilmar thought then said.

"He may have been the Trojan horse we have been looking for,"

Barnabas nodded thoughtfully. The creepy feeling had increased which made me even more anxious. I placed a hand on Barnabas's shoulder, leaning in close.

"There's something not right about this place," I said in a hushed tone.

"Yes," he answered in a similar tone. "I felt it when the wall came down."

Barnabas kept his eyes on Bialek's horror stricken death mask.

"Don't you think it'd be a good idea if we got the hell out of here, like right now" I said in what I hoped didn't sound like a frightened forceful tone.

Barnabas hesitated, thinking.

"I found something," Bart yelled from over by the rim of the crater, near a low pile of scattered rubble.

I turned looking in his direction; somewhat amazed Bart never said anything useful. The others turned to look as well. Bart knelt no more than ten or fifteen yards away from where Barnabas, Wilmar and I stood. Looking at each other in turn with quizzical expressions, each of us made our way over to Bart's location. Race, still in his Werewolf form made it there first. He crouched a few feet to the side of Bart, his hackles up, a deep-throated growl of warning issued from the wolf as his eyes fixed on something.

Race's behavior put us on edge. Adrianna moved cautiously over to stand beside the huge wolf. She placed a calming hand on his arched back stroking the soft black fur between his powerful shoulders. Her tone was soft as she spoke calming words. It didn't take much of this for Race's growl to die away. He didn't relax his posture however. I was fairly certain Adrianna wasn't using glamour. She really didn't need too; her looks along with her commanding way would've calmed the heart of the most steadfast troublemaker.

Standing at various distances from the object we peered down at it. Lying in a small depression loosely covered by fine stone debris was a bent and scarred medallion roughly the same size as an *Eisenhower* dollar. Part of a silver chain of no more than eight inches in length remained threaded through the loop. The medallion appeared to have been made of a similar metal, silver though it was badly tarnished. The design etched in the metal was of a mystic eye encircled by four runes depicting the four elements; wind, fire, water and earth could still be visible through the blackened mark that could've only been made by a powerful magical attack of some sort.

"Master Bialek's amulet," Tilly choked out right before the waterworks started up again.

Remind me never to take him to tear jerker movies. Everyone in the theatre would drown from his balling. Am I sounding like an ass at the moment? Yes I am. He can do all the crying he wants after we're finished with all of this, right now he needs to suck it up. Barnabas read my expression, he flashed a warning glare not to say anything to Tilly and to just let him cry it out. So I just bit my tongue.

"Barnabas is right young Wizard," Merlin deciding to throw in his two cents.

"The Cob Elf has been through quite enough turmoil for his new master to berate him in front of all these strangers,"

Great, now the old man spirit Merlin was siding with Barnabas. Hurray for me. Barnabas remained uncommunicative while examining the amulet from afar. Even Wilmar was keeping his distance. I was honestly surprised that he wasn't down on his hands and knees licking the damn thing. I didn't know, but perhaps they were showing some sort of respect for the dead or perhaps they were afraid to touch it because it was until recently around Bialek's neck. However, I think the most likely answer is that something had them spooked, like something wasn't right with that amulet.

I didn't sense any magic emanating from the amulet itself nor did Merlin, otherwise he'd have said something or at least I hoped he would at any rate. It was nothing more than an innocuous piece of jewelry, yet it's strange that it was just lying out here in a crater. Bialek's murders took an awful lot of time to torture he and Olivia as well as place them on pikes for someone to discover.

The more I thought about the situation the more it didn't make sense. No matter how hard I tried I couldn't see what all this meant. I knew Barnabas, Merlin and I felt that something wasn't right about this place and that amulet. Even Race felt something by the way he acted. We were all just too dumb or just too damn slow to realize the possible danger that may have been lurking right in front of us. Then again, maybe just maybe we were making a mountain out of a molehill and the vibe we were feeling for this creepy place was of our own making. Yeah and if pigs could fly it would be much harder to get bacon.

I looked in Barnabas's direction to gauge what he might be thinking, then started. His eyes were wide with what I assumed was horrified realization. I watched as the color drained from his face. Before I could open my mouth he said.

"I think it would be prudent if we retreated back to the place where we entered."

It wasn't a suggestion it was an order. Without a complaint or challenge to Barnabas's words everyone except Bart began moving in that direction.

"What's the matter Wizard," Bart asked, contempt oozing from his every word.

I was almost positive that we all stopped looking back in Bart's direction. I wouldn't put any money on it, but I was ninety nine percent sure of the fact.

Barnabas remained silent.

"I've gone along with all of your wizard nonsense for the sake of Ms. Thorne," he continued.

"Bartholomew!" Adrianna rebuked.

He continued unperturbed by her tone.

"I expressed my opinion before starting out on this maddening exercise in stupidity that joining forces with wizards was a stupid idea, I went along with it because Ms. Thorne, the head of my house said it must be so, I even tolerated the smell from that mangy flea bag."

He indicated Race with a nod of his head.

"But retreating because the great Barnabas Blackmane is afraid of this little piece of metal is entirely too much for me to stomach."

Bart reached for the amulet taking it in his right hand before any of us could protest his actions. That's when the trap we'd been agonizing over for the last few hours finally closed around us.

# Chapter 24

The sensation of falling from a mountainous height didn't last as long as it sometimes did when traveling by an Egress Gateway Spell. Which is what I suspected we all got hit with back at Bialek's when Bart touched the amulet. The loss of consciousness along with the subsequent binge-drinking throb in my head however made my stomach feel worse than getting off an extreme roller coaster with multiple loops. I've got to give credit though to whoever made it. Normally an Egress Gateway is supposed to be easy to find, They are after all, intended to be used in order get from one place to another.

This particular gateway however wasn't. I didn't think any of us knew what we were dealing with until we found ourselves in an entirely different location, imprisoned inside a containment circle twenty feet in diameter. Our packs and weapons were in another containment circle on the other side of what appeared to be a decayed building that had until recently been submerged in a lake or river.

The skeletal remains of what I assumed was a church, mainly because of a large cross peering down on us through the remains of irregular stone arches. The cross itself stood atop a steeply slanted roof like a carrion bird waiting for death to take us in order to pick our bones clean. The church had seen better days, giving comfort and strength to the faithful. Now with it being abandoned it loomed ominously around us in the eerie light from a half moon that hung in the night sky. A thick musty metallic smell laced with the hint of decaying fish hung in the air like a heavy curtain. What I wouldn't have given for some nose plugs or a clothespin at that moment. All was quiet with no movement outside the containment circle and no sign of our captors.

I was the first to awaken; I played possum until I heard the distinct sound of someone else stirring. The sleep spell, which I assumed had been used on us, was unknown to me, but a sleep spell was the only thing that could've knocked us all out at once. I've been incapacitated by a spell similar to this once before. Another of Barnabas's lessons, I slept like a teenager in the midst of a growth spurt, this time however, I woke fairly quickly without any ill affects. Perhaps having the spirit of a powerful Wizard in my head had its benefits aside from providing me with cryptic advice. Race was the first to stir after myself, he'd transformed back into his human form having the look of surviving a college freshman initiation party. The rest were still unconscious and this may or may not be important but Adrianna snores, like a two-man crosscut saw team taking down a giant redwood. This revelation cast doubt on the saying "sleeping the peaceful sleep of the dead." In any event, I found it amusing.

The sultry night made my winter garb unbearable. Sweat beaded on every inch of my body feeling like I was in the throes of a high fever. I got to my feet stripping hurriedly out of my winter coat and pants attempting to gain some measure of relief from the humidity as well as the heat. I gratefully realized that I still retained my colt defender and three remaining magazines. The enchantments I'd placed on it and the shoulder holster must've been undetectable by our captors.

After discarding my winter garb in a jumbled pile I took the opportunity to investigate our situation seeing that there wasn't much else to do. The floor we rested upon was made from roughly hued stone weather worn from years of harsh elements and neglect. A collection of thirteen translucent green magical symbols bound by four concentric circles glowed faintly from within the stone itself beneath us. The other circle that contained our stuff had similar markings from what I could see.

I decided to stand a few feet away from the perimeter of our magical cell. Given my luck thus far, I wouldn't want to get incinerated just by looking at it. Whatever spell was keeping us contained within the circle was invisible to the naked eye, yet I felt something was there. It felt like a low palpable thrum, like a numb tingling on my skin. It took a few minutes to remember a spell Barnabas had taught me in order to reveal hidden enchantments or wards. Sadly I didn't have my battle staff or wand to channel the spell through, so I had to do the best with what I had.

Raising my right arm, I extended my hand with fingers fanned out, palm facing the invisible barrier. I closed my eyes focusing on the spell, controlling my breathing, it was difficult however to gather energy. The barrier may have been a magical dampening field, cutting me off from the surrounding energy. I was able to gather enough for this spell however. After a few moments of mental preparation I uttered in the spell in a low tone.

"Ostendo sum occultus vox."

A pale blue mote of smoke like energy in the shape of an undulating circle issued forth from my outstretched hand lazily moving toward the invisible barrier. When the smoke ring hit the wall a sound not unlike bacon frying echoed from the impact site. The energy spread out over every inch of the containment wall revealing its shape and size to me. The wall rose fifty feet or so vertically topped with a reverse pattern of symbols the same as what was beneath our feet. A cylinder of magic is what it looked like. As the blue energy faded my heart sank, we were in an absorption field. Any attempt whatsoever in attacking the wall or the stones beneath our feet would result in the strengthening of our cell. I'd inadvertently made the wall minutely stronger with my attempt at garnering its dimensions.

"That was trippy," Said a gruff voice behind me.

I turned to see Race cradling his head in one hand while shielding his privates with the other. Rather nice of him I'd say. I've seen enough of his junk this trip to last me three life times.

"How are you feeling," I asked.

He looked pale.

"I'd be alright if my head would stop spinning,"

He let out a watery sounding belch. Judging by the face he made I'd say a little bile rose up as well. His free hand went to his stomach.

"I can't change." He said. "My head hurts too much."

"Lay back down and rest. We don't need your *Lassie* imitation at the moment."

He painfully nodded his head once then laid back down turning onto his right side facing away from me. I took the opportunity to move around our cell methodically taking in every detail, completing my circuit just as a few more of my companions stirred from the sleep spell. I was fairly certain that whoever created our prison made it with the remaining members of the Octagon in mind. Though I am very thick headed at times, I can connect the dots sooner or later. Merlin to my surprise had remained silent since I awoke. Either he was still out cold or he was observing the situation. I needed to just sit down and think. Something was gnawing at me, something that I may have possibly overlooked or was it just something that hadn't occurred to me. There was still no sign of our captors. I wondered why they decided to be so mysterious. Usually anyone that gets the upper hand in any situation tended to take the opportunity to gloat.

Tilly and Adrianna were groggy as they attempted to make it to sitting positions. I debated telling Adrianna that she was a rather loud sleeper, but decided to just let it go. Now wasn't the time. I moved over to Tilly kneeling next to him.

"Take it easy," I said placing my hand on his shoulder steadying him.

"Yes Master," he replied in a shaky voice.

Satisfied he wouldn't tip over and injure himself, I moved over to Adrianna. At first she spurned my attempts at helping, however the motion of her swatting at my steadying hand caused her to topple over striking her head on the stone floor.

"Ow," was all the verbal expression she could muster.

Her hand rubbed at her temple as I helped her to a sitting position.

"For a Vampire you are pretty hard headed," I said.

"Ha... Ha..." She replied in a cranky tone, but a faint smile appeared nevertheless.

"My intentions are honorable," I said seriously. "I only want to help."

She reluctantly acknowledged my words with a slight nod, which given her lighter than normal pallor was all the response she could manage.

"Besides," I continued, "Had I wanted to take a peek at your *fun bags* or take advantage of your shapely body I had every opportunity to do so while you were unconscious."

A smile erupted from her, as did a charming laugh.

"Then again," I said. "Who says I didn't," I smiled waggling my eyebrows in a knowing manner. "Where are we," Adrianna asked.

I looked around us.

"Not entirely sure," I replied. "I know we aren't at Bialek's place any longer."

She quirked a "you think?" eyebrow.

"*Hassan, India.*" Barnabas's *English* accent calmly proclaimed our location. "Near the *Hemavathi River*."

Adrianna, Tilly and I turned to see Barnabas propped up on an elbow watching us. Even Race rose up to look.

"The hiding place of the Sword of the King, Excalibur."

As we all digested that bit of information Bart took this opportunity to wake up. I'm not talking about a lethargic greeting to consciousness. No, he immediately jumped to his feet moving into a defensive stance, eyes darting around for possible threats. He reminded me of a prison inmate on edge. All he needed was to be brandishing a handmade Shiv threatening anyone that looked at him cross-eyed "not to touch his stuff" to complete the picture.

"Give it a rest," Race grumbled as he lay back down. I think the cool stones against his skin were helping with what ailed him.

"Yeah, Captain I touch everything." I chimed in not wanting to be left out with the insults. "Keep your hands in your pockets next time."

Bart straightened. His eyes resting on mine. He lowered his head, then his vice like hands were at my throat. I didn't actually see him move, but I felt the air he displaced as he took hold of me.

"You don't have your weapons Wizard," he said through a predatory smile. "How about I tear your tongue out just for good measure."

His thumbs tightened on my windpipe as the sound of vertebrate popping in my neck reverberated in my ears. I knew he wasn't breaking any of the bones; still it scared the crap out of me. My hands grasp his wrists attempting to get him off me. His hands were strong like thick metal bands wrapped around my neck. I looked around for help. Everyone seemed to have a difficult time getting to his or her feet. They appeared to be inebriated. The effects of the sleeping spell seemed to still be evident in their sluggish movements. It was sort of comical to watch. I tried for a witty comment, but all that came out was a "gack" sound. My vision reddened around the edges as my head pounded like a snare drum beating time to a rock and roll rhythm. Bart wasn't going to stop; he was going to end me. In desperation, I uselessly punched at his face; all I succeeded in doing was to make him smile more broadly.

"What, no smartass remark," he asked contemptuously.

My vision slowly faded to black, but before my sight blacked out completely I perceived a startled expression on Bart's face, he then abruptly released his hold on me. I fell to the floor in a heap, my knees knocking heavily on the stone as I landed hard on my left hip. A dark hulking form towered behind Bart, a huge right hand wrapped around the Vampire's neck. I heard some unintelligible remark in *German* then Bart went hurdling through the air backward colliding with the barrier. I groped about getting to my knees gasping for air. Stale and foul smelling though it was, the air tasted sweet as it filled my lungs. I turned my eyes toward Bart.

Have you ever sat outside on a glorious summer evening? I'm sure many of you have, who hasn't. A favorite drink clutched lazily in your hand. The heat mild, the humidity low, crickets chirping the first few verses of their night songs. A light breeze gently rustling the leaves in the trees, the creek of a rocking chair on a wood porch and the entire experience cast in a cool blue light of a bug zapper. The occasional electrified crackle of an unsuspecting bug hypnotized by the glow of the death trap as it's body comes into contact with the electrified metal screen.

Now, I want you to imagine a Bart sized bug zapper then you can appreciate the amount of crackling Bart did when he hit that magical barrier. Wilmar brushed his hands together giving a single curt nod in Bart's direction in a "take that" sort of gesture. Everyone was on their feet, except for me of course, shading our eyes to the dazzling light erupting from the barrier. Bart hung suspended five feet above the floor writhing in electrified pain before he was spat - so to speak - back onto the stones in a crumpled mess a foot or so away from me. I scrambled to my feet avoiding being struck with his body as a few sporadic crackles of energy escaped from the barrier before it settled back down becoming invisible once again.

Bart let out a pained groan as he attempted to move. The back of his coat was blackened and smoldering, threatening to burst into flames. The quick thinking Race sprang into action. I'm not entirely sure, but I think we all had varying degrees of the same shocked look of disgust on our faces as Race relieved himself onto Bart's back. Now I've never been accused of being able to judge someone's character or intentions, yet I'm fairly certain Race had Bart's safety and well being on his mind the whole time, not wanting such a valuable member of our group to burst into flames. Race is a kind and giving individual... OK, if you believe either of the last two statements I've made then I have some ocean front property in *Kansas* I'd like to sell you. We turned our gazes to Race as he performed the traditional shake before moving away.

"Was that necessary," Barnabas demanded.

"Yes," Race replied with a smile before he turned sitting back down on the spot where he lay a few moments before.

Barnabas shook his head in a disapproving manner as he scanned around our holding cell. Wilmar leaned in close to him.

"What is our next course of action," Wilmar inquired.

"I'm not sure," Barnabas replied doubtfully. "Our best course of action is to..."

Barnabas's words trailed off. His eyes locked onto something just beyond the barrier behind us. The blood seemed to drain from his skin as his body went rigid. I turned in the direction Barnabas's eyes were fixed. I froze as soon as I saw them; the luminous sanguine eyes peering through a hole in a portion of the deteriorating stonewall. Next to them just above the rim of the wall I noticed another set of eyes peering hungrily in my direction. As I turned scanning our surroundings I saw more, a lot more. Not three or four sets of eyes, but hundreds. All eyes focused on us possessed a deep seeded malice dancing within their depths. Tilly inched closer to me grabbing hold of my left leg.

"What are they," Adrianna asked curiously.

"Bogeymen," Barnabas replied. "Horrible little creatures."

Barnabas was in no way exaggerating with that last statement. Though this was my first time laying eyes on them, I'd heard stories about the Bogeymen. Some of them I've no doubt were flat out fiction while others weren't to be discounted so easily. Perhaps that's why parents make up stories about "The Bogeyman" because they're creatures plucked from nightmares.

Bogeymen aren't imposing specimens in stature at all, three feet high and lanky. Their skin from my observations was obsidian in color, which had a shiny cast like crude oil. What made them dangerous however were the four razor sharp sickle claws on each of their hands and feet. What made them absolutely terrifying were their lifeless blood red eyes and the six rows of shark like serrated teeth set in the jaws of their oval shaped heads. Oh, and as the legends go they're strong physically, highly intelligent and have absolutely no concept of fear.

Bart got delicately to his feet behind us. I turned observing his movements. He looked discombobulated as he took stock of his situation. His puzzlement at the dampness of his coat deepened as he took a section of fabric between pinched fingers giving it a sniff.

"Why am I wet," his question lingering in the humid air a little too long.

Others turned to regard him.

"Your coat started smoldering Sir," Tilly offered up helpfully in the silence. "We feared it may have combusted injuring you."

Tilly was an accomplished diplomat. Had to admire that quality. I think tensions would've been worse had we just told him Race pissed on his back.

Bart nodded in lethargic understanding.

"Why do I smell like urine," Bart asked suspiciously.

That was a question even our little diplomat didn't want to answer. I think matters were made worse by our guilty demeanor and averted eyes. Race's devious or should I say deviant chuckle didn't help matters. Bart stripped out of his drenched coat disgust oozing from his clouded expression. He discarded his coat next to Race with a contemptuous gesture before stalking as far away from the rest of us as our confined space would allow. I perceived his back going stock straight when he finally saw what the rest of us had been looking at for the past few minutes.

"Ahhhhh," Merlin said relish in his tone. "The curtain has risen and now we can experience this little farce."

"Where've you been," I asked perturbed.

I could feel odd stares from those within earshot around me. Tilly released my leg cautiously backing away, his look questioning my sanity. That meant I said the last statement aloud. Better look into getting a few "Insane and Loving It" t-shirts when I get home. I'm pretty sure I'm gonna need a few. I waved a hand for them not to worry.

"Sorry, I just remembered the title of a *Kathy Mattea* song." I said through a smile that I hoped didn't look like I was about to serve tea to a March hare.

"Where've you been," I said to myself this time. "And what do you mean by farce?"

"Be silent and turn round." Merlin replied curtly.

"What," I said incredulous. "I've been waiting for you to say something about all of this and now when you finally open your mouth I get some sort of cryptic reference, then you tell me to shut up and turn around." "If you want to stay in my head you have got to learn to work and play well with others."

"Turn round," Merlin commanded.

So I turned around, reluctantly.

Standing just inside the doorway of the church holding a gnarled staff was the tall Wizard that attacked me in Stumpwater's, the silver Janus mask still covering his face. He considered us for a short time before moving further into the remains of the structure. He stood near our prison facing Barnabas. Following close behind him were around thirty individuals in all. Four were dressed like the tall Wizard right down to the silver masks they wore. Moving along with them to their left was Whitey. When the group of what I presumed to be other Wizards hiding their identity came to a halt behind our albino friend. Whitey moved over to stand at the tall Wizard's left. Then came the sultry Vampire duo, Zoe and Isabel, they were flanked by six individuals wearing the garb of the Ashari assassins. They resemble the ones that attacked us at the *Thorne* building. The remainder of the people in the precession appeared to be - and this is just an assumption – more Vampires. Bringing up the rear of this parade of doom lumbered three Yeti ape beasts. They took up positions at the doorway glaring daggers of hatred at me as well as Wilmar.

Barnabas and the tall Wizard exchanged a series of intense looks as the group halted behind the tall Wizard and Whitey, arranging themselves in an irregular semicircle. The tall Wizard raised his arms in a mocking salute then said.

"The great Barnabas Blackmane and his lackeys."

A wave of laughter swept through those gathered then died away as quickly as it sprang up.

"A washed up Wizard, a pair of misguided Vampires, a monster right out of the pages of a novel, a mangy flea bitten Werewolf,"

"Hey asshole," Race interrupted. "I ain't got no fleas!" Then, he scratched self-consciously behind his ear.

"A poor excuse for an Elf," the tall Wizard continued unperturbed. "And an impudent apprentice that lacks any real talent for the magical arts."

I raised a hand grinning unfazed by his comments.

"Present," I answered in my best annoying tone.

Barnabas remained silent as I gravitated toward him as an unconscious response to the insults. I noticed the others had moved a bit closer to him, lending our meager support. Everyone except Bart, he continued to stay as far away from the rest of us as possible.

"You play an interesting game with the lives of your friends and associates," the tall Wizard said truculently.

He then turned making a beckoning gesture for someone behind him. He indicated to the cross atop the crumbling church. One of the Yeti huffed out a deep-throated rumble that sounded like "Yes". The beast shambled gracefully up the ruins of the walls all the way up to the cross. His huge hand closed around the shaft and with a quick powerful jerk, broke it off where the cross met the stone. The beast moved down the wall faster than he ascended, within moments he was placing the cross at the feet of his master in a deferential manner. The Yeti moved back to lurk with his brothers as the tall Wizard picked up the cross by the small end near the patibulum.

"Gather unto Caesar all that is Caesar's," he spoke with awe in his tone.

"The correct wording of that verse is; Render unto Caesar the things that are Caesar's, and unto God the things that are God's," I chimed in correcting our captor.

The tall Wizard regarded me with distaste for spoiling his moment. Granted, I couldn't see his expression through the Janus mask, but I could read body language. I realized after a few moments that all eyes were on me. I gazed around self-consciously.

"What," I asked innocently. "After spending years in a *Catholic* orphanage it irks me when people don't get *Bible* quotes right."

I heard the palpable disapproval rolling through the gathered assembly like the spontaneous wave at a football game. The tall Wizard raised the cross high in the air.

"Ostendo Sum Thy Specialis," the tall Wizard's cacophonous spell rose up echoing off every surface of the stone ruins.

The weather worn stone of the cross disintegrated, simply blowing away like desert sand shifting over dunes in a gentle breeze. What was revealed beneath the stone was a beautifully crafted Celtic inspired sword that was once held by an extremely famous king, Arthur.

"Excalibur," murmured Merlin in my mind.

Judging by the tall Wizard's posture, he gazed at the sword with what I assumed was avarice. I was fifteen feet away, yet I could feel the power radiating from the blade of this weapon. I was both awed and terrified. Awed for the swords beauty and power, terrified because this guy now possessed it. He didn't care about the swords historical significance, nor did he appreciate it for what it was, a terrible weapon of immense power.

"To see you brought low and beaten at your own game gives me immense pleasure," the tall Wizard said relishing the moment. "Tell me Barnabas, how does it feel knowing you have been finally bested by a Wizard more cunning than yourself?"

Barnabas remained silent. I didn't know what he was waiting for. In the past, - when I witnessed a few of his fights - he'd always banter with his adversary before quickly vanquishing them. Was he scared? Was he being cautious because he didn't have any of his magical tools at hand? Was he remaining quiet as to not anger the tall Wizard in order to spare the rest of us? His calm silence made me feel uneasy.

"You always thought of yourself as the cleverest of all Barnabas," the tall Wizard said. "But we know now that was never the case."

The tall Wizard lowered the sword passing it off to a Vampire that placed it into a wooden box held by one of the Yetis. The tall Wizard then raised a gloved hand, which he held out in front of him. Between his thumb and forefingers was a crystal, Tilly's crystal to be exact.

"Where is the soul essence that this vessel held," the tall Wizard asked coolly.

"If you are more powerful and more intelligent than I, you should know the answer to that question," Barnabas replied curtly.

The tall Wizard let out a chuckle filled with arrogance and contempt.

"So brave yet foolish, haven't you realized that you've lost,"

The tall Wizard turned to one of the Yeti's behind him, beckoning with a jerk of his head. The Yeti let out a grunt moving to the side. A pair of Yetis lumbered toward us dragging a body in each of their powerful hands. The bodies made no independent movements.

They stopped in front of the field raising the beaten and bloodied bodies high in the air like a fisherman holding prized catches. The features of the bodies were so mangled they were unrecognizable. Glancing to my right I could see the expression on Barnabas's face. He knew the deceased, three men and a woman.

"Yes," the tall Wizard oozed satisfaction. "You know who they are, your old friends Victor Felderbach, Rodfar Groakus, Zerial Thrum and last but not least Montagar Greybeak."

A feral chortle rose up from the throats of the Bogeymen, like the mocking laughter of a pack of ravenous hyena.

"Greybeak proved to be the strongest of the four, he nearly died before he gave us the hiding place of the sword." He said. "But, Zerial gave us the location of this," he continued flinging a beckoning hand out to the side the way a game show model might showcase a prize. "She began talking the moment I applied the Searing Stone."

A Searing Stone for those of you interested is a nasty torture device. It's a volcanic rock, which comes from the *Mediterranean Sea* near what use to be *Pompeii*. The stones are normally the size of a chicken egg. Sizes can vary however. The stones are polished to a mirror finish, and then magic runes are chiseled into its surface. An incision is made somewhere on a victim's body and the Searing Stone is placed inside. The stone activates when it comes in contact with living blood. The longer it remains within the body the higher the temperature becomes. It is not uncommon for a Searing Stone to burn right through a victim's body.

One of the Vampire twins stepped forward a small box held in her hands. She stood next to the tall Wizard as he opened the lid with a flourish revealing an ornately made ring, A Signet Ring.

It wasn't much of a stretch to puzzle out that King Arthur once owned this ring. From what I've seen so far, this guy possessed two of the artifacts and was dangerously close to getting a third from me. Our only wild card was Oswald and Glum. As long as they evaded capture we could keep tossing monkey wrenches into his plans.

Whatever they might be.

"That looks nice, did you get that thing out of a *Cracker Jack* box," I said, trying to get a rise from him.

The tall Wizard stared in my direction. Then he said with no emotion.

"We will see how funny you are when I peel the skin from your body,"

He made a "get rid of those things" gesture with his hand indicating the bodies. The Yetis grunted, hurling them in the direction of a dense group of lurking Bogeymen. They fell on them like ravenous dogs, screeching and growling over the sounds of flesh being torn from bone. I didn't have a clear view of what was happening and I thanked God for that. At that moment I realized that we're all going to die. Whoever this guy was he wasn't going to let us go. We were a liability to him. He was going to kill us no matter what happened and no one was going to come to our aid.

That thought depressed me. Don't misunderstand me; I've always known that I'd die one day, eventually. Just not so soon, I felt cheated in a way. Even though I was sort of a nerd that had horrible luck with women. I did however look forward to one day - as remote as the prospect might be - meeting a woman that tolerated my unusual quirks and lifestyle. A woman who loved me for me and of course my dashing good looks. - No chuckles please - A woman that looked a lot like Adrianna minus the fetish for blood drinking. Granted, if I watched the things that came out of my mouth when I opened it I could potentially live for quite a few centuries.

I slumped visibly exhaling a deep breath. I had what the tall Wizard wanted, but I couldn't let him have it. I let my eyes travel from one of my cellmates to another, Barnabas, then Wilmar, to Race, then Tilly. I completely overlooked Bart. My gaze rested on Adrianna, our eyes meeting. She stood calmly with her usual self-possessed nature, as though this situation was as inconsequential as picking up her dry cleaning. Given the world she was Lord and Master over a situation like this was quite possibly commonplace. Despite her mask of confident resolve I detected a glimmer of emotion directed at me. That made me smile. She did care about me. Given our brief time together I didn't know if that emotion was akin to infatuation or if she genuinely had feelings for me. It was a shame that we'd never get the chance to see where our emotions or lust would lead us. We were after all standing on a sharp cliff overlooking the bleak endless chasm of death. I smiled a resigned smile. I detected a minuscule break in her composed emotional mask when she read the expression on my face. I turned my attention back to our captors.

"Now," the tall Wizard began again as he held out the crystal. "The location of the soul essence if you please."

His question was met with silence, save for the gnawing of sharp teeth on bone off in the distance to our right.

"Must I resort to violence," he said exasperated.

"Apparently," I replied.

"Solomon," Barnabas chided.

"What," I broke in before he could continue. "He's going to kill us no matter what we do,"

I turned to glare at the tall Wizard.

"Isn't that right," I demanded.

"Of course," he said matter of factly. "But I assure you all that it will be quick and painless."

"See," I said pointing at our captor.

Have you ever found yourself in a position where you didn't know what the hell you were doing? I was in that situation now. I just couldn't stay quiet any longer. The odds stacked against us sucked. We were unarmed and imprisoned. Surrounded by hundreds of things that wanted to kill and eat us.

"I detest using barbaric means to gain information from my captives but I am on a schedule and require the information," he said coldly, then added "Now."

I grinned sardonically at him.

"Even if I tell you where the essence is and that is a big if, you are still one relic short," I countered. "Sort of throws off your schedule doesn't it stretch."

The tall Wizard struck a mocking thoughtful pose as he crossed his arms tapping a gloved finger against the mask.

"You're right," he said. "But you are operating under a false premise, I never indicated one way or the other that I didn't have the crown."

The tall Wizard glanced to his left and the group of Yetis near him parted once again. This time what entered sent icy pangs of horror and sadness coursing through my veins.

Mindlessly shuffling toward us was Glum. He looked like they beat him brutally with rubber hoses. His skin was a mass of welts and dark black bruises. Glum's clothes were tattered and bloodied with one of his shoes missing. In his arms cradled like a sleeping infant was the unmoving form of Oswald Gleason. Oswald appeared to be as bad off as Glum injury wise that is. His left eye appeared to be gone and his left hand was swollen to twice its size mangled horribly. Given his position in Glum's arms I couldn't see the extent of his injuries, I knew he was in bad shape. The sound of his shallow labored breathing carried to my ears over the distance between us. He was still alive.

The most unnerving thing about this sight was Glum's eyes. They were gone. Well, not gone per say, but devoid of the irises replaced instead by a faint green glow. Over his right breast was something, a round metal object attached to his skin by large serrated hooks. The object was roughly the size of a teacup saucer glowing the same faint green as his eyes.

"A mind taker," Merlin said disgusted. "The work of the Dark Elves."

My emotions kept me from speaking, but my body tensed in rage and I wanted to kill that asshole with the mask. Frustrated angry tears flowed from my eyes. Glum gently placed his adoptive father on the stone floor in front of Barnabas then moved away, standing before us slack jawed. I noticed tears were flowing from his swollen eyes as well. Barnabas stared remorsefully down at his friend. Adrianna moved in behind him placing a comforting hand on his shoulder. He didn't even notice it. The other Vampire twin moved toward the tall Wizard carrying a box. I knew that it contained the crown. He placed his hand upon the lid caressing the wood. He turned to Barnabas gesturing for the crown to be placed by the other two relics.

"Now, I hope that you understand the situation better," he said. "I will kill each and everyone of you until I find the essence starting with this dandy fat body and his troll." His extended index finger tracked over each of us like a marksman aiming for a bullseye landing finally on me.

"And finishing with the smart ass,"

We were fucked.

The tall Wizard raised a disinterested left hand to Glum.

"Kill him," he said boredom in his tone.

"Kill Oswald Gleason."

Glum lurched toward Oswald raising a powerful-balled fist above his head. Barnabas yelled for Glum to stop and I averted my eyes closing them tight.

# Chapter 25

When I opened my eyes, I was standing in the familiar circle of light near the pool of quicksilver. Merlin leaned on his slender staff regarding me.

"Why am I here," I asked my head darting around. "What happened to Oswald?"

"Rest easy young Solomon time passes quickly here but at a snail's pace in the conscious world," "Oswald remains alive for the moment, we must talk."

I composed myself.

"About what," I protested.

Oswald is about to have his head caved in by Glum and he wants to have a chat. Someone needs to have a talk with Merlin about his priorities.

"Since I know what you know I wanted to discuss what you thought was going on at this very moment," he said patiently.

"Haven't you been watching everything through my eyes and listening through my ears," I asked incredulously, "Oswald along with the rest of us are about to die!"

"Yes I have and yes I know what is at peril. But the question you need to ask yourself young Solomon is have you?"

Of course I've been watching and listening. Haven't I? What the hell does he mean, "Do I know what's going on here?"

I paced around the pool of quicksilver. My head lowered in thought running events back through my mind.

OK.

We were trapped in a circle of magic that absorbs energy, which makes the barrier more powerful if we attack it. Our belongings and our weapons were taken away. Obviously our captors weren't underestimating our abilities or taking any chances. Which possibly meant they were frightened of us. But, why be afraid when they had us surrounded and outnumbered by things that wanted to kill us. Most of the tall Wizard's accomplices arrayed against us were Mid-Realm creatures. Who would benefit by using them in the mortal world as soldiers? Someone that either didn't have enough muscle of his or her own or someone that didn't want to call attention to themselves.

Then of course there was the tall masked Wizard collecting the relics. Why was he collecting them? What was he going to do with them once he got them all? More importantly, how was he able to find out who the people were protecting the relics and how did he get close enough to grab them. That last question was singularly important, especially in Bialek's case. Bialek lived in the magical equivalent of a fortress. His compound was well known throughout the magical community to be as impregnable as Fort Knox. Everyone including Barnabas had to send word to Bialek before they visited. Barnabas never just popped in to say hello. That's why Bialek had the stone circle five miles away from his place. Bialek hated surprises. The magical defenses Bialek had arrayed around his place would've stopped an army. Judging by the bodies or what remained of them around the area, they had.

Which meant...

I turned abruptly to lock eyes on Merlin's. A twinkle danced in his blue eyes when he saw realization in mine. A vulpine smile stretched across his face.

"It was an inside job," I said stunned.

"Precisely,"

"So, that tall Wizard is Bialek? Did he fake his own death," I asked excitement in my tone.

Merlin's smile faded as he arched a reproving eyebrow. He let out a long-suffering sigh.

"No, if you recall Tilly's words after your encounter with the albino and the Vampire twins the answer lies there," he said frustrated.

I rubbed a hand over my face, thinking. Then I began.

"Tilly told Barnabas that he saw Rham stab Bialek in the heart,"

"Which means?"

"The tall Wizard couldn't be Bialek," I said deflated. "Then who?"

"Think on what you know," Merlin said. "There were eight Wizards in the Octagon, correct," Merlin asked.

I nodded in agreement.

"When you thought you were taking the crown to Stumpwater's, Barnabas went to Orm's home where he saw Orm's body with his own eyes,"

I nodded again.

"You should be able to put the pieces together now," Merlin encouraged.

I glared at him frustrated. Couldn't he just tell me the stupid answer instead on having me go through all of this supposition?

"OK," I said with just a bit of heat. "Barnabas is in the cell with me,"

"One," Merlin said holding up a crooked index finger.

"Oswald is lying on the stone outside the cell in pretty bad shape,"

"Two," Merlin said raising another finger.

"OK," annoyance rising in my voice. "Could you not do that,"

Merlin lowered his hand in disappointment.

"Bialek is dead, that's three,"

"Orm is dead or at least Barnabas says he is and that makes four... Victor Felderbach, Rodfar Groakus, Zerial Thrum and Montagar Greybeak were killed and their bodies devoured by the Bogeymen, which accounts for the remaining four,"

"Very good," Merlin said in a sarcastic tone. "Now young Solomon, who is left?"

I shrugged my shoulders. Then a thought occurred to me.

"Well, we've accounted for everyone except the apprentices,"

Merlin inclined his head in an encouraging manner.

"Well, there's me of course, but I didn't do anything,"

"Obviously," Merlin chimed in.

"Olivia is dead, Oswald didn't have an apprentice, I don't know if the other four had apprentices, so the only person we have yet to account for is James, Orm's apprentice,"

"Ah, now you've come to the heart of the matter," said Merlin,

"Heart, what do you mean by heart," I asked. "Is James the tall Wizard,"

Merlin moved around the circle of light my eyes and body tracking his steps.

"Why did Orm pick up his ingredients at the magic shop," Merlin asked.

I thought about the morning where all of this started. Staying up most of the night with Abner and his pack, then manning the front counter sleep deprived as Oswald and Orm came in to do some shopping.

"Orm said that he was punishing his apprentice, something about rusty carpet tacks,"

Merlin nodded thoughtfully.

"Had Orm ever come to pick up his ingredients in the past,"

I ran through my memories. He only came to the shop to meet with Barnabas on occasion and those were rare. It was James that always came to the shop to do menial tasks.

"No," I said.

"Why would Orm decide to pick up his ingredients on this particular day and not send James, his lowly dull witted apprentice," Merlin asked.

I shook my head uncertainly as I turned away from Merlin. I didn't have a clue as to why Orm would decide to do something so beneath him as to run errands… My thoughts trailed off, unless…

"James was already dead the morning Orm showed up at the shop, wasn't he,"

Merlin inclined his head minutely acknowledging my progress in thinking.

"So that makes Orm the tall Wizard,"

"Most definitely," replied Merlin.

"Why couldn't you have just told me the information instead of having me go through all of this Yoda crap?"

Merlin smiled.

"A knife cannot cut unless the blade has been properly sharpened nor can a mind be used well unless it has been made to do so,"

I rolled my eyes.

"That still doesn't explain how Orm was able to get through Bialek's defenses," I asked skeptically.

"Does it not," Merlin replied. "Use your mind."

I groaned exasperated.

"I don't want too," I whined.

Merlin considered me, disappointment evident in his eyes. I averted mine. Then I sighed.

"OK," I said. "We'll do it your way."

I paced back and forth ordering my thoughts then I said.

"There was really only one way for someone to get past Bialek's defenses and that was for someone to deactivate them from the inside,"

I turned to face Merlin.

"There were two others in Bialek's place that we know of… Tilly and his apprentice Olivia," I began. "I'm fairly certain that Tilly had nothing to do with Bialek's death," "He had the crystal and was pretty badly beaten up when he arrived at the magic shop."

I pondered that piece of information for a moment.

"So that leaves Olivia," I said scratching my chin. "But her body was at Bialek's place,"

"Are you sure of that fact," Merlin inquired.

"No,"

Then a thought hit me.

"Olivia let Orm and the Vampires into Bialek's compound... It was her,"

I shook my head can't believing that none of this had occurred to me earlier. Then I said.

"But if Orm and Olivia are alive that means that the body we thought was hers at Bialek's was really James's made to look like Olivia using a masking spell of some sort,"

I turned away from Merlin.

"Which would explain all the dark magic around that place," I continued. "Orm must've laid down various spells to throw us off the identity of Olivia's body."

Where was she hiding herself? I thought. She couldn't have been lying low while all this was going on she... Then the answer came to me. I turned back to eye Merlin.

"The albino... Olivia is the albino," I said triumphantly. "Orm had to have known about Rham through Bialek because he was with Oswald and Barnabas the night that the real Rahm was sucked into the collapsing doorway... Orm used Rahm's appearance as some sort of psychological weapon," "Bialek's expression must've been one of surprise just like Barnabas's was when he saw Rahm in the shop,"

Merlin smiled approvingly.

"Orm conspired with Olivia somehow turning her loyalties away from Bialek... He killed James or had him killed the day everything happened, he couldn't have any witnesses... Orm knew everything about the Octagon, it's members and how the relics may have been protected but maybe not the locations of all the artifacts,"

I paced around a bit more as my train of thought kept on chugging.

"But something went wrong when they tried to get the crystal from Bialek... Even though he was caught off guard he still managed to thwart their plans... That's why Olivia had to come to the magic shop following Tilly... Neither her nor Orm expected Tilly to escape with the crystal. It happened all so fast,"

My head throbbed from all the thinking, but I kept my brain chugging along like the little engine that could.

"Very good young Solomon sadly you have overlooked one important detail," Merlin said in a chiding tone.

Crap! Here I thought I was doing so well. I sighed heavily searching my brain for scraps of thought overlooked during my initial deductions.

"The marks," I finally offered. "How did Orm get past the effects of the marks that bound the information only to the members of the Octagon,"

"Very good young Solomon," Merlin beamed.

Thoughts and ideas came more freely now.

"Barnabas said that if any of the members of the Order attempted to speak of the secrets they held to an outside party, that they would suffer terrible pain which would ultimately incapacitate them.

"Yes, that is true," said Merlin. "And what creatures have Orm and Olivia surrounded themselves with?"

It didn't take long for my brain to hit upon the answer. I shook my head however not wanting to register the implications if that thought were true. A Wizard is a powerful being in their own right, but if you were to add the strength, speed, immortality and power of a Vampire to what a Wizard could do already, you'd have a dangerously frightening being on your hands.

"Are you saying Orm is a Vampire?"

"Yes," Merlin answered bluntly.

"That's impossible," I began. "There were things in place like spells and charms and *God* knows what else to monitor the life of each member of the Order. Barnabas had a woodcarving with jewels in it that changed color and Oswald had his rings... I can't speak for what the others had in the way of monitoring devices, but they all would've known when Orm had become a Vampire... You know as well as I do that a person must die in order to be reborn as a Vampire,"

"A quandary is it not," Merlin said.

He lifted his head looking about somewhere above him.

"It is time for you to return to the conscious world," he said... I want you to taunt Orm as mercilessly as you can, do not restrain yourself... Tell him that you are the new vessel for my essence,"

"But..." I protested.

"Do as I say, make him angry. Tell him you are the new vessel." Merlin commanded, sharply cutting me off,

"Now off you go,"

I don't think I can accurately describe the feeling of returning from my subconscious mind, but I'm fairly certain the sensation would feel a lot like being flushed down a toilet. Though I've never actually experienced being flushed down the toilet, I'd have to also surmise dizziness and heavy sweating would be part of it.

\* \* \* \* \* \*

I returned to the same place I'd been standing before Merlin called me for the chat. Which of course I would've anyway seeing only my mind checked out. Glum's arm was more or less in the same position when I left. Recalling Merlin's instructions I called out.

"Hey Orm why don't you do your own murdering for a change,"

Orm's masked face jerked in my direction. His right hand shot up staying the blow that would've surely crushed Oswald's head. Glum tottered back on his heels as the abrupt stopping of his movement unbalanced him, but he managed to right himself.

"Yeah, I thought that was you, the smell sort of gave you away"

Barnabas glared dumbfounded in my direction like I had three heads and a tail. I turned giving him a reassuring glance.

Orm regarded me for a long moment before his hand went to the mask, removing it from his face. He dropped the Janus mask to the stone floor with a clatter before pulling back his hood.

"Yeah, even a mask can't hide that ugly mug of yours," I said.

I think I've described earlier that Orm was not a handsome man. Apparently becoming a Vampire didn't improve his looks much at all. Though his eyes had the piercing jade green color that all Vampires shared.

"You can lose the disguise too Olivia," I said staring fixedly in her direction.

I noticed in my peripheral Wilmar visibly started at my words. The imposter Rham glanced in Orm's direction then back to me. Rham's appearance erupted in undulating ripples. His features melted away in mere seconds, leaving a plain looking yet attractive young woman in her early twenties standing before us. Rahm's clothes hung loosely over her frame as she clutched the medusa cane stiffly in front of her. Wilmar took a step forward, his eyes fixed on the woman that now stood in front of us. She flashed a smug pitying smile in Wilmar's direction.

"Poor sweet silly Wilmar, you never really knew me at all," she said emphasizing the word "silly" in an accent I thought was Russian or some other Slavic dialect.

Wilmar's lips moved, but words were just not there to express his emotions.

"You were blind to who and what I really was just like Hans. Both of you thought I was a weak helpless little girl that needed saving." She said hatefully. "I didn't need him and I never needed you," she spat then pressed on. "Cooped up out in the middle of nowhere miles away from anywhere with only a horny old man and an Elf to keep me company… He never wanted to leave that stupid compound of his… I couldn't listen to his stupid ramblings of the good old days any longer… He was boring, He was lazy, He was filthy and he smelled. The man couldn't keep his hands off of me, he even tried to get me to go to bed with him on numerous occasions,"

Olivia's body visibly cringed at the thought.

"Pathetic worm,"

Wilmar stiffened, his eyes filling with tears. Olivia regarded him with emotionless eyes as she stepped closer to the barrier.

"Poor Wilmar, did you honestly think I could have feelings for an abomination like you, the only reason I visited you was to get away from Bialek and Tilly… Later that excuse allowed me to make trips to my new Master,"

She turned inclining her head to Orm.

"Traitor," yelled Tilly as he lunged at Olivia.

Race held him back. His tiny balled fists punching erratically at empty air.

"And Tilly," she said fixing her eyes on him. "All you were ever good for was washing our clothes and fetching my tea."

"He trusted you," he spat through tears. "We trusted you,"

"And where did that trust get you," she asked harshly, cutting in on him. "Hans is dead and you'll follow him shortly,"

Orm held up a silencing hand.

"I think it's time to stop all this talking... This unmasking of myself and my accomplice is most unfortunate Solomon," he said haughtily.

His high-pitched French accent had returned. The mask must've had some sort of voice modulating spell on it.

"You must think of yourself like a famous fictional detective cast in the same light as *Sherlock Holmes* or *Hercule Poirot*, yes,"

Orm chuckled.

"No, you are like neither of them. "At best your are a pathetic novice and like all novices you overlook the obvious."

"And what's that?" I asked feigning genuine interest.

Orm flashed an arrogant smile.

"There is always an unseen accomplice," he said wryly. "Bartholomew, would you care to join us out here."

I turned to Bart, stunned. The magical field pulsed behind Bart. The field, invisible up to this point flared to a bright azure color bending inward flowing around him like a wall of water separating Bart from the rest of us.

"I'd be glad too, the smell of wet dog is rather pungent in here for my tastes," Bart said moving over to stand to Orm's right once he was clear of his prison.

The field snapped back into place with an audible crackle. The light faded as the field became invisible once again. I hoped that no one saw my jaw drop open in surprise. I was embarrassed enough as it was.

I knew that Bart was a jerk of epic proportions, but I really didn't see that one coming. By the look of everyone's stunned expressions I'd say they didn't either, all except Adrianna that is. She didn't show much emotion at all. Hell, even her body language didn't give anything away. I'd hate having to play poker with her.

Strip poker maybe...

OK. Yes I know I have to focus, but cut me some slack. I'm about to die here. Her eyes fixed piercingly on Bart.

Bart flashed a satisfied smug expression as he stripped out of his tattered and wet winter gear. He was given fresh clothes by a Vampire lackey, I realized looking at the man that he was one of members of Bart's strike team that helped out in the conference room at

Adrianna's building. Avery, I think was his name. But he wasn't a Vampire then, he must've been turned recently.

"You may glare at me all you wish Adrianna, but I want you to remember something. You were far too careless and far too trusting, you alone created this situation not me" Bart said pulling on a new t-shirt.

"Why," Adrianna asked.

"Why," he replied indignantly. "I thought my reasons for betraying you would be clear even to you,"

Hate clouded the smile on his face.

"Power,"

He focused his eyes on hers.

"When I kill you I'll be the head of Thorne house and will be in control of all its money and influence."

He grinned triumphantly.

"With it and the help of the other houses I can once and for all exterminate these Werewolf abominations and cast humanity down into the role it was meant for... Food,"

Funny isn't it, how this whole situation turned into some kind of second-rate soap opera. Sort of makes you wonder if *God* actually likes drama and has it embedded in our genetic code. That line of reasoning would go along way to explaining why we love winners, but love it even more when they crash and burn.

Adrianna quirked an embittered smile.

"Food… You must be one of those Outlaw fanatics," she said scornfully.

"One of them?" He replied laughing. "I created the Outlaws and I did it right under your nose and you never even realized it... I funneled manpower, resources and millions of dollars through shell companies which I created as well as hiding the movement of money in the balance sheets of a few of your legitimate subsidiaries and you were none the wiser,"

He laughed derisively.

"Haven't you realized yet that it was I who sent the assassins after you?" He asked. "I had that team standing by to kill you for weeks when these three idiots showed up,"

He said indicating Barnabas, Race and myself.

"Then I saw my perfect opportunity, I'd have the Ashari kill you, then blame it on the Wizards and the Werewolf."

Well, that explained how the Ashari got there so fast. They weren't trailing us like I initially thought. How could they? Bobum and his people were watching everywhere around the shop and the twins were cleared of any possible magical bugs or trackers. Those assassins were meant for Adrianna as Barnabas surmised which explained why they were carrying only Ash daggers. I should have realized during the attack or at least right after it, that none of them carried weapons to kill Barnabas and me or Race.

"But," he continued. "What often happens in regard to betrayal of this magnitude, the execution of my plan was off and you all survived."

"You executed prematurely..." I asked mockingly. "It could happen to any man... It's never happened to me of course, I've never had that problem... But given your age and quickness to anger you might want to look into getting a prescription for the little blue pill,"

I turned to Adrianna giving her a sly wink. Her expression remained controlled, but I knew she caught my meaning. Bart was outwardly unfazed by my comment, though inwardly, however I knew he was questioning his manhood and the pair of pants he chose to wear.

"Fortune smiled upon me again when you Adrianna agreed to accompany these two half-breed lovers on this mission with none of your faithful bodyguards," He said emphasizing the word - faithful - sarcastically. "I was overjoyed by this news and contacted my second team for them to be ready... Unfortunately the storm prevented the Yetis... he said indicating the shaggy beasts with a gesture. "From arriving at the portal in time to intercept all of you," he continued. "And this freak," he spat glaring in Wilmar's direction. "Appeared from nowhere spoiling my plans and in the process killing four of my mercenaries and wounding two others,"

"So it was you that brought all these Mid-Realm beasts to fight for you," Barnabas interjected.

"No Barnabas, I brought them here," Orm said proudly. "They owed me a debt or two and now they are paying them off... Though a few have expressed interest in staying around this realm for a while,"

A maniacal chorus of laughter rose up all around us. The Bogeymen were laughing as well, though it sounded more like a ham butt caught in a clunky old garbage disposal.

"Man, you two are a pathetic pair aren't you," I said. "Orm needed to go to Mid-Realm for some muscle and you Bart, you just can't catch a break,"

"I eventually did, Orm traveled back to the site of Bialek's compound arranging everything there while you were off resting in the freaks cabin and Barnabas was sitting idle worrying about his oafish apprentice,"

At some point during his monolog Bart had taken out a little knife and was fitfully twirling the blade through his fingers.

"All I had to do was to get one of you to touch that medallion. Since you were all too leery of it I took it upon myself to spring the trap spiriting us all away from that site of carnage,"

Bart's satisfied expression turned to thoughtful remembrance. He turned to Orm.

"Why were there so many bodies of my people at Bialek's compound Wizard," Bart asked coldly.

"It was a matter of necessity in order to fool the keen eye of Barnabas," Orm answered unruffled by the question.

Bart nodded once then made a gesture with his right hand. Vampires fell upon the four Janis mask clad Wizards. Their vicious attack was a horror to witness. When the Vampires were finished all four Wizards lay dead in an ever-expanding pool of blood mere feet away from Orm. Fury welled up inside Orm as his eyes went wide in shock and he wheeled upon Bart.

"Why did you do that," Orm spat the question at his co-conspirator.

Energy swirled around Orm's clinched fists. The Yeti's and Bogeymen tensed for possible action.

"Balancing the scales Wizard... Balancing the scales," Bart spat the words. "Blood for blood,"

"You shouldn't have killed them uselessly. We could have used their abilities,"

Bart turned to glare into Orm's eyes.

"The same could be said of my people Wizard. "We'll be the ones to spill the most blood in this revolution while you Wizards remain relatively unscathed. However, this is not the time, nor the place to have this discussion. Let us finish our business and talk about this later," Bart said placating his partner.

Orm struggled to bite back the words poised on his tongue. He seemed to compose himself as the magic around his fists faded. He nodded once turning his attention back to us. Their relationship it seemed was built on mistrust. Perhaps that could be used to our advantage. I felt a tap on my shoulder. I turned finding no one to my right or left. I heard the clearing of a throat. I caught a few of my cellmates staring at me wondering what the hell I was doing. I gave an embarrassed smile. Then I realized it was Merlin attempting to get my attention.

"What?" I thought ungraciously.

"Did I not tell you to taunt him," he asked.

"I'm working up to it," I replied.

"Work harder and make haste our window of opportunity grows ever shorter,"

I shook my head attracting more stares from my cellmates.

"And how do you fit into all this Orm," I asked. "What's your angle, are you the boss of this little drama or just someone's errand boy bitch,"

Orm, Olivia and Bart leveled their eyes at me. To be completely honest everyone assembled was looking in my direction. Except for Glum and Oswald that is, for obvious reasons.

Orm chuckled hatefully.

"I'm the mastermind of this so called "drama" you insignificant cretin, but I serve one more powerful than myself." He said with reverence. "One who will deliver us from the insanity, destruction and greed of man,"

"Oh," I said. "You're a do Gooding nut job then,"

"Nut job," Olivia spat. "You know nothing,"

Orm silenced her once again.

"It was I who thwarted the great Barnabas Blackmane and it is I who will deliver these weapons," he indicated the three wooden boxes that now contained the signet ring, crown and Excalibur. "To my Master,"

Orm moved closer to our cell standing directly in front of Barnabas.

"You thought yourself so clever, but I figured out how to beat you... Death was the only way you would allow us to escape this spell. Oh sure... I could have come to you all and said I wanted to leave the Order, but you would've taken my memories of my time spent guarding these relics... If I did that I wouldn't have been able to profit from my unique knowledge and experience... Do you know the shame of being poor Barnabas," Orm asked with contempt in his voice.

"All of you, save myself were wealthy beyond belief and you kept me poor for years living out there in that godforsaken wilderness away from the cities which is where I wanted to be... None of you compensated me or allowed me to make money as to not draw attention to our organization,"

He laughed harshly.

"No Barnabas, You wanted me to remain penniless and wanted us all to take our secrets to the grave,"

Orm made a wide dramatic wave of his hand.

"Who better to speak with about death than a Vampire and an ambitious one at that,"

He turned inclining his head to Bart before addressing the assembled gallery of baddies.

"Blood,"

His voice reverberated around the ruins.

"Vampire blood was what I needed to make my plans... The only problems with that were how to get the blood I needed and how to keep the monitoring stones you had in place from notifying everyone that something was a miss," he said sweeping back to face Barnabas.

"For three years I drank small vials of Vampire blood that I received from Bartholomew which acted as a protective shield against your binding spells, camouflaging my intent," he said. "If anyone was looking at the monitoring stones when I drank the blood all an observer might see is a faint change in color for the fewest of seconds," he finished with a smile.

"The plan was ingenious, my Lord," Olivia said awe dripping from her every word.

Orm turned to his accomplice placing a gloved hand affectionately against her cheek. She closed her eyes leaning into the touch.

Yuck.

Orm was a heck of a lot uglier than Bialek as men go. How could she be attracted to him? Either she was into him for his big brain or something else equally as big...

Like, his enormous ego.

Yeah, you thought I was going somewhere else with that didn't you.

Pervert.

Then again maybe she was one of those people attracted to power and money. Though Orm already said he wasn't very wealthy as Wizards went. In point of fact he didn't have a pot to piss in. So it couldn't have been his money that she was attracted to.

"The effects of the Vampire blood were astounding," he said letting his hand fall to his side, again turning to Barnabas.

"Not only did it allow me to converse with other parties about the members of the Octagon, the relics, possible locations of the items in question and the means to obtain them, I was intrigued by my increased strength, heightened senses and speed."

A flash of movement barely perceptible, followed by a sharp sound carried to my ears. Orm stood over a fist-sized hole that appeared in the stone. A fine mote of dust rose from the newly formed depression.

"I couldn't let this new power slip through my fingers." I am now the most powerful Wizard in history," "More powerful than you Barnabas and even more powerful than Merlin himself… It was then I decided to turn, but not before I knew Bialek was dead… That was the only way you see that I could've had an unshakable alibi, if both he and I were dead then who was the betrayer,"

His head dropped in remembrance.

"Sadly James wanted no part of my scheme and I had to kill him,"

I laughed, a rich mocking laugh.

"You aren't even in the same class as Merlin." I said. "If you two were cars, Merlin would be a *Bentley* equipped with all the bells and whistles while you Orm would be a *YUGO*. Both are cars, one is luxurious and awesome in every way, the other however, just sucks,"

I looked in Olivia's direction.

"Or are you the one who... Sucks," my question laced with innuendo.

Her shocked reddening face gave me the answer that I was looking for. A triumphant smile played on my face.

"Does Orm have an impressive wand," I asked moving my hands up and apart indicating the possible length of his unseen member. "Or is it not regulation sized equipment."

I brought my out stretched hands closer until they were about two or three inches apart.

"What do you know of Merlin," Orm spat. Judging by the hue of his skin I'd say he was past the point of being pissed.

"Happy now," I thought.

"Yes," Merlin replied through what sounded like a grin.

"I know, because I'm the new vessel for Merlin's spirit," I said like he should have known this fact all along.

"You are the new vessel of Merlin's spirit?" He asked mockingly.

"Yep," I replied. "I thought that the most powerful Wizard in the world would've been able to detect the aura I now project."

Orm's eyes narrowed as my subtle insult registered in his brain.

"One second," I said holding up a finger turning my head to pretend to listen to what Merlin might be saying.

"Uh huh, Yeah, Uh huh... Are you sure?"

I leveled my gaze back on Orm.

"Merlin says that you are a tiresome prat that isn't good enough to polish his staff... So to speak,"

Orm's hands clenched into tight fists, I was hoping he was about to blow a gasket.

"Oh, he also says that you're a douche bag and that you won't leave this place alive."

If that statement didn't get a reaction, nothing would.

# Chapter 26

Orm's arms flashed out. Thick bands of energy exploded from the fingertips of his outstretched hands piercing the containment wall. They coiled around my arms, upper chest and waist drawing me in tight constricting my breathing. Barnabas, Wilmar, Race, Adrianna and Tilly rushed to my aid, but the writhing bands of strong energy kept them at bay thwarting their efforts.

"Expertly done young Solomon," Merlin cried out in my head.

"Thanks," I managed. "Glad I could help." I couldn't conceal the sarcasm, but I didn't think Merlin picked up on it.

Pain coursed through my body. I felt blood rushing to my head as the bands tightened, I dared not exhale for fear of passing out. Perspiration welled from my skin running into my eyes. I struggled to no avail. I knew that if the pressure on my body continued my head was going to pop like an overinflated balloon. Suddenly, a thought occurred to me. One I had not entertained before, mainly because it hadn't crossed my mind.

"You're going to bring the field down once you're free of my body aren't you," the question hung in my quickly clouding head.

"That is my intention, yes," Merlin responded.

"Would you be able to make the others hear me," I thought through blinding pain.

"Of course," Merlin said amused. An exceedingly simple spell."

"Good," I said. "I need to talk to them,"

A faint light flared to life in the depths of my mind, steadily growing in intensity until finally the light filled my field of view. Then, the most amazing thing happened. I could see simultaneously through my cellmates' eyes. The alien sensation was unsettling at first, but after a few short moments I became accustomed to the feeling.

I said. "Don't panic, it's me, Solomon,"

Sensing everyone's bewilderment at hearing my voice in their minds I took the opportunity to grin even though my mind and body were a flame with pain. I'd been hearing the same voice in my head - along with quite a few others - for years now and it's time they got a taste of what I've had to put up with.

"No questions please, when the containment field drops... That'll be the time to make your move... Good luck," the connection broke as I felt my stomach churn and roil, bile rising in my throat.

Behind me off to my right, I thought I heard Wilmar cracking his knuckles. I dared a glance to my right. I saw the big man glaring murderously at the assembled clutch of Yeti's. Race must've been feeling better because he had changed into his wolf form arraying himself in the direction of the Bogeymen. Tilly, appeared as though he were going to follow him into the impending fray. I glanced to my left catching a glimpse of Adrianna. Her eyes fixed on something ahead of her. Bart I thought. I hadn't a clue as to what she was going to do to him, but I was pretty sure it wasn't going to be pleasant. Barnabas stood a short distance away from Adrianna. A pained expression haunted his features. He remained silent, only inclining his head in my direction.

A violent jerk pulled me through the magical field depositing me roughly onto the stone floor. The coils however, still held me fast, the pain was indescribable. Muffled cries of concern came from Adrianna or Tilly or maybe Barnabas, I wasn't sure. Blood poured from my eyes and nose, the coils continued to tighten. I choked out a breath unable to hold it any longer and wasn't able to take another. My lungs had no room to expand; the coils drew ever tighter around me.

"So Merlin is inside you is he," Orm spat scornfully. "Whether he is or not we will soon find out."

Orm glanced obliquely in Olivia's direction. She inclined her head. Without a word she produced an object wrapped in a dark cloth from one of the pockets of her coat. She pulled the cloth from the object revealing a crystal sphere the size of a racquetball. Orm made a gesture with his hand and I was once again upright hovering a few inches above the stone floor facing her. She lifted the crystal ball holding it in front of my face as Avery, Bart's Vampire security guard pulled a pistol from the inside of his coat placing the muzzle against my temple. An icy chill ran through me, but I didn't panic. The barrel felt cold yet pleasant against my skin despite knowing that was to be the instrument of my death.

"I wish I could say that I hate to do this to you, but I would be lying," Orm said, emotionlessly.

I closed my eyes waiting for what was to come next. I thought of...

Nothing.

Absolutely nothing came to mind.

What a jip.

I cannot tell you how many times that I've read stories in which there was always a character facing his or her own death. More often than not a doomed character recalled memories of relationships not yet realized, long lost loves, missed opportunities, children or a favorite toy. Why I even read a story once where the last thought on one of the characters mind was of his old faithful, yet dearly departed Beagle.

A Beagle.

And what have I decided to look fondly back on? Nothing!

So unfair.

Why couldn't my last thoughts be of the view I was able to get looking through the top of Adrianna's glass desk at her delicious bare legs and slightly opened robe. Because the universe sucks that's why.

I felt a slight motion of the pistol as Avery pulled the trigger. The heart stopping sound of the gun firing was deafening in my left ear. I think my very last thought was I hoped that the Bogeymen choked on my bones.

As I waited for an angelic light to appear to guide my spiritual departure, something strange occurred. I heard the faint sound of a small metallic object hitting the stone beneath me. Followed by a round of gasps that came from the arrayed group of bad guys, shortly after that many pairs of feet shuffling away from me. If that weirdness wasn't enough the constricting coils of dark magic that were strangling the life out of me disappeared. I had the briefest of moments to ponder that fact when gravity and its unforgiving nature abruptly drop me heavily to the stone floor.

My eyes popped open. A figure bathed in warming ethereal light stood mere feet from me, a slender Wizard's staff held firmly in his left hand while the other was up, fingers out stretched. Orm, Bart, Olivia and the rest of our captors looked scared. I had the impression based purely on their body language that none of them expected this turn of events. Hell, even I didn't expect this.

It was Merlin; he appeared to be angry and ready for battle. He glanced down at me flashing a smile and a reassuring wink. Without warning or preamble, Merlin turned to his left launching himself into Avery's body. Avery convulsed immediately on contact with Merlin's spirit, dropping the pistol he held. Orm along with most of his entourage took a few more unsure steps away from the man. Bursts of random intense white light escaped from Avery's eyes, mouth and ears as he jerked violently in response to what I assumed was a monumental struggle going on inside his body for possession of it. The battle lasted for the briefest of seconds until it culminated in what could only be described as an explosion. Everyone standing outside the containment field was rocked back on their heels by an unseen force. The blast caused all assembled to shield their eyes from flying dust and debris.

When I was able to focus on the scene again, Avery stood examining his hands. A satisfied smile playing across his features, beside him laid a spirit, which wasn't that of Merlin. The spirit that lay upon the ground looked like Avery, sort of. Where Merlin's spirit was bathed in pure brilliant white light, this spirit was shadowed in a dark blood red color appearing to be sort of deformed. Not that Avery looked like the *Elephant Man* or anything, he just looked odd, unfinished. I realized that the bad guys were creeping closer to Merlin, morbid curiosity on their faces. Avery's spirit stirred, attempting to get to a sitting position, but was having trouble. Not because he was weak I surmised, but because he had no actual practice with his new intangible form. After some fruitless efforts, he ran a hand over his face in frustration. Startled he drew it away staring at it befuddled. Then he held up his other hand to compare it with its mate. His eyes roved over his body panic setting in, he scanned frantically around searching. Surprised eyes locked on the standing figure of Avery a few feet away. He groped feverishly trying to get back to his body, back to safety. Unfortunately his fingers and hands could not find purchase.

As I watched this sad scene a sound echoed around the hushed silence of the skeletal remains of the church. A sound that didn't originate from anyone or anything assembled here, distant rumbling sounding like the bellow of an angry bull elephant moments before it charges. Only this particular bellow sounded deeper in bass like it came from something far larger and the sound came from beneath our feet. Fear skittered down my spine like a dachshund puppy running to and fro on a hardwood floor. My eyes were fixed on Avery's spirit as a thick reddish black tentacle resembling an appendage you might find on an aquatic animal residing in the deep unexplored canyons of the *Pacific Ocean* erupted from the ground. Boney hooks flexed hungrily as I watched it slither across the stone floor seeking out prey.

If that sight wasn't disgusting enough, another rose up next to the first followed by six more tentacles all blindly groping along the stone toward Avery's spirit leaving a thick mucus like trail.

Avery tried his best to scuttle away from the probing tentacles; sadly his efforts were in vain. Fear and horror consumed him as an unworldly tentacle latched onto his ankle jerking him violently toward the other seven. Terror filled his eyes. His mouth frozen open in what looked like a blood-curdling scream though no sound issued from his lips. The other tentacles wrapped around him covering most of his body except for one pleading eye peering through a gap between two tentacles as he was pulled down into the hellish realm where the beast existed.

"Shit," Was the only word I managed once my fright abated.

Looking about I found I was no longer standing in the same place I'd been. I hadn't realized that I'd moved, but apparently I did. I found myself standing to the side of the magical cell, away from where those tentacle things emerged. Orm and his people had moved a respectable distance away from Avery's demise, the Bogeymen however hadn't retreated at all and in fact they moved closer.

Merlin, who was now inside Avery's body hadn't budged. He remained right where I'd seen him a moment ago only this time he was laughing, then locked eyes on Orm.

"You've lost," Merlin said coldly in Avery's silky smooth baritone voice.

Merlin's eyes flared yellow consumed by a spectral light. Orm and his people moved forward unsure of what was happening, but their need to stop Merlin from whatever he was attempting outweighed their fear.

They reacted far too late, hesitating too long. Merlin raised his outstretched hands bringing them together in a clap creating a sound so loud it was deafening, like the first spine stiffening thunderclap of a storm heralding the approaching untamed force of nature.

Light brighter than the sun flashed out from his hands. I shielded my eyes. Though I couldn't see, I could hear the agonized wails of the Bogeymen and Vampires. Light, it would seem was not their friend. Adrianna even let out a pained whimper. I felt bad for her. The last time I saw her, she was still wearing most of her winter gear, which should afford some measure of protection. She'd also been applying liberal amounts of sunscreen to her exposed skin religiously.

When the spots pulsing in my closed eyes had dissipated I opened them. Merlin was nowhere to be found and the wooden boxes that contained three of the relics were gone. I searched around the ruins of the church, not seeing him or the boxes. I hoped to God that he'd taken them. Vampires' lay on the ground unmoving, their skin charred black from the light. One of the twins, I wasn't sure which, Zoe or Isabel were among them as was Olivia. The Bogeymen retreated this time and I could see blobs of goo resembling the remains that we found at Bialek's place.

I spied Glum off to my left. He had his hand cupped over his forehead swaying in place. He looked dazed as well as confused. I glanced down at that thing on Glum's chest and to my surprise the glowing disk was gone. Only a torn bloody patch remained where it had been attached. The shattered remains lay on the ground at his feet. Glum was free. Hope leapt up inside me for the first time since we found ourselves in this mess. I was so excited that I moved cautiously over to him. I realized at that moment - like the fool that I am - I was still outside the containment circle.

I wiped sticky blood from my face with the end of my shirttail then drew my pistol from its holster, summoning my battle staff with a flick of my wrist. It flew into my outstretched hand, grateful fingers closed around the worn scarred wood.

Hold on a second.

I shouldn't have been able to summon my staff if the other containment field was still up. Which meant if the barrier that held our weapons and personal effects was down, then maybe the field for the cell was down as well. Merlin must've cast a counter spell when he let loose his blinding light assault right before he got the hell out of here. I had to tell the others. I had to give them a fighting chance to get to safety. Before I could call to the others I heard a scrabbling scratching sound behind me. Turning, I spied three Bogeymen heading in my direction. All three creatures had pushed their way through holes no bigger than tennis balls in the crumbling walls to attack. Their movements were quick yet at the same time reckless, no order to them at all, only blind instinctual rage. I leveled my pistol at the closest Bogeyman firing off two quick rounds taking the thing first in the left shoulder then through its right eye. It went down twitching.

I then took hurried aim on the second Bogeyman quickly closing the distance on me firing four badly aimed shots. I missed with three of the rounds; the fourth however hit the thing in the leg just above the knee. It went down hard face first. Tattered bloody flesh hung from its face when it raised its head, eyes zeroing in on me once again. It did its best to come at me on its three uninsured limbs. The third picked up a loose stone hurling it at me as it bounded off a pile of rubble hurdling itself in my direction. I dodged the stone holstering my pistol whirling to my left. As I came round I lifted my staff defensively preparing to come to grips with the living nightmare.

In my peripheral vision I saw a black blur rocketing past me from behind. It took my mind a second to register that it was Race. He leapt at the Bogeyman, his massive jaws closing around the thing's right shoulder. Race's bulky frame collided with the horrible little creature slamming it into the stone floor where he proceeded to tear it apart.

Six more of the creatures zeroed in on Race making a beeline for him. The way his body was turned, there was no way he could see them. Thinking quickly, I leveled the head of my battle staff directly at the center of the rapidly approaching group. I had a spell poised on the tip of my tongue ready to let loose, when Tilly ran between my legs knocking me off balance nearly sending me sprawling to the ground. Regaining my balance I watched him casting spell after spell at the Bogeymen. The first spell he cast incinerated the Bogeyman I'd wounded in the leg. Tilly hurled a ball of green pulsing energy at two of the oncoming six creatures. When the ball of energy made contact with them they simply fell apart into four neatly sliced pieces. One of the other creatures smacked into a large stone that erupted from the ground blocking his path. While the remaining three were impaled on a mass of ice shards about three feet long protruding at acute angles from beneath them. Race barked approvingly as the two of them tore off in the direction of another group of approaching Bogeymen.

I turned checking on the others. Glum's gigantic body huddled over the unmoving form of Oswald while he frantically fought off a group of Bogeymen trying unsuccessfully to drag off his unconscious body. One would distract Glum then another rushed forward grabbing an ankle or a hand before Glum smashed the thing with his dangerous fists. The scene looked eerily like a mother *Wildebeest* fighting off a pack of ravenous hyenas bent on killing her calf. Glum appeared to have them under control for the moment.

My eyes tracked right spying Yeti's piling onto Wilmar. It looked almost like the big man was fighting against the tide as a massive white-capped wave of Yeti's overwhelmed him. I stepped forward to help. Then like a drowning man he surfaced from beneath the white wave of fur holding one of the huge beasts in a headlock. Four of them went hurdling ass over teakettle in different directions away from him. Another of the beasts lay prone unmoving on the ground. One of them however was perched on Wilmar's back viciously tearing at his back and neck. The Yeti's claws and teeth weren't making it through the fur coat. He was handling the situation and probably didn't need my help.

Movement to my left compelled me to look that way. Adrianna rushed boldly into a clutch of six or seven Vampires. Merlin's intense light show had decimated their fighting capability, but there were still enough of them ambulatory to be trouble. Her attack was so sudden and so fierce that they were taken completely off guard. Three Vampires lay dead on the stone floor in a matter of seconds, one of them being an *Ashari* assassin. Sadly, Bart was not of their number. Adrianna was a blur of motion, almost like a tiny white whirlwind. Two of the Vampires took advantage of her concentrated attack rushing at her from the left, which was her blind spot. I planted the end of my staff on the ground then moved it in a wide stirring motion as I uttered the following spell.

*"Trinus tentatio,"*

The attacking Vampires' legs were scythed out from under them. Their faces smacked hard into the rough stone floor with a bone-breaking thud. Blood pooled in ever expanding irregular circles around their heads. Adrianna paused long enough to flash me a smile of thanks before going after two fleeing *Ashari*.

I didn't see Orm or Barnabas in the immediate area. I did however see a rather impressive light show going on some distance away outside the walls of the church. I could only assume it was being caused by the two of them dueling. I pondered the titanic battle between two powerful Wizards taking place, then realized Bart - our resident traitor - was nowhere to be seen. That thought made my hackles rise. Instinctively I drew my *Colt* from its holster once again, ejecting the spent magazine, replacing it with a full one.

I turned to my left sensing motion. I was immediately struck hard with a well-executed *NFL* tackle. The force of the tackle was so powerful it drove me hard to the ground. My head struck the stone on the initial impact. The left side of my head erupted with a sharp stabbing pain. When I got a look at my attacker I expected to see Bart on top of me. To my surprise however, it was one of the twins Zoe or Isabel. Not entirely sure which one, all I knew for certain was that the other twin lay dead beside Olivia. Nevertheless, this twin was unscathed and pissed.

The Vampire screeched in a high shrill tone reserved only for lunatics.

"You killed my sister!"

Straddling my torso, she rained painful blows down on my head and chest. I bobbed and weaved as though my very life depended on it, which it did. Her full weight pressing down upon me however restricted my movements. The arm, which held my staff was pinned under her knee. I struck the Vampire across the cheek with the butt of my pistol, which was ineffective. Parts of my face and chest burned from her heavy fist falls. Not liking the thought of being beaten to a bloody pulp my survival instinct fired up in earnest. I pressed the muzzle of my pistol against her rib cage under her left armpit. I pulled the trigger once.

No effect.

The bitter tang of gunpowder mixed with the tinge of charred leather wafted to my nose. The report of my pistol was barely audible given the tumult around us. I fired again.

No effect.

Having nothing to lose, I pulled the trigger four more times in quick succession. The pistol made a muffled - *Pop... Pop... Pop... Pop...* - sound. This time the Vampire twin clutched her side in excruciating pain scrambling off my chest and away from me. Normally in situations such as this where I find that I'm getting my ass handed to me on a serving platter, I'd spring to my feet and do a completely manly thing. Run like hell.

Unfortunately, I'd taken quite a beating over the last ten minutes. My body, which has never failed me in my twenty plus years, did. I wanted desperately to get to a sitting position and then from there a standing position, my mind even registered these commands. The foreman however as well as his crew that oversaw the workings of my bones, muscles and tendons was either out to lunch or on strike. I just lay there on my back barely moving, limbs flailing impotently like an overturned turtle struggling to right itself. I knew that if I didn't get up in the next few seconds the Vampire twin would've healed enough to come at me again and frankly I didn't have the strength to fend her off.

With what can only be described as an uncoordinated effort, I managed to turn onto my right side, discharging my pistol in the process. The bolt locked open on an empty magazine. The round, unaimed ricocheted harmlessly off a stone wall on the far side of Wilmar grappling with his remaining assailant. The rest of his attackers appeared to be dead at his feet. If only that bullet could've acted the way bullets act in movies. Bullets almost always tended to ricochet off something. Be it a car, a mailbox, an upraised shovel or even a large bronze statue. The bullets, appearing to have minds of their own seem to hit the bad guy, even when said bad guy is at an impossible angle for the bullet to even come anywhere near him or her. I guess physics is only loosely represented in that particular medium.

I could hear purposeful movement behind me. An icy chill flowed down my spine. The Vampire it would seem was recovering quickly and possibly coming for me. Only a few feet separated us. I remembered what Merlin had told me about my body healing more quickly now. He'd done something to my mind as well as the healing mechanism that evolution had given us humans. He removed the limits placed on me by nature. I think that was what he'd said. As I thought about it, I was in pretty bad shape when Wilmar found me. A day or two later when I was able to get up and step onto that cold cabin floor, all I had was a headache along with a few aches and pains. The key to my immediate survival lay in Merlin's handy work. I began to clear my mind. A difficult task for me to accomplish, I know.

I let all thought drain from my mind like pulling a stopper on a full sink basin. I concentrated on an image of swirling water as it disappeared down the drain. The water represented my physical and mental pain of which I had plenty. The last forty-eight or perhaps closer to seventy-two hours has quite possibly been the worst hours that I've spent in this world so far. That isn't to say that I haven't had other hours that were just as bad. There were to be sure.

As my thoughts cleared I could feel a prickling sensation thrumming softly through my body. I remember when I was eight or nine years old, all the kids in the orphanage got to go on a trip to a monastery in upstate *Michigan*. Now at this particular monastery, the monks made cheese. I don't remember where the place was located, but I do remember that it smelled. By that I mean both the cheese and the monastery. The smell as I recall was a mixture of old books, candle wax, aged hardwood and *Parmesan* cheese. Anyway, we had to stay overnight at a cheesy - no pun intended - roadside motel called the *"No-Tell Motel"*. A name anyone that's ever stayed there wouldn't soon forget. The place even advertised vibrating beds. A few of us kids decided to take one for a test-drive, which cost fifty cents a vibe.

The sensation I was feeling was not unlike that. I felt my body hard at work repairing itself with each passing second. It was an unsettling feeling, but at the same time quite exhilarating. I moved my left arm finding that it no longer hurt and to my surprise I still held my staff. I got to a sitting position then to my knees. So far, little or no pain plagued me. Then with one final push of strength I stood on two shaky legs staggering about in an irregular circle.

# Chapter 27

What came next can either be listed under the heading of chance or kick a man when he's down. As I've said, I staggered about a few feet finally orientating myself in the direction of my attacker, steadying my stance for an imminent attack. Behind me I heard a deep throated grumbling that sounded almost like a riding lawnmower that needed a tune-up. I turned, Glum stormed toward me in a rage. There was no recognition of me in his expression. My eyes widened as he drew back one of his meaty blood soaked fists. I'd apparently gotten too close to Oswald and Glum saw me as a threat. When a Troll goes into fighting mode they are not unlike the fabled *Berserkers* of lore, they kill anything in front of them and move on. I took a stuttering step out of the way of Glum's fast approaching fist. His reach however was considerable.

The blow caught me on the lower left side of my chest. I heard as well as felt a loud crack as I was thrown back into the remains of a stone riser. My pistol flew out of my hand in a direction I wasn't able to follow. When my eyes stopped rolling around in my head from the excruciating pain I took stock of my situation. My ribs hurt, making breathing difficult. I also had no idea how bad my injuries were. To make matters worse, I sustained another blow to the head to go with the one I received moments earlier. For most of my life I've been lucky enough to avoid serious injuries, I don't even think I've had so much as a broken bone.

Stitches were another matter. I've had plenty of them, especially when you look after the kinds of animals I do. Now in the last few days I've sustained more injuries than in the entire cumulative years I've been in existence. My pistol was lost, but I managed to hold onto my trusty staff. The thing must be super glued to the palm of my hand.

I struggled to a sitting position leaning against weathered stone stairs that led to what I thought was the former altar. Pain erupted in my left side. It felt like I'd been beaten repeatedly. I rode out the wave of pain huffing out curse words through clenched teeth. The pain subsided to a manageable level, but I feared to move lest the pain flare up again. Without any warning or sound, a Bogeyman attacked me from behind clamping its powerful jaws around my left shoulder. I tensed which caused the pain to return more intensely than before. The fingers of my right hand sought out eyes to gouge as razor sharp claws raked my back while it's head made erratic jerking motions attempting to tear flesh from my shoulder. Having absolutely no luck fending off the beast with a well placed thumb I brought the head of my staff up awkwardly leveling it a few inches from the Bogeyman's head. I closed my eyes as I yelled the *Latin* phrase,

"*Lux lucis ex nusquam,*"

A narrow conical beam of intense light issued forth from the head of my staff. The heat given off by the beam was intense. I knew that the left side of my face was going to be burnt, possibly resembling *Richard Dryfass's* face in the movie, *Close Encounters of the Third Kind*. I opened my eyes. The Bogeyman's head had disintegrated. One moment it was there with gnashing teeth sunk deeply into my flesh, then nothing but a charred neck stump, limp hands and arms loosely attached to me. I struggled to free myself, my ribs protesting strongly with every movement. I remained where I was, my shirt torn and tattered, shoulder bleeding liberally. I looked like a tenderized rump roast waiting to be seasoned and frankly I was too tired to care. I managed to remove the Bogeyman's claws from around me, which felt considerably better. I began to get grossed out by the slimy feel of its skin against mine.

My staff was wrenched from my hand. My eyes being orientated at the ground, I spied a pair of blood spattered black leather high-heeled boots. I didn't have to raise my head to know who stood over me. It was the other twin. I raised my head high enough to catch the sight of a half dozen deformed bullets drop from an outstretched hand. They fell harmlessly to the ground making metallic sounds of finality. I smiled; my eyes met her murderous expression.

I said, "Nice boots. What comes next? Are you going to grind the heel of one of those boots into my crotch? Cause if you are, I want you to know I'm not into that sort of thing."

I knew my staff was a nice sturdy piece of oak when I chose it out of hundreds of saplings from the *Lloyd A. Stage Nature Preserve* located outside *Detroit* in *Troy, Michigan.* I didn't know however, the pain it would cause when swung like a baseball bat when it connected with my head. My vision faded black, then returned blurry and out of focus. I realized as my senses returned, that I'd fallen over, my right cheek now resting against the cool stone. I cannot tell you how good that felt as I watched a slowly expanding pool of my blood mixed with drool flowing freely from the corner of my mouth.

The Vampire let out an angry frustrated scream then violently struck my right butt cheek with the end of my staff. My body didn't register the pain because it racked up so much already it had more than enough to deal with. I can assure you however, the blow wasn't anywhere near a love tap. I rolled dazedly over to look blearily up at her. She raised the staff above her head, a look of calm murderous intent shown in her expression, as if killing me were nothing more than going to the store to pick up a loaf of bread, a gallon of milk and a stick of butter. For any of you reading this that grew up watching *Sesame Street*, you'll hopefully get that reference. Even in death I'm a funny guy.

Then she hesitated, turning to listen behind her, surprise evident in her face. I heard it as well. The sound, sand rubbing against stone intermixed with creaking leather made the Vampire drop my staff as she rushed to the side of her twin sister. Apparently she wasn't dead, which was good for me, her twin however appeared to be in terrible shape. I glanced in their direction. The twin that wanted to end my life cradled her sister's head and upper body affectionately. Tears of relief streamed down her face. She noticed my eyes intruding in on her emotional moment. Her eyes met mine. She flashed me an "I'm not done with you" look, then scooped up her sister and vanished. Please don't misunderstand, I don't mean they disappeared into thin air like a Wizard might, what I mean to say is they were fifteen or twenty feet away from me, then they were gone. I think my eyes had a delayed reaction in tracking the Vampire's movements. Her quickness just didn't register in my mind.

I sank back down onto my back lying there listening to the fading tumult around me. Our group must've been running out of bad guys to kill or I was just falling into unconsciousness. Whatever the case, it was fine with me. I tried my best to clear my mind once again to heal my body so that I could get to my feet. That proved to be more difficult this time. A song, *"Feelin' Groovy"* which was written by *Paul Simon,* but sung by a group that went by the name of *Harpers Bizarre,* kept pushing it's way into my emptied mental space. After a few failed attempts I just went with it, singing the lyrics out loud, proud and off key.

    A thought supplanted the golden oldie from my mind as my horrible singing trailed off. If the other Vampire twin wasn't dead, only badly injured, then it was possible Olivia might wake up as well and be in an unhappy mood about the situation. That thought alone compelled me to get up, painfully. I had an unpleasant act to perform before I could feel at ease. Standing on wobbly legs, I recovered my staff leaning on it as I hobbled stiffly over to Olivia's unmoving form. Half her face and most of her right hand was charred black from Merlin's light magic. Even through the ugly wounds she sustained, one could still see the beauty her features once held. She was so very young to meet her end in this manner. It was her choice after all to follow the path that she ultimately found herself on, whether it was wittingly or unwittingly her bad choices added up and the bill sadly for her had come due. Without hesitation I drew my sword concealed within the shaft of my staff severing the head from her body. I performed the same act on three other Vampire bodies that lay in close proximity to Olivia's remains. I was amazed yet disgusted by the detachment and ease in which I mutilated four bodies. I didn't even gag or retch from the sound of the sword stroke cutting through flesh or the sight of the heads coming to rest once the deed was done. I'd have more time to dwell on my actions this night for the rest of my life.

After I administered the final cut to a male Vampire that looked a lot like *Justin Bieber*. I sat my pained, tired ass down on part of an eroded wall that ended up being a serviceable seat with a high supporting back. I awkwardly sheathed my sword as I surveyed the battlefield.

Wilmar had dispatched his Yeti adversaries and moved over to help Glum mop up the remaining Bogeymen. Race and Tilly were out of my field of view so I had no idea what they were up too. The duel between Barnabas and Orm continued with increasing ferocity. Thunder-cracks followed by flashes of light shown off brightly in the distance, their mayhem appeared to be drawing nearer to the church. Adrianna gutted one of the two remaining Vampires with an ash dagger before plunging the blade deep into his forehead. The last remaining Vampire however had his neck broken by a vicious twist administered by his former employer. I recognized him as well. I don't recall his name and it really doesn't matter for this story. Adrianna used more force I think than she'd intended, because she twisted the man's head right off its shoulders. A fountain of black blood gushed from the torn flesh of the neck spraying her impeccably clean white winter jacket. She had a surprised yet annoyed expression of a person that just opened a can of *Coke* only to find some asshole shook it up moments before and the contents were now everywhere except in the can.

Adrianna dropped the disembodied head with a disgusted look, removing her expensive blood spattered coat followed by the matching gloves. Her face received a few spats of blood, which she quickly wiped away with a clean part of her coat before she discarded it. The removal of her winter coat revealed a white tight fitting turtleneck shirt that accentuated all of her curves. Despite the current state of my injured body, I was in danger of reliving my embarrassing moment in Adrianna's office. Funny, how men can think of sex in less than ideal situations. I averted my gaze when she looked at me. I didn't want her to know I was ogling her tight fitting shirt or more accurately what was underneath.

Duncan! That was the headless man's name, my apologies for the random thought. Isn't it funny that when you think too hard about something it results in a frustrated mind lock with no answer, but when you stop thinking about that subject the answer comes to you more quickly.

When I looked back I found Adrianna kneeling next to me examining my shoulder wound. Her fingers glided over the bitten and torn flesh tenderly moving the tattered remnants of my t-shirt out of the way. The wound was bleeding, but it didn't look as though the Bogeyman's teeth hit an artery.

"Where's Bart?" I asked.

"He fled with a few of his followers right before the fighting began," She replied, and then added. "He's a survivor unfortunately and will be difficult to find. I'll hunt him until the end of days to make him pay for his treachery and there isn't a place on this earth he can hide from me,"

I nodded soberly.

"And his followers," I asked.

She remained silent. Her eyes fixed on mine. Then hers returned to my wound.

"This looks nasty."

"Tis but a scratch my lady," I replied.

A broad smile appeared on her face as she giggled.

"You're this badly injured and you still have enough good humor about you to quote *Monty Python*," she said impressed.

I returned the smile, though I think mine wasn't as bright as hers.

"You watch *Monty Python*," I asked amazed.

A guilty expression played on her face.

"They're quite funny and if you get to be as old as I am you have to experience new things on a regular basis otherwise you'd go insane. I refuse to be like many other stoic examples of my race that do nothing but wear outdated clothing and pretend to sleep in coffins,"

I pondered her answer for a moment, then of course the "Solomon Child" of my brain decided to chime in, and then I said.

"If I understand correctly about what you're saying is that given the lust we both share for one another I'll eventually get to see you wearing something made by *Victoria's Secret*,"

"You're incorrigible... I wasn't saying anything of the sort, but it's not out of the realm of possibility," She said cocking a sexy eyebrow.

My smile widened then I coughed. Pain coursed through my body. I would've fallen off my stone seat had Adrianna not held me in place. I tasted a coppery tang; I placed my fingers of my right hand inside my mouth. Bright red blood shown on the tips when I withdrew them, Glum's blow must've been far worse than I suspected. It was possible that a broken rib had punctured my lung with that cough. My breathing constricted and it felt like an elephant was sitting on my chest.

"Medical kit," I managed to gasp between waves of pain. "Backpack."

Adrianna nodded making sure I wouldn't fall off my perch before she returned. She stood then raced to the area where our belongings were.

Off to her left, a thunderous detonation outside the church walls rocked the surrounding area. A large dark object hurtled through a weakened section of the already decrepit structure impacting on a stone support dislodging debris and a thick cloud of dust. The object in question turned out to be Orm, I recognized his ugly countenance as he extracted himself from a pile of still falling rubble. He immediately raised his left hand. A shimmering translucent shield of what looked like diamonds manifested in front of him. It's a good thing he had great reflexes, because a lance of white-hot fire struck his shield a second later and was reflected straight up into the air. I looked in the direction of where I thought the lance had originated and caught a glimpse of Barnabas hovering a foot above the recently demolished wall. His eyes obscured by furious storms of tiny bolts of electricity. Barnabas clutched his staff with his left hand, his right alight with magical power. To my left appeared a wall of intense yellow fire hurdling toward my mentor. The wall, twelve feet wide, ten feet high and three feet thick, incinerated everything in its path; nothing remained of the bodies I'd decapitated. Which in a purely weird way comforted me. Out of sight out of mind as they say. Adrianna stood frozen in place; her eyes locked on this titanic battle. Any thought of retrieving the medical kit had apparently been forgotten.

Barnabas flicked his outstretched hand seconds before the wall of fire struck him. The fire simply flowed around him turning into a billowing cloud of harmless steam. Orm cursed a string of unwholesome words in *French* through clenched teeth. Barnabas hovered down onto the stone floor. He stood facing his opponent, the distance between them less than forty feet.

"You will not defeat me Barnabas," Orm spat. "Do you hear me"?

"I hear you," Barnabas replied.

"You're weak," Orm continued. "I am strong!" "I have the blood of the Vampire flowing through my veins,"

Orm hurled a ball of azure fire the size of an oversized beach ball at Barnabas. My mentor simply turned it into a shower of confetti with an intricate movement of his right hand. Movement caught my eye to the right, I watched Glum gently pick up Oswald moving him away from the action placing him near a sturdy portion of the wall. Wilmar sat to the side of the wall near Glum, watching not only the fight taking place, but also making sure nothing dangerous made an appearance. Both were blood spattered. Glum however appeared to have had the worst of it. I was surprised he was still standing. Tilly and Race were still nowhere to be seen.

"I have the favor of my lord," Orm screamed.

Orm moved the head of his staff in a figure eight, raising his right hand clenching it into a tight fist. The ground beneath Barnabas shifted, roiling violently. He planted the end of his staff in a crook in the worn stone, pole-vaulting himself out of danger. Orm cursed again. This went on between them for a good ten minutes. Orm would thrust a magical spell at Barnabas and he would harmlessly parry it away. Even though the pain in my body was increasing with every raspy breath, I was interested in finding out how this fight would end.

Right at that moment, Race ran headlong between the two dueling Wizards with Tilly, my Cob Elf riding atop his back and a horde of Bogeymen trailing in their wake. Race headed straight for Wilmar and Glum's position with his tail between his legs. Wilmar and Glum rose to their feet poised for battle. Glum let out a ear bursting roar as he and Wilmar charged the oncoming horde. Tilly hopped down off Race's back moving in to protect Oswald. Race turned following the two gargantuans into the fray. Adrianna was back at my side having shaken off the hypnotic trance of the duel. She even had the presence of mind to grab the medical kit. My ministrations would have to wait however; Adrianna was about to be extremely busy fending off these little creatures. I was in no condition to fight, but I was prepared to at least make their advance difficult. My staff lay across my lap, I struggled aiming the head of it in the general direction of the rapidly approaching Bogeymen. I called out in a weak raspy tone.

"*Parietis of vis,*"

Coming into existence twenty feet in front of me, a misshapen wall of translucent yet solid force raced toward our attackers. To the casual observer the wall would've looked like a large block of melting ice, only moving very fast. The force of the wall hit our attackers like a bowling ball knocking down a set of ten pins. The block sent them flying off in several directions. My staff fell from my lap. I no longer had the strength to hold it. My body soon followed suit. I landed next to my trusty wooden staff in a heap. Pain erupted once more, but I didn't have the energy to care. My position on the stone floor afforded me a sideways view of my surrounding as my breathing became more labored.

Orm cackled as he watched the Bogeymen head for Barnabas.

"My re-enforcements have arrived, it's time for me to leave Barnabas, I hope you won't be offended if I don't watch you die," Orm chortled.

Barnabas conjured a dazzling blue spherical shield in place around him, which protected him from their onslaught. The Bogeymen ran into the shield thinking I suppose that with their large numbers they could overwhelm it, instead they bounced off the surface like a bunch of kids in a *"Chuck E. Cheese"* bouncy house. Orm raised his staff preparing to smite the end on the stone in what I assumed was his way on making a dramatic exit. His arm however never came down; in fact he stopped moving altogether, as did the Bogeymen. Beneath their feet seeping up from the ground was a steady stream of coal black smoke. At first, the whole scene befuddled me, but then I recalled what happened at the magic shop when Olivia arrived dressed as the albino, Rahm. Barnabas and Oswald had frozen her and the Vampire twins in place. I glanced in Barnabas's direction. He appeared to be as befuddled as me.

"You always did talk too much Orm," said a weak, tired and pained voice.

I glanced in the direction of the voice. Oswald was propped awkwardly against a wall. His badly injured right hand outstretched with dark menacing black swirls of power roiling around it. One eye peered hatefully at Orm. The other sadly was swollen shut and sunken. He looked like - *and I hope you'll pardon this overused expression* - death warmed over. Now that I had the opportunity to really look at him, I think my eyes welled up with tears. His skin was a sickly ashen color in spots, the remainder however was a mass of puffed dark purple bruising and dried blood. His signature black crushed velvet suit or what was left of it hung in rags on his still ample frame.

"I should hand you over to the Black Guard and let them have you," he continued.

"But after what you've done, there's only one punishment suitable for the likes of you," Oswald spat.

A look of fear clouded Orm's eyes as Oswald uttered the spell.

"Nex vobis!"

Orm, along with the Bogeymen twisted in pained terror. Their bodies dropped to the stone floor lifeless and unmoving. What remained in place above their now motionless bodies were motes of the same black smoke that seeped from the ground beneath them, only this time the smoke took on the forms of those they hovered above. I thought they might have been their souls if they had any or at the very least life essence similar to that of Merlin. The dark visages looked around dazedly, then after a few moments the smoke began to dissipate taking the forms with it.

The haze brewing in my mind grew thicker. I felt my lung slowly filling with blood after each labored breath. The last few things I recall clearly as my heavy eyelids closed, was Oswald collapsing, succumbing to his injuries. Glum appeared unsteady. He stumbled more than rushed to his father's side, his injuries finally taking their toll on his body. Bitten, bruised, torn and covered in blood as well as fragments of the bodies of his foes, Glum collapsed less than ten feet away from Oswald. My heart nearly broke as he struggled the last few feet crawling on the ground to place his huge mitt of a hand affectionately on Oswald's chest. He smiled a weak Troll smile. His eyelids growing heavy finally closing but not before he let out a grunt of what sounded like satisfaction.

I also remember one or two other things. Barnabas rushing to Oswald's side for one and of course Adrianna's knee and thigh blocking my view. I didn't mind that in the least. I even managed to look up into her green eyes flashing her what I hoped was a contented smile. The moment was ruined however, when Tilly cleaved his way into view blocking the sight of Adrianna. I think I may have had the strength yet to say.

"Move Tilly I can't see her legs" or something to that effect.

And if Tilly spoiling my last few happy moments on this earth wasn't bad enough - because I knew at that moment I was dying - his eyes welled up with tears. He leaned into me hard, my chest reintroducing waves of pain that I thought had subsided.

"My poor master is delirious," Tilly replied shrilly.

His deep sobbing followed me into the darkness as I drifted away.

Sigh, death is so unfair.

# Chapter 28

I awoke a little over three weeks later in a hospital bed at the *Henry Ford Hospital* here in *Corktown Detroit Michigan*; surprised Barnabas hadn't taken me to *Treena Greebott's Wizard Sanitarium* in *New York City*. A large percentage of the magical world trusts wizard medicine far more than the "amateurish" variety mortals practice. Barnabas is one of those percents, so why did he bring me here? I guess in the end it didn't matter, he at least didn't tell me to toughen up and rub some dirt on my wounds. I'd slept through *Christmas* and into a *New Year*, thinking on it the whole experience felt surreal as if it happened to someone else and not me. I have to go back and amend the first statement of this chapter; in actuality me waking almost four weeks later wasn't entirely accurate. I have clouded moments of consciousness that I cannot be certain if they were real or manifestations derived from the medication prescribed by my doctors.

In any event, I've never been one to sing the praises or condone the use of drugs of any kind, but whatever they filled my veins with was some good stuff. I barely felt a thing. My injuries proved to be numerous but not life threatening. Aside from the cuts, bites, bruises and scratches, Glum managed to break five ribs on my left side, three of which were so badly damaged that they had to be removed and replaced with medical grade stainless steel. I'll have to carry a little card in my wallet that states I have metal somewhere in my body. The card is purely a precaution should I decide to go to any location equipped with metal detectors; like airports, courthouses or sporting events.

My left lung had been punctured in thirteen places by rib fragments. Surprisingly, it was seventy eight percent filled with blood. The wound on my shoulder inflicted by the Bogeyman that thought it was a chew toy required sixty-seven stitches to close. The attending doctor was perplexed by the bite. For one thing it looked uncannily like a shark bite. He couldn't figure out how I could've gotten it. Because as you know, *Detroit* is hundreds of miles away from the nearest ocean and I was still partly clad in winter gear when I arrived at the hospital. I also had two fractures in my skull along with a nice head thumping concussion. Oh, and my hip was dislocated. I had litany of medical ailments, but it could've been far worse.

Barnabas told me weeks after leaving the hospital that Tilly stayed by my side the entire time I was incapacitated. As you might imagine I was fairly surprised by that news. I'd been a jerk to him at times and yet he still remained kind and loyal to me. At first I thought that it was the braid of iron around his neck that compelled him to remain with me, but after further thought I realized that the spell that bound him to his yoke of servitude compelled him to only follow my orders. Since I'd given him no such order to stay by my side he didn't have to, which meant he wanted to remain with me. There are times more often than not that I'm humbled by the selfless actions of others. I've strived over the years to be a better man, but somehow I feel I've fallen short in my efforts to do so. Recent events have sort of shown me that I am as Mari so eloquently described me as a selfish brat. If there were a way I can help free Tilly from his bounds of slavery I wouldn't hesitate to do so.

Adrianna, I was told popped in a few times for brief visits. Her being in the hospital was purely to check in on me, which was nice. I can remember her sweet melodic voice echoing faintly in the deep depths of my unconsciousness. I have no idea what she might have been saying, but I'd like to believe she was fawning over the way I filled out my hospital gown. Adrianna even brought a bouquet of colorful sweet smelling mixed wild flowers. Mari informed me later that the flowers were species native to Italy and quite possibly from the region where she may have been born as a human. That last part was pure speculation to be sure, but should I be reading something into that gift? There were many things arrayed against us should she and I decide to take this relationship further. The situation in the Vampire world for instance, prevented her from visiting more often. She'd be perceived as weak if she continued to show interest in her human distraction.

I'd heard through the grapevine that Bart was still on the run however; his power, followers and stash of cash were greatly diminished. Adrianna had methodically tracked down many of his illicit transactions and began a purge of personnel at her organization and in her family structure. The other families followed her recommendations as well. Adrianna is an alluring woman that's intoxicating to the mind, body and senses. The flip side of that coin however is she's also extremely dangerous. Adrianna is a predator. I've seen her in action on a few occasions and wouldn't want to be on the receiving end of her anger. Having said that, I'd still risk sticking my head in the lion's mouth if it meant I could be with her.

Wilmar or Frankenstein as I've been instructed to call him, decided to hang around *Detroit* for a while until I'd recovered from my injuries. In doing so he discovered that my original urgings to come back with us proved to be the best thing he could've done. He wasn't treated as the monster he thought he'd be, in fact he gained a small measure of celebrity here in *Corktown*.

He's a favorite guest at parties and occasionally makes appearances on local television. He also discovered the huge following and merchandising phenomenon that Frankenstein had become over the years. Though Wilmar looks nothing like the *Universal Studios* version of *Frankenstein*, many people here in *Detroit* have come to associate him with *Mary Shelley's* character in her novel. If they only knew he was the real Frankenstein and not an actor or *cosplayer*. I'm not sure if he'll try to recover any past royalties from his likeness through litigation though, it'd be amusing if he tried. He went so far as to buy a box of *Frankenberry* cereal. After tasting it he wasn't impressed. I think the things he's most grateful for regarding his return to civilization are the *Internet* and the *Detroit public Library*. He's been absorbing every piece of information he's been able to get his hands on. He even came to the hospital regularly to read a novels to me while I was unconscious.

    Wilmar, I mean Frankenstein informed me that he traveled back to his cabin to tidy it up before sealing it. Apparently, he couldn't bring himself to return to that solitary existence. This world he said, held far too many possibilities not to take the time to examine and enjoy. Truth be told, the reason he couldn't return to the wintry land of *Russia* was because he discovered the little Italian bistro a block or two down from the Magic Shoppe. *Pagonatta's* has some delicious pasta dishes that will make your taste buds rise to attention begging for more. If that statement wasn't compelling enough for a person to check out *Pagonatta's* the items on the menu were also reasonably priced. Whatever his reasons were for staying I'm glad he decided to stick around.

Of our small band that ventured out in this quest or suicide mission or however one chooses to look at it, Glum by far suffered the most injuries. Some of course were physical while others were emotional. A few of which may never heal. Barnabas took both he and Oswald to *Treena Greebott's Wizard Sanitarium* in *New York City* before they dropped me off at *Henry Ford*. Admitting a Troll the size of Glum to a human hospital wouldn't contribute to the healing atmosphere of the place. Glum healed quickly as Trolls do then nearly wasted away not eating or drinking, holding a solemn vigil at Oswald's bedside.

As it turned out Oswald's injuries were even beyond the abilities of the skilled healers at *Treena's*. He died quietly in his sleep on a Tuesday three days before I woke. I wept deep sorrow filled tears when Barnabas told me the news. I think I've said before, it's funny how you don't miss someone until that person is no longer around. Oswald was a kind and thoughtful man; at least to me he was anyway. He was also a good friend and member of our little extended family. I remember back when I was fifteen or sixteen years old, I was mopping the floor in the front area of the magic shop and doing a half assed careless job. Which resulted in me accidentally putting a mop handle sized hole in one of the glass display cases. Luckily, Barnabas was out delivering potions on

*Valentine's Day*. Oswald had been supervising my progress.

Barnabas knew that if no one were watching me I'd go off and read a comic book or something. As I recall Oswald didn't get angry with me or yell as is quite often the norm for old brooding Wizards. I suppose having a Troll as an adopted son you tend to run into instances like these so the aggravation factor has pretty much worn off. He picked up the broken pieces of glass, waved his wand and repaired the glass case. It looked as good as new. Then in uncharacteristic fashion - because Oswald detested manual labor - he helped me finish mopping. Afterwards he took Glum and me out for ice cream at *Farrel's*, an old style neighborhood ice cream shop. Where the proprietor, wore a black bow tie and shirt garters.

I didn't think Oswald ever mentioned the incident to Barnabas because I was never punished for it. I've never considered myself a strong man emotionally or physically like the ones portrayed in the movies. The hero in the movie could lose an arm or a leg and it wouldn't faze them in the least. They'd just rub some dirt on their injury, deliver a signature *"catch phrase"* and go kill hundreds of bad guys. I on the other hand get emotional sometimes and I'm not afraid to say it. I don't trust anyone that can't express his or her emotions. It's just not normal. As I think on it, I felt bad now about thinking Tilly should just suck it up when he was crying about the death of his master. Talk about being an unfeeling dick.

I was told that at the end, after many fruitless attempts, Mari had finally gotten Glum to let go of Oswald's hand. He'd held it during his entire bedside vigil and for three and a half hours after the last traces of life left Oswald's body. Mari being Mari, decided to bring the big guy home with no objections from Barnabas. Glum, she would later say, needed stability and a loving home. Oswald gave him that and so much more. Oswald's funeral was scheduled for this coming Friday. Barnabas and Mari tried talking me out of going because of my injuries. My stubborn side won out however and I was going even if I barfed up a lung, not really caring about their objections. I had to go. If for no other reason than to pay respects to the man that saved our lives at the cost of his own. There are times you must put reason aside and let insanity run freely, I find it liberating.

They came to the hospital to collect me early that Friday morning for Oswald's service. Barnabas, Mari, Glum and Tilly were all dressed solemnly in black. The protestations of the medical staff didn't deter them from entering my room unannounced, nor did the subsequent threats of calling security as my entourage helped me to get ready. The doctors and nurses may have been frightened by Glum. He was after all an imposing figure, though the last month or so has left him thinner than I'd ever seen him. I'm not certain if the hospital's staff grumblings were about my health and well-being or if it was the fact that we absconded with one of their wheel chairs. Mari brought something appropriate for this somber occasion; surprisingly it was easy for me to get into. A simple white long sleeved dress shirt, a pair of black slacks and tie along with a few other accoutrements to complete my ensemble. I talked her out of the suit coat, there was no way I was going to be able to wear that through the service with my injuries. When all was ready Barnabas took out his enchanted token and said *"Whitby"*. A portal opened and we stepped through.

The stark surroundings of my hospital room were replaced by a lush green meadow overlooking a quaint seaside town. I'd later learn that we were in a little town called *Whitby*, on the east coast of England, the place where Oswald was born. Two things struck me, first the town though lovely reminded me of the English town in *"Bram Stoker's classic, Dracula"*. I hoped that we'd get to walk around it a bit before we had to go back home. OK… I'd be rolling. The others would be walking. The second thing that I was struck by was that it was the middle of winter and the surrounding area for a quarter of a mile was green and vibrant as though we were in the height of summer. When Barnabas wheeled my chair around one hundred and eighty degrees, my lower jaw fell open in amazement. Standing near a low roughly made stonewall was an enormous oak tree with wide inviting branches full of green lush leaves. It was the kind of tree children would spend their summer days climbing as high as the branches or their courage would allow. It was a safe tree, a good tree. I'd imagine quite a few lovers spending time under this tree watching glorious sunsets or professing undying love to their sweethearts. Barnabas pushed my chair up a gentle rise the base of the tree coming more sharply into view.

Beneath the bows of the tree was a small assemblage of thirty-to-forty people and creatures from the magical world. Some were sitting, while others stood and still others lurked, which was their habit. They were gathered loosely around a highly polished white rectangle stone slab set horizontally into the soil. The grave marker was six feet long by three feet wide and was some six to eight inches in thickness.

Standing the farthest to the left, away from the others was a group of Wood Elves, eight in all. Tall and beautiful, the Wood Elves exuded stately charm and authority. All were dressed in robes comprised of various shades of shimmering emerald greens. Each had the same long flowing chestnut hair all Wood Elves possess. Encircling their heads - at first glance - were what appeared to be tree branches woven into crowns. On closer inspection however, they were actually various types of precious metals crafted into intricate designs that mimicked natural materials. One of the Elves stood out from the others. He was a few inches taller than the rest and far more athletic in build. A sash of gold encircled his slender waist and the same colored metal accented the designs of his regal robes. The crown on his head rose higher than all the others, resembling an ornate rack of Elk antlers. King Foxmoor, Lord of all Wood Elves. I'd never met him in person, but I've seen illustrations of him in books covering magical beings. Frankly those illustrations didn't do his appearance justice.

My eyes tracked to the right settling on another group. If someone wanted to draw a contrasting comparison with the Elves all one needed to do was look to the other side of the gathering where a small group of six Dwarves stood. I didn't recognize any of them, but they resembled any run of the mill Dwarf you might encounter in our world. Based upon their dress of dark colors, blacks, browns, reds, and the choices of material making up their wardrobes being mostly comprised of tanned leather along with gruff expressions on their faces, I would venture a guess that they belonged to the Rothgar Clan. The same Rothgar Clan responsible for the rank ale I described a while back. Just don't utter such things within earshot of a Rothgar, because they are quite sensitive to criticism. Which may explain why these particular Dwarves were conspicuously without weapons. No axes, shields, maces, hammers or daggers. A sight that was as rare as listening to a politician telling the truth.

Among the larger group of magical "people" closest to Oswald's grave were a few Goblins standing next to the stone grave marker. Standing would be a loose description of exactly what they were doing. In actuality the Goblins were minutely examining the stonecutter's work as they bickered amongst themselves on the estimated cost of the stone and the words cut into its surface. Goblins are the *"Yankee Traders"* of the magical world. I'm in no way saying that they're not dangerous, because they are, folklore and fairy tales describe them and what they're capable of pretty well. Ever since Goblins discovered the allure of all things valuable and their uncanny ability of acquiring said valuable items, they've shied away from their more violent tendencies. Preferring instead to settle disagreements with payments of precious metals, gemstones, works of art, collectables or any item they can sell for gold.

  I was overcome with a feeling of surprise mixed with a healthy dose of terror to see three members of the Elder Council along with their entourage of Black Guard, six in all standing to the right of the grave marker. Oswald must've been someone of consequence in the Wizard hierarchy to have these particular individuals at his funeral. With my luck however they're here because of the excursion we took to *Russia*. All of the Elder Council members assembled here I knew, but not personally.

  Yoshida Kogon, the shortest of this trio was by far the oldest member on the council at just over eleven hundred years old. He was of *Japanese* decent and represented the *Asian* Wizard community. His baldhead shone brightly in the sun making his bushy cottony white eyebrows more pronounced. Though over a thousand years old, he surely didn't look his age. He stood stock straight in flowing red and white robes. The staff or walking stick, he held was made of a dark wood slender in size and shape, carved with characters from the *Japanese* alphabet I assumed. He projected an aura of honor and nobility not often seen in our cynical modern world.

Tasetta Ranpu, the only woman on the council was of *Egyptian* descent. Tasetta was a few inches taller than Yoshida and like him also sported a hairless head. She was of average build and though her features were not striking she was an attractive woman. Her eyes were large and searching, set under perfectly manicured black eyebrows encircled with full long eyelashes, her eyes appeared not to miss much as they scanned the gathering. Her robes were made of an opulent gold material that appeared to gather around her like an early morning mist after a gentle rain. She carried no staff or wand that I could see, but she wore thick bands of gold around her arms and wrists along with a few rings upon her fingers.

The third member of this trio was a giant of a man. He stood nearly seven feet tall with broad muscular shoulders and in actual fact every part of him was muscled. He had the kind of physique that you'd see gracing the cover of bodybuilding magazines. The man looked like he could've opened a pickle jar using only his neck. Magnus Azeroth, the leader and most powerful member of the Elder Council exuded strength and confidence in every conceivable way. From his lion's mane of wheat blond hair right down to his care free adventurers stance.

All three simply inclined their heads in my direction acknowledging my presence, which was also the greeting that Mari, Tilly and Glum received. Barnabas however received deep bows punctuated by wary looks of suspicion. The Black Guard merely looked standoffish as they often did.

As we drew closer to the gathering I spied Race and Morgan standing near the trunk of the tree. Well, to be honest the tree mostly concealed them. Their body language was indicative of two people deeply in love or possibly lust. The lipstick and hickeys covering Race's neck was a dead give away at what they were up too. It was my opinion that they needed to get a room or be hosed down.

Race was dressed conservatively in something that wasn't comprised of leather, so it would seem that the money Barnabas had given him for his services went to good use. Or at least I assume Barnabas paid him. I've been out of it for a while. I didn't know exactly how much he received but whatever the amount he earned every penny of it. Morgan looked absolutely beautiful in a simple black dress and heels.

Wilmar, sorry Frankenstein decided to come as well. He'd cut his hair short during the time I was incapacitated, it looked like he had been visiting a tanning salon or invested in some sort of spray on tan product because his skin was significantly darker.

Nevertheless he looked good. The tailored suit and long coat he sported made him look like an *NFL* lineman out on the town. It appeared that the twenty first century suited him well.

Adrianna accompanied by two of her people, made it a point to attend Oswald's services, though they garnered looks of suspicion and mistrust from most of the mourners present. Adrianna, a haunting visage dressed all in black from her onyx jewelry, her tight fitting dress, right down to her hose and heels. She was a welcomed sight; though the non-sexual part of my mind continued to strongly warn me that she was a Vampire. - A fact that I was all too familiar with - In my weakened state however, I decided without any deliberation to listen to my rational sense of danger. Predators always went for the weak and helpless. I've had a little time since waking up to think on what happened between Adrianna and myself.

Obviously there was something between us be it infatuation or needful lust there was no way to be sure. For me I'd like to think it was a little more than base animal need going on, but how genuine can a person's feelings truly be for another after only spending, what three or four days with that person? She was the head of the largest Vampire family in the *United States*. She wielded great financial and political power as well as supernatural power. She had the ear of Presidents and Kings. What could I offer her? I had my heart and my soul, but what were they truly worth to a woman like her? In reality or at least in the reality of my mind, I was nothing more than a distraction or an oddity to her. Just like Bart said, she wasn't able to quantify my existence because she couldn't use her glamour on me, thus I drew her attention. I had no delusions regarding our relationship.

There wasn't one.

Circumstances coupled with a lack of sex created the illusions in my mind. Still, that doesn't mean I can't appreciate something beautiful, yet deadly. One of her bodyguards stood next to her, holding a large black umbrella over her even though all three Vampires were within the protective shade of the oak tree. She made a gesture for her guards to remain in place as she came forward to meet us. A wide greeting smile with a hint of sadness clouded her expression.

"Sol," she said. "You look well. It's good to see you out of the hospital."

Behind me Glum let out a low growl. Mari stepped forward to keep him calm. Adrianna appeared not to have noticed Glum's reservations of her being so close to us. Then again, maybe she did and it didn't bother her because she continued nonplused.

"May I relieve you of your burden Barnabas," She asked indicating my wheelchair.

# Chapter 29

Barnabas hesitated and then smiled. Nodding his agreement moving aside to allow Adrianna to push my wheelchair. We were about twenty feet or so away from the rows of folding chairs set up for the service. Adrianna however wheeled me the same distance in the opposite direction at a lackadaisical pace.

"How are you feeling Sol" she asked.

I didn't answer right away, my mind drifting back to the time we briefly shared and my recent thoughts regarding Adrianna.

"I'm on the mend and getting a little better everyday," I replied and then added. "Do you regret anything that we said or did?"

She chuckled in warm remembrance, which put me at ease.

"No... Do you," she asked. I could hear her apprehension.

"No," I replied.

"Good," she said sounding happy. "We need to talk however,"

"OK." I said.

I could sense her hesitation choosing her words carefully.

"I like you Sol, I really do," she began. "You're the first man in more years that I care to count that's made me feel this way,"

"And what way is that," I broke in a bit too anxiously.

"Young and alive," I could hear the smile through her words.

"See,"

She stopped pushing the wheelchair. Her hand drifted to my neck. She placed her fingers against my skin. They felt warm to the touch. I tensed then relaxed, my mind racing.

"How is that possible," I asked perplexed.

Once a person transforms into a Vampire the body loses the warmth you enjoyed when you were alive. A Vampire's body is essentially in a state between life and death. A state I can't fathom because it's as alien to me as being truly dead. In our world, - *the magical world I mean* - it's completely unheard of for a Vampire to regain body heat or the *"life spark"*, once a person has turned. What's going on here is amazing, yet unsettling at the same time.

"I don't know," she replied. "But it's a wonderful feeling,"

"But," I began. "There are so many questions to be answered,"

She kissed the top of my head as I attempted to turn toward her forgetting my injuries, which was a stupid thing to do because they reintroduced themselves in earnest.

"There's plenty of time for questions later, don't ruin the moment by analyzing and over thinking it," she said in a whisper.

I shook my head as my pain bled away, my body settling back into the wheelchair. I managed to keep my mouth shut though it took some effort. She was right however, I'd be thinking about this turn of events for a long time to come.

"Thank you," she said after a moment.

"You're welcome," I replied but it sounded clipped.

She pushed my chair, talking as she walked.

"I want you to understand a few things Sol, "

She went silent. When she spoke again she sounded pained.

"You have no idea how difficult this is for me... My world is in turmoil at the moment and it needs my full attention,"

Another pause.

"What Bart and his followers have begun is far larger than any of us have realized... Even though we've crippled much of his organization we are in for a long drawn out confrontation."

I remained silent as she continued.

"In some of the families his influence is frightening," she paused. "Lines are being drawn and allegiances are tenuous or out right changing, even I don't know whom to trust anymore... The truth of the matter is it will take much longer than I had initially realized to root out our enemies and destroy them."

Adrianna stopped. She stood in silence and then she said.

"My world is on the brink of civil war and we the few old ones that are left cannot let that happen,"

She placed a gentle hand on my shoulder stroking my neck with one manicured finger. The touch made gooseflesh erupt up and down my body.

"You would be a distraction and a dangerous liability for me,"

I heard and felt the emotion in her words. I felt them too because I knew what was coming next.

"That's why I can't have you in my life, if anyone knew about my feelings for you they'd use you against me... They would hurt you to get to me and I can't let that happen... You and I can never be together,"

I didn't try to look at her. I didn't want her to see the tears welling up in my eyes. Though I had mentally come to this very conclusion, I guess no one bothered to tell my heart.

"Well," I began, the lump in my throat making my words sound hollow. "I understand... Both of us are going to have a lot on our plates in the coming months... It'd be silly for us to complicate our already complicated lives,"

Adrianna came around the wheel chair, squatting in front of me as I wiped the tears away. We gazed into each other's puffy eyes. She placed her hands on my knees. I grasped hers with mine.

"I'd gladly suffer that pain if it meant I got to spend a day with you," I said.

Meaning every word.

A half cry, half laugh escaped her lips. A tear ran down her right cheek. I gently wiped it away being careful not to smudge her makeup.

"I know you would," she said kissing the inside of my palm. "But I couldn't bare it if you came to harm,"

We stayed like that for a moment, two love struck individuals staring longingly into each other's pained eyes, forever separated by a chasm of family hatred and hostility. Had it been a play and *Shakespeare* were still alive, he would've written our story. Adrianna was first to break eye contact as she gently squeezed my thigh then stood. I felt the bottom fall out of my existence. She was going to be a difficult crush to get over. Adrianna glanced in the direction of her bodyguards then down to me, a quiet impudent smile shown boldly on her face. She bent down and gave me a kiss...

On the lips.

It was the kind of kiss reserved only for soldiers heading off to war. Everything she felt for me was contained in that one kiss. Passion mixed liberally with desire. Happiness laced with sadness. I could even detect a dash of hatred. Hatred not for me per say, but for a possibility unexplored. I have to tell you this kiss was so good it made my toes tingle. After what seemed like forever, I reluctantly broke our kiss.

"Even my heart isn't immune to something happening to you because of me," I said, my eyes glancing behind us toward her guards.

She thought about it for a second and then gave a curt nod.

"You really know how to spoil the mood don't you,"

I shrugged giving an impish smile.

"I'll miss you Sol," she said.

Our hands lingered in each other's until she let go of mine. She moved around to the back of the wheelchair. Adrianna turned it around wheeling me back to the service. Most everyone had already taken his or her seats. The priest appeared ready to begin.

"I haven't forgotten about you saving me... Twice,"

"You can forget about that," I said. "I have, besides, you saved me so we're even."

"I most certainly will not Solomon Drake," she said. I could hear steel rising up in her voice.

"I owe you two debts and should you require anything from me I will not hesitate to help if I can,"

I felt her hand leave one of the handles, I heard her pull something from her skirt pocket. An expensive looking business card appeared in my peripheral vision.

"My personal cell number is on this card, only a select number of people have it."

I took the card examining it. The paper was a heavy stark white cover stock printed on one side in black ink with just a phone number. I slipped it inside the pocket of my dress pants.

"Thank you," I said. "How many people have this card," I asked for no particular reason.

"One," she replied quickly.

I'd be lying if a tiny smile didn't appear on my face after hearing that. Adrianna leaned in close to my left ear. I could feel her breath on the side of my neck. The smell was intoxicatingly sweet just like it was in her office.

"Sol," she began. "I owe you two debts... I don't like owing anyone anything, so even if it takes a hundred years I expect a call from you for something,"

My mind wandered to topics that would make porn stars blush. My mouth turned up into a wide grin. It hurt, but I still enjoyed the feeling.

I said. "Well, if you have your heart's set on doing me a service you could hike your skirt up - covertly of course - and let me see if you're wearing any panties... That would square both your debts to me,"

She wheeled me up next to Barnabas engaging the wheel brakes.

"Nice try," she said in a hushed whisper. I could hear the grin in her words.

She turned to go stand by her bodyguards at the far back of the assembled guests, Barnabas however wouldn't hear of it, instructing her instead to sit in the row behind us where there just happened to be three empty seats between Race and Frankenstein. She gave him a grateful nod. Adrianna and her bodyguards took their seats as the priest began.

The service was beautiful and as far as I could tell there wasn't a dry eye through the whole thing. Though I confess that it was difficult to gage the emotions of the others through all the tears I was shedding. A few of the mourners got up and said some very nice things - albeit in their own way - about Oswald at the father's urgings.

The first to speak was Drabmud Rothgar, the leader of that particular Dwarf Clan I had mentioned a bit earlier. He wore nothing that distinguished his position from the other Dwarves seated next to him. It appeared that "plain" was the look he and his clansmen were trying to achieve and they succeeded tremendously. Drabmud spoke at length of Oswald's kindness and helpfulness when it came to the Dwarf people. It was difficult to hear him because he had a soft-spoken voice, something completely out of character for Dwarves, because they tended to be loud and obnoxious. At one point he said something that I hadn't known before. Oswald, apparently was a large investor in the Rothgar ale business, a complete surprise to me. The strongest thing I'd ever seen Oswald drink was lemonade. The Rothgar's were close to losing their ale business when Oswald invested in it along with giving them a few tips on making their ale taste better. If what they sold was the best they made, I'd hate to have tasted Rothgar's original recipe.

The second speaker was one of the Goblins, which had been arguing over the grave marker before the service. He spoke in an animated tone. Sadly, he rambled on and on about various topics, many of which had nothing to do with Oswald. Though passionate, his speech was incoherent making absolutely no sense at times.

The last person to speak was Yoshida Kogan, Elder Council member. He spoke in an eloquent tone laced with the subtle hint of a Japanese accent. His words made me and I hoped everyone else feel good about the moment we were all sharing, like a breath of fresh air in the height of spring when all the leaves and flowers are in bloom. Yoshida didn't speak for very long, only a few minutes but those few minutes were inspiring. At first he said that it was unfortunate that we all had to meet under such circumstances. He went on to say, had Oswald been here observing us he would've ask if we all didn't have anything better to do than mourn over a piece of stone. That received a few chuckles and a smile or two from the mourners. He avoided many of the standard cliché people tend to speak at a funeral.

"*He's gone to a better place or his journey is now over and it's time for him to rest,*" that sort of thing.

Instead he chose to speak about when he was a little boy in Japan way before he knew of his gifts. His father - a noble at the time - had made and presented Yoshida with his first bow and arrow. He described it in detail. The bow was far taller than him, made from a sturdy cherry wood cut from his family's orchards. He recalled how the bow felt when he first gripped it in his tiny hands. The silky feel of the bowstring as he plucked it. He was overjoyed to finally get one because he'd remembered seeing the larger boys in the village being taught how to use theirs. He still had that first bow which hung prominently in his home.

Yoshida finished by saying when he first met Oswald, getting to know him over the years, it was just like receiving his first bow. It was a feeling of complete joy and happiness at each meeting, so even though there would be a hole in his heart for the loss of his friend, he'd fill the void with those good feelings. It's the responsibility of the living to remember those who have left this world before us. As Yoshida took his seat, he glanced in my direction giving me a smile followed by a kindly wink. I returned the smile coming away with a respect for this man, which I hoped I'd get to know as a friend one day.

Father Miles Fitzpatrick finished up with the Lord's Prayer. He was rather young for his station, but he was capable and charismatic. He wasn't at all boring as some of the *Catholic* priests that I'd been subjected to in my youth as an orphan. I learned after the service and before we headed into town for some lunch that Father Miles knew more than the average mortal when it came to the magical world. He'd said that he believed in the *Father*, the *Son* and the *Holy Ghost*, how could one not believe in Fairies and Goblins.

When the memorial ended people stood and began filing away. Mari, Glum, Tilly and Frankenstein walked over to stand near Oswald's grave so Glum could say one final goodbye. He held up well, but his eyes were wet and puffy from crying. Some of the mourners left immediately like Adrianna and her people. She and I exchanged forlorn glances and then I watched her walk out of my life. Two of the Elder council members, Magnus Azeroth and Tasetta Ranpu followed shortly behind her. Yoshida, however along with two of the Black Guard remained. A few of the other guests stayed to offer their condolences to Barnabas before departing. The first person to step forward was Yoshida Kogan. He placed a comforting hand on Barnabas's arm as he spoke.

"Oswald will be missed my old friend," he said. "You and he did the only thing possible under the circumstances presented to you."

"Thank you," Barnabas replied. Then he asked in a significantly lowered tone. "Is that the council's official position or yours?"

Yoshida's hand dropped from Barnabas's arm. A completely humorless smile appeared on his face.

"Mine... I'd be lying if I said I was not disappointed as well, many questions are left to be answered."

The smile faded replaced with a thoughtful expression.

"But now is not the time for such things, we will be in contact both myself and the full council... Be prepared for the usual protocols,"

"Nonsense?" Barnabas asked.

"Sadly, yes..." This time Yoshida managed an ironic smile. "The council is never usually in agreement unless there is something they feel threatens their power and control,"

One of the Black Guards leaned in saying something that the rest of us could not hear. Yoshida turned his head giving it a slight nod.

"It would appear my friend that the council requires my presence,"

Barnabas nodded.

"Until our next meeting," Yoshida said turning walking away followed by his bodyguards.

I had no inkling of the magnitude of the hornet's nest that Barnabas stirred up with his secret organization. The magically fortified relics from Arthur's reign or the deaths of seven powerful junior members of the Elder council, but from what I knew of the magical communities predilection for scapegoating and vengeance for blood any contact with the council wasn't good by any stretch of the imagination. I felt for him.

Barnabas lost what constituted the bulk of his close friends and colleagues, now he'd have to suffer through an inquest that may cost him more than he could ever possibly realize.

The next to step forward was Lord Foxmoor and his people. They moved like tall wheat swaying in a lazy summer breeze. Their movements were fascinating to watch. Lord Foxmoor stopped a respectable distance from Barnabas placing a hand on his right bicep, the traditional Elf greeting.

"Tis well to see you again Barnabas,"

"Lord Foxmoor," Barnabas replied by placing a hand on Lord Foxmoor's left bicep - the proper response to an Elf greeting - "It is agreeable to see you here,"

Lord Foxmoor inclined his head as he let his hand fall regally from Barnabas's arm.

"Oswald was a good man and a good friend, I could not honor his memory by keeping my distance from this gathering,"

He looked about admiringly.

"Do you think Oswald would have approve of this day for his memorial," he asked fishing for a compliment.

Wood Elves are notoriously vain, requiring a steady stream of compliments. Should any of you reading this encounter a Wood Elf, be sure to complement their hair or shoes it'll save you about an hour and a half of them talking about themselves. Trust me.

Barnabas looked about as well, a satisfied smile on his face.

"He would Lord Foxmoor and Thank you for your efforts,"

"Twas the least I could do,"

"Wait," I interjected. "You're responsible for this weather?"

Lord Foxmoor turned wearily in my direction. My question appearing to be a nuisance, like a buzzing mosquito. I immediately regretted my outburst. He locked his gaze on mine. His eyes were deep and unfathomable like peering at a wall of approaching storm clouds. Beautiful, yet potentially deadly in their gathering fury.

"Lord Foxmoor, I'd like to introduce my apprentice Solomon Drake," Barnabas said hurriedly attempting to help my ineptitude at Elf etiquette.

Lord Foxmoor's dark brown eyes grew wider peering deeper into mine. Though he didn't speak, I thought I saw recognition. The whole event creeped me out especially when it felt like I was being drawn into his eyes, I could sense a deep unfathomable chasm awaiting me. Luckily I had enough presence of mind to push back against his efforts with my own mental defenses - as meager as they were - to get him to stop. If he wanted to, he had the power to fry my brain with just a thought. Instead, Lord Foxmoor languidly closed his eyes breaking our thinly tethered link. His look of recognition fading replaced by his distant regal mask.

"You'll have to excuse him Lord Foxmoor, he doesn't have the knowledge of your people nor the proper training in etiquette, please accept my apologies," Barnabas said, bowing deeply in supplication.

"Yes," Lord Foxmoor replied thoughtfully. "As with all things in nature and in life there are always first steps," he continued. "When next we meet I hope that you are not so, disrespectful... I would dislike having to make an example of you," he finished with an icy edge to his words.

Abandoning my usual manner of mindless banter I remained quiet. What just happened may have been... To be honest I had no idea what just happened, but I knew I didn't want Lord Foxmoor's attention fixed upon me again. I was far from recovered from my wounds and didn't want any new ones to deal with. Yeah, I know I should be asking a few questions, because let's face it that episode was creepy, but self-preservation was more important at the moment.

"As a favor to you and those who wish to visit this place again, I will leave the enchantment in place for one full moon," Lord Foxmoor said.

"Thank you, Lord Foxmoor," Barnabas said bowing deeply. "Your generosity knows no bounds,"

His mouth quirked up into a self absorbed smile. Lord Foxmoor puffed out his chest inclining his head impressively, the way a rooster might right before he crows.

"I will take my leave of you now," he said.

He turned to leave, his eyes lingering on me as they had before, but only for an instant. The look of recognition was still there, yet it looked more certain this time. He and his people moved toward the oak tree. When they got within a few feet of the massive trunk, their bodies seemed to shimmer, changing or transforming into a majestic herd of Elk, vanishing one by one as though they were walking through an invisible doorway and were gone.

"What was that all about," I asked my eyes still focused on the point they disappeared.

"We'll talk another time," Barnabas replied after a hesitation. "When you're healed and better rested."

Which meant, if I stave you off long enough you'd forget about the whole thing. That wasn't going to happen this time, there were too many questions I've stored up to ask. I pondered this new piece to the puzzle of my past as Race moved over to Barnabas shaking his hand. Morgan was conspicuously absent from his side.

"Sorry about Oswald," Race began. "I didn't know him, but you did and that's good enough for me."

"Thank you Race and Thank you for your help," Barnabas replied.

Race smiled a cocky smile.

"You pay me like you did this go round and I'll do whatever you want," He paused then amended his statement by saying, "Within reason of course. I won't do any sexual favors or anything sick like that,"

"And nor should you," Barnabas replied.

"Maybe I'll make a living out of this mercenary thing, I've been checking around and you can make some good money at it,"

Barnabas nodded.

"Did you take the money I gave you to that financial planner like I suggested," Barnabas asked.

"Yep, he's putting it away for me so it'll grow over time and I won't have to worry about money. I gave some of it to Abner cause he's been pretty good to me, seemed only right," Race said.

"Good man," Barnabas said proudly. "Abner needs all the help he can get,"

"Where's Morgan," I asked forcing my way into the conversation.

"She had to go back with her boss, she said something about that was part of her agreement in order to be with me... The whole Vampire, Werewolf thing," He said disappointed.

I nodded thoughtfully.

"Aren't you afraid that her being one of Adrianna's junior familiars that she'll betray you one day?" I asked.

Race snorted.

"Trust me, she ain't got no mark anywhere on her body,"

Barnabas's ears colored in embarrassment; I think I just sat there stunned and slack jawed.

"Well," he continued. "If you ever need me again Barnabas you know where to find me."

The two men shook hands once again.

"Thank you again Race and give my regards to Abner,"

"I will,"

Race turned toward me.

"You did pretty good out there, Take care of yourself Sol."

Then the bastard slapped me on my bad shoulder walking away disappearing at the point near the tree where all the others did. Payback was all I could think about.

Everyone else had departed except our little group. Mari, Glum, Frankenstein and Tilly joined us. Glum's eyes looking even puffier than before. Barnabas moved over reluctantly by the stone marker for his turn beside Oswald's grave. I got a good look at what was chiseled into the stone from my vantage point. There were only a few lines on the grave-marker. His name was at the top in large bold letters "*Oswald Archibald Gleason*".

Huh...

I knew the man for over a decade and never knew his middle name was Archibald. I need to ask more questions. There was no date indicating the year in which he was born, nor the year he died. Below Oswald's name was only a quote that I didn't recognize it read.

"*Be happy for this moment, for this moment is your life.*"

I pondered the words in quiet thought. It was just like Oswald to think of others before himself even in death. It was as if he was telling us it's OK to stop mourning and just move on. My troubles are over while yours are still on going. There was also another meaning contained in those words. Be joyous because you still hold the gift of life.

"I'll do my best Oswald." I thought. "I promise."

"How are you feeling," asked Mari.

Sluggishly I came out of my deep thoughts about the words carved into the grave-marker. I shrugged.

"I'm doing OK... The pain isn't bad at the moment," I replied.

"I'll give you another pain pill when we stop for lunch,"

I nodded.

Barnabas turned back to us. Though he was good at shielding his emotions from most people, I could tell he'd let a few tears fall. Mari went to him. She took him into her arms. They hugged in a loving caring embrace. I averted my eyes as not to pry into their moment. After an intimate pause, they broke their hug both looking in our direction.

"Well who's hungry," Barnabas asked. "I don't mind telling you all I'm famished."

That seemed to perk everyone up, as the mention of food often does. Even Glum whose normal appetite has been stunted of late, seemed interested.

"I've been told that there is a little pub called *The Dolphin* in town that serves a palatable crab sandwich,"

He and Mari turned walking ahead of us followed by Glum. Frankenstein pushed my wheelchair chatting with me the entire way. Tilly kept pace beside us interjecting tidbits of information as we started off toward *Whitby* for a lunch that proved to be filling, yet somber.

# Chapter 30

I sat at my desk fending off a tired yawn, logging out of an online game I play. I won't say which one it is so don't ask. Suffice it to say if you see a toon named *Solomon Drake* running around in an *MMO* you frequent chances are good that it's me. I pushed away from the desk, leaning back in my office chair shutting my eyes. It wasn't terribly late, maybe around eleven thirty, but I still felt fatigued. It was a good bet I'd fall asleep in that chair even though my bed was three or four feet away. A little over a month had past since the funeral and the reading of Oswald's Will. Which was on the same day as the funeral.

After we finished our lunch in *Whitby*, we traveled to Oswald's lawyer's office. Mr. Bubblesby read us the will. Most of his fortune was placed in a trust for Glum and his eventual needs. I was glad that Mari was the one overseeing his money. I knew that she would take care of it and Glum. Barnabas received all of Oswald's magical equipment as well as his home and other properties. Oswald gave his stake in the *Rothgar Ale Company* back to the Rothgar family, who were ecstatic to get those shares back. Oswald also provided a small inheritance to me as well. I was stunned to say the least. The sum wasn't a fortune, but it was enough for me to put away for a rainy day. Things, as they tend to do got back to a normal routine. For me that consisted of chores in and around the magic shop, though Mondays have become somber and uneventful of late.

Barnabas decided to give me a break on cleaning out the Brood Worm tank as well as tending to the other animals, which was nice of him. He said I'd go back to doing those unpleasant tasks after my body healed. That unfortunately was proceeding a lot slower than I'd imagined even with Merlin's assistance. Whenever I moved quickly, coughed or breathed deeply I suffered sharp pangs of shooting pain in my ribs. My doctor says this too shall pass over time and insists that I should stop being negative about my situation, because research shows having an optimistic attitude decreases recovery time.

What does he know any way?

My mind along with my body gradually relaxed as I drifted off to sleep. I like sleep. To me sleep is better than doing drugs or having sex... When you're not actually doing either, of course. You don't have to put thought into sleep, it just happens. It's the waking up part I've never been too keen on. Especially when you're having a kick ass dream, then waking up is like that annoying person that talks during movies or texts while they walk. Sigh... Maybe my doctor's right. Maybe I need to be happy and optimistic, cause this line of thought isn't getting me anywhere.

"Perhaps you'd be more comfortable resting in your bed, young Solomon," said a voice that didn't originate within my mind.

The voice came from my right. My eyes darted open, my body jerking into action. That's when a wave of sharp intense pain hit me like an uncoordinated belly flop onto a frozen pool of water. I instinctively grabbed at my injured ribs. Which caused me to spill out of my office chair onto the hardwood floor, resulting in more pain.

Before I knew what was happening a pillow was being placed under my aching head and a soothing hand resting gently on my chest.

"My apologies young Solomon, I shouldn't have startled you. But as I've said before, you really are a careless dull wit. Haven't recent events taught you to be vigilant even in your own home?"

I knew that voice. I'd only heard it briefly once or twice before. The last time however, being in the ruins of an abandoned church in *India*. I slowly opened my eyes. Gazing down at me with bright green vampire eyes looking concerned yet disappointed was the face of

Avery. Behind those eyes dwelt an old spirit by the name of Merlin.

"Asshole," I managed.

"I see you haven't lost your wit young Solomon,"

"What are you doing here," I asked. Then added. "How did you get in my room?"

Merlin smiled.

"To have a talk with you of course," Merlin replied. "As for how I gained entrance," he continued. "Have you forgotten that I'm Merlin, Barnabas's wards and defenses though powerful are rather quaint,"

I nodded in understanding. If Merlin wanted to get into a secure place he'd find a way. He's after all **THE** Merlin. An irrational thought occurred to me, which made me tense.

"You're not here to drink my blood by any chance... are you," I asked somewhat concerned.

Merlin chuckled through a wide smile.

"Heavens no," he replied. "I've successfully repressed the Vampiric bloodlust,"

He flexed his hand and arm admiringly.

"And I'm enjoying the benefits of my new stronger body," he added.

I managed a laugh.

"You're not becoming vain in your new body are you Merlin," I asked, a subtle joke contained in my words.

Merlin pondered my question then said.

"Perhaps maybe just a smidgen," he said gesturing with his thumb and finger indicating the measurement of an inch. "And that's not all that's new,"

Merlin reached into his coat pocket producing an *iPhone*.

"I have this as well," he said proudly. "This is an amazing invention, these games however leave something to be desired. Very addicting,"

I shook my head in disbelief.

"Where did you get that," I asked.

"*The Apple Store*," he replied as though I were oblivious to the stores existence.

"I should've gotten the larger phone I think,"

"No," I said interrupting. "I meant how did you pay for that... Where did you get the money," I said incredulously.

He placed the *iPhone* back into his pocket.

"Ah, fortune as it were has smiled upon me," he began. "The previous owner of this body had a good sum of money to his name as well as an established identity, it didn't take much effort to learn how banking and commerce worked in this modern world,"

I nodded thoughtfully.

"Aren't you afraid that Bart or his people will come after you... They know Avery and where he lived," I asked.

"Come now young Solomon," Merlin said in a hurt tone.

"Do you honestly believe that I've been sitting idling on my laurels eating fast food and playing with electronic devices," he asked.

I thought about it. No, Merlin would be the last person not to be prepared for the inevitability of revenge. He'd survived more danger and intrigue than I'd had birthdays.

"Don't worry, I won't let any upstart hooligan punch my ticket... Did I say that correctly," he asked?

I burst out laughing, then Merlin followed suit.

"I guess not," Merlin said.

Which made me laugh even harder. I rolled around on the floor, at last the laughter between us died down. A serious expression filled Merlin's features as he looked at me.

"I just wanted you to know that I'm grateful that it was you that my crystal eventually came to," he said.

I smiled nodding.

"Don't get all emotional on me now," I said.

He returned my smile with one of his own. Then it faded. He became serious once again.

"I also wanted you to know," he said continuing. "That the remaining three relics are safe... I've hidden them securely, which should satisfy all parties concerned," He hesitated then added. "If in the future, should you require the use of them, they will forever be at your disposal,"

That's one burden off my mind. I'd worried that those powerful weapons hadn't been properly hidden away. I should've had more faith in Merlin. He'd saved my behind quite a few times. Come to think of it, he'd given me the tools to improve my magic as well as the control I had over it. Though still being a long way from being good with magic as Barnabas, I was at least on the right and faster track getting there.

He reached into his inside jacket pocket, producing an envelope sealed with red wax.

"I want you to give this to Barnabas," Merlin continued. "It's for the Elder Council and will help sate their lust for the facts of what transpired,"

He placed the thick and heavy envelope on my chest getting to his feet.

"Don't waste your time trying to open the envelope young Solomon, only one of the five members of the Elder council may do so,"

I think the look of feigned innocence plastered on my face gave me away. He knew me far too well.

"Curiosity and you are intimate bedfellows,"

He turned to go.

"No, wait," I blurted out.

I moved quickly getting to my feet keeping him from leaving.

"I have so many questions,"

That was an understatement. Questions raced through my fertile mind. A number of metallic things clanged beside me on the floor. I looked down and to my surprise there were three curved pieces of highly polished stainless steel metal at my feet. I reached to pick them up. My fingers hesitated however. My mind figuring out what these metal pieces were. That was impossible. There was no way I could be looking at these now. They were supposed to be surgically attached to my broken rib cage. I examined my damaged ribs through my shirt. I couldn't feel the rough edges of a scar nor the uneven ridges where my ribs didn't mesh together with the artificial ones. I couldn't believe it. Merlin had done in minutes what the surgical team took nearly seven and a half hours to accomplish. He healed my damaged ribs making them as good as new. I looked up to see Merlin smiling a vulpine smile in my direction.

"Humans make great things, sadly they're lacking in the healing arts,"

He turned to leave.

"Wait," I pleaded. "You have to answer some questions,"

Merlin turned back, sporting a long-suffering look. He let out a dramatic sigh then said.

"All right, I will allow you three questions,"

Just three I thought. There was no way I could get all the information I wanted with just three measly questions. My mind raced. I had to make them good ones. I couldn't waste them by asking silly questions like, why is the sky blue or how many licks does it take to get to a *Tootsie Pop* center. My mind finally set, I asked.

"When that gun was pressed to my temple... in that church I mean, how did you prevent the bullet from ripping through my brain and killing me,"

Merlin waggled his fingers mysteriously.

"Duh... magic,"

I scowled at him.

"That's not what I meant and you know it..."

Merlin held up a hand silencing me.

"Be careful what you say young Solomon, Your words might be taken as a question when you didn't intend them to be,"

I nodded thoughtfully.

"Thank you," I replied.

He inclined his head. Merlin was trying to save me the frustration of inadvertently blowing a question by asking careless ones.

"OK," I rubbed my hands nervously together. "I know this is going to be a frivolous waste of a question, but is there a chance Adrianna and I will be together,"

Merlin quirked a disapproving eyebrow and the best scowl I'd ever seen. Better even than Barnabas's legendary scowls. Then he said.

"Do I look like one of those *Magic Eight Balls* to you,"

"You said I had three questions, that is my second,"

Merlin sighed deeply.

"Fate though unpredictable at times does on extremely rare occasion prove to be sympathetic to the desires of love struck young men... So the answer is, it's possible,"

I smiled. Merlin gave me a fine thread of hope, which I was glad to latch onto. Adrianna left a lasting impression on me; I'd hoped that I had the same effect on her. My smile faded, turning from Merlin thinking of my last question. There was really only one other thing that truly bothered me. I began thinking about it after meeting Lord Foxmoor and his searching eye. The only question for me was did I want an answer to my question. I shook my head free of trepidation, turning back to Merlin.

"At Oswald's funeral... I met Lord Foxmoor, King of the Wood Elves,"

"I know who he is," Merlin said.

I gave a curt nod.

"Well, he took particular interest in me... He tried to pull me into a mindlock, but I was able to resist him. It was as though there were something or someone he'd recognized in me,"

Merlin gazed at me blankly.

"Did Lord Foxmoor know either of my parents," I asked.

Merlin took his time answering. I expected his usual condescending tone. When he finally spoke, his tone was surprisingly gentle and understanding, which confused me for a moment.

"A very good question indeed... Yes, he knew both your parents, but it would've been your father that he'd have been more familiar with.

I swallowed nervously. My father. He'd been a nonexistent figure in my life so distant in my past that I haven't given him much thought until recently. Having never met either of my parents, they both are more imagination for me rather than reality. I deeply miss not having those relationships, especially a relationship with my mother. She after all had the burden of carrying me for nine months. I was told she took her last breath the moment I took my first. That sounds more like dramatic license to me than the truth, but it probably isn't too far off.

"Are you satisfied with the answers to your questions," Merlin asked.

"No," I replied. "I'm not... But I thank you for what you've told me,"

Merlin smiled placing a sympathetic hand on my shoulder.

"Being unsatisfied with answers is most healthy... It means you are ready to search for the full truth... Just remember this young Solomon, you might not like the answers to the questions you ask, "

Boy, isn't that the long and short of it. I'd asked questions about my parents over the years. Some basic. Such as, what did my parents look like? How old were they when I was born or did they love me? Some were not so basic. Such as, why did my father leave, did my mother die alone and is my father still alive? Frankly I'd given up asking questions about my parents because of the lack of answers I'd been receiving. It took me all these years to realize I'd been asking the wrong questions.

"There are others that knew your parents, Lord Foxmoor isn't the only one to have made their acquaintance," Merlin said, emphasis on the first line.

I looked into his eyes finding a level of compassion I'd never seen in them before, even when he was a spirit trapped in my brain.

He stared hopefully at me and then said.

"I must be going,"

I nodded. I had so many more things to ask, but now apparently wasn't the time.

Merlin smiled placing a finger to the side of his nose giving me a sly wink. A swirling cloud of white glimmering magic rose up around him, obscuring him from my sight, then in the blink of an eye he and the swirling cloud were gone. I needed to put a call into Santa Claus to tell him that Merlin stole one of his signature moves.

I looked down at the floor picking up my stainless steel ribs. I smiled happily placing them into the draw of my computer desk. I still held the envelope Merlin had given me, I figured I might as well find Barnabas and give it to him.

I searched fruitlessly through the apartment, then the store. After that the basement and also the garage, I ran into Mari who just happened to be holding a plate of freshly baked *Macadamia Nu*t cookies. I eased her burden by removing three from the plate. They were delicious just in case you were wondering. After receiving an admonishing look from her she told me where Barnabas was.

I found Barnabas in *Whitby*, seated on a red tartan patterned blanket, his back propped up against the oak tree. The spell Lord Foxmoor cast was still active. Making it feel more like a late May evening rather than the blustery weather *Whitby* was experiencing just beyond the canopy of the sprawling oak. Six glass brandy snifters were arranged in a line on top of the white grave-marker. The some of the snifters were filled with what appeared to be *Richard Hennessy Cognac* - based upon the shape of the nearly empty bottle standing next to the snifters - Three had been drained while a fourth was held casually in Barnabas's right hand.

"Is this a private party or can anyone join," I asked.

Barnabas turned; the effects of alcohol hadn't yet impaired his movements. He gave me a cordial smile.

"The blanket appears to have ample room for us both," he said jovially, gesturing to a spot directly next to him.

I parked myself beside him placing an *Aldi* grocery bag near me. Before I left for *Whitby* I grabbed a few essentials. I opened the bag removing a cold bottle of *Samuel Adams Winter Blend.* – Since *Pinhurst* has yet to be offered in a bottle, I had to settle for a human beer - Barnabas gave me a look of disapproval.

"I don't know how you can drink that swill," he said as he took a long pull from his snifter.

"Well," I began. "First I remove the cap," Which I did with a flourish, carelessly discarding the bottle cap over my shoulder. "Then I raise the bottle to my lips taking a nice long drink," I said demonstrating each individual action with alacrity. "Once I finish making the swallowing sounds I follow it up with a satisfying Ahhhhhhh."

Barnabas smiled, chuckling.

"You never fail to bring a smile to me when I need it most," he said going back to his quiet brooding.

I took another drink of my beer. Though fond of beer, today I found it tasteless, using it merely as a prop. It is impolite to let someone drink alone.

"So how long have you been doing this little ritual," I asked indicating the snifters with the neck of my bottle.

"Since Oswald was laid to rest," he began. "I drink with my friends as often as I can." He indicated the five snifters with the one he held.

"And how often is that," I asked.

Barnabas shrugged.

"At least once a week, perhaps more,"

He looked at me suspiciously.

"You don't have any twelve step brochures on you, do you," he asked annoyance rising in his tone. "Did Mari put you up to this,"

I raised an interrupting hand.

"No to both of your questions," I said protesting. "I'm just concerned about your health and financial well being... At thirty five hundred dollars a bottle for that cognac you'll go broke before your liver gives out,"

Barnabas smiled wryly.

"Nothing but the best for my liver," he said draining the snifter then rose to replace it with a full one.

I pulled the letter from my shirt pocket, hesitating. Should I wait for him to sober up or just deliver it now? Given the amount he says he's been drinking there was no time like the present.

"I had a visitor today in my room," I began.

Barnabas turned, a surprised look on his face.

"Well I hoped you used protection, ghastly diseases these days,"

"No, Not that kind of visitor," I said defensively getting to my feet. "God, get your mind out of the gutter,"

Barnabas shrugged disappointed.

I didn't want to talk about sex with my adoptive father and mentor. There were so many levels of gross associated with a discussion like that. I didn't think my insurance covered that sort of psychiatric counseling.

"Merlin came to see me today,"

Barnabas showed no emotion, he said.

"Did he now... How bloody kind of him," he raised his glass in mock salute taking a sip of cognac.

"He gave me a letter for you to give to the Elder council,"

I moved closer to Barnabas handing him the letter. He took it reluctantly.

"What does it say," he asked.

"I didn't read it,"

He stared skeptically at me.

"I didn't," I said defensively. "Merlin said he placed a spell on it and only a member of the Elder council can read it,"

He nodded his understanding, sliding the letter into his hip pocket.

"Well let's hope it has some constructive things to say on my behalf," Barnabas said bitterly.

He sighed heavily turning to me.

"I'm sorry son... How are you feeling," he said changing the subject.

"Much better today," I said.

"Glad to see that those abominable implants are finally taking root,"

"Yes they are," I said not revealing the fact that Merlin did a little surgery of his own.

"Did I tell you," he began turning away from me. "That Frankenstein will be moving in with us," he gazed at me obliquely, judging my reaction.

I had nothing against Frankenstein; I thought he and I got along well. I was sort of pissed that Barnabas was trying to bait me into an argument. I get the fact that he's in a low place and I'll do what I can to help him out of it, but I won't bite on his little lure.

"Fine with me," I said. "I just hope he doesn't snore, two people snoring in the apartment would be unbearable,"

Barnabas smiled wryly; obviously gratified I was able to sidestep his little trap. After a moment his smile faded, his usual deep thoughtful expression returned. After a good ten minutes he said.

"I'm sorry that I got you mixed up in all of this,"

He turned to me, a pained expression on his face.

"All of this could have been avoided had I just trusted the council more," then he added. "Oswald would still be alive... They all would."

Tears welled up in his eyes, but didn't fall as he drained the fourth snifter replacing it with the fifth. He cleared his throat composing himself. It amazed me how well he was able to control his emotions.

"You didn't know," I finally offered.

"No," he spat, "But I should have... I should have,"

He moved to the trunk of the tree placing his free hand upon it, looking off into the distance.

"You began your life with so many difficulties," "No mother, no father, no home to speak of... Just an innocent newborn babe left to fend for yourself."

He glanced back to me.

"Did I ever tell you that Mari, Sister Mari at the time, found you in a brown corrugated box on the front steps of her orphanage."

He smiled in fond remembrance.

"A little beaded bracelet around your right wrist spelling out your name along with a hurriedly scrawled note on *Hotel Drake* stationary that simply read, "please take care of him,"

I remained silent. I'd heard most of this over the years. I still have that name bracelet tucked away in my wall safe, however it wasn't until this very moment that I realized where I got my last name. Most everything I received during my childhood years were borrowed hand me downs of one sort or another, why not my last name.

"I never intended you to come to harm or have you experience pain of any sort... But, we all know that the road to hell is paved with good intentions don't we," He said, his last words trailing off.

I let the silence hang between us for a bit before I spoke.

"Is that the reason you've been tough on me all these years," I asked.

"Partly,"

"And why you've been teaching me weaker spells,"

Barnabas snorted ruefully.

"Did Merlin tell you that," he asked.

"Yes,"

"What else did he tell you," asked Barnabas.

Should I discuss what Merlin and I talked about with Barnabas in this state or should I wait until later. Granted what Merlin laid out before me was still freshly on my mind, I still needed time to think about it. Questions about my parents would keep until later. Right now I had to be here for Barnabas. It looked like he needed someone to talk to.

"Not much more than that… Mostly generalities,"

Barnabas nodded, then said.

"Well my boy, he's right... I've been teaching you weaker spells... The main reason for that is you're without doubt one of the strongest Wizards I've ever come in contact with, that fact alone coupled with your immature nature and impulsive behavior compelled me to instruct you in the manner which I chose..."

"Because you were afraid history would repeat itself and I'd turn into something resembling your former apprentice, Rahm," I said interrupting, no anger in my words only stating facts.

Barnabas nodded once.

"Something like that, I'm sorry Solomon that I didn't trust you either... I should've listened to Mari years ago,"

"There's no need to apologize," I said moving to stand next to him. "Thank you, I don't know how I would've turned out or where I would've ended had it not been for you... You gave me a family and a place where I belonged." Though the whole Brood Worm tank cleaning thing did at times give me vivid fantasies of murdering you in your sleep,"

Barnabas chuckled.

"Humility doesn't come naturally, you have to learn it, that's what my master taught me... Though his lessons involved scraping the calluses from the bottoms of his feet," Barnabas gave a disgusted shake in remembrance.

"Yeah, I'll stick with the gross worms thank you,"

There was a long pause between us and then Barnabas said.

"Life as we knew it has changed and not for the better... You'll be tested in the years to come my boy... Evil will find you whether you look for it or not,"

"I know," I replied as I took a sip of beer. "I sort of figured that out when Whitey and the twins showed up at the magic shop,"

Barnabas nodded thoughtfully.

"Do you think you're ready for what awaits you," he asked.

I shrugged.

"No," I said with a mild chuckle untouched by humor. "But I think I can handle it,"

Barnabas nodded then drained the snifter. He looked at the sixth smiling ruefully.

"I think five will be my limit today," he said.

We both turned our gazes to the east. The night sky was giving way to a dazzling spectrum of color. Deep purples fading into deep reds, then to brilliant shades of orange as the first slivers of sunlight began to push their way into the waiting day. A day, which on the surface promised mild weather and a dazzling blue sky for the sleepy town of *Whitby*, I finished the last of my beer wondering to myself how many more peaceful days I'd be able to enjoy as the years progressed. I pondered the glorious scene before me glancing down at Oswald's grave. A pang of sorrow stung me, as guilt crept into my thoughts. I was alive while he'd paid the ultimate sacrifice. The thought left me humbled yet wondering what fate had in store for me. If the last few months were any indication the rest of my life was going to be anything, but boring.

*I'd like to **THANK YOU** again for reading **RELICS: The Chronicles of Solomon Drake**.*

*As a **SPECIAL ADDED BONUS**, I am offering a **SIGNED RELICS BOOKMARK ABSOLUTELY FREE** to anyone that emails me a confirmation for purchasing my novel. If interested, please email your confirmation to **rbyork1969@gmail.com** in order to receive the bookmark.*

*If you enjoyed this book, the next book in this series called, **Dead Reign: The Chronicles of Solomon Drake** is due out **SUMMER** of **2019**. Drop me a line and I'd love to send you the first chapter for this next installment in the nine volume series.*
*rbyork1969@gmail.com.*

**Robert York**